Before  Cuba

Bora Bora Express

Jeff Hartdorn

PREFACE

"Isn't it great now that Cuba has opened up!" I've heard it a hundred times. Friends know I have spent years visiting the island. Americans don't have a clue. Or worse, they have pre-conceived notions that are just plain wrong. Due to recent events, there seems to be a lot of interest. The more we "open", the more the Castros, or their successors, will shut it down. It's a prison. Once one conceptualizes the island as a prison, it begins to make sense. Any reservations that Cuba was indeed a prison were laid to rest the day Fidel died. I was there. With a snap of official fingers, the island was locked down. No music. No laughter. No gasoline. My prison analogy was not only confirmed, but surpassed.

The following narrative is based on facts I observed, or were told to me by neighbors, between 1991 and 2017, in and around the suburbs west of Havana. The Vali character was in prison for fourteen years and is now in a decrepit family compound in Santa Fe. You can visit her. It was her sister that escaped from the marina. My neighbor on Calle 234 was stabbed at the Rumbo, defending another neighbor's daughter. Coco died a couple years ago, he was a friend and a good man. Esteban still raises and fights gamecocks. It is indeed possible to walk into the surgical theater of the local hospital and I have made the swim, under the noses of the guards, out to sea for three miles just to see if it was possible.

Don't let my experiences deter you from visiting the island. It is unique. Just don't do anything stupid and you will be fine. Perhaps you will pick up on the undercurrents that rule every moment of their existence. Consider renting a car or hiring a driver and getting out of Havana. Once they discover you are more than just a tourist, you may be surprised at how quickly you will be welcomed into their homes and hearts.

In many ways, Cuba is much better off than Venezuela, Honduras or El Salvador. But its existence reinforces the concept that ***when a society sacrifices freedom for security, it risks losing both.***

ISBN: 0692066845
ISBN 13: 9780692066843
Library of Congress Control Number: 2018901758
Before You Go To Cuba: Bora Bora Express New Smyrna Beach, Florida

CHAPTER ONE

Charles Sutton was worried about a mutiny.

"Will this damned wind ever stop blowing?" The tone of his first mate Allen's question seemed only to verify Charlie's fear.

"Fucking wind," Charlie agreed and spat into the waves that conspired to impede their progress.

After quiet reflection, Charlie acknowledged that the wind—God's gift to mariners—was the energy source they would ruthlessly exploit to carry themselves across the surface of the earth, and the waves merely an uncomfortable testament to its efficacy. How could they curse a force of nature?

"Fucking direction?" Charlie asked no one in particular—well, maybe he *was* pleading with the wind just a bit. That didn't work. Nevertheless, the obstacle confronting the captain and crew of the *Bora Bora Express* was as tangible as any mountain range or desert. Charlie and his crew were becoming impatient.

They had waited nearly a week for the wind to switch or lay down, but the May trades in Ft. Lauderdale blow hard from the southeast for weeks at a time.

Being stuck on a mooring at the Las Olas Bridge was hardly the adventure he had promised Allen and his new girlfriend. Charlie noticed their conversations had shifted from palm trees and deserted beaches to student loans and dental appointments. At any moment, his crew—comprised solely of Allen and Jenna—could bail, and there was no way he was going to single-handedly sail to the Bahamas, much less their ultimate destination of Antigua, thirteen hundred fifty miles to the southeast.

Other captains had advised him to wait until the end of hurricane season and ride the November northers. At that time of the year, there were big winds that came through like freight trains on a schedule, howling from the north or northwest for a couple days, gradually clocking through north to the northeast, then petering out from the east. Soon the wind would pick up from the southeast, strengthen from the south, and the pattern would repeat itself.

A modern sailboat could safely run before a gale, and the trip would be an easy sleigh ride without the current complications that Charlie and company were experiencing. By Thanksgiving these fronts extend all the way to St. Thomas. But November was six months away.

On the morning of May 8, 1998, Charlie watched as the trade wind cumulus clouds moved briskly over the Intracoastal Waterway heading to Lake Okeechobee and beyond. There they would rise over the warming peninsula, condense the moisture they had accumulated on their trip from Africa, and explode into spectacular thunderheads, visible even over the horizon at two hundred miles. And that is where he wanted to be, two hundred miles, or two thousand miles away, anywhere but here. "We're leaving in the morning," he'd proclaimed to his crew.

At first light the next day, the *Bora Bora Express* had slipped its mooring and motored south through the Seventeenth Street Causeway bridge, bound for the distant Leeward Islands and the waters, the conditions, and the charter market for which she was designed.

Despite the name, Charlie never had any intentions of sailing through the Panama Canal and across the Pacific to the island of Bora Bora. Nor was his yacht an express to anyone who knew about racing or hull design. To Charlie, his boat's name captured the joie de vivre, the exultation of spirit, the siren call of the eternal sea, the mystical allure of the undiscovered country, the anticipation of exotic cultures, the perpetual optimism of striving for the unattainable, man's immutable desire for conquest, nubile virgins on remote palm-laden shores—his boat's name was a stern-mounted, free-floating Rorschach on which any man or woman could project his or her hopes, aspirations, or interpretation. Anyway, the *Bora Bora Express* beat the hell out of the name that had been painted in sun-faded letters on her stern when he'd bought her—the uninspiring platitude to mediocrity, *Martha.*

Charlie Sutton was an off-color Renaissance man. Although he had been a *B* student in college, he excelled in physics, marine biology and minored in Spanish. A voracious reader, he wasn't by anyone's estimation a stereotypical bookworm. He was an athlete and could sprint, swim, or sail with the best, when he wasn't hung over. He was born to the water, a star swimmer at the University of Florida.

Charlie was good at reading people, too, and he delighted in shocking people out of their comfort zones. In the eyes of polite society, he was, at times, alarmingly profane both in speech and action. There seemed no occasion too proper, no event too solemn, no icon too sacred, no conversation so engrossing that it could not be impaled by an off-color joke. However, many recipients failed to embrace his humor's probative value and were permanently and resoundingly repulsed. Jenna wondered if he was leaving the United States voluntarily or had been thrown out of the country and asked never to return.

He had smiled at her joke. The truth was that he wanted to travel in the full sense of the word, to immerse himself in new cultures, sample native cuisines, climb misty mountains in exotic lands, walk in the footprints of Marco Polo, and—while pursuing these noble endeavors—perhaps share time with a woman or two.

3

"Raise the main," Charlie said.

Allen stripped off the sail cover, rolled it, and stuffed it into the cockpit. Shielded in the lee by a row of condos, Charlie brought the bow to weather. Allen removed the sail ties, attached the shackle, and cranked the main halyard winch while Jenna belayed. They had practiced raising sail in the anchorage, but the situation was nothing compared to the conditions in the choppy inlet.

Charlie close-hauled the main in preparation for the wind funneling its way through Port Everglades. Making the turn to the east, the mainsail flapped like a flag in a hurricane.

"That's called flogging," Charlie yelled to his companions. It was hard to yell above the pitch of the wind. It was also a poor day to begin sailing lessons. "The sail can destroy itself in a minute, whip itself to pieces. Prepare to fall off on a port tack!"

Jenna looked at one side of the boat, then the other. *Port tack, remember, that's when the wind comes over the left side of the boat and we lean to the right, remember, starboard.* Jenna recalled Charlie's explanation for port and starboard. They were constant. Always on the same side. Now that she was facing him, her left was his right, and the system began to make sense.

They used the boat's motor to push through the traffic of sportfisherman, motor yachts, jet skis, and tugboats and out the Straits of America into a sloppy, breaking, head-on sea of four to six feet. Jenna scrambled below to secure items that, having sat motionless for a week, were now jumbled and airborne. Within their first thirty seconds on open water, the cabin sole became a repository for books, settee cushions, spice bottles, navigational tools, binoculars, and anything else not secured, tied, bungeed, boxed, or braced.

"Fuck a duck," Charlie opined.

As Charlie veered to the south, the short-sheeted main filled, and the *Express* was unceremoniously dumped on her starboard—

4

her right side—with an ensuing crash as items on the port side yielded to a new gravitational metric. Both starboard-mounted heads, now well under the surface of the ocean, gushed green water until the seacocks were closed.

Easing the mainsheet reduced the angle of heel as Charlie remembered the mariner's adage: *if it occurs to you, do it*. It had occurred to him to put the first reef in the main while safely in the harbor and now, overpowered, he regretted not heeding his instincts.

On a beam reach like the run from Martinique to St. Lucia, the Out Island was dry and steady at eight knots, even better on the slightly off-wind return. Heading into the wind, however, was a different matter. Rough sailing like this was not what Charlie had envisioned when he'd bought the *Express*.

Charlie, a licensed general contractor turned accidental day trader, had bought the *Express* up in Jacksonville and promptly moved aboard. She was a far cry from the sleek racing hulls he was used to. Her beam of thirteen-foot-nine-inches was equal to the width of a sixty-foot racing machine. At one time or other, he had competed in everything that floated. His specialty was helm and sail trim, but he was knowledgeable, to a certain degree, in all aspects of seamanship, having devoured a library on the subject. That which he read, he put into use while racing sailboats or delivering yachts.

Charlie had begun reading the sailing classics when he was a teenager. He had seen the world through Joshua Slocum's eyes as the soft-spoken old man refitted the *Spray* and struck out on his journey around the world. He marveled at the wanderlust of Sir Francis Chichester, in his various air and sea incarnations of the *"Gypsy Moth"*; the tenacity of Robin Knox-Johnston; the inspirational voyages of Ernest Shackleton through the frozen southern wastes on the *Endurance* and felt that Sterling Hayden's *"The Wanderer"* should be compulsory reading. Charlie had studied Chapman for general seamanship, the U.S. Coast Guard's *"Aids to Navigation"* and Donald Street for anchoring and sail trim.

5

The *Express* had been purchased during the last hurricane season, and Charlie had sailed her only in the Ortega section of the St. Johns River. Rather than a slow racer, Charlie thought of the *Express* as an ocean-going bachelor pad with the ultimate waterfront view. The *Express* had a queen-sized double berth in the private aft cabin illuminated by two stern-mounted rectangular portholes thirty-six inches above the waterline. He wasn't handsome in the classic sense, but women seemed to enjoy his muscular physique and enthusiasm. He was eager to please. Under autopilot, the young captain discovered it was possible to be making love to Kim, his ex-girlfriend, and, when she was properly positioned, gaze simultaneously into the roiling wake bubbling along behind the boat—a view that incorporated the best of both worlds.

Allen Larkin was a six-foot-two MIT engineering graduate who thought that a Caribbean voyage with his new girlfriend would be romantic. He looked like a string bean version of Tom Cruise. His cautious, analytical approach to problem solving counterbalanced Charlie's renowned recklessness. They were a good team. Allen was in the process of learning how to sail, therefore excited to accompany Charlie through the Bahamas, the Caicos, the Virgin Islands, and down to Antiqua where Charlie had been promised a chartering gig. On this trip, it would be Allen and Jenna enjoying the view of the disappearing wake from the aft cabin.

Moments after sticking their beak into the Atlantic, it became abundantly clear they had pissed off the weather gods. Charlie tried not to sound apprehensive as he queried aloud, "How the hell are we going to push fifty miles into this madness?"

They spread a chart over the cockpit table. On a north wind of fifteen knots, they could have been in Bimini in about eight hours. However, a strong southeast wind presented a formidable logistical and navigational challenge. The northbound Gulf Stream, whose surface under a south wind runs faster than the Mississippi River, had to be considered. Due to shipping traffic, it was best to minimize the time the spent within the Gulf Stream.

One option was to drop sail and motor. Under perfect conditions, the *Express* could cruise at eight knots. But in this sloppy, breaking sea, she would make little headway. Even if she could manage three knots, she would have to crab her way across the stream. In the Gulf Stream's axis, motoring was a last resort. They could be headed due south and still be going north at a knot or two.

They could begin tacking immediately, but the math didn't work out. Their course was directly into the wind. Charlie and Allen tried to compensate, but no matter how hard they tried, the *Express* couldn't do any better than due south. Each wave lifted her bow, absorbed the wave's momentum, and threw her head to leeward. This resulting course brought them to Miami four hours later, which placed them three miles closer to Bimini but changed the rhumb line to due east.

That afternoon they secured a slip in Miami Marina and walked the art deco neighborhoods of South Beach. By the time they got to Joe's Stone Crab, they were pleasantly intoxicated. After five or six more drinks, Charlie couldn't keep his mouth shut and launched into a litany of tasteless gay jokes then ethnic jokes. A group of weight lifters—maybe not true weight lifters, but they were certainly physically fit—at the next table apparently picked up on the word *gerbil* and failed to see the humor. Jenna did her best to intervene, but it was by luck alone the boys made it back to the boat unscathed. Climbing over the rail, an unsteady Allen verbalized their collective hopes.

"There always a chance that the wind will slack by morning," he slurred.

It didn't.

Their hangovers provided an excuse for delaying departure. At noon, they once again sailed south, navigating down the beach, to a point nineteen miles due south, roughly east Elliot Key. Any farther south and they would be sailing away from Bimini and reaching a point of diminishing return as the Florida Keys began its gradual turn to the west. It was midafternoon when the *Bora Bora*

Express flopped over to the starboard tack, heading east into the heavy seas.

"Hang on," Allen yelled to Jenna as she struggled up the companionway steps. The wind was sufficiently powerful to blow tops off the larger waves, creating a foam that organized itself into rows of spindrift. Mother Carey's Chickens—a type of storm petrel—floated inches above the breaking crests, dancing impossibly on an ethereal surface, all the while picking out tiny scraps of food from the froth and clumps of Sargasso weed. Charlie wondered where the birds went during calm weather. Flying fish exploded from the steep-sided waves, always into the wind, their tail fin sculling frantically. Some soared, but most crashed into the oncoming waves.

The Straits of Florida were a choke point for most of the east Atlantic's commercial shipping. The *Express* would have to thread her way through southbound ship traffic, hugging the shore to avoid the current and the northbound vessels, riding the magic carpet created by the earth's Coriolis effect. Virtually all the traffic from the Panama Canal, the Gulf of Mexico, South America, and the central Caribbean was funneled between Miami and Bimini, bound for the east coast harbors or far away European ports. Most of these ships traveled at about fifteen knots and crushing a forty-one-foot sailboat wouldn't scratch the paint or wake the crew.

Despite preparations, their tack was accompanied by the crashes and rattles of objects below decks seeking new accommodation. The only level surface was the top of the gimbaled propane stove, its fiddles locking down the cast-iron skillet. The course they had picked—or rather, that had been handed to them by circumstance—would have brought them to Bimini if they had been on a static body of water—for instance, Lake Superior. Within fifteen minutes of leaving the shoals, however, the *Express* entered the invisible clutches of the stream. By the time they were making any headway, they were being swept a full four miles north every hour.

Charlie was glad to see his crew adapting to the uncomfortable conditions. It was unfortunate that their first night at sea had been a battle against the elements. He had hoped to use the crossing as a teachable event for Allen, but all they could do was hold on for dear life and hope the boat didn't come apart. As he listened to the effects of the steep-sided waves smashing relentlessly into the hull, the rattling of the rigging, the strain on sails and sheets, he could not help but curse the fates and mutter to himself, "The wind, the fucking wind."

CHAPTER TWO

Mourners were assembling at the house of Alvaro Cruz. Some had endured voyages from as far away as Camaguay and Santiago. The lucky ones made it in time. Others were lost in transit, perhaps trapped on the sugar train or waiting half a day for a bus to be fixed. Many were elderly and remembered when traveling had been so much easier. Dressed in their finest, family members were spilling out of the tiny front room onto the porch. The women formed a loose circle, the men leaned on the railing—resolute, waiting, resigned to a cheerless day under a blazing sun.

Valentina Olivera knew that Alvaro had been murdered. Her mother had heard it from Mrs. Nunez. The story, passed from one person to another—that's how word spread—told that a young man had been attacking Esmeralda, a neighbor's seventeen-year-old daughter, and that Alvaro had intervened. Valentina thought that the heroics were a waste. Esmeralda had been getting into trouble since she was thirteen and if anyone in Jaimanitas was going to suffer the consequences of bad decisions, it should have probably been Esmeralda. A knife had landed a single stick to Alvaro's heart.

Heading down Calle 234 toward the bodega, she reflected on the old man's life, and how he had spent it all in Cuba. As she rounded the corner, she could see the crowd of mourners on the porch of the Cruzes' house.

Built in the 1930s, Mr. Cruz's house was old even by the standards of Jaimanitas. Tires and concrete blocks, some wired together, added weight to the corrugated iron sheets whose fastenings had long since deteriorated along with the rotten wood of the original roof. Adjacent houses, only three feet away, were newer and built entirely of concrete. When Mr. Cruz rode a bicycle, he would occasionally come home with a board or other scrap of wood that was quickly incorporated into the structure, perhaps as siding or window trim. One day the finely turned original corner post of the porch crumbled, threatening to bring the roof crashing down. Neighbors arrived with two-by-fours, through-bolted together, as a temporary support. Now, its green paint almost as faded as the rest of the house—the patch had become permanent.

Yet, despite the disrepair, the little house on Calle 234 had always been cheerful and inviting. The tattered couch was covered with a colorful blanket, movie stars torn from popular magazines danced and dazzled above a tabletop illuminated shrine of La Virgen de la Caridad del Cobre, the island's patron saint. The cement floors were swept and mopped every morning as was the street to the edges of the property. Due to a contact within Eteska, the Cuban phone company, the Cruzes had a telephone, and their home had become an unlikely center of communication for that part of the barrio.

As she walked past the house, the smell of freshly brewed Cubita hung in the air. Many of the people on the porch were strangers from cities far away; others were neighbors. Nevertheless, they were all familiar with Mr. Cruz and his family. There were few secrets on Calle 234. At one time, the Cruz family had owned vast tracts of land. They had been cattle ranchers and had grown row crops such as potatoes and lettuce. When Fidel Castro and Che Guevara had adopted a Marxist template as their blueprint for social progress, the Cruzes' farms and lands had been seized and nationalized. Alvaro's brother, Julio, had joined an anti-Castro resistance group but had been eventually captured and executed at El Paredon, along with hundreds of others. Once capitalism had been renounced in the new constitution, the Cruz family had had no legal means of making money, so they had moved in with relatives in Jaimanitas.

11

Perhaps Alvaro was Che's *Nuevo Hombre,* the New Man, an enlightened form of human being that put the interests of society ahead of his own or his family? It was possible. But a requirement for the New Man prototype was that he work tirelessly from morning until night to further the cause of revolution. After Alvaro lost his ranch, his business, and his brother, he just sat, on mornings like this, in his chair on the rickety front porch.

The street knew that Mr. Cruz had not played an active part in the Revolution, hadn't been a member of the Communist Party, hadn't been aligned with Batista back in the capitalist days. Nor was he a member of the Committees for the Defense of the Revolution, the neighborhood snoops. CDR operatives received perks such as extra rations. As far as Vali was concerned, Mr. Cruz was a coward who had never taken a chance or done whatever was necessary to advance himself or his family. To her, his unremarkable death was a fitting tribute to communist sycophant. *He's better off dead. I am not going to live that way. I'm not going to die that way.* But it was strange. Perhaps she had misjudged him. He was killed, after all, defending Esmeralda.

A large mulatto woman on the porch, part of the group, caught a glimpse of Vali. The inquisitive nature of her glance was an immediate signal to the other women—like the gazelle in a herd that spots the lion—and they all looked. Then the men on the rail turned their heads to watch Vali as she passed. It was hard not to. The morning sun silhouetted her waist-length black hair and made her backlit yellow, cotton sundress semitransparent. She was graceful, elegant, and a vision of innocence, with a strangely familiar face that transcended anonymity. The men, each in his own way, wondered how, no matter how improbable, how incredibly unlikely, they could juggle space and time in such a fashion that this vision of loveliness would be naked, sweating, struggling beneath them, her fingernails clawing at his back, begging for more, begging him not to leave, before the burial at noon. Men think like that, Cuban men more so.

Neighbors had watched the little girl from Third Avenue metamorphose before their eyes. She was even prettier than her mother had been at eighteen, though slightly taller. She carried herself well and dressed in a manner that displayed to the world she was fashion light-years ahead of the neighborhood girls with their spandex shorts and tube tops. Vali had learned long ago that she could be wearing a space suit and men would somehow ascertain every detail, every concealed nuance of her tight little body. It was a mystery how—maybe they were born with X-ray vision—but they all could do it. She didn't need spandex.

Some things on Calle 234 never changed. The haunting cries of the collared doves mingled with the muted din of a thousand waves crashing on the nearby coral shore. The street even looked much the same as it did on the first day of the Revolution when it had been a vibrant, working-class neighborhood freshly painted under the same sun and sky. At that time, the street had been filled with hope and optimism. The Cuban people had freed themselves from the tyranny of the last of a series of rapacious dictators. They had been masters of their own destiny and justifiably jubilant that they had finally lifted the yoke of two hundred years of colonial oppression. The citizens who had supported the Revolution felt justified to expect to participate in the rebuilding and restructuring of a free society. Thirty-eight years ago, the residents of Jaimanitas— and the rest of Cuba—had looked forward to a new world of hope, freedom, and prosperity. But it hadn't worked out that way for Mr. Cruz or his neighbors.

Like a grand game of musical chairs, once the music had stopped, the entire country was frozen in space and time. Building construction ground to a halt. Potholes on Calle 234 lingered for years. Small businesses closed, and major ones were nationalized and destroyed. The importation of consumer goods had been severely interrupted. The quality of life for the residents of Jaimanitas began to deteriorate.

Goods began disappearing from shelves; those that remained became more expensive. Rolling blackouts became common. Water was turned on for an hour or two every day. Beef became contraband. There were shortages of lifesaving drugs. The system began to unravel to the point that the specter of malnutrition haunted every province. For several years, there was hope that the Americans would intervene—after all, how could the United States tolerate a despot only a hundred miles from its shores, in a country they helped liberate sixty years before—but even those hopes evaporated when President Kennedy agreed to leave Castro alone as part of a deal with the Soviet Union. Virtually overnight, Cuba became a prison in paradise, locked by bizarre ideology into stagnation, deprived of hope, robbed of a future, as was Alvaro, who sat, as if waiting, for almost forty years.

This was the reality into which Vali had been born. It was the only life she had ever known. For her, the system had been immutable, omnipresent, unchanging. In that respect, it offered permanence and security. The status quo was not to be questioned. Even prisoners establish a routine and have reasonable expectations of tomorrow based on what happened yesterday. Life under communism was easy and predictable. In exchange for obedience, the system provided the pretext of health care, education, food, and housing. For Vali and five million other youthful Cubans, this pact with the government—this birthright—was inviolate. It was guaranteed by their constitution. But Vali had seen, growing up here, that those promises were as thin as a month's rations.

For the past several years, the government had not been keeping its part of the bargain. The government could no longer be counted on to provide basic necessities. Things were changing. Vali, her neighbors—indeed, most Cuban citizens—were trying desperately to adapt to a system in transition where the rules were unwritten and the penalties for breaking those rules were severe. The system, which had always been inadequate, had broken down. It hadn't happened overnight, which would have been much better—a new government sweeping out the old, one that had learned from mistakes of its predecessor and offered hope with fresh faces and new ideas.

Instead, it was a decay over a period of five years. People slowly adjusted. There was never a day, a tipping point, where the people said, "Yesterday was all right, but today is intolerable." Nevertheless, the day always arrives when a patient is at death's door, and without intervention, he or she will be dead within hours.

14

That day had arrived in Cuba during 1994. And that had been four years ago.

Before the Special Period—a time when Castro refused US aid but capitulated to limited domestic capitalism in a desperate attempt to save the Cuban economy—citizens didn't have much, but it was enough to survive. As such, the rhetoric of the Revolution was a fair match for the reality of existence. Individuals, families, and communities were bound together in a true equality—poor but equally poor. As long as the state provided the bare essentials, the society was at least on track toward achieving a country populated by Che's New Man.

Residents grudgingly accepted Castro's socialist model. They had listened to thirty years of rhetoric decrying capitalism as the basis for most of the world's evils. This enmity was articulated within its constitution and enforced every day through a constant barrage of propaganda. Without an independent means to verify or contradict the official news, the residents of Jaimanitas knew they were being lied to and manipulated, but, since the media mixed fiction with truth, they had no means or method to parse the degree of deception.

Virtually overnight, Vali and Alvaro were thrown into a new economic order. Under the Special Period, the ownership of dollars was legalized. Laws governing banking, credit, and wire transfer were liberalized. Simultaneously, various highly regulated schemes allowed the average Cuban to participate in a new dollar-denominated economy.

This spawned a panoply of unintended consequences— among them, a wedge that soon cleaved the populace. There were the lucky few that had access to dollars, and the rest of the population was mired in the *moneda nacional*, the peso economy. Everything Vali and her family had been taught about their existence in a socialist society was upended. Suddenly there were *haves* and *have-nots.* People with dollars *had*, and everyone else *had not*. Shattered was even the pretense of social equality. Che's New Man was a now an uber-capitalist in a '57 Chevrolet convertible.

Previously, the state's monthly ration system had supplied thirty days' worth of necessities. After 1993, the libreta yielded only ten.

In order to survive, the Cruz family and the other residents without access to dollars were immediately compelled to enter and participate in the *mercado negro*, the underground economy. Therefore, breaking the law in Cuba became the new necessity. Thus, de facto criminal behavior took on moral overtones; resistance to governmental oppression became a human right.

Vali held Mr. Cruz and his family in contempt. In her eyes, he had been a traitor to the cause of true freedom and the rights of the Cuban people. He wasn't like his brother and had never lifted a finger to fight against the tyranny of Castro or his cronies. He had been silent when the communists took control of Havana and destroyed a functioning economy. He had never protested as his neighbors and his brother were hauled off to prison, or while sitting in the dark after the electricity failed. When their food ran out, he and his family tightened their belts, ate rice soup with fried lard, and played dominoes.

Everyone knew Mr. Cruz had never tried to leave the island. Escape by any means, or just the desire to escape, was an act of resistance. Real men put their families on boats, crafts they had stolen or cobbled together with rope and inner tubes, and headed for Miami. Even if they died trying, it was better than living as a slave. Others, like his brother, had stayed in Cuba and fought in the resistance; some were just getting out of prison after thirty years. He had never applied for the lottery, one of the only methods that allowed a citizen to leave Cuba. Mr. Cruz had accepted the status quo and never fought to better himself, or his family. He endured, regardless of the obstacles placed before him. He had never questioned the system, or, if he did, he kept his thoughts to himself.

He deserved to die, thought Vali as she passed his house, *since he never lived.* She did her best to avoid making eye contact with the group at the Cruzes' house and the old men she knew would be leering. In a similar fashion, she ignored the new tenant in Coco's rental house, although he was only feet away, sitting encased in the metal cage porch. No, this morning she would not be distracted from making her rounds.

A catchphrase had entered the vocabulary of Vali, her family, her friends. Indeed, it floated on the tips of the tongues of most Cubans, like the dark antithesis to Costa Rica's *Pura Vida.* One would hear it mumbled in the bus queues, whispered in line at the pharmacy, or over the dinner table. It was a universally shared acknowledgment of defeat and frustration—*Vida es imposible.* Life is impossible. It had been worse just four years ago, during the starving. Vali remembered when the cats and dogs had disappeared from the streets. She had recollections of the first time her mother had fried a strip of dog meat with onions. Cats were different. They were always ground up and used in soup stock.

Vali navigated the obstacle course of cracks and potholes. Calle 234 was coming to life, a blended symphony of background TV, crying babies, roosters crowing, engines being started, dishes clanging, music, news, voices, and footsteps, harmonically overlaid by the homogenized drone of vehicles on nearby Avenida Quinta.

Vendors pushed through their morning rounds. There was a smiling, toothless Angolan veteran propelling an iron cart with tiny wheels, selling cones of roasted peanuts, his musical shout—*Mani*— was superfluous, since everyone could hear him coming a block away. Muscled young spearfisherman, dripping wet, having emerged from the rocky beach only three blocks to the north, delivered *pargo*, parrotfish, and if one had the right connections, contraband lobster. Horse-drawn carts carried sand and cement for the foundation of the video rental store being constructed on the corner. Scooters sputtered as they weaved their way through the rolling mayhem that Cubans called a transportation system. Schoolgirls in their white blouses and golden skirts walked snakelike paths around piles of rubbish to the primary school on the other side of the park, making Vali long for the relative innocence of her school days.

Every house on Calle 234 was unique, each a reflection of its owner. Some were little fortresses hidden behind masonry walls, topped with spikes or broken glass, or fortified with wrought iron gates on screeching hinges. The house to the right of Mr. Cruz's was a sheathed in green marble with an elegant door of hand-carved teak. On its upper story, a veranda of classical balustrade rail under a barrel-tile roof. Others had automobile garages, or flower gardens, or, like the Cruz family, a simple, wooden porch. It was easy to see which families were receiving *remesas*.

Vali intercepted her neighbors as they assumed the patterns that defined their intertwined existence. "Buenos dias," Mrs. Nunez greeted Vali as they crossed paths.

Mrs. Nunez went off every morning to help her husband, who had a job at CUPET, allowing him to steal gas, which she then sold in two-liter glass bottles in the alley beside her house. It was during these sales—clandestine exchanges at the Nunez house in the evening—that Mrs. Nunez had heard about Alvaro being killed at the Rumbo, and she passed the news along.

CHAPTER THREE

The beginning of an ocean voyage is usually accompanied by an assignment of watches. Three people would fall easily into the schedule of three hours on the helm, six hours off. Without REM sleep, crews get cranky and bad things happen. But in their white-knuckle blast across the stream, there was little thought of sleep. Ships would appear with startling speed and regularity on the black horizon and start to bear down. Even huge ships were marked with deceptively simple navigational lights—a high, white light on the stern superstructure, a low, white light mounted on the bow, a red light on the port side, and a green light on the starboard.

There was little by which to gauge their speed and heading. It was a guessing game. Would they pass to the stern, to the bow, or establish the horror of constant bearing/decreasing range—shorthand for a collision course? Just in case, Charlie stowed the twelve-gauge flare pistol in the binnacle pocket and stood ready to hail on the emergency radio.

"We are like a turtle crossing I-95," mused Allen as a northbound freighter passed to the bow within a quarter mile. "They would squash us like a bug."

Charlie tried to lighten the mood. "Why do they call camels ships of the desert? Because they are filled with Arab semen."

"Yuck," Jenna said as she turned away, looked across the bow, and stared into the darkness. By midnight, they were twenty-six miles north of Bimini.

"If that's a ship, it's not moving." Allen strained to focus on a patch of black off the starboard bow. "There it is again."

The flash of the Great Isaac Cay Lighthouse swept its way over the curvature of the Earth, a tiny pinprick of intermittent light on a monolithic black horizon. Not even a day out of Florida, the crew of the *Express* was confronted with the reality of their insignificance in a huge and unforgiving sea. Only a fool wouldn't be humbled. The crew sat and stared at the lonesome white light.

Hours later, the wind slacked as they entered a long southerly tack past the shoal known as Hens and Chickens, heading to the calm waters in the lee of North Bimini. Using the depth sounder, they rode the ten-fathom curve to avoid the current. Off their port lay the expanse of the Great Bahama Bank, a massive column of limestone rising three thousand feet from the abysmal depths, its great plateau stretching three hundred miles to the southeast with a water depth averaging twelve feet.

Morning's light found them sleeping under a quarantine flag at anchor in crystal clear, flat water. They had traveled 137 miles.

"Oh my God, this is beautiful!" Jenna's breath was taken away as she beheld the Bahamas for the first time. The sun had just risen over North Bimini. The gin-clear water led to a postcard panorama of coconut palms, interspersed with cottages and nearby Alice Town. The wind, which had beguiled them for the past twenty-four hours, was broken by the long, thin wisp of rock and sand that stretched before them from north to south. The sea was calm, flat, and inviting.

"Are there sharks? Can I go swimming?" Jenna's enthusiasm was infectious.

Charlie unpinned the stern ladder and lowered it into the water. He was surprised when Jenna emerged from the cabin wearing only a bikini bottom. She sprang to the cabin top and dived over the railing, making barely a splash. Apparently there was more to his new crewmember than he expected. Allen had met her only a month before up in Atlanta. She had recently graduated with a useless degree -history? – anthropology? – it didn't make any difference because with her credentials she needed to embrace unemployment. However, it was immediately apparent she must have excelled on the swim team. It was refreshing to see her go native so quickly. He had been concerned she might get seasick and take the first plane home.

"With a body like that she could make $500 a night as a pole dancer," Charlie joked. Allen shot Charlie a glance with raised eyebrows and a shrug of his shoulders. He was surprised, also. But there she was, pivoting around after a perfect dive, brushing the water from her eyes, and slicking back her blond hair as she returned the stare of her onlookers.

"Good score, Allen, you found a freaking mermaid."

***

The customs office was located only a quarter mile away in Alice Town, but to get there, they had to travel south and enter the sand-bottom channel that separates North and South Bimini. All visitors to the Bahamas were required to make a customs declaration upon arrival. Technically, no one was to set foot on any land mass or to fish in Bahamian waters without clearing customs. As a practical matter, if a boat was headed in the direction of the nearest international port of entry, they didn't generally get hassled.

They passed the rocky southern point of North Bimini, its casuarina trees shading the carcasses of rusted cars, discarded refrigerators, and concrete-building debris.

21

"It's a lot poorer than I expected," observed Allen as they passed the Loyalist Cemetery and the skeletal remains of the old Bimini Hotel. Construction along the water's edge seemed to be devoid of modern urban planning—unpainted shacks stood beside bright, new multistory, fisherman-friendly hotels, their docks reaching all the way to the channel. Piles of conch shells—the same ones found in shell shops across the world—seemed to be everywhere. They were deposited at the foot of docks, dumped in the weed-strewn vacant lots, and they lay scattered and bleaching across the narrow beaches. The *Express* passed Chalk's seaplane ramp and Sweeting's Dock as they headed for the customs office located at the Bimini Big Game Club.

They could hear it before they could see it. The sound of a steel band increased as they motored north. Colorful flags greeted them, straining in the wind, displaying Bacardi's iconic bat in a red circle. Advertisements festooned the outer docks. Banners swayed from palm trees around the pool area. It was apparent that the crew of the *Express* had stumbled into one of the Northern Bahamas most prestigious fishing tournaments. Other posters paid homage to local icon Ernest Hemingway, a longtime visitor to Alice Town.

The *Express* tied to the outside slip under quarantine, the yellow flag flying just below the spreader—a notice to the world that she was under process. As captain, Charlie was allowed to leave the vessel and walk directly to the customhouse. As he carried their passports and a leatherette file containing the ship's papers, he passed the empty slips of the sportfishing fleet, their satellite dishes and mooring lines awaiting their return. He continued toward what appeared to be a hotel. When he reached the swimming pool, he reclined on a lounge and absorbed his surroundings.

"Now this is more like it."

It felt good to get off the rocking boat. Manicured lawns led to palm-covered walkways and the upscale yellow hotel. Where the walkway intersected the building, a covered gazebo, containing— yes, he could hear it, the cascading diamonds that illuminate every sailor's dream—a free ice machine.

"I could get used to this."

Feeling curious, he thumbed through the passports. Allen, he knew, but who was this mermaid? According to the declaration page, she was Jenna Ann Morrison, born December 5, 1975, in Minneapolis. How the hell had she learned to swim like that in Minneapolis? Sex: Female—seemed right. Her picture looked like the product of a glamour shoot. His looked like a mug shot.

The customs office was located at the end of a strip of pastel-pink commercial shops. Charlie handed the passports to the customs official and filled out the paperwork. Yes, he had no guns. No cigarettes. Some liquor. No scuba tanks. Yes, he had fishing equipment. No trigger-operated spears. He explained he needed a cruising permit since he would be traveling all the way down the chain, exiting at Mayaguana, or Great Inagua, depending on the wind. No problem. Pay $120. Bang. Bang. Bang. Three passports, three stamps—Bahamas Immigration, Admitted May 11, 1998, with the notation: OWNER MUST NOT ENGAGE IN GAINFUL OCCUPATION.

Since the *Express* was here for just one night, she could remain on the outside dock. It cost $1.45 per foot with a five-dollar electric-and-water hookup fee. He paid with a hundred-dollar bill, receiving change in pink-and-blue Bahamian currency that looked more like tickets to Sea World. Returning to the dock, he passed the bar.

"Can I get anything for you?" asked the bow-tied bartender from behind a row of Bacardi bottles. He was wearing a Bacardi shirt, beneath a twenty-foot-wide Bacardi banner dancing in the wind. Charlie wheeled, walked to the tiki hut, and sat on a stool.

"Absolutely. You have any Ron Rico Rum?" he asked, screwing with the man.

Without hesitation, a three-ounce premixed drink in a flimsy, clear-plastic cup appeared on the bar before him. The bartender must have had a line of them concealed behind the counter.

23

"They are free all weekend. Bacardi is sponsoring the tournament."

Charlie took a sip. "Oh, thanks, I love rum and coke."

Looking up from the sink, the bartender informed, "That's a Cuba Libre. It ain't no rum and coke."

Taken aback, Charlie was compelled to ask, "Sorry, what's the difference?"

The bartender responded, as if by rote, "A proper Cuba Libre is two ounces of white rum, one lime squeezed and husked with its husk acting as a bitter, and Coca-Cola in a tall Collins glass, with three big cubes of ice."

Wiping the bar top with a folded rag, the bartender continued, "Lines are out of the water at four o'clock. Weigh-in starts at five. Free burgers, free rum, and the band plays until nine."

Charlie, always the smart ass, said, "But this is a plastic cup with one cube of ice."

The bartender was cool. "Maybe not the glass. People drop them on the pool deck, you know, but that's the real deal inside. You know what they call them in Havana? They are called *minteras* if it's a tall glass, or *minteriditas* in a short glass. *Mintera* means 'lie' in Spanish. That's what the Cubans call them, 'cause Cuba ain't free."

"You been down there?" Charlie sipped his drink, suddenly interested.

"All the guys go. For cigars. We buy them for three dollars each and sell them for twenty-five, thirty, sometimes sixty dollars. Montecristo #2 as high as seventy-five dollars a pop."

"As an American, I can't go."

"You can go. Anybody can go. Just climb on the Cubana Air flight out of Nassau. Takes an hour. When you get there, just put five dollars in your passport and ask them not to stamp it. Flight leaves every day at noon. You can book through Havana Tours. Here's a long article on Cuba in *Cigar Aficionado* magazine. I just finished it. Here, take it."

Charlie chugged his drink, tucked the proffered article in his pocket, tipped the bartender, and carried three Cuba Libres past the empty slips of the sportfishing fleet, to the end of the dock, to the now legal, now free-to-do-whatever-the-hell-they-wanted-in-the-Bahamas crew of the international, headed-to-Antigua, world-traveling *Bora Bora Express*.

After affixing fenders, setting spring lines, and hooking up to electric, the crew of the *Express* raised the dodger and flopped into the cockpit. Charlie looked across the shallow, turquoise bonefish flats that extended a full sixty miles to the east. As the rum kicked in, he reflected on the trip and the events of the day—the peacefulness of a protected harbor out of the wind, the indigo-blue water of the Gulf Stream, an independent country only fifty miles from Miami, Jenna diving from the boat. Life was good.

Around four thirty, their peace was shattered by the return of the first of the tournament boats. Ranging in length from forty-five to ninety feet, these multimillion-dollar machines were toys of the ultrarich, each using more diesel in a day than Charlie would use in three years. They carry hundreds of thousands of dollars worth of the latest electronics and upgrade continually as technology improves. Professional captains, piloting from one of the upper stations or the flying bridge, were eager to display their talents. With three thousand horsepower at their disposal, these fiberglass tributes to conspicuous consumption were surprisingly maneuverable. Charlie marveled at the speed at which they pivoted and backed to the weigh station, their raw power vibrating everything within a one-hundred-foot radius. He watched one move sideways when its stern missed by a couple of feet—a trick achieved by counteracting a pivot with the bow thruster. The prizes for which they competed were are as high

25

as a million dollars, which was often surpassed by the Calcutta—the cash bets between crews, captains, and owners.

Only the largest fish made it to the scales. Marlin under five hundred pounds were generally released, as were bluefin tuna under six hundred. Smaller fish, such as sails, dolphin, and wahoo were weighed and measured since they were included in the overall tally. Charlie watched as the catch, after being weighed, was hoisted to the back of a rusted Toyota and brought to a cleaning hut located at the base of the farthest dock. Once off-loaded, the captains rocketed forward, found their place on the dock, and backed into their slips with equal dexterity, one after another. Charlie lost count. Two million here, eight million there—there must have been a hundred million dollars' worth of floating stock in the marina.

Seizing the opportunity, Charlie grabbed his razor-sharp, fifteen-inch Forschner fillet knife, threw it into a five-gallon bucket, and headed for the cleaning tables. He knew there were more fish than could be eaten by the crew and help with the hot and bloody job was usually appreciated. There are many ways to clean a fish, but an experienced fisherman can size up another's technique and proficiency in about thirty seconds. The mates watched as Charlie began the tail incision on a forty-pound wahoo, following the pectoral ribs to the spine and over the backbone ridge, letting the dorsal ribs guide his knife to the far side without leaving meat on the carcass. Passing his test, he struck up a conversation.

"You all fishing the circuit? Where did you come from?"

Oscar Grisby, mate on the fifty-five-foot Striker *Bill Collector*, described his trip from Caracas, Venezuela to San Andres Island, then north to Grand Cayman, the voyage timed to intersect major tournaments. They had tagged a record twenty-seven sailfish in eight hours. Then they'd caught the Hemingway Tournament in Havana.

"Havana? I didn't think Americans could go to Havana. I looked on the computer. There are huge fines, and they can confiscate the boat." Charlie was starting to think that they were the only Americans in the Bahamas who hadn't just come back from Cuba.

The mate seemed unconcerned, "There are exceptions. For instance, the owner got permission to attend a hosted tournament. I think he had to promise not to spend more than a certain amount per day, something like fifty bucks. Of course, we spent twenty times that the first night. There were lots of boats from the US in the marina."

"But it's communist, right? What in the world can you buy or do in a communist country?" Charlie continued to dress fish as they spoke.

"Anything you want," Oscar said emphatically. "If you have money, the country is wide open. Cabs cost fifty cents. A bottle of Havana Club Rum is just over a buck. A lobster dinner for five dollars. We had to stop the women from climbing aboard. For Cubans, it's a daily hassle. For us it an E ticket to Disney World."

"Women?" Somehow communism and women seemed incongruous to Charlie. "You mean like the women in Russia, the ones that look like Boris Yeltsin in a dress—buffalo faces with a scarf on their head?"

Oscar laughed. "They are probably there, but the ones at the marina were young and healthy. Some even spoke English. The guards brought them to the boat. If the girl came aboard, we had to give the police five dollars. We were thinking about bringing one back with us, but they check every inch of the boat before we were allowed to leave."

After an hour of fish cleaning, Charlie was allowed as to take with him as many fillets as he wanted. He filled his bucket halfway with dolphin, wahoo, and thick, red slabs of bluefin tuna, topping it off with a layer of ice.

Walking back to the dock, Charlie remembered details from his internet research. Cuba was on a short list of forbidden countries that included North Korea and Iran. These were sworn enemies of the United States, as defined by the Trading with the Enemies Act. Penalties for violation were severe and included fines and imprisonment. Yet in a single afternoon, he had learned that regular people seem to come and go without reprisal. And when they went, they seemed to like it there. Perhaps in five or six years, when he was on the return trip home from Antigua, he would make a port of call in Havana.

That night thunderstorms raked the western edge of the Great Bank with squalls and downpours, disturbing the local winds. But when the sun rose, the storms evaporated, and the trades reasserted themselves, blowing fifteen knots from the southeast. The *Express* left the dock midmorning under full sail, making eight knots at 185°. It was the conditions for which the *Express* was designed, and she flew to nearby Piquet Rock, anchoring in its lee. There they donned fins, masks, and weight belts in anticipation of Allen's first spearfishing lesson.

"Diving is a state of mind," instructed Charlie as they dangled from the swim ladder. "Supercharge your body with oxygen." He demonstrated by hyperventilating for thirty seconds. "Then go into a deep sleep, kicking ever so slowly and letting your weights carry you to the bottom."

Allen tried but hit a wall about ten feet down. "My ears," he cried when he reached the surface. Charlie had forgotten to show his student how to clear his ears. On his next dive, Allen made it to twelve feet, but found himself completely out of air and clawing for the surface. Jenna could make it to twenty feet but had never used a spear. Worse, the fish fled long before she was near enough to get a shot.

As they all bobbed on the surface of the water, Charlie shared his thoughts on fish psychology. "If you drop in on top of them, they know you are a predator. You must act casual. Swim to a position on the bottom about ten feet away and approach slowly at their level. Whistle, divert your eyes, act casual, and by the time they figure out you aren't another fish, it's too late." Allen and Jenna tried but couldn't match Charlie's downtime of two minutes and change.

The night was spent on the hook in the lee of tiny Piquet Rock. As the sun rose, they continued south under the main, headed for Gun Cay on a beam reach. Charlie had a chance to teach Jenna about a little about the sails and sail trim.

"That big sail up front is the jib, also called the genoa, or genny—almost your name. When it is unfurled, it can provide far more horsepower than the main. It is mounted on roller-furling gear, and just like the name says, we can furl it around the headstay to reduce it to the size of a handkerchief. We can control its size with the furling line—that's the rope that comes back to the small winch. Then we control its shape with the sheet—that's the one attached to the sail and comes back to this big winch. Both the main and the jib are like huge bird wings, mounted vertically. Here, I will show you."

Charlie released the sheet, and the jib started to flog. "We just crank it in until it stops luffing. There, you can feel it pull. It becomes a wing, pulls like a mule, and then it's off to the races."

Referring to the Bahama Guide, Allen called out navigational waypoints. "Turn east, right here, under the Gun Cay Light."

"*Key* Light. It's pronounced *key*, like a car *key*," Charlie corrected.

"All right, that's the Gun *Key* Light, and we enter the Gun *Key* Cut just to its south. Stay on the north side of the channel."

Charlie started the engine and put the *Express* in gear as he turned to port and into the teeth of fresh breeze. There was insufficient room to tack. Jenna and Allen ran amidships as blue water blasted over the bow, rattling the anchor in its chocks. The swinging, jumping boom became a deadly weapon. A rack of drying dishes smashed to the galley floor. The incoming tide, squeezed between the rocky islands and thrust against the relentless wind, created a confused, four-foot riptide that stopped them dead in their tracks. Sailing was impossible. Charlie pushed the throttle forward and increased power until the diesel screamed. Slowly the *Express* crept its way onto the bank.

Although the wind screeching in the rigging sounded the same as when they had been in the Gulf Stream, the seas and the motion of the boat were very much different. With only six feet of water beneath them, the waves didn't have time to develop into rollers. Instead, they were short and steep, with a period of three or four seconds.

"Did you buy this boat with a built-in headwind?" Allen shouted above the roar as he tried to secure the swaying dingy. *Blam. Smack. Bam.* Every couple of seconds, the spray from the waves smashing the starboard quarter was blown over the gunwale, coating the canvas awning that covered the entrance belowdecks with a crust of salt.

"Holy shit," moaned Jenna, "How far do we have to go?" She steadied herself in the companionway with the look of despair in her eyes.

"Sixty-eight miles across the bank," Allen answered glumly.

"Will there be a hotel there?" she pleaded.

Charlie hesitated, not wanting to be the bearer of bad news. "No, that's to get us over the bank to Tongue of the Ocean, then it's fifty more miles to Nassau." He switched on the autopilot, propped himself with a cushion on the aft of the cockpit, and tried to look comfortable. "This is why they make rum! Please hand up the bottle and a couple cokes." Smashing their way east at four-point-two knots, they passed the afternoon trying to get drunk and playing "Name That Fish" using Bohlke's *Fishes of the Bahamas* as a guide.

As the alcohol brought its merciful relief, Charlie cast his eyes upon the loveliness of Jenna. Thin and playful, she would by now seem overdressed had she been wearing her bikini top. Perhaps the weather gods in their infinite wisdom had sent her firm and young breasts as compensation for their inability to create favorable winds. *All things go better with titties and rum—it's a universal truth*, thought Charlie as he took possession of the big blue book with a parrotfish on its cover.

"Ah yes, this is indeed an informative book." He pretended to read. "Says here that in several regards fish are very much like humans. Some fish, like groupers, exhibit a trait known as sequential hermaphroditism; they are born male and turn female. Yep, says so right here, and other fish turn homosexual—it gives statistics—the same as gay American men: 60 percent change naturally, and the other 40 percent are sucked into it."

Jenna rolled her eyes. "If we ever get out of here, I'm telling people that we had to leave the Bahamas because *they* kicked you out, too."

CHAPTER FOUR

S ince 1962, Vali's family depended—as did all Cubans—on the
Libreta de Abastecimiento, the rationing system for food and
necessities distributed through the barrio's bodega. Each family unit
was issued a palm-sized blue book, the *libreta*, into which was
recorded the receipt of monthly rations. The original system had
been codified into law by the Cuban constitution in 1976, making it
a birthright of every citizen and, for most, the only legal avenue for
obtaining food and other items. Names, ages, and the domicile
address were contained on the declaration page of the *libreta*, as well
as any special dietary or medical information. The pages on the left
chronicle rations of meat, chicken, and fish. On the right, less-
regulated commodities such as rice, milk, matches, coffee, and
laundry soap. There were spaces for nonstandard and seasonal
products such as plantains, yucca, and mangos.

Vali carried two plastic bags, her family's *libreta,* and a
small, yellow coin purse. Inside her bag was a five-hundred-milliliter
plastic TuKola bottle. She hurried since she wanted to return home
before the late-morning sun turned the narrow streets into an oven.
Her purse contained two hundred pesos, about one-third of the total
monthly amount earned by herself, her mother, and her thirteen-
year-old sister, Rowena.

Her mother recollected when the peso had been on par with the dollar, or at least when it had cost a dollar to buy a peso, and vice versa. Just ten years ago, if a tourist paid thirty-five dollars for a hotel room, the rate charged a Cuban would be thirty-five pesos. Now, of course, Cubans were not allowed to stay in hotels, even if they could afford it. During the Special Period, the government responded by overprinting money until inflation devalued the peso to a low of 160 to the dollar. But today—May 13, 1998—its official value was $0.0492, or just under a nickel. Pesos were further divided by one hundred into centavos.

Bodegas serve anywhere from six hundred to two thousand customers. Jaimanitas's bodega served 957. A family's *libreta* was honored only at the bodega that served their district. Traveling to a different district, even for only a night, required a visit to a government office—the OFICODA—to update the booklet's data. Thus, by controlling a person's diet, the government controlled and tracked their movements around the island.

Today Vali's rations included five eggs, four pounds of sugar, five pounds of broken rice, a half-pound of beans, half a bottle of cooking oil, four ounces of coffee, one pound of spaghetti, one kilogram of whole milk powder, one liter of soy yogurt, and cooking gas. Children seven to thirteen, like her sister, got additional items such as one kilogram of salt every three months, one pound of chicken, five additional eggs, a phosphorous supplement, and one piece of bread daily.

Items were taken off the ration list when supply was unable to meet demand. However, these items were usually available at the dollar stores, albeit at prices sometimes ten times or twenty times the subsidized rate. Luxury items such as fresh milk and meat were usually the first to disappear when agricultural production decreased. Sometimes there were additions—for instance, when there was an unexpected abundance of an agricultural product such as pineapples or bananas.

Meat, fish, poultry, and pork were distributed through the *carniceria,* the butcher, allowing a half-pound every fifteen days.

Shortages might last from an hour to a month, and queues often stretched around the block. As a monument to Stalinist efficiency, the bodega, the *carniceria,* and *the panaderia* often lay in far-flung outposts of the distribution district.

Vali fearfully anticipated the line as she rounded the corner. She was in luck. The line hadn't spilled into the street, as it did so often, which meant she wouldn't have to wait in the heat of the direct sun.

There had never been a name above the door of the bodega, nor had one ever been necessary. It had served Vali's mother and her mother before her. Located in the middle of the block, east of the intersection of Via Blanca and Calle 236, it had changed little in thirty years. It was a squat, concrete bunker with a wide, blue door, a poorly lit interior with faded white ceilings, industrial pale-green walls supporting wide shelves that spoke of better days before the Special Period, and a wall-to-wall deteriorating Formica counter, at its center the shrine of the ration state—the ubiquitous Russian-made antique balance beam scale with an oversized, galvanized steel basket. At the scale's side rested the slotted cast-iron counterweights, that, when added or removed from the dangling metal rod attached to the balance arm, meted out, to the quarter ounce, the protein, carbohydrate, and fiber that kept Vali and her family alive.

The rationed items listed in her *libreta* were mirrored on a chalkboard that loomed over the attendant's head. The top line— PRODUCTO, PER CAPITA, PRECIO, INICIO, and VENCE—meant the type of product, the amount allotted per customer, its price, and the dates that the pricing would remain in effect. Out of fifteen listed products, on a good day perhaps twelve would be available and the price on the board only an approximation.

PRODUCT	QUANTITY	PRICE (pesos/unit)
Rice	2 pounds	0.90
Beans	0.6 pounds	1.80
Sugar	4 pounds	0.15
Coffee	4 ounces	4.00
Cooking oil	1 pound	0.40
Pasta	1 pound	1.80
Whole milk powder	1 Kilogram	2.50
Soy yogurt	1 liter	1.00
Chicken	1 pound	0.70
Eggs	5 eggs	0.90
Salt	1 box	0.35
Matches	1 box	0.40
Bread (daily)	French bread loaf	0.05

Other products were optional depending upon supply or seasonality. Fish, yucca, mangos, various soaps, and toothpaste were usually available at some time during the month. Vali endured, shuffling with the other customers, awaiting her turn. Some leaned on the counter, resting on elbows, staring at a blank wall or watching Luciana, the clerk, go about filling orders. Rice and beans were stored in metal drums behind the counter against the wall. They were filled from polypropylene sacks stacked high against the wall of the back room. The waist-high receptacles were always located within scooping distance of the scale, and the clerk was well practiced at approximating the correct amount. Vali placed her order for five pounds of rice, then her one-point-eight-pound allotment of beans for three people, and finally for eight ounces of coffee.

Luciana, who had worked in this bodega for twelve years, carefully funneled 250 milliliters of cooking oil into the TuKola bottle without spilling a drop. She was always cheerful and seemed to love her job. It was a mystery how she could work in these conditions and keep a smile. Handing the bag of rice over the counter, she hesitated, her eyes absorbing and studying the features of her customer's face.

"You know, Vali, you really *do* look like Selena."

35

Vali had heard the comparison before. It was flattering to be compared to the singer. *But*, she thought, *I'm sure that Selena never had to stand in line for rations.*

The bill came to thirty-six pesos, ninety-four centavos, or $1.85, which included a stick of bread. Vali received 180 pesos per month, about nine dollars. Her mother earned both the wage and, since she was single, a pension of five dollars, for a total of fourteen dollars. Her little sister received 180 pesos also. If the average Cuban were to somehow survive on government rations, and only those rations, he or she would wind up with about five dollars at the end of the month.

This five dollars must provide that which the government did not. Therefore, shoes, clothes, refrigerators, furniture, bicycles, bottled water, kitchen items, gasoline, lipstick, sanitary napkins, and other necessities had to be acquired by barter, through the *mercado negro*—the black market—or in the dollar stores. This is the paradox in which most Cubans find themselves. This was the main reason why life was impossible—the government failed to provide the goods, services, or economic means necessary to survive, forcing vast portions of the population into the status of outlaws, which in a Machiavellian twist that could only be dreamed up by a group like Castro and his pseudo-revolutionaries, magnified the repressive power of the government over its people.

In addition to rationing, some citizens received about four hundred pesos Cubano in wage and pension. This could be spent in any government operated peso store or converted at the rate of twenty-to-one for the American dollars necessary to purchase goods in the state-run dollar stores. Friends of Vali that received *remesas* could shop at Palco for luxury goods such as canned peaches and birthday cakes. She had been to the dollar store with them. It was a glimpse into the world of the rich—a parallel world within her own community. It was glimpses like these that fueled her desire to escape.

Castro also kept an iron grip on the distribution of information. The two state newspapers were little more than propaganda sheets that were regularly used as toilet paper since they were cheaper. A Cuban library could fit on two small shelves—the communist rantings of Marx, Engles, and some of the homegrown crazies. Radio seldom strayed from the party line, and anti-Castro broadcasts from the Florida Keys were jammed. The evening news never discussed crime or gave statistics on murder or robbery, but an increase in bauxite production was worth half an hour. Yet in the nearly impenetrable wall of isolation, there was a gaping hole through which any Cuban could glean a non-edited view of the outside world.

Vali knew, as did all Cubans, of the world that lay beyond their shores by watching the bootleg nightly movies on state TV. The Argentinian novella on Canal Tres, filmed in opulent homes of the Latino superrich, displayed an unrealistic but universally envied lifestyle. Any foreign movie, regardless of its plot, gave a view into the lives and luxuries that were standard in the rest of the world. For instance, though the plot of an American film might be irrelevant, Cubans viewers could see the characters winding their way through the labyrinth of a free society. They gained an unobstructed glimpse into the minutiae of everyday life in foreign lands—consumer items that boggled their minds, computers, cell phones, manicured neighborhoods, new cars, blenders, refrigerators brimming with food, clean streets, and, most of all, the freedom to enjoy it all.

It was through the movies that Vali gained a view of life on nearby islands such as Puerto Rico and St. Thomas. She had seen how they lived in Australia and could identify the skylines of New York, Chicago, and San Francisco. Hollywood did more to undermine the legitimacy of the Castro regime than the Helms-Burton Act—the United States latest embargo against Cuba—could have ever hoped. She saw it all and wanted what she saw. She dreamed of the beautiful home, the elegant kitchen, the beautiful kids in the swimming pool. She imagined driving a car—or, better yet, being driven. She knew she was pretty as any of the stars, probably more beautiful since she didn't need or wear makeup.

Vali had vowed to do whatever it would take to interact with tourists. It was her only option. It was only through tourists that dollars could be acquired, and it was only dollars that could free her and her family from the peso culture and the bodega. Her only other option was to sell herself, but her friends who had gone to Havana to work as *jineteras* were quickly identified by the police and placed on warning. Some had been caught turning tricks a second time and were on probation. After a third strike, they would be arrested and do time in a prison or an agricultural work farm.

Vali had considered entering the *jinetera* business but concluded the risks were too great. She shuddered, thinking about the horrors that she had heard described about Cuban prison. Just the thought of being locked up for even a short time was incomprehensible. It wasn't that she had a moral objection to prostitution—for freedom, she would very nearly sell her soul—but even if she entered the trade, the competition was fierce. There were a million pretty girls in the big city, and most were eager to rent out space in their vaginas on a short-term basis. She had no contacts in Havana. There were no police on her payroll. There was no safe room in which to hide when the police swept the streets. It seemed an insurmountable problem. The police had demonstrated that they were ruthless in their quest to keep Cuban women from consorting with foreigners. And the police were on every corner.

***

Tourists traveling west from the Malecon blast through Vedado, Miramar, Nautico and Playa in about 18 minutes if they catch the lights. After the arches of Club Havana, they and their dollars shoot through Jaimanitas in about a minute, in route to Marina Hemingway, Santa Fe or all the way to Mariel. There was little reason for outsiders to stop in Jaimanitas and almost no reason for a tourist to get out of his or her vehicle and mingle with the natives. Vali stood on the corner and watched the visitors with their money whizz by. The tourists on Avenida Quinta might as well have been on the back side of the moon.

But in all of Cuba there were few young ladies, if any, that were a dead ringer for Selina.

Meanwhile, saving for the bicycle she wanted, which cost $78 in the Havana dollar store, would take years.

CHAPTER FIVE

The relentless pounding was beginning to take its toll on the *Bora Bora Express*. Slamming into twenty thousand walls of water every day put a terrible stress on the mast, spreaders, and the rest of the standing rigging. Slack in the stays indicated they needed to be tightened. The sounds of previously unheard creaks and groans belowdecks lent credulity that the *Express* herself was crying out in pain. If she did weaken and crack in two, what irony would it be to founder in a sea so shallow that land was but six feet below her keel?

After ten hours, and with Sylvia Beacon to their stern, the battered crew anchored and slept through the night under the faint glow of the masthead light.

The next morning, the sun cast a pink hue on the backs of the endless army of marching whitecaps that impeded their progress. The combined forces of wind and waves became a definable enemy with anthropomorphized malevolent intent. At anchor, the *Express* "weathervaned" directly into the wind and took the waves squarely on her bow, a configuration only slightly more pleasant than motoring. Taking advantage of the relative calm, Jenna prepared eggs and coffee as Charlie checked the engine oil level. By six o'clock, they were again underway, bound for an invisible point on a plastic chart where the currents of Great Bahama Bank, the Tongue of the Ocean, and the Northwest Providence Channel fought each other for dominance.

Seven hours of hard motoring brought them to the Northwest Channel, a narrow gap between the sand bores of the Northwest Shoal and the treacherous reefs of Joulter Cay, just off the north coast Andros. A feeling of foreboding crept over Charlie as he felt the *Express* rise and fall to an underlying swell that hinted of the conditions that lay before them. From a half mile, he could see the water change color from turquoise to purple. The new heading for Nassau brought them dead into the wind. On the bank's knife-like edge, growlers combed and broke steeply. The sailing ahead of them promised to be even tougher.

They pressed on. Even at full power, the *Express* struggled to make headway. All the machinery of the sailboat, the running and standing rigging, the roller-furling headgear, the furled main were now an aerodynamic drag, conspiring to push her backward. The energy of the pumping mast drove her bow down, even the position of the keel worked against them as it formed a pivot point, an axis around which the bow of the *Express* would rise then plunge into the oncoming sea.

Jenna focused on a clump of Sargasso weed. "We're not moving!"

It was as if they had fallen into a trap. Behind and to the north lay the breaking sand shoals of the bank, to the south the jagged coral reefs of Joulter and Andros.

Charlie yelled to Jenna, "Take the helm. Keep us dead into the wind. We need to second reef the main."

"Fall off to port!" Charlie yelled to Jenna when the reef was completed, wildly gesturing to the left side of the boat. Suddenly, the *Express* put her rail down and took off, catching the young skipper on the low side and nearly throwing him into the water. After recovering and adjusting, they flew at six knots to the northeast. Within ten minutes they were back on the edge of the bank.

The *Express* was on a high-speed roller coaster ride. "We are making good time, but in the wrong direction," observed Allen.

Even the wrong direction was preferable to the beating they had taken over the past twenty-four hours. When they sighted the breaking reefs north of Andros, they tacked again, this time taking an hour and a half to encounter the bank. The chart showed that if they adjusted course, they could make Chub Cay by cocktail hour. Although Chub Cay was only fourteen miles from the bank, it would take almost fifty miles of sailing to reach her. It was a serpentine, circuitous course, but Charlie had a plan to make it easier.

"Time for some rum." Charlie emerged from the galley with three glasses, rum, coke, and ice. It was a good time to drink. It was a good time not to think or to be analytical. Charlie was afraid that Allen and Jenna would start to do the math—the distance divided by speed, multiplied by discomfort—the irrefutable logic of extrapolating the previous one hundred miles to the twelve hundred miles that lay before them. Up until this point, the crew had not complained, but it was obviously not the trip they had signed up for. Charlie couldn't complete the trip without them. Best to have them distracted, get them drunk. Best to have them entertained.

Handing a drink to Jenna, Charlie launched into a story.

"Ah yes, I remember it well. The bucking of this fine ship does recall me a memory. T'was long ago but feels like only yesterday. On a steed, I was, a fine and noble animal, racing across the plain at full gallop with me on its regal back, hair ablowin' in the wind and a pistol at my side. Many miles we had traveled at such a pace, but lo, unbeknownst to me, my saddle had loosened and slid, did I, to the underside of the beast, its thundering hooves only inches from my shell-like ear. Struggle, I did, but to no avail. Distressed, I was, and lo, did I call out until a crowd appeared and summoned the K-Mart manager, who then came out to the parking lot and pulled the plug. Here's a drink for you, Allen."

Five hours later the *Express* rounded the jetty that led into Chub Cay Marina. Charlie's apprehension was mounting. There was an airport on the tiny island, therefore transportation that could whisk his crew away and leave him stranded. He remembered the advice he had been given in Ft. Lauderdale—*wait until after hurricane season.*

Running the numbers in his head only made matters worse. One hundred forty miles off the Florida coast in four days of hard sailing. Less than forty miles per day toward the target which was, he calculated—was it possible?—thirty more days to reach Antigua. And not thirty *cruising* days. A knot was forming in his stomach as reality hit home. Thirty more days of bashing to weather day and night. A sentence of thirty days of semi-isolation with hard labor. Even if the crew could take it, the boat was already starting to come apart. He wasn't even sure if Jenna and Allen had planned to be away from the States that long.

As soon as the *Express* was secure and fees had been paid, Allen broached the subject.

"Listen, Charlie. We gotta talk." Allen looked uncomfortable.

Charlie received a glance from Jenna that let him know they had been discussing leaving the voyage. They were waiting for his reaction, but it was clear they had already reached an understanding.

"A little lumpy out there, isn't it?" Charlie tried to make light of the subject. Even if he wanted to continue, it would be impossible without a crew. But there was no argument. He had already reached the conclusion that there was no place on earth worth going if one had to get there by sailing into a twenty-knot wind. "Wait before you abandon ship. I have an idea."

Charlie slipped the rubber band from chart 11013 and rolled it over the surface of the cockpit table. "Look, we could head south along Andros Island and cut across here." He pointed to a sand bore north of Lark's Nest. "Then west to Hurricane Flats. From there it is a straight shot to Havana. That way we wouldn't have to sail against the Gulf Stream."

"Cuba? You want to go to Cuba?" Allen sounded incredulous.

"Sure. Why not? Let's go to Cuba." Charlie moved his hands across the chart. "It's a huge island, almost six hundred miles from tip to tip. American boats are going. It's supposed to be cheap. Rum is just a dollar a bottle. You were along for an adventure. What could be better than going to a mysterious, forbidden communist fortress?"

Allen looked at Jenna, then focused his attention on the chart. "You want to sail through that?" He pointed to a massive coral formation that extended through the thin waters south of Andros for more than fifty miles.

"Yeah, I saw that, but look here." Charlie pressed his finger on the chart. "There seems to be a passage that's about two miles wide. It will take some careful navigation. With the sun at our backs, and the water clear, we should be able to spot the coral heads. After that, it would be smooth sailing for the next three hundred miles. It's a part of the world that's pretty much unexplored, and we will be on our own, but it should be doable."

The sound of the wind could be heard racing through the tops of the casuarinas that surrounded the marina, its catspaws clawing their way down to the dock, grasping at the *Bora Bora Express* even within the sanctuary of safe harbor. It reminded the crew that the wind had the become the enemy—or perhaps the messenger—of malevolent forces. It had a demon's face; they had seen it in the crest of a thousand waves. It had a hideous howl, its vocal chords comprised of the mast and rigging from which it raged in its pulpit above them with a sermon replete with fire and brimstone.

At night, they had heard the wind mouth words of crystal clarity within its spooky blend of moans and wails and shrieks. The wind had taken on a chilling presence that transcended physics. It was a relentless foe that ultimately threatened their very existence.

Even as they pondered its persona, they could hear it still, beckoning just above the masthead, eager to enjoin them in the next round of battle. It was his youthful exuberance, his arrogance, his blind reliance on luck, that had brought his boat and his friends to gaze into the eyes of nemesis.

We're lucky, thought Charlie. *I screwed up, and nobody got hurt.* Antigua, at this time of year, had been a bad decision.

"Cuba, anyone?" He looked hopefully at his crew.

"It's a no-brainer," concluded Allen. "But it's up to Jenna."

Jenna looked relieved. "If we can stop sailing into the wind, I will go anywhere—Cuba, Bermuda, Denver, anywhere. Do they have beaches there?"

Although they reached the conclusion on day four, they realized the trip to Antigua had been doomed from the start.

CHAPTER SIX

Drinks were prepared and the change of course duly celebrated. Any misgivings they might have had about the dangers of Cuba were erased by alcohol and the relief of knowing that they would soon be on dry land. Before the second round, the wind abated, and a thick cloud cover descended over the Berry Islands, as if the wind gods—determined to demonstrate the futility of the voyage—could now relax and get on with their job of changing the weather.

A morning without sun found the *Express* leaving Chub Cay on a southerly course. The wind had backed to the northeast and diminished, its highest puffs failing to reach twelve knots. Allen was surprised at how quickly the sea had laid down. Under full main and jib, they maintained a leisurely five and a half knots. "It's time to strike terror into the hearts of the local fish population," exclaimed Charlie as he wrangled a rod from its mount on the overhead of the aft cabin. Charlie slipped the butt into the rod holder affixed to the stern rail, set the drag to twenty pounds, and watched the silver-sided lure throw its purple laser shafts of light as it wobbled its way through the gin-clear water two hundred feet astern.

Under a new wind regime, the sinister sea had become a benevolent ally. Instead of pushing through mountains of water, the waves now passed effortlessly beneath them. The pressure of the wind in the sails steadied the craft as she glided over a deteriorating southeasterly swell.

"This is more like it," exclaimed Jenna.

The *Express* slid in an easy motion across the welcoming surface of a sea over a mile deep, all the time keeping the eastern shore of Andros on the near horizon. Jenna emerged from the companionway. "This calls for a bottle of wine." Three glasses were poured in celebration. "Now this is how sailing should be!"

"Did I ever tell you about my uncle in New York City?" asked Charlie.

"Oh no, here comes another one," Jenna braced herself. Allen laughed. Morale onboard was improving.

"Yea, he was one of those raincoat guys, a flasher. He'd jump out of an alley and flash people as they walked by. I asked him if it was tough during the winter. He told me the cold was getting to him, but he was going to stick it out for one more year."

Before anyone could react to Charlie's sick joke, *zing!*—the drag on the reel screamed as a fish tore line from the spool. Charlie grabbed the rod and increased the drag.

"Furl the jib to slow us down!" Charlie shouted.

Jenna and Allen jumped to adjust. As soon as the mahi stopped taking line, it rocketed into the air, twisting violently to throw the hook. Charlie kept tension on the line, which he began to slowly retrieve. The powerful fish changed its course and raced toward the stern, Charlie cranking furiously to maintain tension.

"Start the engine!" Charlie bellowed. Allen flipped the switch and threw the transmission in forward to keep the fish behind the boat and under control.

The mahi broke the surface of the water only fifty feet off the port. One could see why the Spanish name for the fish was *dorado*—or "golden"—a name that failed to do justice to its iridescent blend of green and turquoise, which glowed beneath a veneer of yellow.

"Get the gaff!" Charlie broke away from staring to focus on hauling in the fish. Allen retrieved the four-foot-long hook from stowage beneath the cockpit cushion.

"Allen, I'll walk forward to the spreaders and bring him alongside the boat. You ever gaff a fish before?"

The dorado, which had appeared to be weakening, doubled its effort when it caught a glimpse of the hull, taking line and heading for the bottom. Time and again, Charlie would bring it within gaff range, only to have it veer off on another run. Finally, Allen was able to get the gaff beneath it, snatch it from the sea, and hoist it over the lifelines.

But the aft of the *Bora Bora* was not the working cockpit of a sportfisherman. Allen deposited the frantic fish on top of the aft cabin, where it tried to destroy the hatch. It slipped the gaff and slid down the blood-soaked, slippery fiberglass and was instantly thrashing on the narrow deck between the combing and the rail, only inches from sliding back into the sea. Allen tried to corral the fish with his feet, and then, before Charlie could stop him, he reached down to grab its gill.

In a blur, the hook extending through the crazed fish's jaw impaled Allen in the web between his thumb and index finger. Allen screamed. He was now surgically attached to thirty pounds of thrashing fury. He dropped to his knees to smother its movement, but in the frenzy of blood and slime, the fish was making its way over the side, ripping at Allen's hand and threatening to drag him under the lifeline.

Charlie tried to restrain the fish's head—with its attached hand—by winding the monofilament line across the cabin top and securing it to the starboard aft cleat, but as he pulled the fish's head, he simultaneously contributed to the forces that threatened to destroy Allen's hand.

"Winch handle!" Charlie hollered. Jenna, horrified at the sight of her boyfriend in anguish, was stunned into paralysis.

"Winch handle!" Charlie yelled again. Jenna fumbled for the handle as Charlie struggled to get into a position between the stern rail and the fish's head, from which he could deliver a deathblow.

Jenna leaned across the cabin top and stuffed the three-pound stainless steel tool into Charlie's outstretched hand. Charlie focused on the exact spot where the blow needed to land, raising the handle like a meat cleaver, trying to aim at the top of the fish's head through the narrow gap between Allen and the cabin's side. Allen screamed even louder.

"Are you crazy? You're going to break my arm!" Charlie maintained his striking crouch, waiting for the perfect time. Allen panicked. "Get a knife—a knife—cut its fucking head off!"

As Charlie contemplated the change of plan, Jenna flew into the cabin and emerged with the razor-sharp, fifteen-inch fillet knife. The blade, placed behind the gills and only inches from Allen's wrist, helped restrain the dorado's wild thrashing as it sliced its way into the flashing gold-green skin, through the vertebra, and out the lower side. Once separated, Allen cradled the fish's bleeding head in his left hand to relieve the pressure on his right, but the battle had driven the hook deep into the web of his hand, effectively riveting it to the side of the jaw. Charlie cut the fishing line and helped the traumatized angler over the cockpit combing, where they placed the head and hand on the narrow table.

The relief of separating Allen from the body of the dorado was short-lived. The hook emerging through the right side of the bony jaw was large and rusty. It was attached by two screws firmly to the body of the stainless-steel spoon, impaled deep into the meat of Allen's right hand.

49

"Holy Jesus!" wailed Allen, "Can we cut it off with a hacksaw?"

Charlie stood back and tried to analyze the problem that lay before him. "No, sorry, that's not going to work. We are going to need the entire hook and the shank. Does it hurt?"

"Does it look like it hurts? For Christ sake, do something!"

Since the jaw and the hand were welded together, it was difficult to see how to get the knife between them. One slip and Allen could easily lose a finger. The bottom of the lure was pressed to the inside of the jaw, making it was impossible to get at the screws.

"Here, lift your hand and let's see if I can get the point of the knife in." He placed the spine of the knife along the back underside of Allen's wrist and slid the point to the where the hook emerged from the jaw. "Move your hand over the edge of the table." Allen gently shifted the bloody mess as Charlie raised the winch handle. With the point of the knife at the exact place where the hook pierced the jawbone, the young captain took aim and—*whap*—the knife penetrated through the bone and into the mouth of the fish. Holding the knife with the precision of a surgeon, he then enlarged the slice by tapping the knife through the jawbone with the winch handle. A few minutes later, the hook was released and the slit sufficiently wide to allow extraction of the entire lure. The bloody head was jettisoned overboard.

Charlie unscrewed the hook from the spoon. The three stared with wide-eyed, muted revulsion at the hook still impaling Allen's hand, its barb embedded deep in the muscle. It would have been much easier had the barb come out somewhere. But the barb of the hook, embedded deep in Allen's hand, was going to be painful to remove. "You're not going to like this," warned Charlie.

"I don't like it now," replied Allen. "How are we going to get it out of there? I am going to need a surgeon."

Charlie looked at the hand. "We can get it out. There's no rush. You have plenty of time for a drink." Allen chugged straight from a bottle of rum, then Charlie poured the remaining rum over the shank of the hook.

"It's an antiseptic. It's the best we have," said Charlie as he clamped a vise-grip onto the upper portion of the hook's shank. He knew there was a first-aid kit onboard, but nothing was as potent as the rum. He waited ten minutes for the alcohol to take effect on Allen. "You ready for this?"

Allen nodded grimly. Jenna turned her back.

Grabbing the vise-grip with both hands, Charlie twisted the shank until the barb was just under the fibrous skin of the palm between the thumb and first finger. And there it stopped. No matter how hard they twisted, the tip would not penetrate the tough skin. When they pulled, it simply raised the entire arm. Jenna turned around eventually and tried to watch but felt herself becoming dizzy and nauseous.

They readjusted the vise-grips, and both Allen and Charlie twisted with all their might, but the hook could only be rotated so far. It hovered just below the skin of Allen's palm. They would have to force the barb through the skin so that they could cut it.

Charlie placed the tip of the hook between the jaws of a pair of wire cutters while Jenna held the shank tight with the vise-grips. Charlie then smacked the wire cutters with the winch handle, forcing the skin over the tip of the hook and exposing the barb. Allen, to his credit, never flinched. Turning the wire cutters on their side, Charlie snipped the barb, doused the hand with rum again, and gently rotated the now barbless hook out of the tissue.

Allen's arm, wrist, and hand were covered in blood, creating the illusion that his arm had nearly been torn off. Jenna gently removed the slime and crusting blood with a towel soaked in rum. Minutes later, there was little evidence of the past fifteen minutes of panic. The two tiny puncture wounds instantly sealed themselves, and the hand looked utterly undamaged. Charlie slumped upon the cushion with his exhausted shipmates, staring at the beheaded fish that lay on the deck.

"You ready to catch another fish?"

***

An arbitrary point on a map of the earth, specifically 23° 30′ north latitude, 77 20′ west longitude defines a feared, isolated, dead-end cul-de-sac where few mariners dared to venture—an instant transition from a water depth of six thousand to six feet at the southern terminus of the Tongue of the Ocean. The shallow reefs and sand bores south of Andros had been off-limits since the days of Columbus. There weren't even wrecks, since few captains had been foolish enough to enter. Unlike the recreational Bahamas—only 150 miles to the north—any boat encountered there should be approached with caution, as smugglers had claimed this shallow sea as their own.

But the *Bora Bora Express* was designed for skinny waters. Charlie timed his 10:00 a.m. arrival at the edge to have the rising sun at his back. Heading due west, he skirted the shallow sand bars that threw a luminous turquoise glow into the sky above the southern horizon. The wind diminished and eventually died altogether. The transformation was profound. Soon the wake of the *Express* was the only ripple for a dozen-mile radius, and even that was soon absorbed and dissipated. Without the wind as her tormentor, the face of the sea became a mirror of the sky above, the two merging seamlessly together. It appeared the sea was the sky's portly twin sister, resting temporarily on the firmament as she slowly evaporated and became one with the heavens. Mercifully freed from a breeze to rile its surface, which splintered the sun's rays into a million shards, he viewed with exquisite detail the earth gliding only a few feet below the keel. Visible now were giant yellow starfish, black sea cucumbers, and conch too numerous to count.

As they motored toward the southern edge of the dreaded Curly Cut Cays, isolated coral heads off the starboard bow sprang into view, each a small black oasis bursting from a desert of ice-blue sand. Sailors are generally well-advised to avoid reefs, shoals, and pointy objects that could easily pierce the hull. However, the day was of such exception due to its stillness and tranquility that usual precautions could be forsaken. Without trepidation, they ventured into the midst of the enemy coral heads, so near as to anchor and spend the day snorkeling.

The year before, on summer break, Allen had had the chance to visit Alaska. In preparation, he'd purchased a book, *A Guide to Alaskan Wildlife,* with full-color plates of the various animals one might reasonably expect to encounter. He looked forward to seeing the bears, marmots, pine martins, and a host of other critters that were depicted in his book. But after ten days, the only animal he'd encountered had been a moose that ran across the road in front of his vehicle. Based on that sobering experience, he was amazed to discover that dozens—perhaps hundreds—of fish he had recently seen in Bohlke's *Fishes of the Bahamas* could be found on a single coral-reef system. He instantly recognized and pointed out to Jenna the Nassau groupers, French angels, queen triggers, butterflyfishes, grunts, barracudas, and clownfishes—as if they had swum off the pages and were there on display.

That afternoon they saw hawksbill turtles, green moray eels, harlequin shrimp, and a cleaning station set up by the local wrasses, where a multicolored explosion of fish came to be nibbled clean of parasites. The crew marveled at the untouched beauty—the profusion of brain and staghorn coral—some reaching the surface—encircled by dazzling shoals of fish in a habitat totally undisturbed by the hand of man.

Thus, the most dreaded thirty miles of the voyage to Havana became the best day they had experienced so far. And Allen's hand didn't bother him a bit all day. By evening, they were safely on the other side of the treacherous coral heads, over Hurricane Flats, seventy-two miles north of the Cuban mainland but 312 miles from Havana. They sailed through the night, crossing the western edge of the Great Bahama Bank and through deep water toward Cay Sal Bank. The fickle wind, whose dereliction of duty they had well exploited, resumed its preordained path, making the journey from Africa to America at fifteen knots.

The four- and five-foot waves that had proved such a formidable obstacle now loped alongside, each giving up a tiny portion of its energy in the form of a gentle push in the right direction, their flopping tops splushing harmlessly beside into a foam of seething bubbles. A line, known as a preventer, was attached to the end of the boom, run forward through a snatch-block affixed to the toe rail, then brought taut on the spinnaker winch. This held the boom rigidly to starboard so it didn't slack as the waves crawled their way beneath the boat from stern to stem. Late the next day, refuge was sought behind desolate Anguila Cay, where they anchored and put their heads down for the night.

CHAPTER SEVEN

*Y**ou know, Vali, you really do look like Selena.* It was the second time this week someone remarked on the resemblance. The seed of an idea began to grow. The more she pondered, the more it occurred to her she had nothing to lose. But she would need help.

And Vali immediately thought of her friend, Anna.

Vali had met Anna while attending the English course sponsored by the Archdiocese de San Cristóbal de la Habana. Anna needed to learn English for when—or if—she was allowed to visit her family who had made it to the United States. Vali envied Anna. Her family was rich. They had everything—a color TV, window air units, hot water, a new refrigerator, and a dependable 1954 Plymouth Belvedere. Anna was taking piano lessons in Vedado, wore designer jeans, and had the latest electronics.

The taxi to Miramar to visit Anna cost Vali seven pesos. A DVD from the rental store on Eighty-Sixth cost four pesos more. With traffic, stops, and a minor breakdown, a fifteen-minute trip turned into an hour. The prerevolutionary houses in the beachside suburb recalled a time of opulence when money was not a constraint and residents competed for architectural grandeur. The most

55

exquisite homes were formerly owned by high government officials and members of the Mafia. Some had been turned into foreign embassies. Others had been crudely partitioned into labyrinths of tiny apartments. Anna's house, one-story, small but elegant, had changed little from the old days.

Vali paid the cab driver, let herself into the courtyard of Anna's house, closed the gate behind her, and knocked on the freshly painted red door.

"Entre," Hector bellowed. He was drinking and playing dominoes. "Bienvenidos a la Casa De Gusanos!" *Welcome to the House of Maggots.*

Anna's father was infamous for his drunken tirades. He worked for the Ministry of Industrialization but had decided to take the day off, as had his friend Pablo, a physics professor at the University Havana who worked nights as a waiter. Hector was wearing a torn and stained Che Guevara T-shirt.

"Maggots, that's what we are. We just heard it again on the TV. Two maggots playing dominoes. And we are the worst maggots since our money comes from Miami. That's right. In the world of maggots, there are good maggots and bad maggots, and we are the bad ones. Here, Vali, sit with us dirty old men and have a drink. You know, you are looking good these days." Before she could decline, Hector plunked a water glass, half filled with rum, on the table.

She sat down. "If you are maggots, then I want to be a maggot, too. Getting dollars is nearly impossible." Vali didn't touch the rum. Nothing would deter her from her mission today.

"You are not supposed to have dollars. We are not supposed to have dollars, either." Hector made his move, a dominoes tile smashing the top of the hardwood table. "El had no choice." Hector's hand instinctively went to his chin. The name Fidel was seldom spoken lest it be overheard and interpreted as derisive. The leader was often referred to as *El*, or *He*, as a Christian might refer to Jesus, but the usual reference to the Comandante Supremo was a barely discernable gesture made with the V created by the thumb and first finger, stroking an invisible beard.

"You know, he could put a stop to *remesas* with a snap of his fingers. But he won't. One-fifth of the island's income arrives through Western Union in the form of *remesas*. They don't tell you that in school, do they? Instead, they call us maggots." Pablo gestured as he spoke, the level of rum in his glass much lower than the rum in Vali's.

"No," Vali said. "All I know is that without dollars, it is very difficult to survive. We learned about the Special Period in school because of the *bloqueo* and the Americans trying to starve us to death."

"We can trade with a hundred other countries. They don't tell you that on the news, either. Don't blame the Americans. Blame the Russians," Hector said as he watched Pablo consider his next move.

"Are we still in the Special Period? My mother says life is a lot harder now than when she was growing up. She says there are two types of people, those with dollars and those without. We have no access to dollars. Russians? I thought it was the Americans." Vali was suddenly interested in what the men were saying. It wasn't often that she heard anyone speak so openly about the realities of Cuban politics.

Hector poured himself another drink. "The Americans didn't help, but it started with the Russians. When their economy went to shit, they cut us off. That was eight years ago." Hector stroked his chin, pantomiming Castro. "He declared dollars to be our second currency and went after the tourist market."

"The Veradero Initiative," interjected Pablo.

"Yes. That's what they called it. A plan to replace the money made from sugar. Good luck. Hundreds of new hotels on the pristine sands of the most beautiful beach in the Caribbean. It was perfect, because it's a two-hour drive from Havana, and tourists would never interact with the Cuban people. They didn't teach you this in school because it was our government's attempt at returning to capitalism."

"We were told the tourists were stopped by the embargo," Vali supplied.

"That is partially true," Hector slurred. "But the government simply didn't have the money to construct new hotels. Then the Special Period came. Regular Cubans could obtain licenses to rent rooms and establish restaurants in their homes. You remember when everyone started opening *paladars*? It was brilliant. With the stroke of a pen, El Commandante created a virtually unlimited supply of rooms to rent and kitchens at the ready to feed an army of tourists. But there was one problem with the plan."

"The law of thermodynamics!" Pablo could not restrain himself. The opportunity to apply the physical laws of nature to social architecture was too wonderful to pass up. He picked up the story. Vali could picture him standing before a classroom, students scribbling wildly as he pontificated.

"The homes and their kitchens were in and around Havana, not far away Varadero. Tourists had dollars. The population had pesos. Dollars meant freedom from the constraints of the peso economy. The physical and social barriers created by sheer distance dissolved overnight. The forces of thermodynamics took over as two substances once isolated now touched, interfaced, shared information, and began the immutable process of establishing equilibrium. It happens in nature. It happens with people. That's why it's a law and not just a theory. The proximity sparked a gold rush which reverberated from Maria Gorda to Guantanamo. You remember? Air force pilots rushed to get jobs driving taxis. Teachers quit to become waiters. Dentists dropped their drills, donned monkey suits, and became bellhops. Thermodynamics! *Jineteros* and *jineteras* came from near and far to hustle tourists and perhaps make more in a day than in a month's work."

Pablo paused for breath, and it was then that Anna appeared in jeans and a halter top. "Don't listen to them. They don't know shit. What's up?" Vali shook her head slightly. *Can't explain here.* They went to Anna's room where Vali broached the reason for her visit.

"Do you have a DVD of Selena Gomez?" Anna had a hundred CDs. Bootlegs of excellent quality were available on the black market for ten pesos. It was the go-to cottage industry for anyone with access to a computer and a DVD writer. "Sure, which would you like to see? 'No Me Queda Mas,' that's my favorite."

Anna's TV had a built-in DVD player. Vali had seen Selena on state television, but poor reception and burned-out phosphors offered a ghostlike image. Anna's Panasonic brought to life the smallest of detail—the diamond sparkle of every sequin on Selena's black and white gown, the cherry-redness of her lips, the sheen of her jet-black hair. Selena personified archetypical Hispanic beauty, subtle yet enchanting, her movements sweeping and fluid, reminiscent of the old style. Her costumes, often featuring a bare midriff, were provocative yet conservative.

Selena's combination of traditional Latin beauty, vocal range, and cutting-edge Tejano cut like a laser beam into the Latino heart and soul. Although technically a foreign import, Cubans embraced Tejano as their own. They loved the sound and the artful, unpretentious way it was presented. In an age of rap and reggaetón, Selena's presentation was a refreshing anachronism—a pretty girl in a beautiful dress singing love songs, sometimes soft and romantic, moments later with a fully orchestrated ensemble that had the audience standing on their chairs and swinging in the aisles. Her appeal cut across generations, and her concerts were populated by young and old alike.

More importantly, this was the first opportunity Vali had gotten to get a good look at the face everyone said she resembled. "Do you think I look like her?" she asked. *Claro que si* was the answer.

"Of course," Anna said. "Even more so with your hair down. She looks taller, but I think that is because she is wearing heels."

"Do you think I could become her?" Vali shifted nervously.

"What do you mean? She's dead."

"On the stage. If I dressed like her, moved like her, would people—could I—do you think if I wore the right clothes, the right makeup, I could put on a Selena show?"

"Why would you?" Anna seemed incredulous, but Vali knew she didn't understand desperation.

Vali's one-word reply tied all the loose ends together. "Tourists."

Vali didn't have to explain further. She knew that Anna would realize that the plan was a potential pathway for her friend, Vali's ticket out of the peso economy, perhaps offering an escape from Jaimanitas and the country. Vali's face and body were a competitive edge and offered the ability to capitalize on the implausibility of looking like someone famous, someone everybody knew and loved. More importantly, Selena had a worldwide following. Tourists from Italy, Spain, and America could relate. More than just a lip sync rip-off, if done correctly the act could stand as a living tribute to the murdered diva.

In the wake of the unexpected *Buena Vista Social Club* film phenomenon, which translated into inestimable goodwill and positive propaganda, the government eagerly encouraged new and innovative acts. It was estimated that the knock-on effect of the six old musicians had put over $200 million dollars into government coffers. Happy tourists spent more dollars. Happy tourists told their friends, and they booked more rooms, spent more at restaurants, and continued the cycle. A reincarnated Selena might strike a responsive chord. And, most importantly, if the dollars went straight from the tourist's wallets to Fidel's pocket, it was legal.

"My father knows the manager at the Cecilia. Sometimes he comes to our house and drinks."

"Do you think he will help me?"

"I'll ask him." Anna left the room and returned ten minutes later.

"What did he say?"

"He said human beings are not ants. That's why communism always has to be jammed down their throats."

"No. Not that. About the manager."

"Oh. He says no problem. He will set up a meeting."

Vali felt her plan transforming from a dream into reality.

CHAPTER EIGHT

One enters the walled compound of the Cecilia under a wrought
iron gate that leads through a tree-lined garden. The yellow sign
on Avenida Quinta, sporting the silhouette of a horse-drawn
carriage, proclaimed *Bar and Restaurant*, but the Cecilia had long
been known as one of Havana's top-ten nightclubs. Dressed in
borrowed shorts and a red blouse, carrying a small, battered suitcase,
Vali walked the path through manicured gardens, past the pavilion,
toward the pool.

"Halt!"

She wheeled to find a security guard on her heels.

"What are you doing here?"

Vali explained she was here to see the manager, Jorge, and
told the guard that she had a meeting. She was escorted, as if under
arrest, through the open-air amphitheater, around the kitchen, past
the stage, and into a labyrinth of corridors. He stopped at an
unmarked door, shot a glance that asserted his authority, and
knocked.

Vali heard a chair slide, steps, then the door swung open to reveal a well-dressed, crew cut mulatto, perhaps forty years old.

"Come in, young lady. Don't tell me. You're the girl who's friends with Hector's daughter. What do you do?" It was obvious that Jorge had seen it all and wasn't the least impressed by a pretty girl. Further, he seemed annoyed to be interrupted from whatever he'd been doing. Vali knew that if she hadn't had Anna's help, he never would have seen her.

He eyed her as if he were inspecting a horse. She could tell she was failing the interview before it had started. "All I want is a sound system and ten minutes, thirty seconds of your time," she said. Mechanically, he walked her to the door, instructed the guard to deliver her to Fabian, give her anything she needed, and to call him when she was ready.

The guard's demeanor changed as they neared the soundstage. "The boss doesn't give everyone a crack at getting on stage. He cares about making money and keeping the customers happy. You do something that will accomplish both?" She shrugged but didn't have the courage to start a conversation.

She wanted to ask how the boss made his money—after all, the managers, kitchen staff, performers, gardeners, stagehands, the guards, everyone was paid 220 pesos per month. Only the coveted positions of wait staff and bartenders bridged the physical gap between clients and their dollars, allowing them access to tips. Vali could only imagine how quickly those tips disappeared into sweaty bras and pockets.

The sound booth was located to the right of the stage on an elevated platform. Inside they found Fabian, a twenty-something black gay, blond hair spiking beneath oversized headphones. "Hola, muñeca, usted está aquí por alguna acción?" *Hello, doll, you are here for some action?*

She was surprised to encounter a person that far out of the closet. Homosexuality, despite forced egalitarianism, was not consistent with the machismo culture of Cuba. Lesbianism seemed not only accepted but also encouraged, assuming it included an *hombre* in the mix. It was different for guys—transsexualism, transvestitism, trans-*anything*, did not sit well with the male Latin's psyche. She found Fabian's unabashed flaming enthusiasm refreshing, and soon they were talking like sisters. He listened to her demo tape and declared it to be of poor quality. He could do a lot better with future recordings, and he could electronically fiddle with this one to make it better. He disappeared beneath his earphones and made adjustments with his mixer while Vali transformed into Selena in a changing room downstairs, struggling to remember the moves that she and Anna had practiced over and over for days. The guard was sent to fetch Jorge.

She had visualized her audition a hundred times. She would lock onto the faces of her judges, seated in the front row, just as Selena would have. Emerging from the darkness into full spotlight, she would have time to seamlessly slip into synch and character. But this stage was fully lit since the interior of the pavilion was open to the sky, surrounded by covered concessions. The manager entered through a side door and sat, impatiently, arms crossed, at the far corner of the darkened bar. She couldn't see his eyes. Sounds of the kitchen mingled with a weed-eater as a gardener edged the walkway.

A dog was barking, and people were splashing in the pool. Fabian's voice—*listo*? Ready? Then—*bang*—Selena's raucous opening blasted from surround-sound JVCs at one-hundred decibels, catching Vali flatfooted. Within seconds, however, she was dead-on in sync, her own voice carefully mouthing the words, lost in the sheer volume. She danced step-for-step the moves she had seen on the videos, effortlessly channeling the energy, spirit, and exuberance of Selena, her eyes embracing an audience of ghosts. For ten minutes and thirty seconds, the little girl from Third Avenue in Jaimanitas *was* Selena. Her sound was artificial but her joy genuine.

The music over, reality returned with a vengeance. The silence was jolting, sobering. Jorge stood up, pushed in his bar stool, and exited through the same side door. There was no applause, no words, no eye contact, no clue. She hadn't rehearsed this part and was bewildered as to what to do next. Had it been that bad? Her stomach churned. Sweating and out of breath, she climbed the stairs to the sound booth.

"The boss wants to see you. Don't change. Go as you are to his office," Fabian said. She tried to glean insight into her performance from Fabian's expression—it was somewhere between admiration and hate, indifference and compassion. She had seen that look before. It was jealousy.

"Close the door behind you," Jorge muttered as Vali came in. Vali complied and placed herself in a chair in front of the manager's desk.

"Do you have a phone?" She was surprised by Jorge's first question. She told him that she did not. "Then get one. I must be able to contact all my performers. I can work you in between the other acts as they set up—I've needed a short routine. Work out the details with Fabian—the lighting, how many songs can you do. You will need at least a dozen. Arrive at ten and stay until three unless the night manager says you can go."

She was stunned. Jorge had already analyzed her performance, saw its strengths, assessed its weaknesses and its flexibility as a fill-in act. Jorge continued, "Offstage, wear your costume and stay in character. You have more costumes, don't you? It's your job to encourage customers to buy drinks at the bar or tables. From now on, when you are on the grounds, you *are* Selena. If you leave with a customer that you encountered anywhere on the premises of the Cecilia, you will give fifteen dollars to the night manager. If a waiter or waitress brings a customer to you and you leave with that customer, he or she will receive five dollars. Always ask the night manager if you can leave early. If you try to screw us, we will know, and you will be immediately fired. We know everything."

She couldn't believe what she was hearing. She had barely dared to hope that she would be allowed into the Cecilia, let alone be able to work at the infamous club. Now, a new avenue was being offered. The management of the Cecilia was way ahead of her.

Here, prostitution wasn't just condoned—it was encouraged. It was part of the business plan! It all made sense. These people were just like her, struggling in a world where *vida es imposible* and survival was a right. They were the lucky ones, riding the tenuous and nearly unobtainable train that bridged the distance between foreign money and regular Cubans—an opportunity to span the divide that had perpetually existed between the haves and have-nots, a chance to steal across and extract golden nuggets through an improbable wormhole, a tiny rent in time and space piercing the physical nexus of the peso/dollar interface. She was not alone, or unique. On the contrary, she was about to join a group of kindred spirits ruthlessly exploiting a flaw in the system—one of the few but necessary weaknesses in the government's headlong pursuit of cash.

Faced with the inevitability of prostitution, why not channel it into de facto brothels, generally referred to as nightclubs? Tax the hookers as they come through the door. Tax the johns through overpriced drinks and dinners. Tax the employees as they leave with a client. Now it was obvious to her why the *jineteras* in the streets were regularly rounded up and warned, fined, or arrested—they were free agents and paid no tax, or the fine was the tax. They weren't arrested because they were hookers—there was no morality involved, no social judgment—they were simply beating the system by earning dollars without giving the government its cut. It was all so clear now. She was being invited inside the multimillion-dollar investment that was the Cecilia. Its bar, its stage, the waiters, waitresses, its managers, all were her officially sanctioned *chulos*, or—in English—her pimp. It was folly to believe that the twenty or so nightclubs in and around Havana were operating under the radar. This was Cuba; the police knew everything.

Maybe this *should* have been her plan all along. Not the common practice of a street girl, but the use of her physical gifts to get close to men who had what she wanted. Old Havana and the environs around the Tropicana were once world famous for the sexual garden of delights that awaited the well-heeled traveler. The tradition from days of old never left the collective conscience of the populace; people remembered the mystery, glamour, and opulence of the cabarets, hotel ballrooms, and clubs as if it were yesterday—the allure was a heritage perpetuated in numerous films, books, and art. Tourists would pay for what Vali had to offer, and though she was no *jinetera,* she was no innocent, either. There wasn't enough in her family's rations to allow her the luxury of keeping her innocence.

Vali knew she was leaving one world and entering another. Lip-synching and dancing, that was easy. How would she stack up against the other female performers, each more beautiful and talented than the next, each competing to sell themselves to the highest bidders? And the girls—she had seen the lines outside the gate—were they all professionals? She had never been with a tourist before, although she had heard rumors. Some girls were beaten; others had been pissed on—what about old guys with limp dicks? What kind of freaky shit would they require? But it really didn't matter. This was her chance, probably the only shot she would ever get at leaving Cuba and becoming the wife of a rich man.

Vali left the Cecilia with her mind made up. She didn't have to plead with Anna to borrow more clothes—all Anna had to do was ask Hector sweetly for a few dollars while he and Pablo were having another of their philosophical dominoes games. Hector had given Anna more money than she had asked for, along with an unsteady lecture on how little it all meant in the long run. Vali had come away with a week's worth of costumes, a few bottles of TuKola, and a new gratitude for Hector's cynicism.

On Thursday, Vali worked with Fabian to create a medley that included "No Me Gueda Mas," "Fotos y Recuerdos," and "Tu Solo Tu." It turned out to be impractical to lip-synch the ad libs between songs, so it was decided she would go with fill in with a live mic. They practiced through the day. Rather than a mirror image of Selena's performance, they put together an act that used Selena's moves but conformed to the size of the stage. It felt more comfortable. It flowed better. Occasionally she was joined by other performers—professional dancers—who picked up and improved on her moves in a matter of minutes.

Vali told her mother about the job at the Cecilia. At first, her mother was trepidatious, but Vali's reassurances—and the promise of dollars—quieted her fears. By the time Vali arrived at the Cecilia on Friday night, the first band had already set up. It was a male vocal performance with three fly girls, five musicians, and a fully integrated light show. At the end of their program, Selena was waiting in the wings. The lights went dark. Vali's stomach was in knots. Fabian cued the CD just before she entered under a single white spotlight, the darkness behind obscuring the breakdown of one band and the setup of the next.

It was a tough act to follow. With the change of pace, the hundred or so customers who had been whipped into a frenzy were caught by surprise. *What's this, something new?* It was the moment of truth for the Selena surrogate. Customers were wary, quiet, subdued. They listened. They were the ultimate judges. Vali knew that in a split second they could react like animals, throwing beer cans and crashing the performance. It had happened before.

But, apparently, they liked what they heard and saw, for soon they were dancing beside the tables and in the space around the bar to familiar songs and a familiar face they had loved and accepted into their hearts years before. Like a magician, she lured them with smoke, mirrors and, sleight of hand into a fantasy of her own creation. Like a thief, she stole their incredulity. And the audience played their part, allowing themselves to enter a state of willing suspension of disbelief. They loved it. Selena received a standing ovation. Vali glowed with pride—and relief.

She could see several men in the crowd eyeing her as she exited the stage. But how, exactly, would this translate into dollars? This was unfamiliar territory, and events were happening at lightning speed. She was more nervous now than she had been going on stage. She knew how to service the local boys—she had been screwing since she was thirteen. She could read their dirty little minds. They were all the same. They would use her body and be out the door in ten minutes. They were macho piglets who believed it was cool to be cruel and disrespectful to women. However, she knew where they lived, she knew their mothers, and she was never in much danger of being injured.

She had thought that she would do anything to improve her situation. But now, the thought of driving into the night with a faceless stranger from a far-off land was terrifying. She had never really considered it a possibility, but here she was, heading into a crowd of ax murderers and offering her time, her body, her life. If they slit her with knives, strangled, or chopped her up for crocodile bait, they could be on a plane to the North Pole within hours. No one knew who they were or where they came from. Why were they here in the first place? Couldn't they meet women in their own godforsaken countries? Perhaps they would put a rat inside her. She hated rats. She could feel its sharp little claws and chisel teeth tearing her pussy apart from the inside as it struggled to escape. As she made her way to the bar, it occurred to her that maybe this wasn't such a good idea after all.

For the first time, she had the opportunity to mingle. By eleven thirty, the club was at about half capacity. The majority were local couples, here to enjoy dinner and the show. Well-dressed women arrived in groups and seated themselves at the white linen tables on the grass in front of the stage. Most were local. Men outnumbered women ten to one. The non-Cubans looked like businessmen and hardly fit the Hawaiian-shirt tourist stereotype. As soon as she sat down at the bar, a foreigner approached and asked if he could join her.

Arthur was a physical fitness nut in his forties from Toronto. "I saw you on the stage. It's Selena, right? She's dead now, isn't she?" Vali could see he was overdressed for a tropical evening. His sport coat and slacks suggested he'd thought the Cecilia would be air-conditioned. "This is my first time here. Mind if I buy you a drink?" Jorge had warned her about drinks—specifically, too many drinks. She was an ambassador for the club and was expected to uphold an image.

Canada openly defied the US embargo. Canadian tourists frequented the all-inclusive, hermetically sealed, walled-off

69

fantasyland resorts in Varedero or Comaguay, under total control from the moment they left the plane until a week later when they reboarded, headed home, thinking that they'd been in the real Cuba. As blissfully unaware, suntanned captives, they were pampered by smiling peso-paid government sycophants and party hacks who never strayed far from the robotic official line—welcome to paradise, we love living in paradise. Few Canadians ever made it as far as Havana, and fewer still a remote nightclub five miles to the west.

Arthur was, by Canadian standards, a virtual Lewis and Clark.

"Sure, I would like a whiskey coke."

Arthur told the bartender to make it two. He complimented her hair, her dress, and her selection of songs. He told her she was beautiful and stared into her eyes. He offered another round of drinks, but Vali declined. He asked questions about her family, her schooling, and where would she like to go if she could travel. He wasn't wearing a wedding ring, nor was there a white line where one had been recently removed. Vali allowed herself to relax.

He told her how brilliant she was to leverage her beauty and resemblance to Selena into a stage act. Jaimanitas boys didn't talk this way. She felt special. She knew they were all lies but allowed herself the luxury—just for the moment—of believing they were true. Was he talking to her or Selena? It didn't matter.

Act five was ending, and Vali had to excuse herself. Her second performance lasted fourteen minutes. She returned to the bar to find the drinks had been removed, and Arthur was nowhere in sight. She shot an inquisitive glance at the bartender who shrugged and pointed in the general direction of the pool. Perhaps she'd said something wrong? After twenty-five minutes of dancing in the heat and humidity, maybe she smelled bad? But soon Arthur returned and sat next to her. He seemed more businesslike. Something had changed.

"I assume you will be joining us this evening?" he asked.

Showtime. Jorge had told her to play it by ear. There was no set price. The going rate for a street *jinetera* was twenty-five to forty dollars. Young ladies from the club were generally a little more since they had to pay a cover.

"You want *una companera?* Companionship?"

"Yes, I do," responded Arthur, lifting her hair and letting it cascade gently through his fingers.

"How much time do you want?"

"Until the sun comes up or I get tired and want to go to sleep."

"I am sorry. I don't think you can afford me. I always get *ciento*, one hundred." It was a gamble, but she could always go down on the price.

Arthur didn't blink. "That's no problem. Thank you. I'll wait for you in the parking lot—five minutes?" He paid the tab and disappeared into the darkness.

Ciento! That was more than she would make in the next four months, for five hours of work! The night manager had observed the transaction and gave a nod. She was free to go. Vali collected her purse from backstage, hurried down the flowered path through the gate, turned right to the parking lot at the edge of the property, and found Arthur waiting with a taxi and another girl.

Perhaps he was just giving her a ride home. They introduced each other and climbed into the back seat. Arthur sat up front. There was an uncomfortable silence. Apparently, Mariana—as the girl had introduced herself—hadn't expected competition either. *She's going with us?* wondered Vali. *Was she getting ciento also?*

71

"Hotel Kohli," Arthur told the driver. *How the hell did a Canadian find the Hotel Kohli?*

Indeed, the Kohli was well off the standard tourist route. Situated in its own arboretum of banyan and ficus, it was built on a promontory that overlooked the Rio Mordazo, far from Old Havana or, for that matter, anything else. Despite numerous renovations, the hotel's dated prerevolutionary design was impossible to conceal. Arthur paid the driver and escorted the ladies to the front desk.

"Carnes, por favor," demanded the clerk. The girls slid their National Identification Cards across the counter. The man placed them in a row of a dozen other cards lying face up on a shelf under the keys. One could tell at a glance how many girls were upstairs. Arthur led them to the elevator, and five minutes later they were in his suite.

As Arthur prepared drinks, Vali sized up Mariana. She was a pretty girl of about the same age, brunette, thin, maybe one hundred ten pounds. She was from Buena Vista, only a mile or two away, and had paid seven dollars to get into the Cecilia. She lived so near she could walk home. Mariana seemed totally relaxed as she slipped off her shoes and disappeared into the bathroom, closing and locking the door behind her. Arthur handed Vali a drink as she seated herself in a chair next to the television and across the room from the double bed.

"Have you ever been to the Kohli before?" asked Arthur, having no idea this was her first job. "This is the best room they have." He had removed his sport coat and reclined on the bed, two pillows arranged behind to give support. Mariana emerged from the bathroom wrapped in only a towel. She vaulted over Arthur and snuggled to his side, his left arm pulling her closer to his chest. Vali nervously chugged half her drink. Arthur sensed she was uncomfortable, so they made small talk as the effects of alcohol gradually took hold. He waited until her drink was finished, handed her another and turned on music.

"Bailar!" *Dance*, he commanded, laughing, with his glass held high.

"From now on, you are Selena," Mariana chimed in, pointing to the area beside the chair. "*Bailar*, Selena!"

Vali, feeling the effects of the alcohol, wanted to dance, to move, to enter a comfort zone and gain a degree of control. She danced in the tiny area between the TV and the table, her hands moving sensually over her torso and her eyes glued to Arthur's.

"Sin ropas!" *Without clothes*, encouraged Mariana. Slowly Vali unzipped the back of her gown and let the straps slip from her shoulders. She had been trapped in that tight dress all night, and the cool air on her breasts and stomach was refreshing. She kicked the dress to the side as it hit the carpet. Wearing only panties, she moved like a serpent, spinning and gyrating slowly with her hands above her head, undulating her hips and taking tiny salsa steps. It was more than enough to intoxicate any Latino male.

And it seemed to work on Canadians, also. Arthur ripped the towel from Mariana and kept her from going under the covers. He wrapped his leg around her right leg and pulled it to his center. Pinned on her back, he pushed her left leg to the side and slid his hand between. With his right hand, Arthur turned and opened the drawer in his nightstand, withdrawing a tube of lubricant, which he squirted liberally over Mariana's most private of parts. With Arthur's left arm compressing her chest and her right leg trapped, she resigned herself to inevitability and embraced the tiny circles her captor was making with his index finger. Vali wasn't shocked by any of it. Maybe it was the booze, but she felt completely at ease.

Arthur, now firmly in control of a moaning Mariana, motioned to Selena to remove her panties. He watched Vali dance as a Mariana unzipped his fly and fumbled around, trying to find something to latch onto. Arthur assisted by unbuckling his pants. Now Mariana could easily reach beneath his underwear and make contact. Selena didn't have to be coached. Kneeling on the same side of the bed, she pulled the pants and underwear off her client and mouthed the head of his unit while Marianas's tight white fist pumped the shaft below. Arthur stroked Vali's hair with his free hand, occasionally slipping beneath to cup and squeeze one of Selena's hanging breasts.

After about ten minutes, Selena's mouth began to get tired. *What's holding him up?* she thought. By now the boys in her village would have blasted her tonsils and been out the door. Soon she recognized the telltale signs that Arthur was getting ready to erupt— she could tell by the elevated heart rate and breathing that Arthur was approaching the edge. Suddenly, he jumped up.

"Time for another drink," he said.

Arthur stripped off the rest of his clothes, went to his little bar on top of the mini refrigerator, and made three more drinks. "All right ladies, shower time."

Mariana just laid there, eyes wide, spread-eagle, panting as if she had just completed a marathon. She heard him start the shower.

"Come on, ladies. Time to get clean."

Selena helped her off the bed, and they joined the energetic man from the north in a shower built for one. No sooner had they gotten wet than Arthur turned off the water and soaped every inch of their bodies. Once shining and slippery, he gave them full body massages, and they, writhing and laughing, reciprocated. He drew them to his chest, and the women's bodies touched for the first time of the evening. Vali was not a lesbian and had never harbored thoughts about sex with another woman. But this was business— *ciento dólares.* She lathered Mariana's breasts and played with her little pink nipples as Arthur played with hers.

They rinsed with hot water and were immediately ushered, dripping wet, back to the bed. It was cold in the air-conditioned room. Arthur placed Mariana on her back with her legs hanging over the side. Half on, half off the bed, he spread her legs and dived face-first into her roseate pussy. Mariana gasped, arched her back and grabbed him by the ears. Selena, literally out in the cold, slid on her back between Arthur's legs and, using the side of the bed to support the back of her head, diverted the awaiting boner from her eye socket into her mouth. It was effortless. She could stay there all night while her face was being abused, but ten minutes later, she was thrown on the bed as a wild man flipped her on her back and did his best to suck the G spot out of her body. This was a new and strange experience. Sometimes his face would slip down, swishing from side to side, and driving like a human jackhammer, she could feel a probing tongue then tiny kisses all the way up to the magic button.

As she let herself drift into a different dimension, she could feel her body tensing, her legs begin to shake, her insides pulsing rhythmically. *Good God, don't stop now*, she thought, or maybe said out loud as she death gripped the bedsheet, arched her back, pointed her toes, and exploded into Arthur's face. Emboldened, energized, he persisted, locking her in place with a vise-like grip on her ass as she crabbed her way backward across the bed in a futile effort to separate his face from her now hypersensitive lower unit. Pleasure and pain become inseparable as she reached the edge of the bed, dropping, limp, laughing, unceremoniously, over the side and onto the floor.

Arthur made three more drinks and placed both ladies on the bed. Selena, or Vali, or whoever she was tonight, still in a state of recovery, dimly remembered thinking, as she watched him roll on a condom, that she could hang her laundry on his pulsing *pinga*. With Mariana in the middle, he spread her legs and positioned Selena on her knees, between them. With her ass over the edge of the bed, Arthur pushed Vali's face into Mariana's snatch, simultaneously ramming her from behind. Vali had never eaten a pussy before, but she tried her best. She struggled to remember what she had just experienced and find the same spots, but the physiology was far more complicated than she imagined. As she licked and sucked and bobbed her head, *whoa*—something new was happening from behind. Arthur, on his tiptoes, eyes rolled back and about to come, stuck a slippery finger into her upturned ass. Another first for Vali.

She slobbered and sucked and held on as her hips were gripped from behind by hands of steel and her whole body slammed in a synchronized counterpoint by an impaling shaft of fire. The energy from body blows translated through her nose, mouth, chin, and tongue as she burrowed deeper into a receptive Mariana, who by now had grabbed the sides of the Vali's head and was assisting, jamming her face down with such force it was difficult to breathe. As Arthur reached his climax, she felt her vaginal walls automatically try to snap shut like the jaws of an epileptic alligator. Arthur must have felt it too, his grasp on her hips tightened, tightened, his ass pumping like an out-of-control pile driver and then—*blam*—he relaxed, instantly defusing the group dynamic.

The trio disentangled. Arthur went into the bathroom, washed his hands, and flopped on the bed between the two, drawing them to his chest and kissing them gently.

Selena looked at the clock radio on the nightstand. It was four forty-five. She found herself staring straight into Mariana's drooping eyes on the other side of Arthur's unshaven chest. It had been a long day for both. Perhaps they could sleep here. It would be delightful to have breakfast in the hotel and hang with Arthur through the day. There was a pool on the terrace just below their window. Kohli had a bowling alley. That would be fun.

But as she started to wiggle under the covers, Arthur jolted from his stupor. "Sorry, ladies, no sleepovers," he said as he withdrew his arms from around their shoulders and folded them across his chest. He got up quickly, put on his trousers, and motioned for them to get dressed. On the bed, in front of Mariana, Arthur peeled four American twenties, a ten, a five, and five ones from his money clip. Mariana reconstructed the pile and stuck it in her pocket. Vali watched as he lined up four twenties, a ten, a five, and five ones. *Ciento dólares.*

This was a dangerous time.

If something were going to go wrong, it would happen now. The goods had been delivered, what if the client refused to pay? Or he wasn't satisfied with the quality of the product? There was no contract, were no witnesses, just a number whispered through a darkened keyhole of noise and alcohol. Conversely, Arthur had allowed two strangers into his room, locked the door behind them, and had shown them where his money was hidden. Cuban girls often carry knives or mace. They could have slipped him a drug. Scopolamine from Columbia, it was making the rounds. It was possible they could have pocketed items when he was distracted, or they could have wanted to argue about compensation for spending extra time or providing unspecified services—for instance, Vali hadn't signed up to have her asshole violated.

But tonight, there would be no drama. Mariana wrote her telephone number on a slip of paper and left it on the nightstand. They both gave Arthur a kiss, collected their carnes from the front desk, and walked past the dollar cabs parked out front. When they reached Calle 44, they shared a passing peso cab. It cost Vali fifteen pesos to return to her mother and sister in Jaimanitas. Vali's mother almost wept when Vali gave her ten American dollars. The rest, Vali kept secret. She fell asleep with an unsettling sense of joy—she had sold herself a little bit closer to freedom, and it had been strangely easier than she had imagined.

CHAPTER NINE

Midnight of the following day found the *Bora Bora Express* strafed by the beam of the Faro Harnando Cortez, a lighthouse on Cuba's Cayo Cruz del Padre, a small, rocky island off the north coast. Ten hours later, skirting the shore to avoid the Gulf Stream, the muted pinks, greens, and shapes of bare concrete that form the skyline of Havana jutted their jagged heads out of the sea on the western horizon.

Battered dories with patched canvas sails fished the deep inshore waters, reminding Charlie of Santiago, Hemingway's "Old Man" and how each of the anglers looked for all the world like Spence Tracy in the movie. Even the skiffs were identical. As they passed, the grizzled fisherman would look up and wave. "We've made contact," Jenna remarked. "They seem friendly."

Yet the captain and the crew of the *Express* had reason to be worried. They had entered enemy territory, as defined by Congress and reaffirmed through a dozen amendments, each more draconian than its predecessor. Was the enemy designation simply political horseshit, or did the Cubans take it seriously? At any moment, one of the harbor boats could spot them, and they could be captured.

They'd talked about it as they neared Havana. What could they say? *We're lost. Sorry, we must have made a wrong turn at Key West. Viva Fidel!* There would be no excuse. There was no embassy here. They had been warned on the internet not to go, with a punishment equal to that of sneaking into North Korea. If the boat were seized and they were thrown into prison, who would know? Would they be allowed a phone call? Would they have to talk to the operator in Spanish? Would the pay phone take American quarters?

Thoughts turned negative. Imaginations ran wild: ten years in prison with nothing but preconsumed sangria and moldy tacos. Allen scanned the horizon with binoculars for a gunboat bearing down on them. He said he'd seen it a hundred times in war movies—a steel-gray patrol vessel, armed to the teeth, headed right at them, on its bow a cigar-chomping, mustached soldier hunched behind a swivel-mounted howitzer. Jenna peered nervously and took a turn with the binoculars.

"That one kind of looks like a police boat," she whispered. Abstraction had turned to reality. All three shared a common thought. *Maybe this wasn't such a good idea after all.*

It took another hour and a half from downtown Havana to reach the twelve-foot- tall buoy moored in sixty feet of water at the channel's entrance. Elbows resting on top of the furled main, Charlie scanned above the breakwater into the marina, half expecting to see barbed wire, gun emplacements, and shackled prisoners being flogged while bound to palm trees. Instead, he saw a colorful tent of red and blue with huge balloons, a water slide, drunks on jet skis, and a mini-sailing regatta for youngsters.

"They are having a freaking party in there," he announced. Astounded, he cast his gaze past the yachts and sailboat masts, east to a hotel overlooking the rocky beach. There on top of the hotel was a small, square building surrounded by a low concrete wall. Over the wall, Charlie struggled to hold the binoculars steady, was a group of uniformed military types staring back at him through a huge telescope mounted on a tripod.

Allen ran the yellow quarantine pennant to the spreaders while Charlie navigated the narrow, dredged channel to the customs and immigration building located on the backside of a rectangular island created during the capitalist era. The squat concrete headquarters had once been sales offices. The crew of the *Bora Bora Express* found themselves in uncharted political waters, anxious at the opportunities, apprehensive of the consequences. They were instructed to tie to the concrete quay and await their turn.

"No stampa por favor." Two military men approached, climbed aboard and examined the ship's documents. They conducted a cursory inspection belowdecks which was followed by a search conducted with a beagle. "No stampa?" implored Charlie. The customs man insisted that it was required they stamp all passports. Charlie explained that an American passport with a Cuban stamp would be an enormous problem when he returned to the States—suggesting perhaps they should turn around and leave now.

"Come on, work with me here," he pleaded. But the officers simply seated themselves, as if they had taken up residence in the cockpit. They seemed to be waiting. For what? Allen offered them a shot of Johnny Walker Black, which they immediately downed. Then another. Nevertheless, in the air was the uncomfortable specter of miscommunication.

"This is your first time to our country, right?" one of the men asked. Charlie nodded. "Now you want something from me. I want something from you." The crew was intrigued. Were the cops fishing for a bribe?

He went on. "We are required to stamp your passport, but we could stamp the immigration form, which you could then retain in your passport for the duration of your visit in our country. It's a courtesy we could extend to our American visitors. It's customary we receive a tip, usually twenty dollars, sometimes more." Allen reached into his wallet and handed each man a ten-dollar bill.

"And perhaps ..." One pointed to the bottle of whiskey on the table. A minute later stamps were placed on the back of the light-blue immigration cards, folded, and inserted into the passports. The bottle of Johnny Walker was handed over. "Proceed to Canal Number Two," the officer said, smiling.

Leaving the customs dock, Charlie was jubilant. "I love this country already. Crooked cops. Doesn't get any better than this."

They followed the dredged channel on the south side of the island, crossed the center of the little harbor, and entered the canal to the right of the Papa Nightclub. They passed the parking lot on the left and the hotel on the right. Berthed adjacent to the concrete bulkhead was a wide variety of yachts, some of which hailed from the United States. Many more were from Canada. Guards, communicating constantly with each other through their walkie-talkies, directed the *Express* to her assigned berth on the right side of the canal, across the road from the pool deck of the Hotel Aquario.

"We scored!" cried Jenna.

Charlie surveyed his surroundings. It was not what he had been expecting. The marina was modern, stylish, clean. This was enemy territory? The hotel was painted in pleasant pastels. Music wafted from the pool deck. Other yachtsmen assisted as he secured lines. Closer examination revealed the Aquario was badly in need of maintenance, but at least they tried to hide it under a fresh new coat of paint. He remembered the hotel, the one on the beach. With his binoculars, he once again scanned the roof of the hotel. Gargantuan telescopic eyes were staring back at him.

"How many days do you intend to stay?" inquired the dockmaster.

"Quanto cuesta?" "How much does it cost?" Charlie countered.

"For your boat, twelve dollars per day with electric and water."

Charlie shot a glance at Allen. Allen was laughing, shaking his head in disbelief. "Twelve bucks a day? We could live here forever!"

Charlie explained, "We intend to stay for a long time. Let us pay two weeks in advance, then we will pay for the next two weeks." He had the suspicion that the dock fees disappeared long before they made it to Fidel's pocket. *Even the dockmaster is crooked as a snake*, mused Charlie as he paid a ten-dollar bribe. *This is my kind of country!*

Although still Cuba's premier yachting facility, the structures, the seawalls, the streets around Marina Hemingway—virtually everything created by the hand of man—were in the process of yielding to the forces of entropy. Each structure followed its own preordained path, some quicker than others, baking and bleaching in the tropical sun down the road of no return. Projects, some designed by the world's best architects and at great cost, littered the landscape and had become eyesores. Futuristic playgrounds with rusted rocket ships spoke to unachieved aspirations and were now a hazard; children barred from entry by a rusty chain-link fence. Churches were boarded. Theater marquis went unlit. Secondary roads became unpassable. Telephones worked sporadically, as did electric and water.

As they explored their surroundings, Charlie quickly saw that, save for small private holdings, the veneer of decline was a defining characteristic of the island and somehow distinct from that of other Caribbean countries. Cuba's strain under the cancer of collectivism permeated every aspect of the culture. It had its own patina and was instantly recognizable. The Hotel Aquario was no exception.

"Where are you from?" asked one of the guards. Jenna had flopped into the cockpit, escaping the sun's heat beneath the canvas covering.

"The United States," she answered carefully.

"America. I have a brother in Miami." The military man seemed to be staring through Jenna's bikini. "You have two boyfriends?"

"Charlie, you had better come up here," Jenna called. "This man thinks that I could stand you as a romantic partner. He obviously needs a drink."

The sunburned captain emerged from the companionway. Jenna stood and went to join Allen.

"Hey, you want a drink? What's your name?" Charlie sat down in the seat that Jenna had just vacated.

The guard declined the drink with a wave of his hand. "My name is Fernán. What will you be needing?" he asked.

"Tomorrow we will need a car and driver. He's got to speak English," Charlie said.

"An all-day driver will cost sixty dollars. You pay for gas and buy lunch. It's no problem. What do you need for this evening?"

Was this it? This was what the bartender had talked about, that the guards were supposedly pimping for the neighborhood talent—but that could have been all talk. Charlie had never considered hiring a prostitute in Florida. They were generally drug addicts from which a person could receive one or more infectious diseases, some fatal. He would see them on Route One. They had brown teeth and smelled like raccoons. But this was different. This was an exotic country. Things like this were … accepted? Maybe the guard was talking about something different.

"You mean food?"

"You can eat right there." The guard pointed to an elaborate covered walkway across the road and to the right of the pool. *"Companera? Quiere companera?"*

"Claro que si." *Why not?* So that's how they did it. They asked if you wanted a companion. That was a nice way to phrase it. Companionship, everybody wanted companionship. Who wanted to be alone? *Great marketing*, thought Charlie.

"*A que hora?*" asked the guard. *What time?*

Charlie thought for a moment. "Nine o'clock," he said, wondering if the girls charged by the hour and if there was a curfew in the marina. Charlie didn't see himself as the type of man who hired a hooker—this was more in the category of a sociological experiment.

Fernán nodded. The guards departed from the *Bora Bora*, and the crew were left to marvel at their good fortune—a cheap, tropical paradise that would carry no evidence that they had ever been to its forbidden shores. Charlie, Allen, and Jenna relaxed, as if they had dodged a bullet

Nine o'clock came and went. At ten, the lights around the pool deck were extinguished. The music was turned off. Allen and Jenna grew tired of waiting to see what a Cuban hooker looked like and disappeared into their cabin. From his seat in the cockpit, Charlie could hear the latch to their door being turned.

Fifteen minutes later, a blue, Russian-made Lada drove slowly past the hotel entrance and pulled into the parking space perpendicular to the *Bora Bora Express*. Charlie watched. A burly man in an untucked blue dress shirt opened the driver's side rear door. Two women slid out. The driver closed the door and returned to the passenger seat, where he sat in the dark. Like hunting dogs on the scent, the two women beelined across the grass strip, somehow knowing exactly where to go. Charlie asked them to remove their shoes before they came aboard.

Charlie had them speak slowly so he could understand. "Qual son tus nombres?" They told him their names. They were neighbors from nearby Santa Fe. Daniella was thirty-five, a mother of three. She was pudgy, with light brown hair and a moon face, jet-black eyes peering through sun-damaged skin, reminding Charlie of Peruvian Indians he had seen in *National Geographic Magazine*. She was proper in both dress and demeanor, in her folded hands a piece of tissue. Her skirt was knee-length, and she had somehow squeezed her brown, duck-like feet into fashionable pumps. Her voice was pure and soft, as was her smile. *She's a hooker?* Charlie practiced his Spanish, asking her questions. Yes, she was married—that was her husband driving the car.

Her neighbor Miranda was much younger, maybe twenty-five. She was shorter, thinner, but not nearly as lithe as Jenna despite her skin-tight jeans. Unlike her matronly friend, she was bursting with youthful exuberance, squirming in her seat, her eager hazel eyes locking onto Charlie like a cheetah watching a warthog. *This is a no-brainer*, he thought, *but are these two a tag team, or can I split them up?*

Charlie found himself in an awkward position. He hadn't come to Cuba to hurt anyone's feelings. Daniella knew she couldn't compete with Miranda, but it was obvious she had taken a shower, changed into tasteful clothes, put on perfume, hired a babysitter, and hauled her chubby self across town. She was ready, willing, and able to perform. She was undoubtedly a lovely person, but this was business. Sex business. Charlie explained that he had asked the guard for one girl, and although he would enjoy sharing their companionship, the berth in his boat was tiny and would not accommodate three people. He handed Daniella a twenty-dollar bill and watched her waddle her way across the grass strip and slump into the back seat of the waiting car. *It's business*, he reminded himself. *So why do I feel like such a pig?*

"You want a drink?" Charlie asked Miranda.

"Un cola, por favor," Miranda replied as she grabbed Charlie's hand and dragged him into the cabin, massaging the front of his jeans.

"No rum?" asked Charlie. She explained that her stomach had been upset, and she couldn't drink tonight. Maybe tomorrow.

"You are my first American," she told him. Apparently, she too had family members in Miami. She hadn't seen her father in seven years, and her mother was a religious harelip with a penchant for avocados. As they talked, Charlie caught a whiff of something foul in the air. Maybe one of the heads was blocked. That happened occasionally. Perhaps a mouse had died in the bilge. He walked toward the engine room, where the smell seemed to disappear, then back to the table, where it lingered. The fumes seemed to be emanating from just below her seat, but soon most of them were disbursed by the air-conditioning system.

She removed her shirt, and Charlie could see that she was a mother. A web of stretch marks crisscrossed her stomach. He found himself to be uncomfortable, nervous, and apprehensive. Things were happening too fast. He downed an extra potent Cuba Libre. This was unfamiliar territory. The role he usually played with women was reversed.

She massaged the growing bulge in his pants with her right hand and held her cola with the other. He wasn't used to aggressive women. All the foreplay he had honed through college, the delicate dance of seduction, meant nothing to the lady that was grabbing at his crotch. She had ample breasts, and Charlie was sure this was a problem with which he could learn to deal. Nevertheless, he was ill at ease. Perhaps it was time to make another—*blam*, there it was again, but worse.

Suddenly he was engulfed in an invisible bubble of noxious fumes that blew him backward, gasping for breath. He sprang to his feet, unable to believe the little flower before him had delivered a surprise package from the bowels of hell. "Good God! Something crawled up your butt and died! What have you been eating?"

"Frijoles negro," came the sheepish reply. Black beans. "Lo siento," she apologized, looking down at the table, embarrassed.

Trying to gain his breath and composure, Charlie sought refuge near the sink in the galley, but shockwaves from the expanding cloud quickly filled every nook and cranny of the cabin.

As he finished making his drink, he turned to find Miranda placing her folded jeans, along with her G-string, on the seat beneath the book rack. He had been about to reconsider this transaction, but now she was standing naked in his cabin, and he was worried about what the guy waiting in the car would do to him if he sent her back without paying her.

Charlie compared his previous mental image with the reality standing before him. Her voluptuous breasts were the perfect example of the rationale behind the creation of the bra—before now, her knockers had been lifted, separated, and displayed to the world in their best possible configuration. Now, without that support and yielding to the force of gravity, they were just pendulous blobs of adipose tissue. And the jeans, they must have been made from Kevlar. How else could they have constricted the lumpy legs and flat ass into the desirable package that had been sitting before him only moments before? But the fear of the guy in the car, along with the fact that the blood had already left his brain, and all of it made little difference to Charlie. At that moment, she was a goddess.

What she has lost in muscle tone, she'll make up for in enthusiasm, he thought. *Thank you, Cuba. Thank you, Fidel.*

She pointed toward the V-berth in the forepeak. Charlie was back in familiar territory. He not only knew what to do, but also perhaps he could teach her a few tricks. His shirt and pants were jettisoned to the cabin sole before he reached the forward V-berth. She motioned for him to roll on his back as she knelt beside him. He complied, his custard launcher aimed at the underside of the forward hatch, bobbing with anticipation. She placed one hand on the base of the shaft, the other cradling his nuts. She inserted the tip into her mouth. Charlie placed his right hand on her sweaty head and fondled a swinging breast with the other. She applied negative pressure and increased the tempo. *She's a pro*, thought Charlie as he drifted into a better world.

Slowly, but never losing suction, her body rotated toward his right shoulder and, before Charlie had time to interject himself into the decision-making process, she swung her left leg over his head and straddled his chest. He was pinned. His eyes, which had rolled back in his head, took a time-out to focus on the hovering brown crack only five or six inches from his face.

Oh no, she doesn't really expect me to eat that thing.

The answer was clear as she leaned back, forcing the questionably hygienic portal to her ovaries firmly over his mouth and chin. In an effort to burrow through the matted hair, Charlie swished his head from side to side and probed with his mouth and tongue, eventually breaking through to raw meat. He went to work with his tongue, searching for the upside-down magic spots, which, to her delight, he found. She assisted by shifting her body and pelvis, pumping his face with her backside and forcing Charlie to breathe on the upstrokes. She shifted forward, just a bit, but this placed her lover's nose directly against the terminal end of her clenched colon, which chose at that very moment to yield to the hydraulic pressures of stomach distress and the decomposing frijoles that had built up over the past twenty minutes.

Charlie's brain, which had been soaring with the eagles somewhere over the Serengeti, plunged into panic mode. He couldn't breathe. He was nearly blind. Throwing her to the side, he flipped over. Now on his hands and knees, he was stunned and temporarily paralyzed. To eject the rotten gasses from his lungs, he had to first breathe in. But he didn't want to inhale, as the ejection had been accompanied by a spray that had coated his inner nose up to the sinuses. His frantic mind searched for a solution and found one. Dazed, holding his breath, and on the verge of losing consciousness, he sprang from the bed, streaked through the cabin, slid back the companionway hatch, and dived naked into the canal, which attracted the attention of a guard.

He burst to the surface, gagging and clawing at his throat. Meanwhile, the splash and ensuing commotion woke Allen and Jenna, who emerged from aft cabin, dazed and startled. The guard, walkie-talkie to his mouth, trained his flashlight on the swimmer, who was obviously in distress. Other yachtsmen, in tune with the usual sights and sounds of the marina after dark, rushed to shine their lights, fearing, from the sound of it, that a donkey had fallen into the canal and was struggling to escape. The captain of the *Express* tried to breathe, but the offensive vapors had firmly attached themselves to the inside of Charlie's skull. In an act of desperation, he tried sucking water up and into his sinus cavities, which triggered a further round of hacking and coughing.

"He's drowning!" screamed Jenna. Wearing only panties, she dived over the rail to save him. A car full of guards squealed to a stop beside the Lada, yellow lights flashing. Hotel workers, peering through the plate glass windows, assumed a guest was in trouble and rushed to help, followed by curious onlookers. In a desperate effort to dislodge the demon, Charlie gulped air through his mouth and blew it out through his nose underwater, convincing Jenna he was in the final throes of dying.

Reverting to her lifeguard training, Jenna approached the victim from behind, raised his chin above the surface in the crook of her arm, tipped him on his back, and compressed the back of his head to her upper shoulder. Unaware he was being rescued, the young captain interpreted the unexpected stranglehold as a shark attack.

Those people who were not yet aware of the drama unfolding within the canal—guests on the other side of the hotel watching TV or trying to sleep, fellow boat owners surrounded by the din of air-conditioning, indeed pretty much every living soul within five hundred yards—were jolted to attention by Charlie's death scream.

By now the guards had made their way to the stern of the boat. Charlie was still nearly blind, but this time augmented by the glare of a dozen flashlights as they followed his naked journey up the swim ladder, over the rail, and into the cockpit. Allen wrapped Jenna in a towel as she emerged from the black water. After seeing that everyone was alive and admonishing that swimming was not allowed after ten at night, the guards and the crowd quickly disbursed. Miranda, fully clothed, was standing in the cockpit, demanding money.

Charlie sputtered, "How much?"

Palm outstretched, she replied, "*Ciento*. I need to go now."

"One hundred? You want a *hundred* dollars? I am not paying you a hundred dollars. You only make twenty dollars a month. That wasn't five month's work!"

"*Ciento*. I need to go now." She looked over her shoulder at the waiting Lada.

"Listen, I will pay you fifty." His head was spinning. No sooner had he left one uncomfortable situation than he has in another. *What happened?* he wondered. What happened to the compliant young mother? In her place stood a vicious little harpy brimming with hostility, a hateful shrew stridently demanding payment. Did she have a knife?

Her eyes, which had been warm and beckoning only minutes before, were now piercing beacons of venom and scorn. Had she hated his guts when they were laughing and joking? They had seemed to be getting along so well. Perhaps it was something he'd did. Or hadn't done. Or was it because he'd screamed like a girl when he'd been in the water? That was probably it. Perhaps he had failed to live up to a macho code.

"OK, I will pay you seventy-five, but that's it."

Charlie went below, slipped on his pants, and fumbled for his wallet as he was climbing the companionway stairs. In the dimly lit cockpit, he pulled out three twenties, a ten, and a five, splaying it before her scowling eyes. Reluctantly, she took the money. "Ten more." The outstretched hand reappeared.

"Eighty-five? That's too much! We agreed on seventy-five!"

"My driver. Ten for my driver."

Allen and Jenna were gaping at him. It wasn't worth arguing. Charlie was defeated. He reached into his wallet and withdrew a ten-dollar bill. It was worth ten more to get her off his boat. Within a minute, she was safely ensconced within the waiting Lada and disappearing into the darkness.

Charlie slumped onto one of the deck cushions, trying to make sense of the evening. Methodically chronicling the strange sequence of events, he remembered something. It hadn't registered at the time. Just a little thing, probably nothing. When he had pulled the wallet from his pants, it was folded side up. He always folded the wallet and slipped the folded side down. *She couldn't have.* She had been in the cabin by herself while he'd been doing his best impression of a dying seal. His arm instinctively reached behind, a feeling of dread welling up within him. He snatched the wallet from his back pocket, flipped it open, and peered into the secret compartment where he kept an emergency stash of five crisp one-hundred-dollar bills.

It was empty.

He had been in Cuba for less than twenty-four hours and had been gassed, strangled, chastised by the police, and ripped off. Worse, his pussy fund was already down $585, not including the $5 that he still he owed to the guard.

CHAPTER TEN

Cubans joke that if Castro arrived on the island today, he would immediately seek to overthrow the existing government. After forty years of cultivating the cult of revolution in the hearts of every Cuban citizen, Fidel was reaping what he had sown—a parallel, embedded culture of criminals openly defying the system—doubly dangerous since participants were imbued with righteous indignation. Worse, the Cubans' black market was the definition of pure and unfettered capitalism. The underground economy balanced the deficiencies in the government's collectivist market model. Without the black market, the regime could not survive.

"*Mira*, Mama." Vali spread the money on the kitchen table.

"Ciento!" Nicole had seen American dollars before but never in her home. Vali's mother lifted the stack and splayed it in her hands like a peacock's tailfeathers. She was worried about how her daughter had found a way to bypass the peso economy and earn real money. Up until last year, any Cuban—especially any women—found associating with tourists was instantly harassed by the police. Many were arrested. There was an assumption on the part of officials that hustlers and *jineteras* would target the visitors as easy marks. Further, if even one tourist was killed or seriously injured, the entire tourist industry could take a hit.

But the plan had backfired. Foreign television crews and camera-clad visitors had picked up on the heavy-handed treatment of ordinary Cubans who'd done nothing more than strike up a conversation. Videos of these incidents gained exposure, and both the press and human rights groups took notice. It was a view into the reality of repression, and the world began to see how out-of-control Castro and his cronies were—an unintended consequence of opening the doors to all those pesky tourists. Beginning in 1993, the negative press was taking its toll on hotel occupancy.

During July of 1997, the regime reversed itself. In anticipation of the pope's arrival, consorting with tourists was not openly encouraged but seemed to be grudgingly tolerated. There was nothing in writing. The word was simply passed down through the ranks, but its effects were soon felt on the streets, and Cubans responded accordingly.

Repression remained, but the tactics changed. Intimidation became the new policy as ID cards were regularly and ruthlessly scrutinized. The time and place of any detainment was recorded in a small green book carried in the back pocket of every police officer. The message was clear—*we are watching you.* As always, Cubans pushed the boundaries as they struggled to ascertain and survive within the constraints of the rule of the day. Within a month, elements of the general population realized a veil had been lifted as they were permitted to have lunch in a hotel or invite foreigners into their homes. *Jineteras* learned the police would tolerate a girl in a rental car or taxi with a foreigner if it looked like they were on a *sita,* a date. ID cards were still a requirement to check into a hotel room, but the rule of thumb became one girl, one man, one night. It was good news for Vali.

Nicole feared for her daughter's new enterprise, and she told Vali as much. There was danger. The nosey CDR district supervisor lived on the corner, only three houses away. There were few secrets in the barrio, and this one could cost them their house. Police and prying eyes were everywhere. Nevertheless, those dollars—when converted back into the peso economy—were pure gold. Necessities such as cooking oil, grains, soap, toiletries, and the like were available at the peso stores for pennies. A manicure cost twenty-five cents, dresses for under a dollar. Other products—many of them originally purchased in the dollar stores—had migrated into and were bought and sold on the peso exchange.

Mother wanted in on the gravy train. Though Nicole hadn't outright asked Vali to include her, Vali could sense it. At thirty-seven she was still a healthy woman with a good sense of humor who often joked that she knew more tricks than any eighteen-year-old. Never in the past had Vali seen her mother as a sexual competitor—why would she? Before today there had never been a reason.

Mom had her own sex life. Men would drop by, some old enough to be Vali's grandfather. Vali could hear them in there grunting as she tried to go sleep, only a wall away, sharing a bed with her sister. Mama may have received a peso or two, but more than likely her late-night activities were simply to pass the time—an activity more enjoyable than playing solitaire but trumped by the telenovela, which she never missed.

The daughter saw her mother in a new light. Was Nicole marketable? Vali tried to look at her mother objectively—she was stockier, a little shorter. Though she always wore a hat on the way to and from the market, she had sun-damaged crow's feet under her brown eyes, one of which was lazy and drifted to the left. Her legs were stubby, her feet flat, and she was not obsessive when it came to shaving nor was general hygiene high on the list of her daily priorities. Life had been tough on Mom since her husband had disappeared over the horizon on a *balsa*. But, God bless her, she was still ready and able to suck a dick.

Vali plucked the cash from her mother's hand and spread the money on the kitchen table. Five dollars for the waiter, fifteen for Jorge, twenty-five as a deposit with ETESCA for a telephone. Fifty-five-dollars profit! In one night!

That afternoon Vali worked with Fabian on new songs and choreography. She was assigned a locker. They worked on hand signals so Fabian could craft her performance to the mood of the audience. At six o'clock she returned home and took a *siesta* since she didn't know if or when she would return home that evening. She hoped to meet an American. A young one. A rich one. Someone to take her to Miami or the Grand Canyon—anywhere, provided it got her off the island.

After her first show, Selena assumed her station at the bar. Within minutes she was joined by a paunchy, swarthy, balding man, with a round, brown face that reminded her of a bulldog. She knew by his accent that he was from Mexico. They talked. He bought her a drink then disappeared into the crowd. She scanned the crowd for faces that looked American, and she thought she found two of them, but when they spoke, she could tell they were from Spain.

Several *habaneros* joined her. They were young, strong, good looking. They bought her a drink, but they had no intention of purchasing her affections. There was no need. She knew the lifestyle—young men like that who were confident, alpha, they were butterflies that flitted from flower to flower. And she was sure that each had his own garden.

She saw the Mexican stumbling his way through the crowd toward her. He wore a light-blue guayabera shirt, charcoal-gray slacks, and cheap shoes. He sat beside her, reeking of whiskey.

"I want to fuck you."

"How's your wife feel about that?" She pointed to a wide, gold wedding ring. He laughed.

"She would want to fuck you too."

"Did the waiter send you over?"

"No. Why? I just see you, Selena. I have always loved your music. For years I look at you on the stage, and I want you in my bed."

95

"No, thanks. If you saw me naked, you would die of a heart attack. I would be arrested for murder. It's not worth it."

He roared with laughter, choking on his drink and nearly falling off the barstool. "My name is Miguel, I have always loved you, and now I love you even more. I sell Corona beer. Look, see that poster? I give posters to all the bars and restaurants. We are always looking for pretty girls to put on posters."

"I am sorry. You could not afford me, even for ten minutes."

He laughed and ordered them both a whiskey and coke.

She was setting the hook, but was this a fish she really wanted to catch? Vali scanned the crowd for other prospects. The night was young. Clients were still arriving. Perhaps she could polish off this fellow and return in time to snag another one.

"I could afford you. I could buy this entire fucking restaurant."

"I don't think so. I get one hundred dollars for three hours."

"I will give you eighty."

"What happened to the big spender? Talk is cheap."

"This is business, and I am a businessman. I offer eighty. You want a hundred. Let's agree on ninety and all the whiskey you can drink."

Not having to pay a waiter saved five dollars. The up-front telephone expenses had already been allotted. No other fish at the bar were nibbling at her bait.

"All right, ninety. *If* you will pay taxi fare to my house in Jaimanitas."

"Better, my princess. I have a driver. He will return you to your castle. He's waiting for us outside. You have your identification card?"

Twenty minutes later, they arrived at the Capri, near the Malecon in Havana. Vali had never seen the inside of a big downtown hotel. She had tried. Each time she would be spotted as a Cuban and refused entry. But she wasn't Vali from Jaimanitas tonight. She was Selena in a beautiful gown, the consort of a wealthy foreign businessman. This time the guards at the door rushed to assist as they passed through, arm in arm.

"Your card?"

Vali handed Miguel her identification, absorbing the grandeur of the lobby as he slid the card and a twenty-dollar bill to a woman behind the reception desk.

Miguel's room was on the fourteenth floor. The scheme was yellow and white, modern, with a king-sized bed in the middle of the room. Vali threw back the sliding glass doors and stepped onto the balcony. It was breathtaking. Past the Malecon and across the harbor entrance was El Moro National Monument, illuminated by white and blue spotlights for the tourists. Directly across, the venerable Hotel National—the timeless baroque castle featured in a hundred classic movies. To the right was the skyline of Old Havana, which, despite its warts and wrinkles, was still a beautiful sight.

Vali tried to draw on her limited experience. "I've been dancing all night. I am sweaty and need to take a shower."

"No shower."

"If you have music, I can dance for you."

"No music." Vali watched as he went to the closet, opened his suitcase, and withdrew a small black leather box, which he placed on the bed.

"Take off your clothes."

"You promised me a drink. I am going to need a drink." Miguel picked up the phone from the desk. "Two whiskeys and ginger ale. Room 1412." He hung up. "Now stand right there and take off your clothes."

Miguel's demeanor had changed. He was sullen, focused, deadly serious. Vali began to feel nervous. There was only the two of them here, and Miguel suddenly did not seem the gentleman that Arthur had been.

"Can I close the blinds?" She was looking for an excuse, any excuse not to comply with her client's wishes, to give herself time to calm her nerves.

"Certainly. I don't want to share you with the Hotel National."

"Can I turn off the lights?"

"No."

"Are you going to hurt me?"

"If you don't struggle, you won't get hurt." For the first time, Vali saw Miguel as a physical impediment between herself and the door. He was short but powerfully built, with the upper arms and hairy paws of a gorilla. She felt fear welling up. She hadn't brought a knife. Next time she would bring a knife, if there was a next time. Her heart was pounding. She could hear it, feel it. She wanted to flee, but he was still between her and the door.

The door chimed. A waiter entered and placed two drinks on the nightstand. It was her opportunity to make a break, but she didn't take it. As nervous as she was, Miguel hadn't done anything to hurt her. The waiter had now seen her. Her ID card was at the desk, so others knew she was here, at least. Miguel gave the man a tip. As the door closed, Vali felt as if her last link to safety had been lost. She thought hard about the money that she would leave with after he was done with her and tried to detach herself from whatever they were about to do.

"Take off your clothes." Vali let the dress slide down from her shoulders. Miguel sat on the bed and watched, his hand placed on the box as if to keep something inside from escaping. She kept her eye on the box.

Why would he do that? What's in the box? Her thoughts ran wild. "Rats! That's it. He's got rats in the box!" Her worst nightmare was coming true on her second night of work! Instinctively, her hands shot down to cover her crotch. Rats! They are filthy animals. She knew she smelled something funny. Now she could hear them trying to gnaw their way through the top of the box. That's why the gorilla had its hand on the lid. It was just waiting for her to remove her underwear and its giant, hairy anthropoid hands would spread her legs apart and insert big black rats with their beady eyes and claws and teeth. The mental picture was more than she could stand. She screamed, bolted for the sliding glass doors, ran through the opening, and cowered on the balcony, looking for a way down, wishing she could fly.

Miguel walked slowly to the balcony holding a drink, as nonchalant as if encountering a terrified, nearly naked girl—one 150 feet above the ground, trembling in the corner of his balcony—was an everyday occurrence. Miguel put his arm around her and handed her the drink.

"Look at what a beautiful night it is. This is my wife's favorite hotel. My kids like the pool. You are new at this, aren't you? You must learn to relax."

Supportive, soothing, and reassuring, he led her back into the room, closed the slider, and slipped off her panties. Still shaking, she sipped her drink on top of the bed covers. Save for his shoes, Miguel was fully dressed. His voice was gentle, his manner reassuring. She felt embarrassed. She had overreacted. Her actions were neither appropriate nor professional. After all, he was a father with kids and a wife, maybe a dog. He wasn't a monster. Comparing him to a gorilla was cruel. She began to relax and imagined how ridiculous she must have seemed running toward the balcony. He must have thought she was going over the rail and committing suicide. *Silly girl.* She would do her best to control her imagination in the future.

Miguel placed his drink on the nightstand and opened the box, pulling out a jumble of black leather, buckles, and bright chrome chains. Vali dropped her drink and flew over her client as she headed naked for the door. The gorilla pivoted and placed his huge monkey fist against it. She dashed for the only other exit, the balcony. There was another balcony about ten feet away, and she knew she could bridge the gap. She just had to get on top of the rail to push off. She slid the patio chair to the edge of the rail, stepped up, placed one foot on the top in preparation for launch, but was tackled and dragged to the floor by King Kong. She struggled, but the Mexican ape held her in its powerful grasp, smothering her to his hairy chest.

The gorilla whispered in her ear, "I'm not going to hurt you. It's a game. It's just a game."

Here she was, selling herself to try and escape captivity, and this man wanted to chain her up. "Nobody is putting chains on me."

"You have no choice. As long as you cooperate, you will be fine." He picked her up and carried her to the bed. "I am not going to hurt you, I promise." His beady eyes seared into hers he removed a black leather wristband from the entangled pile. The chains rattled. The animal wrapped the band gently around her left wrist, securing it with a thick leather strap and buckle. He did the same to her right hand. "Lay in the middle of the bed." She was terrified to comply and terrified not to. The beast arranged a pillow in the middle, pushed her into position, and laid her head upon it.

"Relax your arms." Slowly, cautiously, he peeled her left arm from her side, extended it to a forty-five-degree angle, and secured it by a chain to the bedpost. It did the same to her other arm, then her legs. Within minutes she was spread-eagled, naked, and helpless.

The gorilla walked around the bed, adjusting the chains to remove any slack. He put a small square pillow from the couch on her chest, just below her jaw, blocking her view of anything but the ceiling. She heard him breathing. He positioned himself at the foot of the bed. Vali was surprised to find her nipples getting hard, but it was cold in the air-conditioned hotel room. Yes, that was it. It was cold in here.

"You're so beautiful." The tone of his voice relaxed Vali a little. He sounded reverent, awed.

She heard trousers unzip and then a rustling. Then silence. The bed creaked as pressure was applied. He was crawling up, between her legs. She could hear him breathing. And then, contact. He touched her. She held her breath, surprised to find that she was anticipating what would come next—without her earlier level of fear. He touched her foot. He enveloped her foot with his claws and commenced sucking her toes, his monkey tongue exploring the cracks and crevasses in between them, making slurping sounds. He slathered, sucked, and kissed the soles of her feet, then the heels, returning occasionally to tongue massage a toe. She could feel the hot saliva as his mouth moved from one part of her foot to another.

Then he switched his attention and his slobber to her right foot. His actions became more frantic. He stopped after five minutes and released his grasp. There was silence. No movement. Suddenly the face of the creature emerged from over the pillow and crashed down next to hers. Huge paws covered with drool grabbed her head, and a raspy tongue found its way into her ear. She felt his little gorilla penis slide into her. There was a grunt then a slump. Her face was crushed into a sweaty armpit. She wiggled from beneath to prevent from being suffocated.

The animal rolled off and disappeared into the bathroom. With the pillow dislodged, Vali could see that he had never even taken off his pants. Laying there—cold, helpless, covered with gorilla slime, it occurred to her that perhaps she had made the wrong career move.

Miguel emerged from the toilet with his face washed and hair combed. He unfastened his slave and didn't even watch as she got dressed. Vali noticed he seemed dazed, in a trance, his face blank. He mechanically withdrew ninety dollars from his wallet. Vali grabbed it and escaped, glad to have survived, glad to have ninety dollars. There was no driver to take her home, so she paid her own cab fare, wondering if Miguel would even notice that she was gone.

CHAPTER ELEVEN

Cuba was a mystery. Who was this Castro and how had he come to power? For a man with such military prowess—which remained a blueprint for dictatorial overthrow—his economic stewardship of the island displayed either a lack of understanding or an outright contempt for the elementary economic laws of supply and demand. Despite his claims to the contrary, once in power Castro had rapidly adopted Che's version of a Marxist ideology—one that predictably destroyed a vibrant albeit corrupt economy. Under centralized planning, Cuba plummeted into a subsistence economy. Perhaps the most visible manifestation of this was the unfinished, unpainted city of Havana and its ubiquitous fleet of aging automobiles.

One of which pulled into a parking space near the *Bora Bora* at nine the next morning.

The driver stood beside the *Express*, looking for signs of life. It was silent. He knocked on the deck. Charlie emerged from the cabin, bleary-eyed. "Can I help you?"

"My name is Esteban. Call me Steve. I'm your driver."

"Oh shit, I forgot. Come aboard. You want some coffee?"

Esteban looked the part of a harried businessman—a wrinkled, striped shirt stuffed into black dress pants, fidgeting as he glanced at his watch. He was perhaps forty-five years old, with the body of an athlete who hadn't exercised in fifteen years. His voice was deep, abrupt, his attitude cynical. He removed his dusty dress shoes and waited in the cockpit, wiping his brow with a handkerchief he kept in his left shirt pocket. He was imminently likable but anxious and guarded as if a piano was about to drop out of the sky and squash him like a bug. He waited as the crew packed their day bags with cameras, baseball caps, and bottles of water.

"That's your car?" Allen pointed to the faded blue-and-white 1956 Chevy Bel Air two-door hardtop. "Is that a Nomad? Didn't they make that in a four door also?"

Allen, the car buff, was in heaven. Esteban folded the driver's seat forward to allow Jenna and him to limbo into the cavernous interior. "Wow, leg room." Allen sprawled on the bench seat. "Damn, I've had smaller apartments."

Charlie, in the passenger seat, looked at the metal dashboard between himself and the window. "I guess there weren't airbags in the sixties. How are the brakes on this thing?" he asked as Esteban tried to jam the transmission into reverse.

Leaving the space-age, poured concrete guardhouse at the entrance to Marina Hemingway, Charlie received his first view of the real Cuba. They waited as the busses, motorcycles, and a rolling junkyard of vehicles made their ways around a wooden wagon. The wagon was mounted on a straight auto axle, pulled by an emaciated brown horse as it clopped its way west on Avenida Quinta, or Fifth Ave. Esteban crossed to the other side and headed east toward Havana.

"This is the Rio Jaimanitas. Look at the boats. That's a fishing club," Esteban narrated. The small craft, like the cars, were holdovers from the days before the Revolution, some painted festively while others were on the verge of sinking. "This river separates the marina from the town of Jaimanitas. You can walk to here in five minutes. There's the Rumbo. Beers are fifty cents. It's a lot cheaper than the marina. And over there, the *farmacia*."

Charlie looked to his left to see Esteban futilely pushing at the floor-mounted shift in an effort engage third gear. That seemed strange since the Bel Air series started life with a column-mounted shift and a hydroglide automatic transmission. "The synchro is gone in the upper gears, and I have to double clutch," said sweating Esteban in a voice that hinted of long-simmering frustration, "There are no more automatic transmissions left." In that case, it was no use in inquiring about the air-conditioning, and Charlie could see that the power steering was either functioning poorly or not at all. He wondered about the power brakes.

The residential neighborhoods east of Jaimanitas were as varied as the throngs of people going about their business. There was a crowd outside the farmacia, another at the PhotoServi on the corner, yet another at the bus stop, its inadequate shelter crammed with those trying to escape the morning sun. Women, often with children, and the elderly stood halfway into the middle of the road, facing traffic, their eyes imploring drivers to stop. They passed a huge Russian-marked dump truck, jam-packed with human cargo ranging from sewer workers to well-dressed secretaries headed for office buildings in Havana. Charlie tried to imagine his mother, dressed in high heels and carrying a pocketbook, making her way up the side and into the bed of an earth hauler belching black clouds of diesel smoke. Two policemen, impeccably dressed in their tight-fitting uniforms, were hitchhiking beneath the shade of a ficus tree.

"What is that—the sign with a camera with a slash through it? Along the road here, look, there's another one coming up." Charlie could see that under each international symbol was printed *No Foto*.

"That's Fidel's house. He lives right here in Jaimanitas. The fence around it is eighteen kilometers. Keep your cameras out of sight," Esteban warned.

"But there are other houses. I can see through the fence."

Esteban glanced through the passenger window. "That's his security. The place is more like a military garrison. Look." The driver pointed to a what appeared to be an outhouse on stilts, set back from the fence about three hundred feet. "There are two guys in there, one with a machine gun and the other is a sniper."

Charlie felt a wave of excitement. Being viewed from within Castro's fortress, with its impending ominous overtones, added to the sense of adventure.

In the midst of moving traffic, Esteban switched off the engine. They coasted a couple hundred yards to the stoplight in Playa where the road divides. "Saves gas. We need to stop at the next station," said Esteban as he poised to jam into first gear. The gas gauge was well past empty, but that didn't mean much. They weren't alone. Next to them a '53 Plymouth carrying—Charlie tried to count—eight people, maybe nine if that bundle on the shoulder of the woman in front was a baby.

"That's a peso cab. Cost ten pesos for Cubans, more for you." As the digital counter that hung above the stoplight neared zero, other cars could be heard cranking their engines and, once started, revving up, since every stoplight initiated a drag race. They flew passed the Commercial Centro de Nautico. The restaurant was bustling.

"You like spaghetti?" asked Esteban, pointing to the modern glass storefront. "Good spaghetti for sixty cents. It's near my home. Better spaghetti than Palenque. My wife likes to eat there. They bake their own bread."

"You live around here?"

"Not far." From the Nautico to the Oro Negro, on the traffic circle, was a straight shot of about half a mile. "I live that way." Esteban pointed to the tree-lined road leading up the hill. Their car was sixth in the queue at the gas station. Esteban turned the off the motor to save gas. When cars pulled away from the pump, Charlie,

Allen, and Jenna pushed the car forward as Esteban steered. By the time they reached the pump, they were all sweating.

"What do you want—cola, beer, cigarettes?" After they'd agreed to all three, Esteban disappeared into the station and returned with a bag. "That will be seventy-two dollars."

"What? How much?" Charlie scoffed.

"Fifty-four liters of gas at $1.18 per liter, that's about $4.25 a gallon, then the cigarettes and the beer." Charlie looked at the pump then at Allen and Jenna. "I thought this place was cheap!"

During the 1930s, Havana had been the Paris of the Caribbean, with its Malecon reminiscent of the French Riviera's and its capital a dead ringer for the one in Washington, DC, only larger. Ostentatious displays of its prosperity extended west along the coast through the neighborhoods of Vedado, Miramar, and Cubacan. But Havana's wealth had been affected by the same crushing poverty that had fomented discontent in Cuba for so many years. During the short drive from Playa into Miramar, within a mile or two, there is a profound architectural and sociological transformation. Esteban slowed to let the crew of the *Bora Bora Express* marvel at the splendid homes and mansions lining the boulevard. Many were now sectioned into multifamily units, others used as foreign embassies or governmental offices—yet their classic balconies and porticos still inspired awe.

"My God, what in the world is that thing?" Jenna scrunched down in the back seat to get a view through the windshield. Looming over the prestigious neighborhood was an incongruous monolithic structure brimming with radio antennas. "I never thought a building could be evil, but that one is. If Darth Vader was reincarnated as a building, that would be it, or him."

Indeed, the Russian embassy seemed the embodiment of malevolent intent as it commanded a view of twenty miles in all directions. "Oh, that?" Esteban said. "We don't even notice it anymore. It's filled with Russians. We hate those bastards."

Since they had no reason to hurry, Charlie had Esteban pull into the shade of the huge banyans at Parque Quinta. Youngsters were playing baseball in the park using a rock wrapped tightly in a sock. Two teenage girls sat on a bench, listening to music.

Charlie rummaged in the bags and spoke to Esteban. "Here, relax. Have a beer. Save gas. Where did you learn to speak such good English?"

"My mother returned to Cuba from Boston at the request of Fidel. They were friends. That was 1961. She was second in command at the Ministry of Industrialization, under Nora Frometer. English was my first language. My father was a doctor and headed the army clinic in Angola, Africa. He died last year."

"And you work as a taxi driver?" Allen asked, opening his own beer.

"A driver! I'm not a taxi driver. I work cruise ships. Been all over the world in cruise ships, some of the world's finest. I speak Italian and Portuguese. Guest relations. I kept everyone happy."

"I didn't think Cubans could leave the island. That must have been good money. Why did you come back?" Jenna asked.

"Money? The pay was terrible. The government billed the cruise line at international rates, took the money, and paid me twenty-two dollars a month. That's all we are allowed to make, just the twenty-two a month that Fidel gives us."

"What?" Charlie was incredulous.

"It's the system. But I could make tips. I made big money in tips. Those Fidel did not know about." Esteban smiled wistfully, as if remembering.

It didn't make sense to Charlie, so he pressed on. "So why are you here driving tourists around in this hunk of junk for sixty dollars a day when you could be on the beach in Rio drinking caipirinhas?"

"Well, it just didn't—I was—that job didn't work out."

"You fucked up, didn't you? We are Americans. Who we going to tell? Come on, how did you screw up?" Charlie needled.

Esteban squirmed uncomfortably, but there was a far-away look in his eye. He seemed to be transported back to his life on the big boats. "You know, those ships carry three or four thousand guests. But those are just the people you see. There are another fifteen hundred underneath. They are invisible, but they are down there. They run everything—the engines, the laundry, the performers, all the singers and acrobats and stagehands. About four hundred of those workers are women—young women—from all over the world. They make very little money and are bored as hell."

"Oh, man, I think I see where this is going." Jenna rolled her eyes as he spoke.

"I had one of the few jobs that mingled with the guests— guest relations. I could go anywhere. If a guest had a problem, they came to me. If they wanted to play ping-pong at midnight, I made it happen. If they wanted a private limousine waiting for them at the gangplank, no problem. If they wanted sex, just tell me when and where. They loved me."

"So you provided desperate young dancers to dirty old men?" Jenna's tone became disapproving.

"Sometimes. Usually, old ladies who wanted a young stud or couples who wanted a young person—sometimes a man, sometimes a girl. A lot of gays. We would split the money fifty-fifty. They would arrive in the room as maintenance workers. If the spouse was out gambling or getting a massage, I had spies that kept track and reported back to me on the walkie-talkie. They were my security detail and got a cut. It was perfect. Everybody was happy. Guest relations. I was just doing my job."

109

"What happened?" Allen asked.

"The internet. The fucking internet. Word got out on the internet. People would call up and want to know how to book a voyage on the SS *Whorehouse* or the *Good Ship Blowjob* like it was a big joke. They determined I was guilty of unjust enrichment, and I was fired."

"Why did you come back to Cuba?" Charlie emptied his first beer and reached for another.

"My mother was sick. She lived in my house."

"What happened to all the money?" Charlie asked.

"The government confiscated about six thousand dollars at the airport. The rest I had already spent fixing up my house."

Allen, who had obviously been thinking in the back seat, piped up. He looked skeptical, as if this was obviously a bullshit story designed to gain their sympathy. "Twenty dollars a month? You mean additional money, above your normal wages?"

"Twenty dollars a month, no matter how hard we work, no matter how hard we study in school. Twenty dollars to buy our food, gasoline, electric, medicine, clothes, shoes. See these shoes? They are from Italy. They cost sixty-three dollars. That's three month's pay if you go by what you're allowed."

"I'm sorry," said Jenna, confrontationally. "I've heard this crap before. That's simply not possible. No one can survive on twenty dollars a month. Look, right here there's ten dollars' worth of cokes and beer in that little bag. We just got here, but for Christ's sake, we're not stupid."

Few appreciate freedom more than those who have lost it. Esteban had risen to a level of privilege denied most Cubans. He had been allowed to travel. Not just geographically, but through a diversity of cultures and characters. He had been free to move through the functioning matrix of societies scattered across the globe, each with its own flavor of political and economic ideologies, many of which validated his concepts of liberty and were readily adopted as his own. He had been allowed to climb the mountain and view the world hidden on the other side, a world he immediately embraced. For the first time in his life, he was not under direct governmental control and, armed with a fresh perspective, realized the extent of the official manipulation that pervaded every aspect of his life in Cuba.

But he wasn't free. Once his fledgling business began to generate profits, his fate had been sealed. Cuba extended its tentacles, and he was on the next plane to Havana. Chauffeuring these Americans, who had no concept of repression and took their freedom for granted, unexpectedly awakened feelings he had worked so hard to repress. Suddenly he was overwhelmed with an unexpected rush of emotions.

"Yes. It *is* fucking impossible!" Esteban broke down, smashing the steering wheel with both hands. His iron-strong voice, which moments before was recounting an incident with resonant clarity, now cracked with emotion. Stunned, the passengers turned to see their tough-as-nails driver wiping the tears from his cheek.

"I try. My family—" He hesitated, staring into infinity through the dusty windshield, his jaw clenched in stoic agony in an effort to hold back a flood of tears. The spontaneous outburst revealed a festering frustration hidden just below the surface. As Esteban collected himself, he was no longer just a cab driver. He was a person. In pain. Holding back his tears, it was as if he were in a trance, bearing witness to a higher power.

"Let me see if I can put this in terms you will understand. Cuba is a prison. It's a prison island. The prisoners aren't allowed to have money. They get little scraps of paper they can redeem at the prison store, and everything in the store is shit. Since they have no money, they can't afford a doctor. They go to the prison doctor. That's why health care is free. You wouldn't send your dog to a Cuban hospital. The prison library can fit into the trunk of this car—

111

Fidel: The Younger Years, *Fidel Taking a Crap on a Lamppost*, Marx, and Lenin. Our prison newspaper is called the *Grandma*, six pages of propaganda. You in America hear we have a ninety-six percent literacy rate. But there is nothing to read except more propaganda. School is free. It has to be—we have no money. And the things we are taught are totally useless. Economics is obeying the government. There is no economics with centralized planning. Gastronomy means you have a shot at working behind a food counter. Mathematics, what a joke. Just hand anyone on the street a pencil and paper and tell them you will give them ten dollars if they can divide one hundred sixty-nine by thirteen. They can't do it. They use calculators. Nothing bad ever happens in the *Grandma*. We don't know if someone dies unless a friend tells us. Half the island could fall into the ocean, and we would never know about it. We are all supposed to be equal, but Fidel has a private jet to go to his private fucking island. The guy that flies his airplane can make more money selling the eggs from three chickens."

Charlie, Allen, and Jenna exchanged uncomfortable looks. Esteban looked off into the distance, but his eyes were vacant.

"And Fidel owns your house. You don't own your house. You don't own your kids. You don't own your own fucking underwear. How do I know? If you try to escape—not leave the island, just escape the system by making money or trying to feed your family or speaking against the Revolution—you are in mortal danger. And what Revolution? The Revolution was over forty years ago. What are we supposed to be revolting against? Oppression? From who? From what? McDonald's hamburgers? We'd love to have McDonald's hamburgers. Fifty billion sold, but not one in Cuba. We're the ones being oppressed, but if we say anything, do anything, think anything that is against the Revolution, we lose our house and our kids and get thrown into a work camp, which is just another prison within a prison. There are signs all over the place. Huge billboards. *Liberty or Death*, *Socialism or Death*, Che's picture, always the same one, but where's my liberty? Why don't I have any freedom? You can go back to America and eat hamburgers. We can't. We can't even own beef. We can't leave. They know that

112

if we do, we will never come back. There are secret police all over the place. Look at that guy. He's on his radio. They read our mail—"

"Whoa, big fella. Calm down," Charlie soothed. The rant had caught them by surprise. Were all Cubans ticking time bombs, or had they just met Esteban on a bad day? "Perhaps we can continue this discussion as we drive."

Esteban composed himself and started the car, still shaking. "Sorry. You are Americans. We can't talk to other Cubans."

As they drove, Jenna wondered aloud about the beaches, Allen played name that car, and Charlie pondered the ramifications of vacationing in a prison. How *did* they survive? Couldn't talk to other Cubans? Secret police? He had a million questions. He took note of the astounding number of armed personnel. There was one on almost every corner. He hadn't noticed them before.

"Those are traffic police?" Charlie asked.

"There's a crackdown this week on *paladars* and prostitution." Esteban supplied.

"What's a *paladar*?" Charlie was still full of questions.

"During the Special Period, about six years ago, Fidel let us open little restaurants in our homes. They required a license. They are closing the ones that don't have licenses, or they have expired, and hassling the honest ones. Happens every couple of months."

"And prostitutes? It's eleven o'clock in the morning. Why in the world would a prostitute be walking around out here in the bright sunshine?" Charlie craned to see out of the window as they passed through intersections, hoping that the street corners would suddenly burst forth with pretty girls like some fragrant tropical market.

"The cops know the working girls in this area. There's lots of them. We passed one about three blocks back. Remember the girl in the green dress standing in the crowd, waiting for the light to change?"

"No." Damn. He'd missed the only prostitute that had escaped the crackdown?

"Well, that was a prostitute." Esteban sounded so casual about it.

Charlie laughed. "How do you know?"

"Eye contact. She spotted you halfway down the block."

Charlie pondered the implications. With increased awareness, he ran the numbers on the police as they drove. One on every corner, four corners per block, eight or nine blocks per mile, one on each side of the road.

"In Florida, you can never find a policeman when you need one. Here there are thousands of them, everywhere. If we can't afford this level of police protection in the richest country on earth, how can Cuba plaster the countryside with cops?"

"You are looking at our country through American eyes." Esteban was struggling to deal with his frustration. "They aren't protecting us. They are protecting Fidel *from* us. They don't cost anything. They get the same as the rest of us, twenty-two fucking dollars a month. You see police. I see guards."

Indeed, through the eyes of Esteban, the passengers saw Havana in a new and disturbing light. Could it be true? If it were true, it would change everything. Rather than being protected, as they had assumed, were they truly under constant surveillance? Charlie gazed into the face of a cop as they sped past. If it was true, they were now in the same fishbowl as their angst-ridden driver, a world now much smaller and defined by invisible walls. Was it likely they had the misfortune to have chosen a mentally unhinged chauffer, one who had reconstructed the world around himself to fit a distorted sense of reality? Was his conception of life within a prison simply a manifestation of his whacked-out paranoia, his hypervigilance the result of a mind that had lost its ability to screen out, weigh, balance, and allocate the flood of information entering his eyes and ears?

But Esteban seemed normal enough. And there *were* police everywhere.

They took the mandatory tourist route and cruised the Malecon, a road that ran from the mouth of Havana Harbor in Old Havana, along the north side of the Centro Habana neighborhood, and ended in the Vedado neighborhood. There was plenty to see along the seawall. They climbed the crumbling castle El Moro, marveled at El Capitulo, and visited various destinations within the maze of Old Havana. Charlie, Allen, and Jenna had forgotten about Esteban's outburst. The group was as carefree as if they had been vacationing in the Bahamas. As they walked from the cobblestone square of Plaza de la Cathedral the half block to Bodequita del Media, Esteban was deep in conversation with Charlie, in the middle of unraveling the myth that Ernest Hemingway was a frequent customer of the historic bar.

Suddenly two uniformed officers emerged from a doorway. They split Esteban from the group. As Esteban had instructed earlier, the three friends kept walking. As they entered the tourist trap through its huge wooden doors, Charlie glanced back to see Esteban, now pressed against the wall, vigorously gesticulating. One officer was scribbling into a book the size of a ledger. The other was peering at a small card— undoubtedly Esteban's *carne*, his national identification card.

Ten minutes later Esteban joined them at the bar, his face red with anger, his hands shaking. "Bullshit. It's just fucking bullshit. They were going to take me in and hold me for two days— interrogation!"

"For what? You are not breaking the law. There are taxi drivers all over the place. Why did they pick on you?" Allen asked.

"I don't have a license. They say I can only work with Cubans, for pesos. Not tourists. But there is a new law, or there was a change in the old law. Nobody really knows. The law is what they say it is, and they can hold you for two days while they figure it out. It's bullshit."

Jenna slid a waiting mojito to the distraught driver. "What did you do?"

"I paid them sixty pesos. Listen, I called my wife, and she is preparing dinner at my house."

They drove El Rampa, which sloped gently down to the Malecon and the crashing sea, turned at the monument, and headed west on Avenida Quinta. Five miles later they slowed as they passed the La Cecilia Restaurant and Bar, entered the traffic circle, and instead of continuing west, followed it around almost to the Oro Negro gas station and then veered south, up the hill. The change was profound. Within a half mile they had entered a unique forest neighborhood of stunning mansions surrounded by gates and armed guards. Esteban double-clutched his way up the winding road where the tops of the trees touched, forming a dark, vegetative canopy reminiscent of a cloistered abbey. Past the Palco hotel. Past expansive lawns and gardens surrounding the stately homes. The group had a hundred questions, but their driver was on a mission to get home. Charlie was surprised when Esteban turned and shot down a side road between two small castles.

The road twisted its way through the forest to a large, three-story concrete structure on the top of the hill. More practical than palatial, Esteban's house was nevertheless elegant by Cuban standards. Its façade of cut coral, vaulted windows, and ornate portico attested to the legacy of its former occupants. Charlie recalled that Esteban's mother had been a bigwig in the revolutionary government, handpicked by Fidel himself. The entire property, perhaps a half acre in size, was surrounded by an eight-foot, ivy-covered concrete wall. Entrance to the car park had been hewn from solid rock and led to a garage below the main house, where they landed. Esteban closed the swinging steel garage doors behind them.

A circular stairway of stone led from the garage to the living area. "My wife must be upstairs with the baby. Have a seat."

The walls, a stately blend of cream-colored coquina with insets of blue marble gave the combined foyer and living chamber an unexpected aura of elegance. The floors were a diamond-patterned travertine with inlays of onyx. Esteban's three temporary employers were agape at the unexpected luxury.

Another winding staircase with classical Greek balustrades dominated the far end of the hall. Esteban beckoned with his arm. Carmen, his wife, was upstairs, propped on a pillow, bottle feeding an infant. She was perhaps ten years younger than her husband, with flowing auburn hair and a magnetic smile. Her English was flawless. *This Esteban is full of surprises*, thought Charlie.

The stairs leading from the second story to the third were blocked off. Esteban explained, "I was in the middle of remodeling when I lost my job. Here, follow me. There is something I have to show you."

They followed him down the stairs, through the kitchen where pots were simmering on the stove, across the veranda into a walled courtyard that was lined with banana trees and hibiscus. The air was heavy with the earthy smell of poultry, steaming vegetation, punctuated with smoke from burning cane fields.

Beneath the shade of a spreading mango were five cages. In each cage, a rooster. But not like any roosters they had seen before. The bird's legs and lower breasts had been plucked, making them appear for all the world like naked red birds that had been interrupted before they'd gotten their pants on. The plumage that remained was strikingly colored, iridescent—one bronze with red streaks, another dappled white and gray, another pure black with a red crest. The cages of the magnificent birds were elevated, immaculate, the dirt on which they stood packed as hard as concrete. They had obviously been well attended. Esteban beamed.

"These are the best birds in Cuba, maybe the world. People from all over would love to buy these birds. They are champions. Reaching into a cage, he clasped one in both hands. "This is *Rusty Nail*. He never loses. That one is *Espirito de Cienfuegos*. The other three are still in school."

"Fighting?" Jenna struggled to solve what to her was a mystery. "These birds are for fighting, aren't they? They are trained to kill each other. How can you do that to such a beautiful animal?"

"They love it. It's what they were born to do." Esteban held the bird close to his face. "We just breed them and try to make them better. Same as horse racing."

"But horses don't kill each other." Jenna protested.

"Stallions do," Allen said, playing devil's advocate. Jenna shot him a look.

"But why do you want these birds to fight?" she asked Esteban.

"Money. Rusty is going to make big money. He is going to make me rich."

That same faraway look had returned to Esteban's eyes.

CHAPTER TWELVE

Over a dinner of steamed pork and yucca, Carmen told of their plans to finish renovations. The half-tiled kitchen was a stark reminder of the day her husband had lost his job on the cruise ship. The hosts were gracious, but between the smiles, the visitors could not help feeling an underlying tension that permeated the household. It was hard to define, as if someone had died or there was a threat of imminent danger. And it was equally hard to forget how Esteban had raged when his simmering existential anxiety had been allowed to bubble to the surface.

Driving back to Marina Hemingway, they approached a girl hitchhiking in the darkened stretch on Avenida Quinta near the Nautico stoplights. Charlie shot a glance at his driver, who knew immediately to stop. She sprinted to the passenger window. Esteban barked an order in Spanish, much too rapid for Charlie to understand. But she did, opening the door and jumping into Charlie's lap. "Damn, I love this country." The new passenger was a twenty-two-year-old accounting student from nearby Sibonet. She lived with her aunt, made her own clothing and owned three pigs. She snuggled with the young captain as if they newlyweds.

119

At the entrance to the marina loomed the blue-and-white art deco concrete guardhouse. A lift gate, like the ones that block cars from crossing railroad tracks, spanned the entrance. The guard, walkie-talkie in hand, not recognizing Esteban or his car, asked the nature of his visit and their destination, his flashlight illuminating the faces of the occupants one by one.

Esteban explained he was returning a captain whose boat was inside. The guard never enquired about the girl sitting in the captain's lap, but as he pressed the button to raise the gate, he was already talking on his radio. As they pulled into the *Bora Bora*'s parking space, two police officers were waiting for them. Charlie recognized one as the procurer of Fartblossom. As if Esteban and Charlie were invisible, they zeroed in on the young lady, now frozen with fear and stiff as a cod. She was kept blinded by the rays of their flashlights.

"*Carne*," they ordered. She reached into her back pocket and handed her laminated plastic identification card. They said something to Esteban. He translated. "She has got to go out now."

Charlie was sure he could persuade the guards to let her stay. "Tell them there is no problem. She is not staying on the boat—just a visitor. She will go out in three or four hours."

"She has got to go now."

"Why?" Charlie was becoming angry. "This is ridiculous. I am paying good money to rent here. The boat is my home, and I can invite whoever I want, whenever I want, to my home."

Esteban pushed the clutch to the floor and ground the transmission into reverse. Charlie could see he was fighting a losing battle. "Tell them she is my second cousin by my fourth marriage. Tell them she is my real estate agent......."

"*You* have to get out now." Esteban was deadly serious as he pointed to the passenger door. Charlie lifted the maiden from his lap, got out, and stood by helplessly in the parking lot. "Tomorrow. Nine o'clock. See if you can get her telephone number."

It was a sobering experience. Charlie had a tiny taste of what it felt like to be a Cuban. Were the cops really that powerful? His reaction was to fight back. The Cubans knew better. They were afraid of the police and instantly compliant. Further, the incident may have been a game changer. The thought of not being able to bring visitors to his boat was, at best, disturbing.

There seemed no room for negotiation. Plans were made for a morning rendezvous. Charlie handed sixty dollars to his driver and watched as his as his long-legged sperm receptacle disappeared into the darkness from which she had emerged.

Ten o'clock the next morning, the old Chevy rattled into the carpark, an hour late. The sweating driver emerged—wrinkled dress pants, rumpled white shirt with long sleeves, dress shoes with socks. Charlie noticed he seemed fidgety.

"Aren't you hot? What the hell happened to you last night?"

"The guards. You never know. Changes all the time. They are controlling the prostitution. They only allow certain girls, and they get a cut. Probably their sisters. Or their mothers, those pricks."

Charlie didn't press him but suggested that for the day, Esteban stay with him and relax on the *Bora Bora*. Esteban shook his head.

"Look around you." Esteban pointed to shiny, black hemispheres attached to the undersides of the eaves of the hotel. "Cameras, everywhere. And over there, across the canal." Charlie hadn't noticed them before, but now that he knew what they looked like, he could see at least five cameras within eyeshot.

"That certainly sucks. I don't want to do the tourist thing today. Allen and Jenna are going to stay on the boat for a while and then go to the pool. Why don't we buy some tile, and we can work on your kitchen?"

"Well, I have some business to attend to, if you want to ride along. But you can't bring your camera."

There was no gate preventing guests from leaving Marina Hemingway, but Esteban stopped and handed loose change to one of the guards, like paying a toll. They headed west, past a half mile of homes concealed behind concrete walls. Most were in need of repair.

"Those houses back up to the canal leading into the marina complex," Esteban explained. "You passed them on the way in."

Horse-drawn wagons grew more numerous as they entered the outskirts of Santa Fe, an overcrowded, crumbling, but vibrant seaside community whose placement on the coast had little to do with the sea and appeared to be a simple accident of geography.

"Where are all the police?" Charlie asked tentatively.

"There are no tourists here. No dollars. Fewer police. Just CDR."

They passed an abandoned airport, now a junkyard of stripped Russian helicopters and a huge Tupolev TU-95 poorly hidden behind a camo-draped chain-link fence topped with concertina wire. "That's our air force," Esteban quipped sarcastically.

Enveloped in a cloud of diesel smoke, they followed a bus as it left Avenida Quinta and headed south. Within a mile, they were in desiccated, rocky, unproductive farmland. It was obvious that there had once been crops grown in the fields; the farmhouses and outbuildings were placed accordingly. Long before pasture, it had been a semitropical forest.

"It's hard to imagine," observed Esteban, "that when the Spanish colonizers arrived five hundred years ago, it was said they could walk the entire length of the island shielded from the sun by the canopy of trees. It took two hundred years to transform the jungle into pasture and farmland." He sounded so wistful that Charlie, again, was hesitant to ask—could Cubans not even farm the land anymore?

Potholed dirt roads lined with broken fences branched from the main road, some disappearing into verdant oases of palm and fig. At the terminus of one of the unmarked roads, they arrived at a concrete apartment building and parked beside a brand-new, black Mercedes 420 E Class sedan. *Holy shit!* Charlie thought. *That car is worth more than my boat!*

"Wait here."

Charlie obeyed as Esteban climbed the stairs and knocked on one of the six doors on the second floor of the tenement. The stark lines of the building screamed *Russian*. Esteban waited then returned.

"Get out. Follow me." Again, Charlie eagerly obeyed. Beside the building was a ravine, containing a forest surrounded by a ten-foot-high wooden fence. Charlie followed his driver across the parking lot to a green welded iron door, set in a metal frame. A sign over the door read *Projibito Entrar*—keep out. Esteban knocked. An iron bolt was thrown, and the door opened cautiously, screeching on its rusty hinges.

"Bueno. Hermano." An arm shot through the door and embraced Esteban. Charlie followed a descending path of flat stones placed into the sloping side of the depression, leaving Esteban to his business. Although it was almost noon on a cloudless day, Charlie had to remove his sunglasses in order to see—the entangled leaves and branches of the encompassing ceiba trees allowing not a single ray of light to penetrate. His eyes adjusted to an amphitheater of covered cages, perhaps numbering one hundred and fifty, attended by half a dozen workers. In each cage was a fighting bird, and every bird was magnificent in its own right. An office with electric lights stood to one side, under a corrugated metal roof that extended all the way to the center, covering a circular ring of sawdust with walls about a foot and a half tall.

Esteban had explained that cockfighting was legal in Cuba. Gambling was not. He'd told Charlie that, before 1959, Cubans were encouraged to bet on jai-alai, cockfighting, horseracing, and other sports within the mob-controlled casinos. It was big business. But since the Cuban Revolution, all forms of betting and gambling had been strictly forbidden. Still, that hadn't stopped thousands of island residents. In fact, cockfighting was such a popular pastime that authorities largely looked the other way, and uniformed police helped park cars. Thus, cockfighting joined a long list of activities that fell within the gray area.

Esteban said that wagering on the outcome of bird blood sport was in the Cuban DNA. He might have been right. The sport of gamecock fighting—as it had been known through history—went back almost six thousand years. Specially bred birds, trained to augment their genetically inherent aggression, conditioned for increased stamina and strength as if they were professional athletes, were given the best of care. Esteban had laughed when he told Charlie that stories abounded of practitioners neglecting their families while doting on their birds.

Cockfights were held in a round arena commonly called a *valla*, surrounded by a small fence around which the spectators are accommodated. The feathers of the chest, hackle, and thighs were removed, revealing the red skin beneath. Detachable fang-like tortoiseshell spurs augmented the natural spurs on the back of both legs of the fighting cocks. Combatants were strictly paired up to fight according to their body weight. The allowed difference in weight between the contenders ranged from half to one ounce. Fights were limited to a single round of thirty minutes, but participants knew that most fights ended within the first five minutes. While not all fights were to the death, the cocks might endure significant physical trauma.

The cages at this facility were immaculate. There was no poultry smell. There was no litter beneath the cages, which seemed impossible. Each cage received water through an intricate system of pipes and tubes. One worker was busy filling the bird's trays with a yellow, powdery feed. Two more, each with a bird clasped firmly in their hands, were prepared to enter the training ring. Even knowing only what little Esteban had told him about roosters and the sport of cockfighting, Charlie knew he had stumbled into a world-class facility. As if viewing masterpieces in the Louvre, he lingered before a cage, absorbing the majesty, the splendor of its occupant, before he moved on to the next.

A worker went into the office and emerged. He set up two chairs on the side of the ring, motioning for Esteban to sit. Charlie watched as a tall man emerged, carrying a clipboard with attached papers. He looked like an Italian movie star. Charlie struggled to remember where he had seen that face before—billboards, print ads in glossy fashion magazines? The guy had chiseled features, salt-and-pepper styled hair, a ramrod frame maybe six-foot five, blue dress shirt unbuttoned at the top, khaki trousers, and shoes that may have been Ferragamos. *Not your standard chicken farmer*, mused Charlie, who inferred from the two chairs that the conversation was private.

As he toured the facility, he glanced in the direction of the training ring and the conversation taking place there. Esteban looked like a child who had been dragged to the principal's office. His head was bowed, his demeanor subservient. The movie star pointed his finger in an accusatory manner, aiming first at the clipboard, then waving the same finger in his student's face, occasionally raising his voice. With his imposing physique and confident manner, he exuded power, and this was his home turf. Ensconced in his monument to bird combat Charlie mused he was as invulnerable as Superman in his Fortress of Solitude. Confronted by such power, Esteban was acquiescent.

The movie star returned to his office. Esteban was visibly shaken as he and Charlie climbed the steps to the parking lot. They drove the dusty road in silence. Charlie didn't know where to start.

"You OK? Who the hell was that?"

125

"That's Tony."

"I thought so. He looked Italian."

"He was born here. He's Cuban."

"You have business with this guy?"

"When I worked on the cruise ships, I had money, big money. I bet on the cockfights. Somehow, I ended up behind. I told you: they took six thousand dollars from me at the airport. That was going to pay down my gambling debt."

"Pay down?

"I was going to use two thousand to pay Tony and the rest to fix up my house."

"How much do you owe?"

"I don't know. It goes up every day. He charges interest. He bought up some of the debt I had with other breeders. Somewhere between eighteen and twenty thousand."

Charlie was astonished. "Twenty thousand? Twenty thousand pesos, right?" Each question he asked gave rise to a dozen others, which he kept to himself.

"Dollars. American dollars."

"Sounds like the Mafia. How are you not sleeping with the fishes?"

"No, not Mafia, it's worse than Mafia. It's the government. Tony is one of Fidel's buddies, a friend of the family, and Alejandro, he runs everything this side of Havana. He's behind the scenes. He's invisible. The only reason that they haven't done anything drastic so far is that they still believe I will make good. They want their money."

The reality of Tony was utterly inconsistent with the bombastic iconography of the Revolution: the ubiquitous fatigue-clad, bearded freedom fighter looming over a grateful citizenry, its heraldic image plastered and painted upon any flat surface capable of being viewed by the public. He was apparently a jet-set communist—an ardent enforcer of a system from which he had been mercifully spared. Charlie recoiled at the hypocrisy. He had read about men like this, Ceausescu, Peron, Allende, and their henchmen, but never expected to see one in the flesh.

Storm clouds were brewing on the horizon. Charlie watched as the cool air from the Caribbean was drawn inland, over the parched, baking patchwork of fallow fields and villages, absorbing the land's heat and transforming themselves into towering thunderheads that rained down upon the earth their violence and fury and in the process, were themselves destroyed, evaporating into thin air and gone forever.

Charlie pondered Esteban's plight. "What happens if you don't pay?"

"They will take my house and my car and put me in jail. They could take my baby. Gambling is not legal. They have reminded me of all of this."

Tragic flaws, thought Charlie. *We all have our tragic flaws. It's Shakespearean.* His driver had somehow taken a bad situation and made it worse. He had created a self-fulfilling prophesy in his prison within a prison. Charlie couldn't help Esteban. He didn't have that kind of cash. He would have liked to help, but ultimately, it wasn't his problem. He had heard of travelers in India stepping over dead bodies on their way to the market. These are the things a visitor encountered when they left civilization and headed into the unknown. He couldn't feed all the hungry children, he couldn't change this socialist shithole into a thriving democracy, and he couldn't bail out his cab driver.

"Why don't we pick up some tile and work on your kitchen?" he suggested.

"Maybe tomorrow. First, there is something I want to show you." They returned to Avenida Quinta, passed the entrance to Hemingway Marina, continued east about two hundred yards through the casuarinas, across the bridge into Jaimanitas, and stopped in front of the tiny pharmacy. Beside the apothecary was a gate that led to an alley then a brightly painted courtyard that served as the common area for several apartments. Esteban knocked on the varnished wooden door. It half opened, cautiously. He had a discussion with a middle-aged, bleach-blond lady who handed him a set of keys.

"We can walk from here."

Charlie noted the concrete pyramid marker set into the sidewalk that identified the street they turned onto as Calle 234. It was a working-class neighborhood with side-by-side houses built directly to the edge of the sidewalk. The asphalt road was cracked and potted, but passable, its sides lined with old cars in various stages of disrepair. There was music. Smells of cooking competed with piles of garbage waiting to be collected. Unlike the dusty agricultural towns of the interior, this street was full of life; people chatted in the middle of the road, they were emerging from one side and disappearing through doors on the other. And there were women. Lots of women, of all ages, many wearing spandex, many of whom shouldn't have been allowed to wear spandex.

Charlie joked, "This place is a tit lover's dream."

Just over halfway down the block, Esteban stopped in front of a two-story building, its front door opening onto a tile porch enclosed by a cage of wrought iron. He fumbled with the keys, searching for the right one. Inside the house was a living room composed of two opposing sofas, one beneath the staircase, a television with rabbit ears and an ornate varnished wooden coffee table. A breakfast bar with three stools separated the living room from the tiny kitchen.

"Look at that refrigerator." Charlie marveled at an ancient General Electric that dated back to prerevolutionary days. "That's impossible. That needs to be in a GE commercial."

The door to the right of the kitchen led to a hall containing three more doors. Door number one opened to a single-car garage secured by hinged metal doors. The middle led to a bathroom with a toilet, sink, and shower, the third to a small bedroom with a wall-mounted air conditioner, illumined by a feeble light fixture in the middle of the ceiling.

"Take a look up top," Esteban suggested.

The stairs, on the left, leading from the rear of the living room were of a modernistic open concrete design covered with inlaid broken tile of all colors. Upstairs was another bathroom with a shower, a spacious bedroom with a window overlooking the street, a walk-in closet, and window-mounted air conditioner. Ruffled pink pillows lay atop leopard-skin bedsheets. On a rickety bedside end table was a ceramic statue lamp of an X-rated Betty Boop with illuminated breasts

"I love it!" Charlie exclaimed. Esteban clicked a switch, and an out-of-balance ceiling fan, mounted above the bed, sprang to life, eventually reaching an uneasy, oscillating equilibrium as it searched for its center of rotation.

"How much?" Charlie braced himself for the answer, remembering the seventy-five-dollar pit stop at the Oro Negro.

"Twenty-five dollars a night, $500 for a month. I have to know quick because her husband needs an answer tonight."

Charlie tried to restrain his excitement. "Does that include electric and water?"

"Electric, water, gas, trash. You get the garage and a guard from nine o'clock until the sun comes up in the morning. Daily maid service. It's a ten-minute walk to your boat. With a bicycle, you can be there in about three minutes. Roberto knows everybody and is in with the police."

"Who's Roberto?"

"Your landlord. He owns this place. Fixed it up. He did a lot of work."

"Can I have visitors?" Charlie recalled his unpleasant experiences with the police at the marina.

"No girls under seventeen and they have to show their identification card to the guard. Also, I get to use the downstairs bedroom."

Charlie didn't hesitate. "Where do I sign?" It was perfect. An apartment gave Allen and Jenna the boat to themselves, and when they wanted, they could use the kitchen, take showers, or use the bedroom downstairs. At five hundred bucks a month, Charlie did the math in his head, he could afford to stay until the north winds of November. At five hundred a month, he could afford to live here for the next five years. A guard? His own guard? Who has a guard? Having visitors was not a problem. He could learn a new language. Ten minutes from the boat. There was no discussion. No need for negotiation. No haggling. Nice house. Nice street. A great driver who loved his chickens. Charlie felt as if he had just won the lottery.

Esteban pulled another key from his ring. "For the roof. You can see the ocean from your roof. It's only two blocks."

They returned to the landlord's house. "Roberto will be back tomorrow. I will need your passport." Raquel scribbled a receipt. Charlie handed her a one-hundred-dollar bill. She handed him the ring of keys. "The garage is tricky. You have to push the key in and then bring it back just a little bit before you turn it."

In that instant, the captain of the *Bora Bora Express* became a temporary resident of an off-limits, forbidden, prison communist island. He was in heaven.

CHAPTER THIRTEEN

"You did what?" Allen was incredulous. "You didn't ask us? I thought we were part of a team." Charlie explained that there was no commitment. The apartment was just a cheap alternative to the boat, a free-floating life raft that could serve as a secondary base of operations.

"Tomorrow, just take a look. I think you will like it. A real bed to sleep in. One that stays still."

Ten o'clock the next morning found the captain and crew of the *Express* struggling with the outer lock on the iron cage that surrounded the porch.

"Houdini couldn't break into this place," Allen complained, inserting one key after another.

As they tried to negotiate the security system, a girl joined their ranks. A maid? The landlord's daughter? She was dressed in a halter top and skin-tight shorts, but all the women of the village were dressed in skimpy. She just stood there, silently, rooted, as fixed and resolute as the nearby lamp post. She followed them inside, brushed past them, and went straight to the refrigerator. It was empty. Even the small plastic ice cube trays were on top.

131

"Cervesa?" she said, folding her arms and landing on the couch beneath the stairs, a scowl on her pouting lips.

"I think she wants a beer," said Jenna, amused.

Confused, Charlie looked on as the girl crossed her legs. She was lovely—perhaps a *trejeno*? Charlie tried to remember the words for the gradations of skin color. She was maybe twenty years old, the kind of girl who would warrant a condo and a new car back in Florida.

"Look," he said, "she's pissed at me before I've said a single word. I feel like I am home already." Allen and Jenna peered into cupboards, checked out the bathroom, and tested the mattress in the downstairs bedroom. The girl grabbed Charlie by the hand.

"*Bom,*" she said, dragging him toward the open door. Charlie assumed correctly that *bom* was a contraction for *vamos*—"let's go." With her arm around his waist directing his forward progress, she shepherded the bewildered American to the head of the street, around the corner, to a fast-food lunch stand.

"Siez cervesas y dos paquetes de Hollywood."

Charlie stood back as the clerk loaded six Bucaneros beers and two packs of cigarettes into a flimsy, transparent plastic sack. "Algo mas?" the clerk asked.

"Chicle," she said.

He reached under the counter for a pack of gum. "Algo mas?"

Charlie began to understand what was happening. She was going to keep spending his money until he stopped her. He stepped forward to intervene.

"No mas. La cuenta, por favor." The bill came to $3.30.

"*Bom*," she said, grabbed his hand, and escorted him back to the apartment.

"Alegre ahora—happy now?" Charlie asked. She sat cross-legged on the couch, drinking her beer. She smiled contentedly, leaning back slightly. She was very limber. Try as he could, he could not take his eyes off her crotch. He had seen a million girls sit with their legs crossed beneath them, but this one somehow projected her pelvis forward, or spread wider, or cast a magic slut spell. It didn't matter. Charlie found himself uncontrollably drawn to her lower unit. He didn't know her name, but that didn't matter either. He tried not to stare. It was ungentlemanly, and he was, above all, a gentleman, but every nuance, gesture or move she made somehow, inexplicably, enhanced the narrow gap barely contained within the fabric of her short shorts. He couldn't concentrate. He couldn't conjugate the Spanish verbs he had been studying.

"What in the world is this thing?" Jenna squawked from the bathroom upstairs. Charlie arrived to find them staring at a showerhead the size of a pineapple. It was a bizarre contraption of wires, wire nuts, and a lever marked *C* on one end and *F* on the other. Charlie recognized the symbols for hot and cold—*caliente* and *frio.* He surmised it must be an on-demand electric water heater—an ungrounded, 220-volt, electric water heater mounted six inches above the bather and meant to be adjusted with wet hands.

"Good God, step back. Don't get near that thing. It's a widow-maker," warned Charlie, drawing on his contractor background. He heard a commotion downstairs, descending to find Beer Girl—who he now knew was named Cindy—and two more girls withdrawing beers from the refrigerator. They passed him as he stood at the threshold of the stairs. Cindy gave him a wink and tweaked his nipple as she walked past, guzzling her second beer, resuming her station on the couch. The other two headed out the door and down the street, beers in hand. *What am I? Invisible? Must be a cultural thing.*

Esteban rattled to a stop only inches from the open door, his left wheels on the sidewalk in order not to block traffic on the narrow street. He had been hired by Allen and Jenna to taxi them to Mariel for the day. Charlie had decided not to go. He watched as they climbed into Esteban's car and creaked their way around the corner.

It was the first time in a month he had been by himself. He looked forward to being alone in his new house in a mysterious land. *It doesn't get much better than this*, he thought. The natives were indeed friendly, the sky was blue, and new adventures seemed to be inevitable. He wanted to know everything, absolutely *everything*. As he walked to the corner store, he absorbed and embraced every new sight, sound, and smell. Six TuKolas, a fifth of Havana Club, a few limes, and a bag of *hielo*—ice—came to $10.20.

Calle 234's newest resident lugged a chair from the living room to the porch, positioned his head so it was in the shade of the overhang, created a Cuba Libre, and took in his surroundings, absorbing the sights and sounds of the street. Across the street and to the right, there seem seemed to be a formal occasion. Men and women, dressed in long clothes that made no sense in the heat— perhaps a wedding, or a funeral—milled about quietly on the front porch of the faded, green wooden structure.

There was a peanut monger, the clop-clop of a small, brown horse pulling a wagon. A lovely young lady, with long dark hair, dressed in a yellow sundress, passed between himself and the crowd on the other side without acknowledging his existence. The intoxicating smell of coffee varied in intensity as the shifting winds hinted of new sources. Babies cried. Roosters crowed. The screeching leaf springs of ancient automobiles, doing their best to carry passengers across tortuous roads, could be heard bouncing their way down adjoining streets.

Charlie wasn't alone for long. A white Lada 2107 rattled to a stop in front of his door, only about six feet away, the dust and exhaust temporarily filling the porch. Two men emerged, popped the trunk, and removed a ventilated metal box, open on one end, which they carried past Charlie who, drink in hand, followed them to the kitchen.

"Hola, me llamo Coco." His landlord extended a strong brown hand. He was built like a rugby player, with an infectious smile and a rubber face. A mulatto? Charlie liked him instantly. His real name was Roberto, but he was known to the world as Coco. The fact that he spoke not a word of English made little difference. Somehow the sheer force of his personality transcended the language barrier. His helper, Guillermo, was an older man, thin, with Castellan features. He retrieved from the trunk a large cardboard box filled with parts. Next, they went upstairs to Charlie's room, carrying tools. Charlie returned to his chair on the porch. He could hear them crashing about upstairs. Twenty minutes later, they had succeeded in moving a large, rusty air conditioner down the stairs and placing it beside the box of parts on the kitchen counter.

"You want a drink?" Charlie asked. Coco and his helper were sweating as they dissembled the rusty AC unit. When Charlie opened the door to the empty refrigerator, Coco laughed.

"You need food?" Coco asked. Charlie nodded. Coco went to the porch and shouted into the street, motioning with his hands after he had caught someone's attention.

"You will like Esmeralda," he said, raising his eyebrows. Five minutes later a short, young, thin, sweating, out-of-breath fashion model with frosted dark hair appeared—an *adelantao*? Charlie tried to remember the names for the dizzying array of non-judgmental categorizations by which the Cubans refer to one another.

God, I love this country. You just yell, and women appear, Charlie thought.

Coco barked an order to Esmeralda, handed Charlie the keys to his car, and told him to be sure to bring his passport. Charlie fumbled with the gears of the Lada. The clutch engaged after a quarter inch of throw. He stalled twice before he got the feel of it. Esmeralda, wearing only black spandex shorts and a pink cut-off T-shirt, navigated as Charlie wove through the neighborhood.

Esmeralda directed their way to the largest dollar store west of Havana.

In many respects, Palco resembled a small modern supermarket—large plate glass windows, four rows of checkout counters, fluorescent lights, meat and dairy in refrigerated cases along the back wall. But there were also differences, one of which Charlie noticed immediately as he tried to push through the bottleneck of shoppers at the exit, delayed as a lone guard detained every customer on their way out the door, comparing what's in the shopper's bag against their receipt.

Store shelves were stocked with products from all over the world. Items changed, Esmeralda explained, on a daily basis. Confused shoppers may find tuna from Norway, ranging from four dollars to nine dollars a can, replaced by jars of Peruvian honey a week later. American goods abounded—Heinz Baked Beans, Ivory Soap, Kleenex—breaking the embargo by being imported from third-party countries. Prices, which seemed to be doubled or tripled, were in American dollars. The only bargains were in the liquor aisle. A large section of shelving was devoted to Havana Club Rum. Prices started at $1.20 a fifth. Charlie placed five bottles in the cart. Local beers started at $.50. Heineken and St. Pauli Girl were $2.00 each.

"Una regala para mi mama—*a present for my mother?*" asked Esmeralda as she held up a bag of Cubita Coffee for $8.10, dropping it into the cart before receiving an answer. Esmeralda took charge. She filled the cart with two-liter bottles of TuKola, lemon-lime Gaseosa, Dona Delicias Mayonnaise, a box of locally made Polvarones—the tasty cinnamon-sugar cookie, Premium saltine crackers, plus Head & Shoulders Shampoo. She chose spaghetti, meat sauce, bottled water, canned peaches from Australia, and a jar of salted peanuts for $6.50. Two sticks of French bread, at a dollar each, had to be paid at the tiny bakery.

Charlie, following like a puppy, mesmerized by her ass, was joyously oblivious. He looked for a panty line. There was none. *My God, she is only wearing two pieces of clothing.* She added a ten-pound bag of Vietnamese rice and a tube of Pringles. Charlie watched as the cart filled up. *She must play a sport. Maybe beach volleyball.*

When she got to the *carnecia*, the meat counter, Charlie glanced at the prices and intervened, gently guiding Esmeralda toward the checkout counter. The bill came to $115.75. Charlie gave a $100 and a $50 bill to the cashier. She demanded his passport, took a ledger from beside the cash register, and handed it to an assistant seated next to her on a stool. The assistant hunched over the ledger, poised to make entries on its narrow lines with a number-two pencil. The cashier squinted into Charlie's passport, dictating the passport's number, the country of origin, the date, his address in Cuba.

"What's my address?" Charlie asked.

"Hotel Valencia," Esmeralda lied without hesitation.

"Hotel Valencia," he repeated to the assistant, who busily scribbled the name into the appropriate slot. She held each bill to the light of the front windows, snapping them with her fingers. She announced the denomination, giving time for it to be transcribed into the ledger, then its serial number. Customers standing in line shuffled as the checkout system ground to a halt for three or four minutes.

Charlie marveled at the monumental display of inefficiency. They lacked the ability to accept credit cards, so all transactions were in cash, recorded in the ledger. Without a bar-code reader, inventory control was at best, laborious. Reconciling the daily receipts with the existing inventory had to be an ongoing manual process, otherwise how would they monitor for resupply or prevent employee theft? The ledger would have to be physically carried to someone, somewhere, who would have to read the tiny handwritten print and manually upload that data into a computer to make it useful or accessible.

Despite its shortcomings, the system maintained the ability to track Charlie and his crew anywhere they went. Coupled with the passport information that was mandatory for registration at a hotel or a paladar, the government could eventually piece together and track anyone with a fifty-dollar bill as they went about their business. That same someone, somewhere, would know that Charlie Sutton, an American tourist, had broken several large bills, the amount he spent, the location of the expenditures, and where he was sleeping that night.

Esteban's words came back to him. *Cuba is a prison, and we are all prisoners.* And now, by the simple act of buying groceries, Charlie was entered into the system.

Upon his return to the house, Charlie found Coco and his helper trying to release a set of rusted screws on the underside of the compressor housing. Esmeralda stacked items into the shelves of the refrigerator. When she placed groceries on the upper shelves of the pantry, her T-shirt lifted, exposing a flat stomach, almost allowing a glimpse of her breasts. Charlie wondered if the woman had any idea of what she was doing to his brain.

"Esmeralda, take him to the beach," Coco commanded.

"*La playa?*" she asked, waiting for Charlie's approval.

She could have said, "Let's go to the dump," or "Let's go kill baby seals." It wouldn't have made any difference. He would have followed her anywhere. She left with her coffee and returned wearing a green polka-dot bikini.

Calle 234's north end terminated at a community center, which was accessed through a door that was monitored by an attendant. The center commanded a beach of coarse, grainy coral sand protected by a low concrete breakwater that extended two hundred and fifty feet into the sea over the rocky coral. The rickety skeleton of a gazebo, its thatched roof in tatters, threatened to fall on anyone using it for a picnic. Since the water was only two feet at its deepest, Charlie wondered who would use the facility— children would be torn to shreds on the sharp coral; adults would slice their feet.

The breakwater provided a walkway to the slightly deeper water outside. Esmeralda led the way. Charlie found a clear spot between the rocks and made a shallow dive. Through his face mask, he watched her lower herself gently into the water.

"I can't swim," she said. "Hold me!"

She lay on her back, half floating, half supported by Charlie's arms, the parts constrained by her bikini top yearning to break free. He spun around, looking over her arched body at the white-capped sea. The sea had become, for him, at that moment, a highway to heaven.

Fletcher Christian, master's mate aboard the HMS *Bounty*, had arrived in Tahiti in 1788. There he'd encountered and fallen in love with the chief's daughter, the young and firm Maimiti. The ship left in April of the following year, bound for England with a cargo of breadfruit seedlings, tearing asunder the bonds that had grown between the two lovers. But their love had transcended time and distance. Unable to live without her, Master Christian had architected a mutiny that would culminate in his return to the island and marriage. This epic love altered history and greatly set back the worldwide propagation and cultivation of breadfruit.

As he held his exotic Maimiti in his outstretched arms, the vast expanse of azure sky and sea stretching before him, Charlie Sutton *was* Fletcher Christian on the fateful day he set eyes on his Tahitian beauty. Their encounter was a momentous event. It was fate. He could feel it. The earth had shifted on its axis. History was being rewritten. Breadfruit futures were plummeting.

It was after four o'clock when they returned to the apartment. Coco was endeavoring to braze copper patches onto cracks in the cooling coils. The house was hot and thick with the acrid smell of industrial welding. Guillermo's wife, Julia, was sitting on the couch, drinking a TuKola. Esmeralda withdrew a beer from the refrigerator and disappeared into the downstairs bathroom. Charlie could hear her taking a shower. He envisioned a number of possible erotic scenarios, most involving soap and being slippery. Fletcher Christian walked stealthily to the door, hoping to surprise Maimiti. Quietly he turned the doorknob. It was locked.

Esteban clunked to a stop behind Coco's Lada. He, Allen, and Jenna had never made it to Mariel. Allen and Jenna looked like survivors of the Bataan death march. Charlie was sure they had lost weight. Esteban's white shirt was streaked with dirt, soiled by oil, soaked with sweat and hanging from his shoulders.

"What the hell happened?" asked Charlie.

Twenty miles out of Baracoa they'd blown a tire. Having no spare, Esteban was forced to backtrack and undergo near-heroics to procure a new one. By the time he'd hitchhiked back, carrying the new tire and mounting the wheel on the car, Allen and Jenna had been baking for six hours, and it was too late to make it to Mariel.

Jenna and Allen seemed amused by all the strangers in their apartment. Jenna prepared a rum and coke for each of them, informing Charlie they were out of ice. Esmeralda emerged from the bathroom, towel drying her hair. Charlie gave her a dollar to fetch a bag of ice from the corner store. Coco's wife, Raquel, arrived, introduced herself, and started mopping the floor. There was a knock on the cage. Charlie turned to find a policeman in uniform, in his hand a spiral-bound notebook. Behind him was Yancy, the neighbor from next door—old, thin, with the look of a witch but the voice of an angel.

Coco introduced Capitan Abrego. He was middle-aged, looked like Gary Cooper, and was dressed formally, differently than the other police who lurked on every street corner. He exuded an air of importance. Coco explained that the policeman was one of his best friends, and since Charlie had indicated he would be here for a month or two, it would be good for them to become acquainted. Charlie made the officer a drink, waiting impatiently for Esmeralda to return with ice.

The cop sat on the couch next to Guillermo's wife. Yancy entered and continued a lively conversation with Coco's wife that had begun while she was in the street. She was obviously concerned about something, voicing her opinions and observations at high volume, waving her arms, pointing to coordinates within the village as if the walls were invisible. Raquel never stopped mopping. She nodded frequently and seemed to be in accordance. The conversation was much too fast for Charlie to follow. Julia lifted her feet to allow the mop head to swish beneath the couch.

It was now 6:30 p.m. The sun lowering in the sky had little or no effect on the heat. The buildings themselves became radiators, releasing the accumulated heat of the day back into the evening air. Guillermo refreshed the drinks for himself, Coco, and his wife. Esmeralda made her own, munching on Pringles, which she passed around.

Charlie returned from a trip to the bathroom to find an unfamiliar butt emerging from the refrigerator, its torso hidden by the open door. It was one of Cindy's friends, returning to raid the refrigerator. Cindy had never returned, to Charlie's dismay. Along with a Cristal, she removed the jar of mayonnaise. The kitchen having been turned into a workshop, she placed it on the coffee table in front of the other couch. As if on cue, Esmeralda joined her, carrying the stick of bread and a knife. Charlie felt invisible, no more than a butler attending a party of strangers that happened to descend from the sky and land in his apartment.

Once they had ice, Charlie finished preparing a second drink for Capitan Abrego. It was good that Roberto—Coco—had set up the meeting. It was comforting to know his landlord had a rapport with the local officials. It might come in handy. But this was a bad time. Cindy's brother wandered in, looked around, and left without saying a word. Charlie watched the world swirl in and out of his apartment. He came to the conclusion that as long as he had an open door and a well-stocked refrigerator, he would never have to worry about being alone.

Two neighborhood girls walking down the street peered through the open door and, observing their friends eating bread, Pringles, and mayonnaise, joined them on the couch. Esmeralda pointed toward the refrigerator, her mouth too full to talk. When they managed to speak, they talked so rapidly to each other they reminded Charlie of parakeets. Each withdrew a Bucanero from the refrigerator, one complaining she liked Heineken better. Their names were Pantera and Claudia, late teens or early twenties, the former a nickname due to her black and red snarling panther tattoo located about eight inches below her navel. Claudia had a long, thin face, a face Charlie envisioned eating apples through a picket fence. He couldn't shake the image. Charlie handed Claudia, who he instantly nicknamed Horseface, a five-dollar bill and sent her galloping to the store for ten more beers.

Pantera asked Charlie if he had any cigarettes. He explained he didn't smoke. "Regala me, por favor—*please, for me, a present?*" On her way to the store to buy a pack, she passed Claudia, who was returning with a bag full of beers. Horseface waited, and they returned together. The AC was ready to be reassembled. Guillermo held the air-conditioning housing at waist level. Coco did the same with the heavy, rusty tray supporting the hybrid compressor, cooling fins, and fan housing. They rushed at each other. They met in the middle, both pushing, their combined energy trying to slide one module inside the other. They were almost successful, but it jammed two inches short. Compelled to identify and eliminate the problem, they had to separate the components, now firmly wedged together by the weight of two adults charging at each other like bighorn sheep.

Anticipating an energetic evening, Charlie went upstairs to his room to open the windows. But the windows had been caulked shut. It was, after all, an air-conditioned room. He heard high-pitched shrieks coming from the downstairs bathroom and found Claudia freaking out as the toilet overflowed. Coco ran to the garage for a plunger. Raquel simply redirected her energy to the area around the toilet. She was a professional mopper. Poetry in mopping motion. If she ever entered the Mopping Olympics, she was a shoo-in for the gold or silver.

Back to the air conditioner. Guillermo attached vise-grips to the side of the compressor housing. Coco used a jack handle as a lever. They separated the parts, isolated, and fixed the problem. This time the components slid into the housing with little effort. Charlie made them a drink as they attached the control panel and the grill face. Charlie watched anxiously as Coco plugged it into the wall. It sprang to life. It was a miracle. One pile of junk combined with another pile of junk to make a functioning air conditioner. Charlie was convinced that, with the same parts, they could have constructed anything of equal mass—a trash compactor, a small motorcycle, an atomic antimatter cyclotron—anything.

Officer Abrigo left as they were lugging the machine upstairs. There wasn't time for any conversation beyond pleasantries. Esmeralda's mother, Sulema, took his spot. She was imposing, raucous, tipping the scales at almost three hundred pounds, wearing a violet muumuu. Short-cropped graying hair, piercing black eyes and quick wit, she was bigger than life and with a voice and attitude that commanded respect. Charlie made her a drink. She called him a *Yuma*. Everyone laughed.

Coco explained, "When Castro opened the prison doors and sent all the convicts to Florida, an operation known to the world as the Mariel boatlift, many were rounded up and kept at the Chrome Ave Detention Center as US authorities tried to figure out who was who. Slowly the identity and history of each detainee were unraveled, and they were dispersed across the fruited plains accordingly. Some were set free or united with relatives. Many were imprisoned. The worst of the worst were eventually identified and sent to a maximum-security prison in Yuma, Arizona. The word inexplicably morphed to include anyone from the United States."

Raquel stashed her mop and bucket in the garage and left, followed by Yancy, who had never stopped talking. Guillermo and Coco announced that the air unit was installed and functioning. Slowly, the place cleared out. Jenna and Allen, exhausted, went to bed.

Soon everyone was gone, except for Horseface. He hoped Esmeralda would return after she changed from her bathing suit. Firm, young Esmeralda. Cindy wasn't bad either. How could she possibly consume that much beer and stay in shape? It was the first

143

opportunity to direct his attention to Claudia, looking lost on his couch, slurping on a Cristal. She was very young, perhaps seventeen, thin but not skinny. Her face had an equine quality with bushy eyebrows and huge eyelashes. Perhaps, he imagined, they helped to keep the flies away. Her head was thin, as if it had been inserted into a wine press for a year or two, the compression forcing her jaw forward, offering a plausible explanation for her buck teeth. Or her protruding chompers could have been caused by a bit in her mouth. Her mane was mottled and looked as if it had been cut with garden shears. Charlie was having fun with the imagery. He imagined her naked on all fours, him riding a tiny saddle attached to her back as she grazed on the carpet. He envisioned hiding an apple in his pants, holding her by the ears as she tried to encircle it with her tongue.

Charlie realized that sexual desire was robbing him of cognitive functions. The Cuban women seemed oblivious to their effects on men, each naively dressed, provocatively, in her own slutty way. Each an accidental temptress. It had been a month since he had consummated a relationship with a woman. The little lady in his apartment may have looked like Sea Biscuit, but she had working girl parts. He fantasized about spreading her legs and hefting a hoof over each shoulder. He knew that his thoughts were no longer normal, or whatever passed for normal in his universe, but it didn't matter.

He closed and locked the door, made a drink, and sat down beside her. He grabbed her right leg and slung it over his. Her short blue skirt slid up, revealing pink underwear. So far, so good. He cautiously sniffed around her neck for any hint of oats, barley, or a barnyard. Detecting none, he put his arm around her, and she instantly reciprocated, turning to snuggle, her hand falling casually to his lap. A minute later her fingers moved and began stroking his member through the fabric of his shorts. He lifted her shirt above her head, revealing tube tits, each hanging like a sock containing a cue ball. He threw the shirt on the other couch and reached for her crotch.

Her hand fell on his, pushing and pinning it to her leg. Did he misread the signs? She was half-naked, sitting on his couch, door locked, stroking his unit—in America this would clearly constitute foreplay. Why did she stop him?

She nibbled on his ear, stuck her tongue inside and gently whispered, "Cincuenta."

The translating part of Charlie's brain was completely out of gear. *Cincuenta*, was that a drink? Did they have cincuenta in the refrigerator. There was a rodent that lived in the Andies, they make coats out of them, chin- … chin- … chinchilla, no, that's not it. Her stroking changed to gripping and squeezing, reminiscent of the fuel bulb between the gas tank and an outboard motor, as if the pumping would reverse the flow and force blood back to his brain so he could concentrate on translation.

"Cincuenta," she repeated. It was hard to focus. *Cin-cuent-a*, he sounded out the word, breaking it into its component parts. *Sin* in Spanish, that means "without." *Cuenta* sounds like the word for "count" or "check." *Sin cuenta*, without a check, without a boundary. She was without boundaries in her lust. Fabulous!

She withdrew her hand, pushed back, and looked him straight in the eye. "Cincuenta." She held out her hand. Her expression changed. He had seen that look before, after he was gassed by Fartblossom. That's it—oh no! She was asking for money, *cincuenta*, fifty-dollars. He was caught off guard. His mind was far from negotiation. "You want what?

"Cincuenta."

"That's a lot. That's two days rent. For you"—Charlie did the math on his fingers—"that's nine week's wages!"

Horseface lifted her leg from on top of his, smoothed out her skirt, and crossed her arms, thus removing her panties from the playing field and barring access to her sausage breasts.

"Cincuenta es demasiado." *It's too much.*

145

She retrieved her shirt from across the room and headed for the door. *Damn, don't these people know how to bargain. Smarter than she looked*, thought Charlie, *she must have horse sense*. Except for her face, jaw, teeth, and chest, which weren't her fault, the rest of her body was well-groomed. *Maybe she wasn't a thoroughbred, but donkeys need love too*, rationalized the horny tourist. The image of Sea Biscuit in a dress was now etched in his brain; he couldn't make it go away.

Charlie had to consider his options. It was a classic approach/avoidance scenario. Pro—she was housebroken, looked good from the rear, was in his room, and had a pulse. Con—she could look through a keyhole with both eyes, seemed to be quite a bitch, and cost fifty dollars.

"Wait." She released the door handle, turned around, and smiled. To her, it was a game, and she knew she had won. The odds had been in her favor. She ripped off her shirt and let her skirt and panties to the drop to the floor. Within thirty seconds she was nuzzling her way between Charlie's legs. She unzipped his fly, rooted around, and found the carrot she was looking for. She stuffed Little Charlie into her gaping elongated face. She grabbed the base with one hand and sucked and slobbered on the top end, making good use of her raspy seven-inch tongue. *She is very proficient*, thought Charlie, *very good ... really quite good ... nice technique. She's a professional. Where did she learn how to ...* And it was all over.

She put on her clothes. Charlie handed her a fifty-dollar bill. She gave him a kiss and was out the door, trotting down the street. It occurred to Charlie that, for a brief moment, at fifty-dollars per minute she was making more than Warren Buffett. Naïve? She had been playing him from the moment she'd sat down. The girls knew precisely the effect they had on men.

Charlie's chair was still on the porch. As the last red rays of the sun set the tops of thunderheads aglow, he tried to make sense of all that had happened on his first day in his new home. Somehow a dozen people had come and gone from his living room. That seldom

146

happened in America. He had watched two men work all day on an appliance that was worth about thirty dollars. That was strange. He'd gone swimming with a beautiful girl—where was she, anyway? He had gone to the supermarket, driven a Lada, and made love to a horse.

A girl appeared at the cage. It was the yellow-sundress girl he had seen that morning. With both hands on the bars, she looked like a prisoner in a jail—was she looking in or out? The girl's face was beautiful in the classic Latin tradition. She looked familiar. She waited for Charlie to speak.

"Le veo esta manana." Charlie attempted to say that he had seen her that morning, but his Spanish was eluding him.

"I study English. I am not very good," she answered, sounding apologetic.

"Better than my Spanish. I will teach you if you will instruct me."

"You are an American?"

"Yes."

"I heard you are an American. And you have a boat. A big boat."

"Yes. Why don't you come with me to America on my big boat? We could have many children and grow fat together."

She laughed. "I just wanted to say hello. I live nearby. I have to go now."

And then she was gone, melting into the myriad of other riotous colors that were blending into the coming night. The guard arrived, positioning himself on the wall beneath street lamp in front of the Cruz house across the street. Though the night was young,

Charlie would go to bed early. The air conditioner sounded like a tractor pulling a trash can down a cobblestone street, but against all odds, it blew cold air.

He realized, as his mind drifted, that he had forgotten to ask the girl in the yellow dress her name. Within minutes, he was asleep.

CHAPTER FOURTEEN

Charlie awoke to the sounds of thumping. Raquel was mopping vigorously, slamming into walls and chairs in her headlong pursuit of dirt and dust. Like a human metronome, once she established a rhythm, she was relentless. Esteban was seated on the couch. The fact that he was there was a testament that he had found no other clients. Music was blaring from Calle 232, at least three hundred feet away. Charlie wondered how the neighbors put up with the racket. What if you lived next door with a baby or worked nights and slept during the day? In a world of ridiculous laws, there had to be a statute that addressed destroying the eardrums of one's neighbors.

By now Esteban knew the American was not the same as the other tourists he typically squired through the city. The Yuma wanted to see how the Cuban people lived. He enjoyed going into villages where no other tourist had ever been seen. Charlie could live on black beans and rice, just like a Cuban. He was a contractor back in the States and therefore handy with his hands and tools. The arrangement was perfect for Esteban since he had a busy agenda that was constantly interrupted by the necessities of earning a living by driving a taxi. With Charlie as a customer, he could go about his usual activities and get paid for it, albeit at a lower rate than the lucrative gigs in Havana. This was fine with Charlie, since having Esteban as a driver was giving Charlie a look at the real Cuba. Since

Allen and Jenna were off exploring again, and Charlie was ever increasingly fascinated by Esteban's Cuba, he tagged along with his driver and was becoming more of a sidekick than a client.

Esteban's first stop was a wooden shack behind a low, white concrete duplex. He carried a two-gallon plastic bucket. The shop's interior looked like a witch doctor's apothecary—above the sacks and barrels on the floor were large glass jars filled with gains, powders, and liquids of various colors and viscosities. Some of the products bore labels printed in English—urea, bone meal, vitamin C, and powdered hog testicles. Charlie watched as a worker, referring to Esteban's itemized list, went from container to container, carefully withdrawing from each a measured amount that he placed into the bucket. He mixed the concoction with his fingers. Esteban paid and left with a pail of lumpy yellow powder.

"It's for Rusty. A special menu, high protein. Secret ingredients. This will get him into shape for his big fight," Esteban explained to Charlie.

Charlie was surprised at the specificity of the underground enterprise. Rippling beneath the stagnant official economy was a dynamic market that made life possible. "If you are buying special food for your bird, your competitors must be doing the same."

"Some of them hire *galleros* to train their birds, like boxers that train in the same gym under the same coach then go out and fight each other in the arena. But I can't afford a full-time trainer."

"And they make their own special feed?"

"Tony buys his feed. He has the best. We try to come up our own recipes. Everybody has their own secret formula. I have been working on mine for twenty years."

"Where does Tony get his feed?"

"Purina. From America. He has contacts with the port and brings in just enough for his birds."

"Purina? Just regular old chicken feed?"

"Did you ever read the ingredients on the side of a sack of Purina Chicken Chow? There are over a hundred. They have spent millions perfecting their formula, they have thousands of scientists and work with universities. They have been making improvements for over a century. It's the best. Tony has cornered the market."

"So our embargo is hurting your cockfighting?"

"It's not your embargo. It's Fidel's embargo. The embargo could be lifted next week if Fidel wanted. You are thinking like a capitalist again. If you think like a communist, it all makes sense."

"You are telling me that Fidel wants the embargo left in place. No way. That doesn't make any sense." Charlie paused for a moment before he asked what could be an awkward question.

Esteban seemed annoyed, having to explain the obvious. "Castro plays your president like a violin. Whatever he wants, he gets. He got Helms-Burton. If President Clinton opens the door, Castro will find a way to close it. The only thing Cuba wants from America is your dollars."

"Helms-Burton? Castro wanted Helms-Burton? That's impossible."

Esteban explained as they walked to the car. "We get news— from your country. The guys in Miami tell us everything. There was talk of ending the embargo. They didn't want any more *balseros* to drown or starve to death out in the ocean. Looked bad on TV. Brothers to the Rescue would fly just beyond the twelve-mile limit. They would spot the rafters, and then speedboats would pick them up. When the wind was right, they would occasionally drop anti-Castro leaflets, millions of them, that would float their way to the mainland—like we don't already know we are being screwed.

"Anyway, your Congress was considering relaxing or eliminating altogether the embargo. Fidel blames everything on the

151

embargo. It's, how do you call it, a scapegoat—we would have milk for babies and medicine for the sick except for the embargo. We would paint Havana and fix the roads, but there is an embargo. So it follows that once the embargo is lifted, things will get better in a hurry. Our news never points out that we already trade with over one hundred countries. The embargo was vital to keeping Fidel in power. There was talk of establishing *el dialogo*—talks between your country and mine. That's the last thing Fidel wanted to hear. So he sent out Mig-29 fighters and shot down two of your aircraft. He killed Americans. He knew exactly what he was doing. Two weeks later, Helms-Burton was passed. Now you see it every night on TV—Helms-Burton this, Helms-Burton that, if it were not for Helms-Burton everything would be perfect. Castro architected the whole thing and counted on your country being predictable."

"So it's in Castro's best interest to maintain the embargo. That's insane. That's hard to swallow. Do you hate Castro?"

Esteban looked perplexed, as if he'd never had to consider Castro in terms of black and white. It was a poorly crafted question. He scrambled for the right words. When they came, it was a shock.

"No, Castro was good for Cuba in some ways. Before his time, there were rich people and poor people, just like there are now, but it was different. The peasants had no rights and were butchered by the thousands. Soldiers could enter your home whenever they wanted. They could rape your wife or your daughter. The government was fractured, and criminals advanced themselves through political assignations. There was a power vacuum. We were a puppet state of your country. A strong leader was needed to stand up to American colonialism. We needed to sweep out the garbage and release the potential of the Cuban people.

"That person was Fidel Castro. He defined and articulated the forces of imperialism. He educated us to the downside of democracy and capitalism. Batista hunted him down like a dog and tried to kill him. They put him in prison. But Castro came back and pulled off the impossible. *La Victoria*. He united our country under one strong leader. But he never got over being a revolutionary. He still gives three-hour speeches in Teatro Marx about the Revolution. It's over. He's the only one stuck in the Revolution. Everyone else is trying to move on. He was supposed to be a man of transition. He was supposed to liberate Cuba and go away. But he is still here. Now he is the problem. We can't get rid of him, but we nevertheless owe him a great debt."

The words coming from such a strong critic of the regime were surprising. Charlie saw El Commandante Supremo in a new light—Castro, the liberator who would not go home. The revolutionary who would be king. The one-trick pony. A magician who, after pulling a rabbit out of his hat, didn't know when to get off the stage. Castro, like a tragic figure from Greek mythology—his strength led his people into the light; his personality flaws forced them back into darkness.

They returned to the house on the hill. Rusty was placed in a perforated cardboard carrying box. After fifteen minutes of potholes, they arrived at a training camp on the outskirts of La Lisa. While its training methods may have been sophisticated, the camp was primitive—a fence of automobile hoods, mattress box springs, and flattened metal that was once the sides of refrigerators and washing machines. Wood from shipping crates, rebar, and banana tree bark had been wired and welded and stitched together to form an enclosure. Extension cords led to a nearby house, supported on bamboo poles, supplied current to five or six dangling light bulbs. Three practice rings about fifteen feet in diameter were flanked on both sides by rows of cages under corrugated metal roofing. There were approximately sixty cages, each receiving water through a web of black plastic tubing.

Esteban explained the setup. Unlike Tony's facility, which was private, this was owned by a syndicate of bird owners—a cooperative that shared the premises, but each member was free to campaign his fighter and be instrumental in its training and diet.

Maintained on the premises was not only a stable of avian champions but also a component of professional losers. Handlers knew the strength and weaknesses of all their charges, which was

153

vital in their physical and psychological training. As contenders worked their way upward through ranks and weight classes, honing their stamina and abilities, it was important that they were subject to increasingly difficult challenges. It was equally important that they emerged victorious from every battle since beaten birds develop negative self-images. There was a parallel to be drawn there somewhere between the birds and their handlers, but Charlie didn't think too deeply about it. Esteban told him that it was up to the trainers to ascertain a bird's opponent in order that it put up a good battle but ultimately lose without seriously injuring its sparring partner.

As a nonsyndicate member, Esteban had to pay to use the facilities. Rusty was evaluated by a group of handlers. He was an impressive bird. They knew him and of his performance in previous fights. He was weighted, and his spur measurements were compared with the records of his last visit. They listened to his lungs for signs of fungal or bacterial infections.

The choosing of Rusty's opponent was cause for heated discussion. It was an important decision. Their compensation was linked to performance—get it wrong and a gallery could lose a client. Word would spread quickly through the fighting industry.

Despite their bare feet and ripped clothing, the handlers were professionals. They were not kids. Charlie figured they were in their midthirties or early forties. Each had an opinion, which was stridently expressed through animated, vociferous squabbling. More than once, they nearly came to blows. Charlie watched the handlers interact.

Each seemed tougher than the next. It occurred to Charlie they were very much like the roosters—bellicose, loud, aggressive, posturing, giving the impression they were ready, indeed eager, to fight at a moment's notice. But why?

Charlie studied the men. He was slowly realizing that, here, the government took the place of a man, as a provider and as a protector. Perhaps machismo was all they had left. In the prime of their lives, they were in a cage as real and substantial as those surrounding the birds. They had been deprived of true education, their ability to perform as fathers or sons, earn money legally, form a viable business, enter into contracts or travel freely. They had been robbed of respect or the ability to earn respect. These are serious challenges to the self-worth of a man.

Their position of provider and figurehead in the family had been replaced by Fidel. Castro put a roof over their kid's heads. Castro put food on the table. The government provided. For Cuban men, at least these Cuban men, there was little chance for advancement or self-improvement. No need for a legacy of any kind. As leaders, if they chose to be courageous and rail against injustice, their lives and their liberty were in peril; those who strayed from the party line risked jail and reeducation. Like their avian charges, they had been reduced to impotent strutting bluster, a fleeting blur of feathers rising in the sky for an instant of fury and glory but ultimately left lying in the dirt.

Once in the ring, the handlers thrust the birds at each other in mock attacks. Instincts and adrenaline kicked in, and the birds locked onto one another, twisting and turning trying to break free and attack. After being whipped into a frenzy, they were released onto the sawdust floor in the center of the ring. They charged at each other like sumo wrestlers. When their chests collided, their combat took to the air, smashing with their wings, each trying to jockey into a position favorable to landing a death blow with its heel spur. To the uninitiated—to Charlie—the birds seemed to meld together into a blur of furious feathers. But Esteban said that the handlers could generally tell which combatant was gaining an advantage. Within the mayhem, he went on to explain, one bird may propel itself just a bit higher, but that height gives it the advantage to puncture an eyeball or drive its spur into the chest of its opponent.

Battling for favorable position continued when they returned to earth. Blood soon covered their heads and hackles. Weaknesses were instantly exploited. Now their beaks came into play, landing blows on the backs of their opponent's head whenever the opportunity arose. Esteban told Charlie that, in a practice match, this

155

was often the signal to separate the birds. In a real match, there was only a slight little correlation between the first head blows and the eventual victory, which may not be determined for another twenty minutes. As expected, Rusty quickly assumed a superior position and proceeded to rain down assaults on the back of the skull of its unfortunate rival. Charlie wondered if the bird had been trained to lose—just as they were training Rusty to win—to gain the confidence, and the money, of their clients.

Despite Rusty's performance, Esteban appeared worried. He placed the bucket of chicken feed beside an empty cage. "He will spend the next week here."

"What happens then?" Charlie asked.

"Then, the big fight."

"This fight is bigger than other fights?"

"It's the big one. The one that will solve all of my troubles. Rusty will take on Tony's best bird."

Charlie computed the odds. Tony had over a hundred of the finest birds on the island. He had the best facility, the best trainers, and he fed his birds Purina. Charlie felt Esteban's faith in his feathered protégé was admirable but misplaced. But if preparing his bird for a fight brought hope to his friend and helped pass the time, who was he to voice an opinion? He was, after all, just another tourist. Just a Yuma.

Returning to Jaimanitas, they picked up a hitchhiker. She seated herself in the middle of the long, vinyl front seat, speaking to Esteban in a machine-gun staccato. Charlie could catch perhaps one word out of five. By the time his brain made the translation, conjugated the verb, placed it into a sentence, and tried to divine its meaning through context, they were linguistically a thousand miles away, increasing the gap at the speed of sound.

Charlie disconnected from the conversation and concentrated on their new passenger. She had been cooking in the sun for an hour and radiated heat like a baked potato, along with the fragrance of coconut shampoo mixed with the musty smell of her sweat. She was a nursing student, he had caught that much, stocky, with shoulder-length brown hair that had been permed within the last week. She was dressed conservatively, her teal blouse tucked into a knee-length cotton skirt that clung to the moisture on her short, stubby, muscular legs.

"Her family won the lottery. She is on her way to Havana to have sex with tourists."

Charlie tried to reconcile the two statements. *What could one possibly have to do with the other?* By the look on Charlie's face, Esteban knew further explanation was required.

"*El Bombo*. Her family won *El Bombo*. They are allowed to leave Cuba and go to America to become citizens of your country. Twenty thousand families each year. More would apply," explained Esteban, "but the government considers all who apply traitors to the Revolution, same as the *jineteros—guzzanos*, maggots. They get less food."

"And she is on her way to Havana to work as a prostitute?"

Gloria turned to Charlie, telling him, in Spanish baby talk, what every Cuban knows. It costs a fortune to leave the island. She went on to tell him her story, her family's story. He was touched. An idealistic student from a poor, outlying village, forced to the big city to sell her body so she and her family could pursue a life of freedom in a far-off, new land. It was heartbreaking. It was a tragedy.

"It will take my family many years to raise the money," she summarized. "I have never been a prostitute before," she added objectively, as if applying for a new job. Charlie tried to imagine her on the streets of Havana. The way she was dressed she wouldn't have a chance. *Hey sailor, want to have a date with a librarian?*

He wished he had money enough to give her the cash. He wished he had the money to give them all cash. Esteban needed twenty thousand. Gloria needed four thousand. Roberto needed a new air conditioner. Horseface could use a set of braces. The people around him weren't lazy, as it had first appeared. On the contrary. They were willing to go to extremes and take enormous risks to better themselves and their families. They were frustrated entrepreneurs, eager to advance themselves through the limited options that presented themselves in a dystopian system.

What other opportunities were open to Gloria? There were no paladars on the south side of La Lisa, no *extranjero* was going to rent the back room of her family's shack. The government controlled all aspects of her life. The one item over which she had limited control was her body, but if she was convicted of prostitution, it could cost up to five years "deprivation of freedom." Charlie wanted to help, but he had to be practical.

"I will give you forty dollars to accompany with me." He was learning the nomenclature. *Accompany* sounded so much better than *screw my brains out for the next twenty-four hours*."

"How much time?" she asked.

"Until tomorrow morning."

"I want seventy-five."

"I will pay you fifty, plus lunch and dinner and all you can drink at my apartment."

Gloria put her hand on his knee. "Almuerzo, ahora? Tengo hambre—Lunch? Now I am hungry." Charlie knew the deal was sealed.

Esteban took them to Restaurant El Palenque, which he said was noted for its grilled pork. It was a favorite for locals, particularly on special occasions like anniversaries, Mother's Day, and birthdays. Al fresco dining under long, thatched roofs. Domestic beers were seventy-five cents, a fried-chicken dinner two dollars and fifty cents. Pulling into the parking lot, they passed golden-brown hogs being roasted on spits over charcoal-fired ovens. A minstrel trio—a male singer, a violinist, and a classical guitar player—worked the room, delighting customers, annoying Charlie.

It was the first time Gloria had been to the Palenque, she said, though she had heard about the restaurant since she was a toddler. Her family never went to restaurants. They saved their money. After drinks were ordered, Charlie asked if she was ready to go to America. It was an offhand, throwaway question. He wasn't prepared for the answer.

"My father was in the Communist Party, a Fidel supporter and active in the local CDR. He worked for the state, rebuilding bus engines in Havana. At night he would restore junk cars. He would buy them cheap, maybe five or six hundred dollars, and work on them for months. He would sell them for a profit, sometimes four thousand dollars, and he would invest the money he made in tools to make his work go faster. He had bought an airless sprayer and not only painted his cars but also worked for his neighbors and other restorers. When he painted a car, people would stop in the street and stare at it."

She sipped on a vodka tonic and told her story without emotion. Just one fact after another.

"We had a large backyard. At any one time, he would have four or five cars, some almost ready to sell, others just starting to get fixed up. My father would travel all over to find parts. One day a tow truck arrived in front of our house. Men from the government had papers. They took my father's cars, confiscated them under the law of illegal enrichment. They said the money he earned was not his. It belonged to the Cuban government. They took all the money from his bank account and sent him to prison on a four-year sentence. It was very hard for my mother. He was released after two years on parole. We were surprised that, since he is an ex-prisoner and no longer supports the government, that we won the lotto. He wants to immigrate to America. That's why he entered El Bombo. That is why I have to make money."

Charlie looked aghast. Esteban nodded and spoke. "We can fix cars for ourselves, but we are not supposed to sell them. Instead, we work out deals under the table. Money changes hands, and the title remains the same. Otherwise, the government can seize the car. They can take your house, too. Her family was lucky."

"Lucky!" Charlie thought about what he had just heard. Gloria seemed so happy. How could she be happy? She was smiling. She had a beautiful smile. How could she smile? How could anyone smile? Men with shiny shoes had shown up and destroyed her family. Her father had done nothing wrong. He hadn't killed anyone, hadn't molested a sheep. He had been working like a dog in his backyard and had been hauled off to prison. And he had been a supporter of the regime, a card-carrying commie! What if he had been a dissident? They would never have seen Daddy again.

"Couldn't he have received a license and operated legally?" Charlie wondered aloud.

Esteban laughed. "You're thinking like a capitalist again. Licensing is a money-making enterprise for the government, not the people. The last thing they want is for the Cuban people to have money. Have you read Che Guevara, the New Man, and all that crap? People have to pay for the license. That costs fifteen hundred pesos. That is just the beginning. There is a monthly fee, and it changes all the time. It always goes up. Legal businesses are subject to inspection. No one ever passes an inspection. Every time they come, the owner has to pay a fine. During inspections, they look at the books. If every penny isn't accounted for, they revoke the license. Most businesses close their doors after a couple months, and the government keeps the fifteen hundred pesos. If someone manages to make a profit, it is taxed heavily."

As Esteban began to order, Gloria said very softly, almost inaudibly, "Yes. It's very hard to make money without breaking the law."

CHAPTER FIFTEEN

The bill came to sixteen dollars and fifty-seven cents. Reaching for the cash in his wallet, he looked for the other bills. There should have been a group of fifties and hundreds to the left of the small bills. There was a single hundred. *What happened to all my money?* The fourteen hundred that had been in his wallet when he'd arrived was supposed to have lasted at least a week, but it had almost been gone by the end of day four. *Where did it go?*

Charlie made a quick mental calculation of his expenditures—marina expenses, Palco, Esteban at sixty dollars per day, and another thirty per day for gasoline. Fartblossom had stolen five hundred dollars, and he'd given her eighty-five more. There was fifty dollars to Horseface then groceries. *Damn, I thought Cuba was cheap.*

"Esteban, I need to go to the bank and get some money."

"Do you have traveler's checks?"

"No. I use my credit card at the ATMs."

"What kind of credit card?' Esteban asked in a tone that sounded as if he already knew the answer.

"American Express."

"An American Express or a foreign American Express?"

"American."

"Doesn't matter. It's no good here. Do you have someone in America who can wire you the money Western Union?"

"I could call my bank, and they might arrange a wire transfer to a Western Union in Florida. Maybe three grand to spend over the next month. How much does Western Union charge?"

"Twenty-nine dollars for a three-hundred-dollar transfer. Three is all you can get through Western Union. Here it's called is CIMEX and can only be used three times a year. But it's for remittances from one family member to another, and those have to be registered with the government."

Charlie was starting to worry. His tropical paradise was turning out to be more complicated than he'd anticipated.

The *Bora Bora Express* had originally been bound for Antigua, a well-established member of the international banking community. Transfer of funds on and off the island were state of the art, completed in microseconds. Before leaving Florida, Charlie had arranged for a monthly direct deposit from his bank into his American Express account, which could then be debited through ATMs once he'd reached his destination. Charlie had done his homework—ATMs provided the best exchange rate and the lowest transactional fees.

What had at first appeared an inconvenience was actually a well-constructed wall, crafted from the interlocking bricks of US policy. Cubans had found ways to get around many of the restrictions—it was in their genes—by using surrogates or hiring couriers. But these options were not available to Charlie or his crew.

"Do you have anyone who can bring money from America?" It was in Esteban's interest to keep Charlie solvent. Flying someone in from Jacksonville with a wad of cash seemed an impractical solution.

"Don't worry," assured Esteban. "There is always a way."

A half hour later, they were in the cramped back office of Havana's Hotel Sevilla. Chief Financial Officer Shlomo Tantara did his best to explain the difficulties facing Charlie and his crew:

"It's a moving target. Changes from one month to the next. First, dollars were banned by Fidel. Then they became the island's official second currency. Then remittances were allowed, then the Torricelli Act tried to shut them down. Then Clinton allowed remittances. Drives us crazy. Now we have Helms-Burton. For a while we couldn't do any credit card transactions, then your county relaxed the rules. Now we can use Visa or Mastercard if they originate in any country other than the United States. We run a lot of business through Canadian banks. If you are going to stay, consider getting a Canadian credit card that draws on a Canadian bank. American Express—forget it."

"That's what I have, American Express." Charlie handed his card to Señor Tantara. "There's got to be some way of transferring funds. Otherwise, we are going to be in big trouble."

Charlie wondered if Allen and Jenna were having any of the same money problems. They hadn't mentioned it if they had. Then again, they weren't financing a small village.

Shlomo scrutinized the card's front and back. "No problem. Using your credit card number, we transfer funds from your Amex to Barclay's Bank in Bermuda. From there, they go to Banco Exterior de España-Argentaria in Madrid, Spain, then into the hotel's account in Banco Financiero Internacional here in Havana. We do it for guests all the time. First, we need to confirm that your card is valid. Can I see your passport, please? How much money do you want to withdraw?"

163

"One thousand US dollars."

They waited in the lobby for twenty minutes before they were summoned back to the office. Shlomo handed Charlie seven hundred and fifty dollars tucked inside his passport. Charlie counted the money. "Two hundred and fifty commission? You charged twenty-five percent?" It was a disaster. He wondered how much of the two fifty had gone to Esteban. Suddenly an expensive country became twenty-five percent more expensive—food, rent, dockage—all instantly up by twenty-five percent. Worse, the price of pussy had just skyrocketed. For two hundred and fifty dollars, he could have sailed the hundred miles to Key West and cashed a check. Of course, doing that, he risked having his boat confiscated by US Customs.

Charlie was still considering the implications as they arrived back at the apartment on Calle 234. The cage door was open, swinging into the sidewalk. Roberto and Esmeralda were on the couch, drinking Cuba Libras. Gloria slipped seamlessly into the conversation. *They are all sisters,* thought Charlie as he escorted his overheated hitchhiker to his air-conditioned room.

He placed her in front of the mirror and stood behind her. She was brown, squat, short, and stocky, maybe five foot three. Slowly, he unbuttoned her blouse, stopping occasionally to massage her shoulders, then as she lowered her head, he rubbed the nape of her neck. She was pliant, responsive, receptive. He removed her shirt and let it fall to the floor. Then her bra. He raised her arms above her head and cupped each breast. They were small, durable, refreshing; the image of Horseface's pendulous tube knockers was still fresh in his memory. Her nipples were like little brown pencil erasers, hard as a rock. He turned her around and knelt before her, sucking one breast then another. She tasted like salt. It made sense. When they'd found her, she had been marinating on the side of the road in the direct sun. She had subsequently spent another five hours in Esteban's rolling sauna. It was a wonder she didn't smell like a goat.

"Bañarte!" *Shower!* He slid her skirt and panties down to her knees, reaming her sweaty navel with his tongue. He walked behind her to the shower. What he thought would be fat was muscle. She had the body of a little weightlifter or maybe a Romanian gymnast. He imagined her cracking walnuts between her iron butt cheeks.

Charlie was terrified of the shower. The water, controlled by one knob, came through the wall on a galvanized pipe and entered an electric heater that doubled as a showerhead. Once in the heater, it activated a pressure switch that sent electricity through a series of heating elements, much the same as a hair dryer. But everybody knows not to get a hair drier wet—here they pumped water through them! Worse, to adjust the temperature required a bather to reach up, with wet hands and manipulate the hot/cold lever. Cold water trickled through for a minute or so, then a small red light indicated the heating element had switched itself on.

He escorted her into the shower and guided her into the water stream. Charlie waited to see if she was electrocuted. But her head was fifteen inches below the voltage; it was a long way for a current to arc. Cautiously crouching, he moved to a position beside her, adjusting his height to match hers. So far, so good. Slowly he raised the top of his head up the spitting stream of tepid water, waiting at any moment to complete a circuit and be struck dead. When he narrowed the gap to five inches, electrons leaped from the coils and began to use his body as a lightning rod. An inch closer and a million electric worms slithered and stabbed the top of his head. It felt good. He moved his head from side to side, and the electric massage traveled in an orbit around his skull—a one hundred ninety-pound bobblehead swaying in a 220-volt halo.

Delighted at having survived another near-death experience, he turned his attention to his companion. He soaped her from head to toe and shampooed her hair. She reciprocated, kissing him as she worked the shampoo into his hair with her fingernails. She soaped his entire body, using his erect member as a towel rack for the washcloth. Charlie rinsed off the suds and carried her, soaking wet and squealing like a little pink pig into the bedroom. She shivered in the air-conditioned room. Charlie laid on top of her, sharing the heat of his body.

"Remember: you said I could drink."

165

But when he returned, he was surprised to find that Esmeralda had made her way upstairs and engaged Gloria in conversation. The mood had been shattered. He was once again invisible and arriving at the conclusion that all tourists were interchangeable, merely walking wallets to be exploited. He pictured himself lying on the floor of his apartment, bleeding, near death, the neighborhood girls stepping over his body on their way to the refrigerator for a beer.

He had never considered himself a romantic man. On the contrary, he cultivated the image of the confirmed bachelor. His humor, when directed at women, was often base and demeaning. But that was just a joke. There were indeed times *he* had been cold to a woman—distant, short, sharp, hostile—but such strong displays of emotion were indicative of relationships and feelings gone bad. In America, he had always sought out women of substance, not sluts or hookers, and when they'd made love, it had strengthened the bond between them. It had meant something. For all the hype surrounding free love and sport fucking, he had tried it and found it ultimately unfulfilling, leaving him emptier than before.

So, what was he looking for here in Cuba? He realized it was unrealistic to expect a bond with the street girls. He had heard the expression *colder than a whore's heart*, and it made sense—they had to protect themselves. Imagine the reverse. Falling in love with every client, having their hearts ripped out on a nightly basis. It would be foolish of them, an act of self-destruction, to allow themselves to have feelings for a tourist, any tourist, one who could pack up at a moment's notice and disappear, leaving them with broken hearts, alone and still imprisoned. No, they had to be cold and distant by necessity.

But the Cuban ladies he had met carried impartiality to a new level. It bordered on contemptuous. He was human. He had feelings. Was it too much to ask for a little eye contact? Sitting on the couch, he could hear them cackling upstairs. *Have they noticed I am missing yet?* he wondered. How was it possible he was in his house with two beautiful women and felt as alone as if he were in the middle of the Sahara Desert?

He looked through the glass door to see Sundress Girl peering through the bars. *Oh no, not another one. I am not the Bank of America.* Still recovering from the body blow delivered by his last companion, he unlocked both doors and led her inside. She spoke English.

"This is Roberto's house. You are lucky to have a friend like him. He will take care of you."

She was well-dressed. Coral blouse, white belt, black skirt. She was five foot five, long and flowing jet-black hair—a classical Latin beauty. She looked high maintenance. Charlie shook his head. *I wonder how much this one is going to cost me?*

To avoid the inevitable, he cut to the chase. "Look, I am having trouble getting my money from America. I'm paying for this house, the marina. I have a driver. My refrigerator is apparently open to the public. I just don't have enough money to pay you right now."

She laughed, surveying the room. "I don't want your money."

"What do you want?"

"I am hungry. Have you been to El Laurel yet? I think you would like it. It's near. Not very expensive."

This was the first time anyone on the island had taken into account that he was not a walking ATM.

"I would love to go, but I have two girls upstairs."

"Have you paid them?"

"Not yet. Only one is on the payroll. The other is a neighbor."

"What's the neighbor's name?"

"Esmeralda."

Sundress Girl went to the foot of the stairs and shouted instructions to the room above. Voices floated back in response. Sundress Girl exuded confidence. Sundress Girl had poise. Best of all, Sundress Girl didn't want money.

"I'm sorry. What was your name again?"

"Vali, *corto*—short, for Valentina"

Charlie changed into khakis and a long-sleeved shirt. They walked to Avenida Quinta. Vali hailed a lime-green 1949 DeSoto peso cab and handed the driver twenty-five centavos. Vali explained during the drive that there was a canal that bordered Avenida Quinta for three-quarters of a mile—almost to the edge of Jaimanitas. Long ago, the canal-front property had been divided into eighty-foot-wide parcels and sold as residential property. Some people bought two or three lots, side by side. One investor bought five in a row. The homes constructed on the lots were as varied as their owners—some simple wooden dwellings, others palatial. After the Revolution, many owners had fled north, and their homes had been immediately confiscated. Other owners had stayed. One such owner had been the Gutierez family. During the Special Period, they'd applied for, and had been granted, the license to operate a *paladar*. That business had evolved into the Restaurante El Laurel.

The DeSoto wheezed to a stop under the partial shade of an enormous ceiba. At the green-gated entrance was seated a grizzled old man. Except for a *machete*, he appeared to be a *campesino*. He stood up and bowed as Charlie and Vali approached, welcoming them with a broad smile and a sweeping gesture. El Laurel was a walled family compound, beside the wooden ancestral home a parking area with eight spaces. A floral pathway led to a wide veranda and dining tables on the edge of the canal.

Charlie instantly regained his bearings—across the canal and to the left he could see the customs building, and to the east, there was the Papa Restaurant and Nightclub. He could see the entrance to his canal, but the view of the *Bora Bora Express* was blocked by the Hotel Aquario. He briefly thought that it had been too long since he'd been back to the boat, and he made a mental note to check on Allen and Jenna.

A rickety dock, its pilings made of palm set in concrete formed with truck tires, supported one dining table and provided a view down the canal. Other docks extended across the shallows, but none made it to deep water, each falling about fifty feet short. He thought it peculiar. Such fantastic boat access to the sea, to fishing and sailing, but it was impossible to dock anything much deeper than a kayak. Nor were there any boats on the docks or tied to the bulkhead.

They chose the table with the best view, located at the terminus of the shaky wharf. Charlie surveyed his surroundings. The ten-foot masonry boundary walls were lined with royal palms, beneath them a manicured understory of frambuesa, hibiscus, and oleanders. A coquina-rock grotto covered with ivy provided shelter to a mercifully silent Scarlet Macaw. The atmosphere was one of peace, shelter, sanctuary. The wall was old, weathered, and had over its hundred years developed a patina. Of the places he had seen thus far, Charlie liked this location the most. It fit him—a verdant paradise beside still, calm, protected water. It was easy to fantasize its purchase. Of course, he would have to deepen access to the dock or extend it to the edge of the navigational channel. And if it squawked just once, the bird would have to go.

Perhaps he could incorporate the existing wall as part of a courtyard behind a cottage of stone, with two stories, and a veranda on the second floor that overlooked the canal. It would have a thatched roof, but beneath it was an underlay of thirty-pound felt in case of a hurricane. Since it was made of rock, the same massive hand-hewn blocks of coral as used by the Spanish to build El Moro and El Cathedral, it too would grow ivy and endure for a thousand years. He could see it. Medieval arched windows composed of mosaic glass. Oak doors fastened with black steel. Three hundred years in the future, tourists would visit his little castle as a shrine—

home to an intrepid American who'd defied authority and fallen in love with a forbidden foreign land and decided to stay.

It was fun to imagine. But there was a practical aspect to his daydreaming—he couldn't live on a boat forever. The *Bora Bora Express* was a vehicle, a temporary plastic conveyance to carry him from one home, one life, one adventure, to another. Maybe that was what he was really searching for, something permanent, something that felt like home. His boat was the antithesis of permanence and security. He was kicking the tires of a new country. Trying it on for size. Charlie Sutton, c/o Restaurante El Laurel, 2354 Avenida Quinta, Santa Fe, Cuba. Yes. A good address. An exotic address.

Why let the fantasy stop there? He would need someone with whom he could share his rock fortress. A queen for his castle. He didn't have to look far since one had dropped out of the sky, landed on his doorstep, and was now sitting beside him on the edge of his imaginary construction site. She was a beautiful woman. Beautiful women were a dime a dozen in Cuba. Yet this one seemed different. He felt as if he had seen her face before. She made him uncomfortable. Charlie had a hard time making eye contact. Each time he did, he found himself falling into her eyes. She was Medusa with a twist—instead of turning to stone, he turned to mush. Somehow, she had the upper hand without saying a word. Her mere presence put Charlie at a disadvantage. How could he talk with this girl when he couldn't look her in the eye?

And talking would break the spell. It always did. At least that was what his experiences had been with American women. Princesses fell from their thrones once they opened their mouths. The cold rain of reality soon extinguished the fire of fantasy. This woman's power was illusory. *She can only use the power I give her.* Charlie had been here before. Choking. Knocked off his game plan. Temporarily stunned by beauty, fumbling, at a loss for words. But it always passed, and it passed quickly.

Oh, sure, first encounters were a blank canvas; fears were swept aside to allow for hope—the hope that this unknown person, mysterious, unexplored, would be the perfect fit; the lifelong friend and companion, the necessary and ultimate counterpart to achieving a love that transcended time. Charlie was not immune to hope with its unfettered potential. Within the woman before him was the sum total of all women. She was a mother, lover, daughter, Helen of Troy incarnate, the embodiment of all things feminine since the beginning of time. It was a fleeting moment to be savored, cultivated, nurtured since it could not last.

She broke the silence. "You have a boat."

"You have me at a disadvantage. You seem to know everything about me, and I know nothing about you."

"There are few secrets in Jaimanitas. Roberto says good things about you. He likes you. He is usually a good judge of one's character."

"And I like Roberto, too. Your English, it's excellent. The girls on the street can't speak a single word. No hello, goodbye, one, two, three—nothing."

"That's because they don't want to improve themselves. We all study English in school. It's required. They just don't want to learn. Have you watched our television at night? We get English movies with subtitles. It's much better than school because it is the way your language is really spoken. When I hear new words, I look them up in my dictionary."

"The girls in my neighborhood, *mi vecinos*, they are your friends?" Charlie asked.

"I grew up with them. They are my sisters. We are all the same."

"But they don't want to improve themselves?"

Charlie watched as she twirled a lock of hair around her finger. "They do. In their own way. I just"—she paused in search of the right phrase—"do whatever is necessary."

The waiter arrived to take drink orders. Vali asked for water.

"You don't drink?" Charlie asked.

"I have just begun a new job. I don't think it's a good idea to show up smelling of alcohol."

"Tonight? You work at night? Where? What do you do?"

"I do a Selena imitation. You know, the singer from Texas. She was killed. I sing at the La Cecilia nightclub. I just started and don't want to do anything wrong."

Charlie remembered he had seen a sign on Avenida Quinta. Perhaps it had been while they were pushing Esteban's car. "Is the Cecilia across from the Oro Negro? By the traffic circle?"

"Yes, it is very nice." She suddenly seemed wary.

"Tonight. Great, I will stop in and see you perform."

Vali's demeanor changed immediately. She reached out and squeezed Charlie's hand as one would a child's. Her eyes drilled into his, her expression stern, hawkish. "I want you to promise that you will never come to the Cecilia."

CHAPTER SIXTEEN

They returned to the apartment to find that Esmeralda and Gloria had gotten into the rum. Charlie thought it a stroke of luck that he hadn't been upstairs with Gloria when Vali had appeared. Vali left to prepare for work. The drunks were escorted through the door and ejected into the street. The fact that it was dark did little to reduce the temperature, but still, Charlie set off walking toward the marina to check on Allen, Jenna, and the *Express*. Through open doors and windows, he could watch the neighbors going about their business—cleaning dishes, sweeping floors, preparing children for bed—on every television, the same show—cartoons, an indication that the other two channels were devoted to political discussion. The smells of coffee, cigars, and kitchens mingled with the aroma of garbage placed on the street for tomorrow's pickup.

Past the Cine Paradiso and the bodega, up the shortcut to Avenida Quinta and the Rumbo on the corner, in the early evening, the open-air mini-mart magically transformed itself into a bar/restaurant/nightclub. Burgers, fries, and fried chicken were prepared under a corrugated tin lean-to propped against a side wall. Patrons could eat at the counter on bar stools or dine beneath a latticework of bamboo and vines. A boom box on the counter provided music that simultaneously entertained people waiting on the corner for the bus.

Between the Rumbo and the Rio Jaimanitas, a parking lot that also served the *Club de Desporte de Pescada,* the village's sportfishing club, hidden away in the casuarinas by a high chain-link fence crowned with rusty barbed wire. Walking over the bridge, he turned to look down the little river. He wondered how many of the fishing craft had disappeared on nights like this, spirited quietly past the line of boats, tied three and four deep, into the sea near the rocky swimming pool where he had swum with Esmeralda. The river took a bend, so he could not see the ocean. He guessed its distance to be a quarter mile. The sea was so close. Anyone could swim around the fence and snatch the vessel of their choice—a motor launch, a large rowboat, perhaps a sailing dingy—all were capable of making the voyage to Key West with a little bit of luck.

Perhaps the boats were guarded, but he could see no one. Even if there were guards, they would probably be bribable. There had to be some reason—and then he imagined an overhead view, putting together the bits and pieces of geography he had seen and trying to arrange them in his head. Jaimanitas was behind him, here was the river, the entrance to the marina directly ahead maybe five hundred feet, and straight down the entrance road was Hotel Viejo y El Mar. That was it. The river emptied into the sea beside the most sophisticated surveillance apparatus on the island. The garrison bivouacked on top of the hotel was not bribable, they were not approachable, and they were not even allowed to be photographed. Of course, that's why the boats were resting so peacefully so near the ocean. They were untouchable. There had to be a curfew, a time past which they could not leave the mouth of the little river and head for the sea. They wouldn't have a chance of escaping. There was no way a fat rat was going to make it past, under, or around the Russian-trained guards hovering overhead.

As he approached the *Express,* he was pleased to see a group assembled in the cockpit. Other yachtsmen had joined Allen and Jenna for drinks. At least they'd made friends in his absence. Charlie climbed aboard and introduced himself. He was well received. Within the small society of Canal Two, he had achieved a questionable notoriety. They had heard of his encounter with

Fartblossom and were delighted to put an embarrassed face with the name.

But Charlie wasn't the only one with a story. One of the sailors, a catamaran captain named Arthur, out of Long Beach, California, was sporting bandages on both hands and his neck. The oozing red blood indicated the wounds were fresh and still weeping. He told a disturbing tale.

"I have spent over two years here in the marina. I know all the guards and many of their wives and children. I have always gotten along with everybody. Never made any trouble. I know everybody at customs and bring them gifts whenever I return. Last year I brought them three Hunter ceiling fans. New ones. In the box from Home Depot.

"When I came through customs this afternoon, they brought a dog on board. A German shepherd. I was down below, arranging sail bags in the forepeak of the port hull. They ordered me to appear. I told them in Spanish to fuck themselves. It was a joke. I always joke around with those guys. They released the dog. It went for my throat. There was no room, you know. It's not very wide up there. There was nowhere to go. I tried to protect my face and head with my arms. As you can see, it did a pretty good job on me. Those dogs are fast. Then the guards insisted on their presents. I had brought them each a box of twenty-four frozen hamburger patties. It's impossible to get a good beef here. I have no idea why this time was any different, but next time I leave, I am never coming back."

The implication was clear. If the police could attack Arthur, they could attack anyone. Usually tourists were immune from harassment. The regime went to great lengths to ensure their vacations were free of threat or hassle since the slightest negative press could have an enormous knock-on effect, threatening the only viable industry on the island. But a sailboat bum who had been here for two years was not the usual tourist. Within the ranks of budget travelers and consummate freeloaders, sailors stood on par with hitchhikers, hobos, bums, and backpackers. What could be expected from a group who use the wind to get from place to place, feeding on fish as they traveled? Arthur may have fit the miserly sailboater stereotype. He was taking up dock space from a potentially profligate millionaire. Arthur had become a nonproductive liability. He was supposed to have spent his money and sailed away. But he hadn't. Perhaps he'd just gotten the message.

Charlie wondered how he would be treated after he moved into his dream fortress on the grounds of El Laurel. Would they put the dogs on him, also? If they were smart, they would let him finish construction before they turned his arms and neck into Alpo. When it came to extracting money from tourists, they *were* smart—Castro had written the book himself.

Though the group continued drinking and socializing, Arthur's story had added a disturbing undercurrent to the party. Arbitrary and capricious actions on behalf of the Cuban government was just one of the concerns on the minds of the group.

"You know," Allen said, "the attack on Arthur may have been in retaliation for the passage of Helms-Burton. It puts yachtsmen squarely in the middle between two feuding governments. The laws governing travel to Cuba have been largely ignored for the past five years. You think the US government doesn't know the names, registration, and document number of every boat in Marina Hemingway?"

Charlie guffawed, sipping a beer. "Hell, they know our passport numbers, what we had for breakfast and the number of barnacles on our hull. They know the nationality, and resident status of all the captains and all the crews. Maybe it's an experiment to see if Cuba tolerates us. Maybe we're being used as embedded agents to advance the American agenda. Anyway, if it were true that America really didn't want us here, we would not have gotten within twenty miles of the marina.

Arthur joined in. "Not a bad theory. That would make every arriving sailor an agent of the United States. As they traveled about the island, they would, by their very presence, sow dissension, incite class envy, and diffuse the party line that America and its people are an enemy."

Charlie raised his beer. "A toast. To being capitalist pathogens injected into a communist host. Bless us free-spending, free-talking Trojan horses, eagerly, if ignorantly, dragged behind enemy walls!"

The other two men raised their drinks. Jenna raised her glass. "To plausible deniability!" she cheered.

Fears somewhat assuaged and patriotism shored up, the group drank until the wee hours. They were consoled by the fact that no sailors had been arrested, nor their boats confiscated by the US government, since the Mariel boatlift.

CHAPTER SEVENTEEN

Vali had her pick of suitors at the bar that night. It seemed everyone wanted to have sex with Selena. Though something about the club was bothering her this particular night, she accepted a proposition from two well-dressed young professionals from Colombia, here to film a documentary. They paid eighty-five dollars to film her performing oral sex in the back seat of restored 1955 Dodge. It was the easiest money she had made thus far. They insisted that she remain in character, which meant not removing her gown and leaving on her high heels. They took her telephone number and her address in Jaimanitas, telling her there may be a chance for more work in the future. She was through by one o'clock in the morning. She would usually have gone straight home, but tonight was different.

On his way home from the marina at about the same time, Charlie encountered a standing-room-only crowd at the Rumbo. It had spilled into the parking lot. He worked his way through two hundred customers to an area in front of the bar. Tables had been pushed aside. The music, through speakers pushed far beyond their performance range, was deafening. Charlie had seen salsa dancing before, or thought he had seen salsa dancing, but it was white-people salsa—mechanical, constrained, scripted. He wasn't prepared for the spectacle that emerged from the dimly lit dance floor.

Within a ring of perhaps two dozen spectators, each yielding to the irresistible beat, was a fluid core of dancers, its number fluctuating as participants exchanged places with eager onlookers. Each seemed to be a professional, each with his or her own subtle variation, each channeling an artistry and enthusiasm that meshed like a well-oiled machine, in unison, with the core. Charlie watched as a single dancer seamlessly became two, not unlike tango dancers, twirling, dipping, then three, as one assumed the position of the pole man, with his arms held high, then four, their faces serious, classical, engaged, sweating in the midnight heat around a single, gyrating axis. Charlie was mesmerized. He had never seen this side of Cuba. It was an unexpected view into the hearts and souls of his neighbors. Somehow, in this dirty roadside cantina a crowd had spontaneously assembled and created something beautiful. He suddenly thought about Vali.

He arrived at his house to find Vali sitting on the low stone wall, talking with his guard.

"I'll have that drink now," she said as Charlie unlocked the cage door.

"I have whiskey and rum. Which would you prefer?"

"Whiskey."

"With water or cola?"

"Ginger ale, if you have any." She was wearing blue jeans and a pink blouse. "I have to take a shower. I just came from work. Do you have hot water?"

"Damn, they used up all the ice and didn't refill the trays." Charlie looked at the counter. "And they ate all the cookies and left the mayonnaise on the counter. Those girls are going to clean me out. The upstairs shower has hot water."

She took a sip from her drink and started up the stairs. "You coming?"

179

Charlie kept waiting for the other shoe to drop, the inevitable discussion of time and money. He found it interesting that, until the discussion had taken place, their roles duly codified by verbal contract, she had all the power. Once a price had been determined, he would be in control—a gentler, kinder version variation of master/slave or perhaps employer/employee. Then he would know how to act and she, by virtue of entering into the contract, how to respond. Establishing a price removed ambiguity. But ambiguity was far from his mind as he focused on her world-class ass leading him up the stairs. His mother wouldn't like her. His father would want to bone her.

She swept aside the shower curtain. "Do you have a shower cap?"

"No, sorry. I have a mask and snorkel." She undressed. He looked at her naked body from behind. "You don't have tan lines."

"I don't own a bathing suit."

The silver backing on the medicine-door mirror had been deteriorating for thirty years, forcing users to wobble around in search of the best reflection. Vali looked into the mirror, tucking in strands of hair that were escaping beneath the towel she had wrapped around her head. Charlie turned on the water, but the pressure-sensitive, on-demand heating element always exercised its own free will about when and if it would start working. Naked, graceful, poised, she entered the shower but stood back, not wishing to get the towel wet. Charlie soaped his hands and proceeded to wash her from head to toe. When he arrived at a sensitive area, she offered no resistance.

Fifteen minutes later, they were in bed. She was shivering, not being used to air-conditioning. The elephant in the room was impossible to ignore.

"What do you want from me?" he asked. Her response was unexpected and caught Charlie by surprise.

"Just hold me."

She fell asleep in his arms. He followed soon after.

Charlie's room on Calle 234 faced east toward the street. Since it was on the second floor and the house across the street was a single story, it received the full blast of the morning sun. The double-glazed windows were protected by an ornate wrought iron lattice bolted to the outside of the building. But that did little to block the sunlight. On the inside, pink plastic lace curtains, sliding on an outer rod, did their best to conceal a heavy blackout curtain. The side of the blackout curtain that faced the street was coated with a silver layer to reflect sunlight, and its heat, back through the window.

This morning a shaft of light made its way through a crack between the two halves of the blackout curtain. Vali was asleep, naked, lying on top of the covers. The brilliant beam crossed her back, carrying a hint of pink as it made its way through the outer curtain. Having awakened before her, Charlie propped a pillow behind his back and gazed upon the stranger in his bed. She was lovely, but all the girls—oops, Charlie remembered Horseface—*most* of the girls he had encountered were lovely. All had young and athletic bodies. All were eager to perform. Why was this one so alluring? Why did she exude an irresistible femininity? Why couldn't he gaze into her eyes without his legs turning to Jell-O?

Perhaps it was because she was still a mystery. She hadn't stated her price. They all had a price. Once she did, she could be categorized, compartmentalized, pigeonholed, her place in the relationship immediately defined. Once she asked for money, she was just another whore on the street. A classy whore, one who had a job and spoke English, but a whore nevertheless. The universe would be restored to order. He would be the client. He could tell her when to arrive, when to leave, and decide what position he would like to try next. Life was easier that way.

He wasn't looking for a mutually exclusive relationship. He wasn't looking for a lover, especially a girl from Cuba. He watched her chest rise and fall. He looked at her breasts. He remembered her voice. It was soft and sweet. *No. Impossible.* He would have to be an idiot to fall for a Cuban girl. But this one seemed different. She was trying to better herself, which was in itself a revolutionary idea. Was she the exception?

Charlie's brain fumbled for an answer. It was infatuation, that's all. She was exotic. She had animal magnetism. Look at that butt. It was the ass of a temptress. Infatuation was all right. It was temporary. Episodic. It was like the flu; it came out of nowhere, hung around for a couple days, then disappeared. Therefore, he should enjoy it while it lasts; drink in and luxuriate in the elixir of infatuation. It was harmless. Temporary. Soon it would blow away in the wind and be just another memory.

Having analyzed the quandary and found plausible answers, he felt better, more secure in his autonomy, more in control. When she finally stirred, she briefly opened her sleepy eyes, turned, saw Charlie, smiled, and crawled back to sleep on his chest. When he put his arms around her shoulders his brilliant analysis crashed to the floor.

Man, I am so screwed.

Vali slipped easily into Charlie's apartment, into his shower, and into his heart. Over the summer, they established a pattern. Vali would conduct her daily chores after leaving the apartment in midmorning; helping her mother, doing laundry, shopping, preparing for the next show. Charlie was free until late afternoon. Sometimes, for dinner, they ate in the apartment, usually, however, it was faster and cheaper to go to one of the local restaurants.

The summer stretched on. Vali never asked Charlie for money. She was accepted by the marina police as a *novia*—a girlfriend, falling into another gray area that hung between policy and practicality. The police got used to seeing Vali come and go to the apartment and not just visiting with Charlie. Considering their backgrounds, Jenna and Vali would seem to have little in common, yet they became friends and traveled together, usually to Havana in the peso cabs.

During the day while Vali was at her mother's or off with Jenna, Charlie would occasionally help Esteban with carpentry and tile work. Sometimes Allen tagged along. Charlie and Allen would have colorful conversations with Coco, who knew everyone and seemed to have influence that extended well beyond Jaimanitas— Charlie called it the *Coco Mafia*. When Allen and Jenna had days when they would go exploring, the free time gave Charlie an opportunity to network with other sailors at Hemingway. They were a tight-knit group and through their combined resources knew a lot about Cuba and its ever-shifting policies.

Vali would leave Charlie's apartment to go to work, sometimes not returning until daybreak. Charlie never went to the club to see her perform. He never asked about what she did all night or how impersonating a dead pop star earned her so many American dollars. He just held her when she asked and cursed himself for the small tendrils of hope that unfurled every time she came back to him.

CHAPTER EIGHTEEN

The Colombian film crew was seated at a table near the stage. Vali recognized them instantly as she performed her act. She had been hoping they would return. Eighty-five dollars for fifteen minute's work. She directed her attention toward them, making eye contact and pointing to them seductively at the appropriate time within her song, as Selena often did. She could tell that they, in turn, were focused on her act. Her performance was being critiqued. When she was through, she joined them at their table.

"We have talked with your boss. We would like to hire you to star in our movie. Would you like to be a movie star?"

"Of course, but I have my job here. I can't miss work. What kind of movie? What would I have to do?"

"You are already doing it. Be Selena. Every man in the world fantasizes about Selena. We want to make those fantasies come true. Selena on the beach. Selena in a forest. Selena in a garden of roses. Fantasy. Pure fantasy. Art and fantasy. Classy, it has to be classy. That's what you are already doing through lip sync. We will just help you bring your act to the next level."

For Vali, this was a dream come true. This could be her ticket out of Jaimanitas and off the island forever. Her heart was pounding. Her imagination was running wild. Vali the movie star, discovered in a tiny cabaret west of Havana, now appearing with Brad Pitt in her first Hollywood production. She didn't even think to question if the movie would require her to perform as she had previously. *But wait.*

"I thought you were filming a documentary?"

"We are. We are almost through shooting. Part of a series on Spanish architecture for Bogota Channel 24, RTN Tele Noticias. All the equipment is already here. The sound man, Sebastian, you remember him, microphones, cameras, everything we need. We have put together a script and a storyboard and think you would be perfect."

"How long would it take?"

"Three, maybe four days. We are willing to work around your schedule."

Vali would have acted for free. If it were possible, she would have paid *them*. But this was business, and the Colombians seemed to have a lot of money. She did her best to look disinterested. "How much would this job pay?"

"We have already worked out the details with your boss. If you agree, your share would be twelve hundred dollars. We provide food and drinks. You can keep the clothes we buy you."

Vali did her best not to fall off the chair. "Yes. I will do it for twelve hundred dollars."

"Good, we thought you would. Glad you are aboard. We are going to need a young girl, a girl under fifteen, to work with you. Do you know any young ladies that would like a chance to become an actress?"

"My sister is thirteen."

185

"We would be glad to take a look at her. If we hire her, she would serve in a supporting capacity. We would be willing to pay five hundred dollars if she was suitable for our needs."

Vali found it hard to restrain her enthusiasm. "When do we start?"

***

Four miles west of Baracoa, Rio Tiburon empties into a bay then flows in an ancient channel through the reef into the Atlantic. Before departing the mainland, the river slows, widens, and forms a deep, natural harbor that could easily hold an entire fishing fleet were residents allowed to moor their craft within its protected waters. On the south side of the bay, Playa Banes, a crescent of secluded coral sand accessible via a narrow, winding beach road. At ten thirty the next morning, a rented van bounced its way down the lonely road, speeding up occasionally to avoid getting mired in the soft sand. Waiting for them when they arrived, an old man with a donkey.

Vali and her sister waited. It hadn't taken much for Vali to convince her sister to participate—the money was too good to pass up. Diego removed a camera and tripod from the back of the van, carried it about two hundred feet, and set it in the sand. With the sun at his back, he had a commanding view of the turquoise sea lapping gently on the bleached white sand, behind, the rocky mouth of the inlet and the expanse of open Atlantic. Next to the camera, Matias, the director, set up two folding chairs and a small table beneath a beach umbrella. Sebastian carried a boom box that he placed on the table. Matias led Vali and her sister Rowena to the umbrella and instructed them to remove their clothes, which they folded and placed on the table. They signaled for the donkey, named Pepe and guided by the old man, to be stationed off camera, to the right.

"Now climb up on the donkey," Matias commanded.

Vali tried to mount the animal, but its back was as high as her chin. She ran and launched herself onto Pepe's back but slid off. Without a saddle, there was little to hold on to. The old man cupped his hands as an impromptu stirrup, lifting her as she mounted the hairy back in a precarious straddle.

"Hold onto his mane and try to look relaxed." Matias pushed a button on the boom box. Instantly the sound of "Como La Flor" from the *Entre a Mi Mundo* album blasted from beneath the umbrella. "Start singing and don't stop until I tell you." The old man grabbed the bridal and paraded Pepe and its lip-synching rider in front of the stationary camera. Back and forth they went, under constant direction. Sometimes Vali would look straight ahead, other times into the lens of the camera. "All right, Rowena, get on behind your sister." Vali reached down for Rowena's hand as the old man boosted from her waist, almost jettisoning the tiny girl across the beast's back and onto the sand on the other side.

This part of the movie was in the style of a music video, explained Diego. The film clips being created today were to be woven into a seamless, artistic, musical tapestry.

"Keep singing."

Rowena held onto her sister's waist.

"Play with your sister's nipples."

Rowena hesitated. Though they slept together in the same bed, they touched only by accident. Vali lifted her sister's hand to her breast.

"Now the other one."

Rowena improvised. Giggling out loud, she squeezed and jiggled her sister's exquisite breasts.

Vali did her best to constrain her discomfort. "Does the old man have to be here?"

"Yes. He does. It was part of the deal. No girls, no donkey. Dismount!" Matias said.

The sisters slid off the back of the burro onto the warm sand. Diego approached carrying a can of warm TuKola. He cupped one of Vali's breasts and filled the cup with cola. He did the same to the other. He instructed her to spread her legs. When she did, he splashed cola onto and around her most private of parts. "He loves cola," remarked Diego.

"Who? The old man?"

"No, the donkey. Keep singing!"

She was instructed to stand at the edge the water. The CD belted out "Si Una Vez," the third song on the *Amor Prohibito* album. Vali knew the words and choreography by heart. Pepe's head was positioned by the old man to a point a foot or so in front of her naked, heaving chest. When it caught the scent of its favorite beverage, it lurched forward, sniffed once or twice before it started licking enthusiastically. The nose of the beast, being irrevocably connected with a mass of muscle capable of towing a fully loaded garbage wagon, pushed her backward. She took a step to balance herself, bringing an instant reprimand. "Stand still, stay in frame."

She put one foot back to resist the pressure of the slurping lips and sandpaper tongue. Her chest was soon covered with donkey drool. In order to steady herself, she inadvertently grabbed Pepe's ears, pulling down, which the animal interpreted as a signal to lower its head. When its nose descended below her navel, it discovered the scent of a fresh new source of delicious cola nectar dripping from between her legs. Pepe's tongue twisted and curved all the way to her backside.

"Don't move!" the director yelled. She planted her feet firmly in the sand, leaning against the force exerted against her lower abdomen by the probing nose and prehensile lips of a powerful animal.

In an unexpected move, the donkey nuzzled his way between her legs, lifted its head, and effortlessly raised her off the ground, flipping her on her back. "Perfect!" screamed the director. "Spread your legs. Don't stop singing."

Vali was increasingly uncomfortable, but she kept thinking of the money, only of the money, and how it could be her ticket to a new world. The animal's muscular tongue soon licked clean her entire bikini area, but it didn't stop there. Pepe probed for more cola. Before she could scuttle backward, the donkey stiffened its raspy tongue and drove it straight down the bore to her cervix. She combat-rolled to secure her freedom, gained her footing in the soft sand, and screamed as she covered her snatch and headed for the safety of the umbrella. But her screams fell on deaf ears. Diego, Matias, Sebastian, Rowena, and the old man were rolling on the sand, laughing so hard they could barely breathe.

With Vali off recovering, now it was Rowena's turn. Diego rubbed cola on her budding breasts and slid his hand beneath her legs, slathering TuKola on her undercarriage. The old man held the slobbering donkey until the camera was turned on. Rowena put her hands behind her back and leaned forward, thrusting her little chest forward in anticipation. Pepe sprang into action but zeroed in on a rivulet of cola making its way from her breast to her hip. Rowena recoiled. She was *cosquilloso,* ticklish, and pushed the nose of the beast from her side and stepped backward. She tried again, and again, but no matter how hard, once Pepe's tongue made contact, she was incapacitated by a convulsion of laughter.

Vali returned to find Rowena and the crew taking a break on the beach. Segment two was the Burt Lancaster and Deborah Kerr *From Here To Eternity* beach kiss. Vali was directed to lie in the surf. Diego lifted the camera from its tripod. Sebastian removed his clothes and, under direction, assumed the Lancaster position. They kissed and writhed as waves washed over their entwined bodies. Diego circled, capturing the lovers from a shaky three-hundred-and-sixty-degree point of view. However, Sebastian improved on the classic by making the scene X-rated. They maintained the kiss as she wrapped her legs around his waist. Waves broke over their writhing bodies as the fake Selena made love with the fake Burt Lancaster. It was a difficult scene that demanded numerous retakes. Next Sebastian held the camera while Matias pounded Vali into the sand. Then it was Diego's turn. The sharp coral sand entered her body and made sex painful. Her pussy would heal itself; her poverty would not.

When they were through with Vali, who was beginning to sunburn, they instructed Rowena to assume Deborah Kerr's position. Up until now, the movie making had been in the pursuit of artistic expression. Vali watched as her little sister was being led to the shore.

"Stop!" Vali yelled.

Sebastian seemed startled. Vali insisted, "No sex. She is too young. She is my little sister for God's sake. She is only thirteen years old. We could all get in trouble." Diego looked perplexed. Vali was adamant. "Art is all right. Sex is against the law. She has to be at least sixteen."

Matias took control. "In that case, it's a wrap. Good job, everybody. Be ready to shoot at nine thirty tomorrow morning." He peeled five one-hundred-dollar bills from his money clip and handed them to Vali.

Sand and seawater are poor lubricants. That evening, hoping to facilitate healing, Vali used her mouth to subdue Charlie's throbbing libido. After Vali had presented her mother with more American dollars than any of them had ever held, her mother informed Senora Montoya, the CDR president who lived on the corner only three houses away, since Rowena had *el gripe* it would be wise to keep her out of school for a few days. The next morning the teenager sneaked through the backyard shortcut to rendezvous with her sister at a prearranged pickup spot near Fuster's Street and Avenida Quinta.

The actresses were spirited to a seven-bedroom villa in Vedado. Although there were houses all around, once the high wooden gate was closed behind them, their seclusion was absolute. Vali was lead on a five-minute tour. Dabbled rays of sunlight penetrated an upper canopy of mango and ceiba. Bamboo spanned the distance from the gardens to the lower branches. It was a grand old house of three stories built in the 1930s, with oak floors and a huge coquina fireplace. From the casement windows on the third floor, a commanding view of the Russian embassy. Within the garden was a ten-foot-tall shrine of the Virgin Mary. A mahogany table had been placed before the statue and on the table an upholstered chair. Beside the chair a glass bowl and a bar of soap.

Matias set up the camera. Sebastian loaded the boom box. Vali was instructed to remove her clothes and sit in the chair, a prop microphone in her right hand. Rowena, who was by now also naked, waited off-camera. *Action*! "Bidi Bidi Bon Bon" blared from the small twin speakers, Vali mouthed the words, reenacting as best she could a video of Selena seated in a similar position.

"Now spread your legs." Vali placed her legs on the armrests, looking for all the world as if she was in the doctor's office preparing for a pelvic examination. Rowena approached, carrying a safety razor. She dipped the towel in the bowl of water, worked the soap into a lather, and covered her sister's crotch with the milky brew. Selena never missed a beat. Rowena was instructed to climb upon the table, lean over her sister's leg, and begin shaving her sister's bikini area, which seemed a futile gesture since it had already been well attended only hours before. Vali tried to picture in her mind the image that was being captured by the camera.

People in Colombia must have a twisted sense of art, she thought to herself. *And where are the gowns I was supposed to wear?* But she must be doing something right. Whenever she looked at the Colombians, they seemed most pleased with themselves.

Shooting continued through the day and became increasingly bizarre. Sebastian and Matias began drinking whiskey and insisted that the sisters share in the refreshment. Diego's girlfriend, Marta, arrived unexpectedly and was pressed into service. As Vali lip-synched on the grand piano, Marta used the handle of the microphone as a dildo. Everybody laughed. Drinks were passed around. Then Marta and Vali in the fountain, followed by a sudsy lesbian encounter as they washed the car. More drinks. Vali lost track of time and didn't realize until late afternoon that she hadn't seen her sister in hours. Distressed, she threw on her jeans and T-shirt. She searched the bottom floor, then the second, where she found her little sister passed out on a dirty mattress.

No matter how hard she was shaken, Rowena would not wake up.

"What did you do to her?" Vali demanded.

Diego's voice was calm and reassuring, "She just had a little too much to drink. She must have wandered upstairs and gone to sleep. She will be all right by ten o'clock tomorrow when we begin shooting. I will give you the rest of your money then."

The sisters were dropped off at the bus stop in Jaimanitas. Rowena had resumed consciousness but could barely walk. She was still groggy at ten the next morning and couldn't remember how she'd gotten to the room where Vali had found her. They still made it to the rendezvous spot on time.

They waited for two hours before they realized they would never see the Colombians again.

CHAPTER NINETEEN

S unday. The day of the big fight. Rusty had been in training for a month. During the previous week, he had been launched repeatedly into the air, a maneuver designed to strengthen his wing muscles. The handlers rode with Rusty between them in the back seat. They smelled of chickens and earth and sweat. Vali was in the middle of the front seat. The usually loquacious driver was uncharacteristically subdued, eyes straight ahead, a two-handed death grip on the steering wheel. Vali looked at Esteban, then back, quizzically at Charlie, who shrugged his shoulders.

They drove for forty-five minutes to a place by a river, south of Havana. From the parking area, they entered an amphitheater hidden by a thick wall of majestic royal palms. The trees, Charlie guessed, were at least fifty years old, attesting to the venerability of this palea. Unlike bouts in the nearby Club Gallístico Deportivo Alcona de Cuba, this was an unsanctioned arena. The attendees, numbering perhaps two hundred, flaunting the "gray area" of Cuban law—statutorily illegal but prosecutorially ignored.

Blankets were spread on the ground near the entrance. On the blankets an odd assortment of consumer goods: toothpaste, a baby doll, cans of creamed corn, a colorful toy helicopter—items pilfered from warehouses or intercepted in the supply chain of the dollar stores. Tethered birds, waiting their turn to fight, circled stakes impaling the rock-hard red earth. A scale dangled before a tally board where the weights of the birds were recorded in pounds and ounces. Beer and whiskey were sold from a hut near the perimeter, next to another selling a combo platter of *pollo frito, arroz blanco* and *frijoles negro*; fried chicken, white rice, and black beans. Under a nearby roof was a long table. The sound of dominoes being smashed into play echoed through the trees. Galleros held their fighters at eye level before the spectators, seated on wooden stools and benches. Each supervised as a spur of tortoiseshell, sharp as a needle, augmented and enhanced the spur that was provided by nature. Applying the spur with a combination of glue, wax, and cotton thread required experience and was the subject of much discussion.

Esteban watched as a spur was attached to the back of each of Rusty's legs. He was slated to fight in the eleventh round of competition. He needed to be ready. With time-outs, a bout between two birds of equal skill could go on for about twenty minutes. Others could be over in less than sixty seconds. After Rusty was weighted, he would be checked by a veterinarian for signs of powders or ointments applied to wings or spurs—poisons used occasionally by handlers intended to cripple, kill, or blind an opponent.

Vali led Charlie through the throng to the entrance of the corrugated metal building that housed the arena—a Mad Max Thunderdome of welded rebars, pulleys, ropes, and a bolted iron referee chair that rolled over the combatants on trussed metal rails. The cockpit was eighteen feet in diameter, with walls two feet high. The floor was moistened sawdust. Wooden planks wired to concentric rows of interwoven steel provided spectators with a tenuous perch. The stands were separated by a walkway of about four feet from the edge of the pit. During competition, the walkway was reserved for galleros and owners.

Betters were cleared from the ring as the first bout was beginning. Handlers carried their charges to the center of the ring in small wooden boxes then removed the birds and thrust them, time and again, at each other. This preparation worked the birds into a frenzy and went on for several minutes. Even at this preliminary stage of the bout, betters watched for subtle clues in the bird's behavior, hoping to gain an advantage. Boisterous spectators covered the *pelea*'s central ring, hurrying to place their bets with each other, haggling over the amounts. Referees cleared the crowd, and the birds were placed on the ground facing each other in the center of the ring and released. Rumors abounded about the amount of money being bet. Even Charlie could see hundreds of dollars exchanging hands between participants.

Whap! Within an instant, the combatants were lost in a whirlwind of dust and feathers, rolling in the dirt, rising into the air. The lowly yard birds had magically transformed themselves into magnificent war eagles, slashing at each other with deadly intent and equally lethal talons. All parts of the animal seemed to be brought into play and weaponized simultaneously—their wings slapped and inflicted body blows, claws on their feet lashed out in an effort to blind their opponent, spurs ready to impale, and beaks landed blows with deadly accuracy to the back of the head. Charlie wondered about the schoolboy taunt—*chicken, are you a chicken*?—where did that come from? Obviously, the originator of the phase had never seen roosters in combat. The birds were fearless, ferocious, with the hearts of tigers and the speed of cobras. He'd never seen anything like it.

The cacophony of spectators reverberated within the metal shell. Handlers blasted words of encouragement to their protégés. Charlie tried to remember if he'd seen earplugs for sale on any of the blankets. The birds tired quickly. One fell on its side, its wing sprawled uselessly above its head. The other swooped in, trying to land a death blow. Just as quickly, the underdog sprang to its feet and flapped its way to a superior position above its attacker's head, its spurs jabbing at its opponent's neck and shoulders. Those betting on the upper bird went wild, standing on their feet and yelling encouragement, but in seconds the tables turned again, and the other half of the spectators cheered for their champion.

The birds whirled to a virtual draw and laid down beside each other, bleeding and exhausted. A signal was given. The galleros lifted their birds, wiping blood from their eyes and cleaning debris from their nostrils. They blew into their noses to supercharge them with oxygen. The birds seemed to recover quickly. A cage suspended from a wire was lowered into the ring. Inside were compartments for the two birds, separated by a partition. When placed inside, the birds could not see each other. When the box was lifted, the cocks seemed startled as a previously invisible opponent materialized before their very beaks. Programming kicked in, and they immediately lunged at each other with renewed vigor.

In seven minutes, the battle had been decided. One bird had lost the ability to protect the back of its head, the other doing its best to break through its skull into the brain cavity. The champion strutted over the wheezing body of its vanquished rival, stopping occasionally to deliver a triumphant death peck. The losing gallero, who had never been more than a few feet away, picked up and cradled his bleeding bird before it was finished off, the cockfighting equivalent of throwing in the towel.

Eighteen more birds entered the ring. Nine were declared victorious. There were no ties. The audience rotated as bets were wagered and settled. But after the tenth round, the stadium filled. Looking through the entrance, Charlie could see that vendors had left their stands, players had put down their dominoes, and virtually everyone was trying to make their way into the arena. The referees waited for the crowd to work its way into every inch of the palea. Charlie waited for the stands to come crashing down around himself and Vali. There was an unexpected air of excitement in the spectators, anticipation—everyone was hushed. It made no sense. This was just fight number eleven, to be followed by ten more before the day was done. But something was different.

Vali leaned to her side and spoke with the man beside her. When she looked back at Charlie, her face was white. She grabbed his arm and cradled it on her leg, staring silently into the ring before them. Into the walkway strode a face Charlie had seen before—the Movie Star. It was Tony, dressed in a gray sport coat. Next to him was his handler, followed by Esteban's gallero, then an anxious looking, disheveled Esteban. Tony's handler displayed his pure white bird to the spectators. *Balto, Balto*, the crowd cheered. They knew the bird. They knew Tony. *Damn*, thought Charlie, *Balto is a movie star also.*

Handlers held the birds like lances and jabbed at each other. The atmosphere had turned electric. The tension was palpable. Something was different. The referee gave the signal, and both birds were half thrown, half dropped toward each other in the center of the ring. They ran at each other and met in a blur that was too fast for the eye to follow. The birds rolled, slashed, stabbed so quickly Charlie had no idea if one was gaining an advantage over the other. The crowd, however, gleaned nuances from each and every microsecond of the confrontation, their collective voices rising and falling on subtleties lost to the Yuma. Owners are allowed to coach their birds. They hovered agilely nearby, careful not to interfere with the fight, which could be grounds for disqualification. Esteban's voice rose above that of a hundred spectators, delivering instructions and encouragement to Rusty. Tony did the same for his bird.

The avian gladiators attacked with relentless ferocity for a full five minutes. Both their heads were covered with blood. Vali pointed with her finger. "Watch the blood. It gets into their eyes and blinds them."

Blood oozed from Balto's neck and head. He rolled onto his side for a second. When Rusty delivered a peck to the side of his vulnerable head, Balto burst to a superior position, flipping over in the air and landing in pecking position on Rusty's back. Charlie was impressed. "Balto was playing possum. He lured Rusty in," he lamented.

The action entered a second phase where the fighters conserved their energy and stalked each other, calculating the appropriate time, the perfect trajectory, to deliver the death spur. They jockeyed for position, their heads entwined and twisting like snakes as they each sought to land a beak on the vulnerable spot on the back of the head. When Rusty was able to push Balto's head below his, he capitalized on the advantage and mustered the energy to launch an aerial attack. Thirty seconds later, Balto would turn the tables and do the same, stabbing from above with his stiletto tortoise spine. It was an aerial knife fight.

After twelve minutes, both combatants were exhausted. The match was lasting longer than any of the previous ones. The birds lay down side by side on the moist sawdust, mirror images, their feet dangling uselessly to their side, breathing heavily to renew their depleted oxygen reserves. Then, as if alerted by a bell only they could hear, they would snap to attention and bash away at each other for another ten or fifteen seconds. Energy expended, they fell to the ground, gasping for breath once again. There was never a hint, a sign, the slightest suggestion, that either Rusty or Balto was considering disengaging from the battle. On the contrary, they pushed through exhaustion to continue thrashing away at their foe.

They had the souls of true warriors and reminded Charlie of Captain Ahab's words that defined single-minded obsession, or was it Khan?—"To the last, I grapple with thee; from hell's heart I stab at thee; for hate's sake, I spit my last breath at thee." They were relentless, focused, resolute. Their determination was admirable. They were preprogrammed to take the life of their opponent, alpha males of the highest order.

Handlers scooped them up, held them at eye level for about five seconds before returning them to the sawdust floor, face-to-face, to reengage in the contest. They would fight until utterly exhausted. The skirmishes degenerated into a slugfest as each bird dug deep to find the energy for another blow. Energy spent, one would lie down to recharge his battery, which prompted the other to attack. When they were both down, they would be cradled once again by their handlers then be placed face-to-face to carry on. It was an even match. The fifth or sixth time—Charlie had lost count—they met in combat, Rusty lost his balance and started to fall backward. Balto launched as Rusty struggled to regain his footing. He propelled himself to a height of two feet, into the perfect position, rotating backward, wings flapping furiously, concentrating every ounce of energy on the tip of the blood-soaked spur that he drove into Rusty's neck. It caught the carotid artery. Blood squirted. Rusty rolled onto his side, never to move again. Vali squeezed Charlie's arm. It was all over.

By the time they reached the car, Esteban was already behind the wheel. He was shaking. He could not talk. Vali slid into the middle. When Charlie started to speak, she hurriedly put her hand over his mouth. Before they reached the hard road, tears were streaming from Esteban's eyes. He pulled to the side, cradling his head in his arms, sobbing. He looked scornfully at Charlie. "You don't understand, do you?"

"Rusty was a hell of a bird. I know you are going to miss him." Charlie was at a loss as to how to comfort his friend.

"You know nothing! We played for the debt," sobbed Esteban.

"You mean the $18,000 you owe Tony?" Charlie was aghast.

"Yes. The $18,000. Double or nothing. I owe Tony $36,000."

Charlie had known that Esteban had bet on the fight, but not that he'd had everything riding on this. Win, and he would have cleared his debt. Lose, and he lost it all. Charlie thought of Esteban's wife and child and wondered if his wife knew how deep he was now in debt. Charlie—a tourist, an American, a man with the ability to sail off at a moment's notice—couldn't fully fathom what this meant for Esteban.

CHAPTER TWENTY

O ne morning, shortly after Vali left for the day, Vali's mother entered the apartment and slumped onto the couch. She explained to Charlie that she was exhausted, having had been up all night. Vali's younger sister had been vomiting since midnight. "I came to see if Vali had left yet. No matter. Probably something Rowena ate," opined Nicole as Charlie prepared a cup of coffee

"Does her stomach hurt?" he asked.

"Yes, she is in a lot of pain."

Before heading out to sea, Charlie had purchased a small book, no bigger than a pamphlet, specific to sailors and the treatment of medical emergencies that might be encountered far from professional medical assistance. *The Sailor's Guide to Common Illnesses* described the setting of broken limbs, puncture wounds, the treatment for severe sunburn and other common maladies that might befall the unfortunate mariner. Charlie located it in the luggage he'd brought into the apartment, and he retrieved it, finding the page that dealt with appendicitis.

Charlie scanned the page. "Is her pain localized? I mean, does it hurt all over or in a certain part of her body?"

"It's her right side. She keeps clutching her right side." Nicole imitated her daughter, her hands encircling a spot above her right hip.

Warning bells were going off in Charlie's head. The little girl might be in trouble. "Take me to her. There's a test."

Rowena's room was dark and smelled of vomit. She was curled on her side, obviously in pain, her face hovering over a metal wastebasket. The child was frightened, tired, her underwear stained from bouts of diarrhea. She offered no resistance when Charlie laid her flat on the bed. Placing two fingers above her underwear, four inches to the right of her navel, he applied firm and steady pressure.

"Does that hurt?"

She said nothing. He pushed harder, hard enough to be uncomfortable to someone who wasn't sick. He then withdrew his fingers, quickly, as quick as swatting a fly, but in reverse. The kid shrieked in pain.

He turned to Nicole. "That's called rebound tenderness. It's a test for appendicitis. I am not a doctor, but the book says she needs a doctor, and she needs one immediately. Can you call an ambulance?"

Nicole shot him a look.

"OK, then a car, any car." Nicole went to the street and shouted to her neighbors. Five minutes later, a peso cab arrived at the door. Rowena was washed with a cloth, wrapped in a bedsheet and placed in the back seat, bucket at the ready.

Charlie wondered how they could get word to Vali. She would be at work by now. They could send someone from the neighborhood. Vali would want to be by her sister's side. "Nicole," he started, "can someone get a message to Vali at the club?"

Nicole shook her head vehemently. "She is practicing. Her job cannot be risked."

Charlie knew that what Nicole was really saying was the *American dollars* that Vali brought home couldn't be risked. He had the urge to argue but refrained. "Can I come?" he asked.

Nicole grabbed a baseball cap and snugged it onto Charlie's head. "Today you are not a Yuma; you are a Cuban. Keep your mouth shut."

He had heard the hype, free medical care, the best doctors in the world. He wanted to see for himself. Further, as a practical matter, it seemed a good idea to know the location of the nearest hospital.

The taxi took them through Siboney, past Esteban's house on the hill, to a three-story military hospital that overlooked a wooded ravine in Marianao.

The hospital was probably state of the art during the 1950s, the swept-back concrete entrance attesting to a time when space travel was manifest in both automobile fins and medical architecture. But it hadn't been painted since; once light-green, the paint was now chipped away to show the bare concrete. What little paint that was left was mottled with mold. Rowena, doubled over in pain, was led up the steps through the main entrance. The doors, four wide, were perpetually open. The waiting area looked more like a bus terminal in a bad part of town. The tile floor was chipped and filthy. Flies plagued the two dozen suffering citizens waiting stoically on flimsy plastic chairs. Fluorescent lights hung in disrepair. A dog wandered in, seated itself in the corner and began scratching at fleas. Chunks of concrete from the ceiling above the waiting area were missing. *Did they land on the patients?* Charlie wondered.

To the left of the entrance an admitting desk. It was large, perhaps twenty feet across, its dark plywood veneer ripped and shredded. It was designed for an admitting staff of four or five, but today it was vacant. Charlie looked for a doctor or a nurse, anyone in a white coat. It was an emergency. A little girl was sick—the sister of the woman he loved. There should have been doctors. There should have been nurses. Nicole led her daughter to a seat in the third row, placing the bucket between her baby's legs. She sat beside her daughter, waiting to be admitted.

After twenty minutes, a sullen woman with a clipboard appeared and assigned Rowena a number. A woman in the front row was led to a corridor. The waiting continued. Charlie was aghast. If he had been in America, Rowena would have had a flurry of hospital staff around her. Charlie looked at the young girl's face, so much like a younger version of Vali's, and felt sick himself. Rowena was in danger. If it was her appendix, it could rupture at any time.

Seeing that security was as lax as medical staff, Charlie lowered his cap and ventured into one of the corridors. He waited to be challenged. Along the corridor were doors and benches. The benches were overflowing with patients, and many sat on the floor. As he passed the doors, which were open, he saw what seemed to be doctors doing examinations, poking and prodding their patients on stainless steel gurneys as others within the room watched, awaiting their turns. The examination rooms were Spartan—a desk, a row of plastic chairs, a shiny metal table under a bank of dusty jalousie windows. Within the corridor, a single public bathroom, the contents of its toilet oozing its way under the door and into the hallway. The signs above—maternity, cancer, X-rays had little or no relevance to the events that seemed to be taking place within.

If this is the hospital, I would hate to see one of their prisons.

The corridor to the left was the same—a bus terminal with doctors. Perhaps the lower levels were strictly diagnostic. Since he seemed to be invisible, he continued to press his luck. What could they do? Throw him out? People probably wondered if he was a doctor. The elevator was broken, so he walked to the second floor. A poorly lit waiting area mirrored its counterpart below. The halls were lined with plate glass windows. Beds were made of simple metal tubes with iron bedsprings. Around each bed, family and friends attended to patients, some of whom were interacting, while others looked dead. Charlie paused and stood in a patient's doorway. Here, too, the windows were open to the outside.

Bugs, what do they do about bugs? he wondered.

To his surprise, he was waved inside a room by a cheerful family. An elderly woman lay before them, arms waving as she amused her visitors with a story. It was a family reunion, and they were making the best of it. She reminded him of his mother, whom he had attended on several occasions when she'd been in Jacksonville Memorial. It occurred to him that something was missing. He remembered his mom's hospital bed and compared the mental image to the scene before him. There were no electronics, no oxygen or oxygen monitor, no PCA for self-administered pain relief, no call buttons to alert the nonexistent staff, no heart monitor, and the IV solution seemed to be hooked directly into her vein without a microdrip adjustment.

He was incensed. He wished he had brought his camera. The world had been duped. He, too, had been taken in. Cuba—his paradise, his summer escape—he found that he had wanted to believe it was true. It was comforting to think that in exchange for sacrificing material gains and upward mobility, for buying into forty years of revolutionary bullshit, for a lifetime of dependency and suffering, the least the government could do was lavish upon its subjects the best health care in the world. It made sense. Quid pro quo. Pot of gold at the end of the rainbow. If they didn't get good health care, what did they get out of the deal? It wasn't just a humanitarian argument; health care was the birthright of every citizen, part of their pact, their deal with Castro's government, codified and articulated in the Cuban constitution and printed for all to see on a faded sign above the reception desk:

Article 50

Everybody has the right to health protection and care. The State guarantees this right;

- By providing free medical and hospital care by means of the installations of the rural medical service network, polyclinics, hospitals and preventive and specialist treatment centers;
- By providing free dental care;
- By promoting the health publicity campaigns, health education, regular medical examinations, general vaccinations and other measures to prevent the outbreak of disease. All of the population cooperates in these activities and plans through social and mass organizations.

—Fidel Castro

Health care was free, and they were getting their money's worth.

The surgical floor was located one story above. Charlie had seen the signs. Though it was improbable that he would make it into the surgical ward, he was going to persevere until he was stopped. Upon reaching the top of the stairs, he was stunned to find another waiting room, filled with the same glassy-eyed people on the same flimsy plastic chairs. Surgical floor? Must be a mistake. No. This was it. Third floor. The belly of the beast. What should have been the sterile inner sanctum of any hospital was a carbon copy of the floors below. Same open windows. Same filthy floor. A monument to disease and cross-contamination. Now he was angry. This was past negligence; this was criminal.

Swinging stainless steel doors sealed a corridor labeled *Unidad de Cuidados Intensivos*—the ICU. The doors should, of course, be locked with access controlled by an attendant. He pushed.

They opened. The corridor was much the same as the one below it, with glass windows and casement doors—cheerless, faded, industrial. The scene reminded Charlie of Mathew Brady's daguerreotypes of the American Civil War surgical field hospitals that depicted patched and bleeding soldiers lying in rudimentary beds, desperately clinging to life. He remained unchallenged. In the middle of the hall was a sign above a door that proclaimed, *"Sala quirúrgica."* Charlie had stumbled upon the operating theater.

The door was open; he stood at the threshold and looked in. The windows had been blacked out with paint, sealed shut with industrial caulking. A three-section stainless steel operating table stood in the middle of the room, surrounded by a ring of lights suspended from the ceiling. Paint above the table was peeling, exposing the raw, cracked concrete. On the wall was a collection of surgical instruments: a saw, a drill, a selection of forceps and hemostats. Below, a deep gray plastic sink. He had seen that sink before—they sell them at Home Depot. A green bottle of oxygen was strapped to a handcart. Next to it a heart monitor on an extension cord. There were doctors here. At least he thought they were doctors—they were better dressed, carrying charts, and they had an air of professionalism. And they were young, perhaps only a couple years older than he was.

Heart thudding, Charlie hurried down the stairs to rescue Nicole and Rowena. "We have to get her out of here."

Large drops of perspiration were streaming down Nicole's face and neck. Some of the front-row sitters had disappeared, hinting at advancement.

"There has to be better hospitals than this one."

Nicole shook her head, as resolute as she had been about not sending word to Vali. "Impossible. I am assigned to this hospital. Same as the bodegas, this is my hospital. You go now. We will be fine."

Charlie hesitated. What would Vali think of him if he just left her mother and her sister?

It was good to be out of the hospital and into the sunshine again. A line of peso cabs was waiting at the entrance. He had learned to haggle for a price before he was in the car. The driver asked for his destination, and suddenly Vali's words from their first lunch leaped into his mind. *I want you to promise that you will never come to the Cecilia.*

The trip to the marina cost forty cents. He climbed aboard the vessel of his new friend Arthur, still recovering from his experience with the police and their dog.

"Charlie! You just missed Jenna and Allen. You headed back to the *Bora Bora*?"

"I need a drink. I just took a little girl to the hospital. I think she has appendicitis," Charlie blurted.

Arthur winced. "You saw the hospital? You wouldn't want to take your worst enemy to a Cuban hospital. They don't have drugs. Since 1992, they don't have many doctors."

"Right. I heard that before. They seemed to be short staffed."

"It's ironic." Arthur gestured with his hand to the west, "There is a world-class medical school down the road in Baracoa. They crank out doctors by the thousands. Literally, this country has the highest doctor ratios in the world. Something like one out of every one hundred fifty Cubans is turned into doctors. This island is a doctor machine. Fidel sends them to Venezuela in exchange for oil. Some are sent to Africa and Central America for PR and propaganda. This is where the Venezuelans come when they get sick. They get treated in special hospitals, and the care is pretty good. Some kind of a deal with Chavez."

"All the doctors I saw seemed to be young."

"Interns," Arthur explained, which just made Charlie's anxiety spike higher. Arthur continued. "Once they graduate, it's off to Venezuela or Angola or some other socialist shitbox. Do your friends have money for drugs?"

"I don't know. Why?"

"You may want to help them buy drugs. If the little girl really has appendicitis, she is going to need painkillers. She will need opioids, morphine, oxi, but they are very difficult to find. Aleve or Tylenol will probably be the best you can get."

"What do you do when you get sick?" asked Charlie.

"You have two choices. If you have insurance, you can go to Cira Garcia Clinic in Havana. It's on a military base, and they won't let regular Cubans in, just the Communist Party bigwigs. They have real doctors there, medical tourism and all that. But if you are really sick, get your ass on the plane to Nassau then Miami or New York."

Charlie returned to the apartment at four thirty, prepared a drink, and dragged a chair into the cage. He had an unobstructed view of the street and enjoyed watching the neighbors go about their business. He noticed an unusual amount of activity in and around the street. Tentatively, people started approaching the cage. He shifted his chair to get a better look. Neighbors started a growing pile on in front of his apartment—a plastic bag filled with toiletries, bedding, a pillow, rags, food, and bottled water.

A woman approached with a bundle and, once empty-handed, headed toward the street. Charlie leaped up to intercept her. *"Desculpame, que pasa?" What's going on?*

With her hand, she made a gesture of knife slicing her abdomen. "Surgery. Rowena is having surgery. These things are for Vali's family. She stays here, yes?"

Before Charlie could answer, a yellow Lada squealed to a stop in the street. And as if by magic, Vali was there. She said something to the driver of the Lada in Spanish, and the driver, an older man, placed the boxes and bags in the trunk. A small crowd gathered around the car. Vali turned toward Charlie's apartment, and the Lada sped off, taking three neighborhood women along as passengers.

Vali's wild eyes landed on Charlie. Her makeup was streaked—she had obviously been crying. He opened his mouth to explain, to tell her why he hadn't been the one to come to the Cecilia to tell her about Rowena, but his words caught in his throat. He wasn't sure if she was angry with him. So he just stood there, at a loss. He didn't have to wait long for his answer. Vali barreled into him, burying her face in his chest. Her sobs wet the front of his shirt, and she clutched at him desperately.

The next afternoon, he returned to the ICU with Vali. Rowena shared a room with three other patients, each surrounded by family members. His diagnosis had been correct. Surgeons had removed the inflamed appendix before it had had a chance to burst and spread bacterially infected fecal matter into her peritoneal cavity. Surgeons had injected the site of the four-inch incision with local anesthesia, which, after twelve hours, had worn off. Rowena clutched the bedsheets, afraid to move, white, and paralyzed with pain. Charlie had expected to find an IV drip carrying morphine or Demerol or something, anything to get her through the next forty-eight hours. But she was on her own.

"What are they doing for her pain?" Vali asked, her face as anguished as her sister's.

Nicole reached into her purse and produced a tin of *asperina*—aspirin and shook her head. Vali had produced precious American dollars and sent two of the neighbors, armed with prescriptions, to canvass the local pharmacies in search of oxycodone. Charlie wondered if the Venezuelans were receiving pain medication, but the answer was obvious: of course, they were—they had value, in oil. Even Hugo Chavez wouldn't enter into a deal where his citizens were denied medication. Cubans, on the other hand, were expendable. In flagrant disregard of the provisions

209

enumerated in the Cuban constitution and plastered on the entrance wall downstairs, if they could not pay for and provide their own drugs, they were out of luck.

In the hope that more dollars would be more persuasive, Charlie set out on his own desperate search for pain medication. Enlisting the help of a peso cab driver, he inquired in pharmacies large and small throughout Miramar, Playa, and even Jaimanitas, without results. As an incentive, he offered to pay five American dollars for every pill of Oxycontin or Vicodin, up to forty pills. For contact information, he left his name, address on Calle 234, and Coco's telephone number. He returned to the apartment after a futile afternoon.

Vali wasn't far behind him, walking into the apartment shortly before six, carrying groceries. Lying in bed after dinner, he told her about his search and the lengths he had gone to.

"You did what? That was a stupid thing to do. You must think before you act. Now everybody from here to Havana knows there is an American looking for drugs."

Charlie frowned. He countered, "I told them it was not for me. If they investigate, they will know I am trying to help a little girl, trying to do what the doctors should have done in the first place."

"You can't help," Vali admonished. "There is a way to do things, a way to avoid notice. The people I sent for medicine know how the system works. The police, they don't investigate. They show up, put you in the back of police car, and bring you to jail. It might be months before you tell your story to a judge, and when you do, they are not going to believe you. Even if they did believe, it would make no difference. Those drugs you tried to find are narcotics; they require a special prescription. Just trying to obtain them without a prescription is against the law. Maybe Coco could help you, maybe not. You were stupid. You can never bring attention to yourself."

The next morning at ten o'clock, a white medical van pulled to a stop in front of Vali's house. With the help of Charlie, Rowena, stooped in pain and clutching her stomach, was led from the van and into her bedroom. Nicole, Vali, and a circle of friends surrounded the young girl.

Charlie spent the next three days with Esteban at his house, mixing mortar and laying tiles. On the third day, Vali brought them lunch. Charlie hadn't seen her since Rowena had come home, but he could tell from the pallor on Vali's face that things weren't good.

"What's the news?" He tried to sound casual.

"She has a fever. Can you come?" Her voice was so small, and Charlie could see that the brave front that she normally wore was crumbling under the weight of her sister's slow recovery.

Charlie arrived at Vali's house on Friday morning, a full five days after the operation. Nicole was attending her little girl. Towels had been placed on Rowena's body, and on the towels were bags of ice. Vali had explained on the ride over that Nicole was trying to bring down Maria's temperature, working on the assumption that her daughter had caught a cold during her stay in the hospital. Her fever had spiked during the night and was now above 103. Neither Vali nor her mother had gotten much sleep over the past week, and Nicole appeared no longer in her right mind. Charlie removed the gauze bandages and recoiled at the sight—the incision was oozing and surrounded by an angry red glow.

"That wasn't there six hours ago," mumbled Nicole.

Charlie mobilized the neighbors, sending one to fetch a cab, another armed with a twenty-dollar bill for antibiotics from the *farmacia* near Coco's house. Within an hour Rowena was back in the same ICU. Charlie watched as nurses hooked her to an IV drip of plain saline. There was no pain medication. She received no antibiotics, and none could be obtained from the farmacia, even with Charlie's money. Rowena went into septic shock and was pronounced dead at two fifteen in the morning

CHAPTER TWENTY-ONE

"What in the world was that?" Charlie was jolted out of bed as blows on the wrought iron cage reverberated throughout the concrete structure. He had just barely fallen asleep, restless, his mind racing after the events of the previous few days. Flipping on the light, he was surprised to find Esteban pacing nervously on the sidewalk.

"What's up Esteban? It's three o'clock in the morning." The guard looked on.

"Come with me. I need your help. Bring your fish knife, the big one, and your sharpener."

Wiping the sleep from his eyes, Charlie stumbled into the kitchen for his razor-sharp fifteen-inch Forschner. "You think it might be a little late for fishing? What's going on?"

Esteban ignored the question. "And your flashlight. Bring your flashlight. Put on a dark shirt. Do you have a black one?" Like a robot, Charlie complied, retrieving his flashlight from the nightstand beside his bed. He slipped on his dark-blue T-shirt.

"Put on your sneakers and get into my car." Charlie had wanted to stay at the apartment in case Vali showed up and needed him, but he was going along out of sheer curiosity at this point. They crossed Avenida Quinto and headed south past the outskirts of Jaimanitas into the darkness of the *campo*.

Esteban drove quickly, silently, both hands on the wheel, a crazed look in his eye. Within minutes, Charlie was lost and disoriented. Esteban was sullen, focused, noncommunicative. Charlie noticed the handle of an ax resting on the floorboard next to his left leg. He thought it strange. With the beam of his flashlight, he followed the handle down to the floor. The head of the ax was covered in blood.

"Esteban, there's blood on you ax. That's not normal."

The springs of the old Chevy creaked as they took corners at a high speed. After twenty minutes, they turned from the main road to a dirt secondary. Then a rutted farm road. On the left side of the road a barbed wire fence. Charlie noticed it was different. Unlike the other fences which were little more than rusty strands of wire draped from trees grown along the edge of fields and pastures, this fence was new, set on pressure-treated posts, its wire glinting in the headlights.

The road terminated at a T intersection. The fence had followed the road almost to the intersection, where it ended in a cross-member terminal structure. They stopped at a double metal gate set at a forty-five-degree angle to the corner. Like the fence, the gate was new, shiny, secured in the middle by a chain with a padlock. The fence then turned left, along the side of the pasture, adjacent to a road that disappeared into the darkness. They crossed through the intersection and went off-road, rolling through high weeds. Esteban braked, put the car in reverse and backed into a thicket. Thorns raked the old car as it pushed into the dense vegetation.

With the lights and engine switched off they were, for all practical purposes, invisible. The driver grabbed the ax, pushed his door shut, and stepped into the darkness. "Don't slam the door!" he whispered.

Charlie pushed the button on the handle and gently latched the door.

"And don't forget your knife," Esteban reminded.

Esteban hurried his way through the weeds, headed for the intersection. Charlie stumbled behind him, wondering how he'd found his way. Charlie was perplexed. The situation demanded an explanation, but none was forthcoming. Esteban seemed possessed. Focused. On a mission.

"Talk to me, Esteban."

Esteban hesitated. His thoughts were scattered, defuse, his answers unintelligible.

"They feed the cows at the gate."

"Who feeds what? Are you drunk?"

"The children. I see them. They pull grass from the roadside and feed it to the cows through the gate."

"What cows? What gate?"

The intersection came into view, the white sand on the road glowing in the starlight.

"Felix was going to help me, he has a tow truck with a hoist, but she ran away."

"Who ran away?"

"The cow, a boy cow, a—" Esteban searched for the word in English.

"A bull or a steer. If a bull has its nuts cut off, it's called a steer," Charlie supplied.

"A steer. He was supposed to help me with the steer. But it ran away."

"It wasn't supposed to run away?" Charlie had to pry the information from his friend.

"No, it was supposed to be dead."

"And you were going to lift the dead cow over the fence with the tow truck. Got it. Sounds like a plan. And this affects me how?"

"We need to find it."

"The truck?"

"No. The cow."

Charlie was trying to put the pieces together. "So the cow was supposed to be waiting for you and Felix patiently at the gate?"

"Yes."

"And why would a cow do that? Are you now a cow whisperer or have a magical control over cows?" As his eyes adjusted to the dark, Charlie could see they were approaching the gate. "Once again, tell me why the cow should be waiting at the gate."

"Valium. Two hundred of them."

"Shit. How did you slip it to him?"

"Mixed in with the grass. Just like the children do."

"What color is it—the steer?"

"Black. I gave him the valium around eleven o'clock. I waited for an hour. Nothing happened. I thought it would just fall down, and I would slit its throat. But it didn't. So, I put grass on this side of the fence. When it put its head through, I hit it with my ax." Esteban raised his ax in mock slaughter. "I hit it good. Just above the eyes. Look at the blood."

"Did you consider a rope? Tying a rope around its neck, secured to a post, before you smashed its head?"

Esteban was silent.

"You really didn't think this through, did you?"

Esteban ignored this question, too. "Come on. We've got to find it."

Charlie looked into the darkness, "How many black cows are out there?"

"Maybe twenty." Esteban threw the ax and followed it over the gate. Charlie climbed and jumped to the other side.

"You know, this sort of thing is frowned upon in America. I think the farmer can legally shoot us."

"These cows aren't owned by farmers."

Charlie got a bad feeling. "Who owns them?"

"Fidel. He owns all the cows."

"Communist cows." Charlie found the unlikely scenario amusing, but he was also starting to get the picture that Esteban was up to something seriously nefarious. He was about to refuse to go further without knowing the full details of whatever scheme had been hatched, but just as they entered the pasture, headlights appeared. There was no cover, so they ran toward the middle of the pasture. At the last moment, they lay flat on the ground. Charlie's cheek rested on the pungent earth. "Esteban, do you know what is brown and sounds like a bell? Answer: dung. I think we are laying in cow shit."

The truck was bouncing its way up the road that led to the left, toward the intersection. It slowed, rounded the corner, and rambled east into the loom of lights above Havana, perhaps twenty miles away. Up until now, Charlie had internalized the foray as a prank, a college stunt. But lying face down in the shadows, hiding from headlights, he with a knife, his friend with a bloody ax, in a communist country he wasn't even supposed to visit, it no longer felt like a joke.

As they moved through the blackness, they could hear hooves pounding the hard ground as an invisible herd stampeded around them. Black forms, blacker than the night, formed a wary perimeter as they moved through the open space.

"Exactly how are we supposed to catch one of these animals?"

"Look for the slow one."

But each seemed nimbler than the next. All seemed in top form as they fled to a safe distance. Racing cows. They would bolt a few quick steps, turn, and snort. *My God*, thought Charlie, *what if one of these monsters is a bull? Or two? Or three? We would never see it coming. And if we did, there is no place to hide. We would be stomped flat as a flitter. Or gored. What the hell are we doing out here?*

And then, quite by accident, they stumbled over the dead steer. Charlie fell to his knees and ran his hands over the animal's back. "It's huge. It's the size of a Buick!" he whispered.

"We need to get it into the car," Esteban insisted.

"It won't fit in the car. Can't we just leave it?" Charlie was getting nervous. It would soon be dawn.

"No. I need the money the steer will bring. We need the tow truck."

Realization dawned slowly on Charlie. By now they were in the middle of the pasture, several hundred yards from the gate in the corner, slightly nearer the fence to the west. Their travels had taken them toward a row of wooden farmhouses bordering the far edge of the pasture. Above the silhouette of the roofs and palm trees, he could see his old friend the Southern Cross. Charlie estimated it at eighteen to twenty degrees above the horizon. It had reached its zenith on the twenty-second of June. Then, night after night, it would lower its way back to its home in the southern hemisphere, invisible for the next eight or nine months. It occurred to him that this was the farthest south he had ever been.

"We can't bring the truck out here. There are people in those houses." As he spoke, a light flicked to life in the nearest house, its glow visible through a row of windows. Roosters were crowing in anticipation of the new day. People were beginning to stir.

"We will have to drag it out."

"It weighs a thousand pounds. You really didn't think this through, did you?"

A crescent new moon emerged in the eastern sky, its feeble glow like a spotlight from a guard tower zeroing in on escaping prisoners. Coupled with the lights of Havana bouncing off passing low-level clouds, there was now enough light to throw a shadow. Charlie felt exposed, visible, vulnerable.

"Hand me your knife." Esteban directed Charlie to straddle and lift the front leg. "Move it up and down, I have to find the joint." As Charlie raised and lowered the leg, Esteban ran his hands over its hide, like a doctor, trying to locate the shoulder joint. The first rays of the morning sun were now visible in the eastern sky. Esteban began an incision where the leg intersected the chest. He cut deep and fast. He followed the ribs the all the way to the spine, then continued down the side of the neck, forming a ring. He straddled

218

the carcass, peeling back the meat until he was down to the bone. Without the muscles, the leg was easily articulated. Charlie moved it in a circle. Esteban probed with the tip of his knife. Finding the joint, he cut straight down, exposing the glistening white cartilage in the yellow moonlight.

He sliced into the joint, trying to find the cleavage point. "Hand me the flashlight." Hidden from view within a foot of flesh, the beam of light illuminated the cleavage spot he was looking for. He positioned the knife where the joints came together. Charlie struck it with the back side of the ax, and the joint was cleanly severed. A few slashes later and the leg was separated from the body.

They moved to the hind leg. It was much heavier. Lights appeared in more of the houses. The glow in the east was becoming ominous. The crease in the skin between the torso and the leg was pronounced and easy to follow. He formed the ring. Charlie was surprised at how easy it was to cut through a foot of solid beef. *Like butter*, he thought. By now he knew the drill and stood poised with the ax.

The rear leg was dragged to the side. They lifted the bottom legs to flip the beast over, and the procedure was repeated. Within minutes four legs lay on the ground. "Help me get this on my shoulder." Charlie estimated the hindquarters weighed one hundred twenty pounds, the front maybe ninety. They raised it to his right shoulder. Esteban bent forward. With Charlie's help, they shifted the weight across his back, and he was off, a crazed hunchback running through the darkness toward the nearest fence. Charlie lifted a front leg over his shoulder and tried to keep up.

Esteban jettisoned the hindquarter over the four-foot-high fence. Charlie had heard that incredible feats of human strength were possible under extreme circumstances. Now he was witnessing the phenomenon. He threw the leg he was carrying beside the one laying on the ground and raced to catch up to Esteban. Morning had arrived. The carcass was clearly visible. They hurried to get the other two legs over the fence.

Esteban threw the keys to Charlie, who jogged to the car. The ax and the knife were retrieved. Charlie parked the car next to the legs. The front legs filled the trunk. Hindquarters were jammed into the back seat. They were both covered in cow's blood.

"You *really* didn't think this through, did you?"

Esteban jumped to the driver's seat and raced down the road toward the farmhouses. People were already outside attending to their morning chores. Several were in the road, moving from one house to another. The old Chevy slowed down, not wishing to attract attention. Charlie glanced into the back seat. One of the hooves was waving in the air at the height of the top of the seat. Anyone peering into the car would be sure to notice. As they crept past an elderly woman carrying a carton of eggs, Charlie made eye contact. If she was able to see him, did she see the hoof also? He wrestled with the hindquarter to reduce its height, then he draped his shirt over the hoof.

"Explain to me exactly how you plan to use the five hundred pounds of meat in the back seat."

"It's worth a fortune. I need the money to pay off my debt to Tony. Tourists pay $25 for a little piece of steak. Felix knows a guy with a walk-in freezer. From there it goes to the *paladars*. He can sell it. It was his idea. We will split the money."

"But we left a cow without legs in the middle of the pasture. I think they will conclude it was not a natural death. What's going to happen?"

"That could be a problem. There is going to be a lot of witnesses. They will have to call the police."

"What happens then? Will we have to replace the steer? That could be over five hundred dollars. I can't afford five hundred dollars. I'm nearly tapped out. Why did Felix think this was a good idea?"

"It's his wife. She works in the Ministry of Agriculture. She is in charge of keeping track of things like pork and poultry production. They have done this before, with chickens and pigs. The government also keeps track of every cow. The records land on her desk, where they are compiled and fed into a computer. She can alter the numbers in the computer, alter the input. One cow? No one is going to miss it. Who counts cows? Even if it were missed, no one cares. There's a space on the form for deceased animals—attrition—she could mark that space. One way or the other, she could figure out how to make a cow disappear. No one would be looking for it."

Charlie shook his head. "Well, if we get caught, you should make Felix pay for it."

The Cuban countryside was a matrix of interconnected dirt tracks and farms roads, many only wide enough for a horse and wagon. Esteban seemed to know them all. When a paved road was encountered, he crossed it immediately or exited at the first opportunity. Gradually, he wove his way back to Cubacan riding pavement for the last mile to his house. There he parked in his underground garage. Breathing a sigh of relief, he closed the doors behind them.

"When is Felix going to pick up the meat?"

"Tonight, I think. He was waiting for my call last night. He works all day."

They dragged the pieces out of the car and stacked them onto a plastic tarp in a corner of the garage. Stooping down, Charlie put his hand on one of the shoulders. "The meat is hot. We are going to need ice."

Esteban had a blank look on his face.

"We are going to need at least a couple hundred pounds. We need the big blocks."

"Bags. All there is are bags."

"In that case, we are going to need a lot of bags." Charlie viewed his accomplice in the light of the basement. He was covered in dirt and blood. "First, you gotta clean up. You look like Charles Manson. Then the car. You gotta clean it up also."

To avoid suspicion, they drove to Marina Hemingway. Under the guise of preparing for a fishing trip, they purchased thirty bags for seventy-five cents each. The ice started melting before they reached Esteban's garage, a puddle forming beneath the car as the bags of ice were removed and mounded over the pile of legs. Esteban returned Charlie to his apartment. They were both exhausted and slept until early afternoon.

Five o'clock. Esteban and Charlie returned to Esteban's house and made a telephone call to Felix.

Felix was furious. "You idiot! I knew it was you. Stay away from me and my wife."

It was not the response Esteban had been expecting. "What's the matter?"

"Out of all the steers in Cuba. You have to choose that steer?"

Felix went on the explain that the herd was a cooperative experiment conducted between the Ministry of Agriculture and the University of Barcelona. They were a special breed, genetically engineered to thrive on the low-protein grasses specific to a high-calcium soil, the type found in north-central Cuba. Agricultural scientists and students were following their conversion rate all over the world on the internet. It was further hoped the breed could cope with tropical conditions better than domestic species. Results had been promising. Fidel himself had taken an active interest in the herd and had visited several times, as chronicled in the *Grandma*.

"How did you hear about it?" Esteban was beginning to get a sinking feeling in his stomach.

"My wife was informed at nine o'clock this morning. The police are looking for the perpetrators. They have witnesses. They took fingerprints."

Esteban was frantic. His fingerprints were on the gate. "This was your idea. You have to help me. We need to get the meat into your walk-in cooler immediately!"

"The police are checking every commercial walk-in, every big refrigerator, every refrigerated chest. They just barge in, unannounced and snoop around. And ice. Don't buy ice. All large ice purchases must be reported. They set up roadblocks, checking every car between San Isidro and Santa Fe. You stay away from me and my wife and don't call again. You are dead to me."

Esteban's life was being destroyed by his debt to Tony. He had been having trouble sleeping. When he did sleep, he had bad dreams. His thoughts were erratic, his judgment clouded. He was losing weight. And now his troubles were compounded by the senseless act of killing a cow. The thought of losing his home was inconceivable; it had been in his family since 1927.

After he was forced to leave the ship, he was ordered to appear in court. Those found guilty of breaking the law are subject to sanctions, in descending order:

a.)   Death
b.)   Deprivation of freedom
c.)   Correctional work with internment
d.)   Correctional work without internment
e.)   Fine
f.)   Warning

He received the two lowest sanctions, a fine and a warning. The judge allowed the confiscation of his six thousand dollars to constitute payment of the fine. The warning is simply a request by the court that the offender not recidivate. Both go on his record.

The debt to Tony had been incurred while Esteban was employed on the ship. His source of income was gone and with it his ability to repay. At the rate of his current quota, 220 pesos for him, 220 pesos for his wife, after deducting necessary expenses, he would have to live for the next thousand years to repay the principal, much less the interest accumulating at a rate of twenty-four hundred dollars per year. Rolling the dice at double or nothing had been a calculated risk. It had been a viable option. However, killing the steer had been ultimately an act of despair and rage, a futile attempt to strike back and injure a faceless monolithic oppressor.

Esteban told Charlie all of this. Charlie surmised that Esteban had, somehow, turned beef into plutonium. It was radioactive and had to be disposed of quickly and permanently. They considered the ever-dwindling options. They couldn't use the car since the police probably obtained a description from the villagers. The ice was melting quickly and could not be replenished; therefore, the legs could not remain in the garage. There was too much to burn. There was too much to eat.

They tried to remain calm as he watched rivulets of blood and water make their way across the garage floor and disappear into a drain that led to a dry well under the house. If the beef couldn't leave Esteban's property, it had to stay. It had to be hidden. Esteban and Charlie spent the next three hours digging a grave in his garden. As they covered the evidence with dirt, it occurred to Esteban that he'd risked his home and his family to bury twenty-five-dollar-a-pound worm food.

CHAPTER TWENTY-TWO

The masthead apparent wind indicator had swung to the west. Charlie and Allen were sitting on the deck of the *Express*, relaxing while Jenna took Vali shopping. Charlie had suggested it, hoping that it would cheer up Vali. Nicole had taken Rowena's death incredibly hard, and Vali had taken on the task of caring for her grieving mother. Charlie related the story of the incident of the cow in the nighttime to Allen, who hadn't laughed at it as Charlie had expected. The mood was serious when the conversation turned to leaving Cuba.

"There must be a low pressure forming over Alabama. We could use that west wind to head east. Where was it when we needed it?" Allen watched as the clouds came toward them from the direction of the setting sun. Charlie poured another drink. "They say the peak of the hurricane season is the twelfth of September. So in three weeks, the probability should start going down. When we leave, I would like to take Vali with us."

"Never take exotic animals out of the jungle," counseled Allen.

"What does that mean?" Charlie asked.

"Here, she is in context. She's Cuban. She eats Cuban food. Thinks like a Cuban. She's not educated. She has never read a good book. All her friends are here. Her mother and sister are here. Sure, she wants to come to America. They all want to come to America. They don't have a clue about America. They think Miami is America. What would she do? She can't drive a car or balance checkbook. She would have absolutely nothing in common with any of your friends or family. You are letting her spin the ratchet on you."

"The ratchet?"

"As you give up power, she takes it, and you never get it back. Every time you say something stupid or make a comment in passion, click, the ratchet tightens. It only goes one way. Everything you say can and will be used against you. She can only use the power you have given her, and you seem to have given her a lot."

"What about Jenna?" Charlie countered.

"She's different. We are soul mates."

"That's hypocritical horseshit," Charlie retorted. "You are exactly right, though. She's not an American girl. She hasn't been contaminated by commercialism or greed. She is pure, untouched, nonmaterialistic, naïve. That's what I love about her. You don't know what it's like when we are together. I have never met a girl like her. She gives freely and without condition. She asks for nothing. No strings attached. She is never jealous. Never asks me where I have been. When she is in my arms, we just dissolve together. It's hard to explain. She becomes part of me, and when that part is gone, I want it back. It's as though I was incomplete without her. I want to be the one who teaches her how to drive and how to balance a checkbook. She's not stupid. She is just stuck in a dead-end country. I want her to grow in America, and I want to be there when she sees the Rocky Mountains and the Redwoods, and we will read the classics together. Besides, we both have ESP."

"ESP? Have you gone completely nuts?"

"Yea, it's true. I have an Extra Strong Penis, and she has an Exceptionally Sensitive Pussy. I love her. I can't live without her. It will be easy. We can shove her into a sail bag some night and smuggle her out of here." He was making light of their connection, at least as he felt it. Coupled with his infatuation for Vali was fear— fear that the island would eat her alive, as it had Rowena, as it was going to devour Esteban.

Allen snorted. "Oh, yeah. Take a look at the top of the hotel."

Charlie lifted the binoculars. He scanned the observation platform on Hotel Viejo y El Mar. There was an unusual amount of activity. Uniformed men were installing an apparatus on a pedestal mounted in the center of the deck.

"That's the new FLIR, forward-looking infrared radar, actually a long-wave infrared radar with thirty-two-power magnification and digital image processing. The ultimate in night vision. Arthur's friend knows about these things. They can spot a hamster at night three miles away and tell you whether it is male or female," Allen explained.

Allen took a sip of his drink and continued. "When you arrive, they search the boat for contraband. When you leave, they search for stowaways. They know all the hiding places. See the *Star Gazer* over there?" Allen pointed to a sixty-five-foot ketch on the other side of the canal. "Her captain was complaining about the holes caused by customs probing his sail bags with a long stainless-steel needle. Customs personnel are rotated every couple of days, so you don't know who to bribe. If you try to bribe one of the marina guards, they will take your money then turn you in for a bonus. Either way," he concluded, "we all end up in jail, and you lose the boat. If you want to get her out, you will have to marry her and go through the system."

***

Parque Lleras, Poblado, Medellin, Colombia. Six men meet in the conference room of the five-star Dann Carlton Hotel. Three are well-

227

known producers of documentary films, employed full time by Channel 24, RTN, with headquarters in Bogata, Medellin, and Cali. Seated with them is their attorney. Across from the table sits Osvalso Munez, president of Video de Amor Azul, the largest producer and distributor of pornography in the country. Beside him, his attorney. The lawyer reached into his briefcase and placed a stack of contracts on the mahogany table.

Señor Munez has concerns. "The girl, for Christ sake, she looks like she is twelve years old." Salvadore slides a release across the table. Attached to the document a photograph of Romena, her signature, and a thumbprint. "She is sixteen. We searched for a girl that was above the age of consent but looked like an adolescent. Here, she signed all the papers. We did everything we could to make sure she was of proper age. We are absolved of liability; therefore, you are also in the clear. You can have the original signed release. We will keep a copy for our records."

Munoz hands the release to the attorney. "You know cassette sales are now fifty/fifty with VCDs. We have to market both formats until everyone in the world has a CD player. What a pain in the ass. After CDs, who knows? There is no way anyone can keep up with the technology. You have provided two hundred forty-six minutes of footage. Twenty-two is B-roll. Your transitions are shaky. You should have used a dolly. But we really like the Selena angle. Where did you find her? She is a dead ringer. Based on your tape, we can dress up some of our local talent and create a celebrity video. It hasn't been done before. People will love it."

"How much footage can you use?" asks Matias.

"We can pay you four thousand dollars up front for everything you have, then a 2.5 percent royalty if and when gross sales reach fifty thousand dollars. We can probably use about thirty-five minutes of your footage."

Contacts are passed and signed. Ten days later, the Selena imposter and her little sister were in thirty-five hundred adult bookstores and sex shops from Tiera Del Fuego to Tijuana.

CHAPTER TWENTY-THREE

Charlie was vaguely aware of the sound of car doors slamming. He awoke to the sound of the cage being rattled. Blue flashing lights illuminated the curtain. There was the sound of a vehicle idling below the window. Vali stirred.

"What time is it?" she asked.

Charlie glanced at the luminous dial on his watch. It was five fifteen in the morning. Before he could get to his pants, four uniformed officers burst into the darkened room. A mustached military type grabbed Charlie by the throat, pinning him to the wall with one hand, pushing a badge into his face with the other. He instinctively raised his hands, demonstrating he had no intention to offer resistance or interfere. Vali was blinded by the glare of flashlights.

"You are Valentina Olivera?" they asked, making it clear they already knew the answer. "Get dressed. You are coming with us."

Lights were switched on. Vali's skirt and blouse, which lay beside the bed, were searched for weapons before being handed to her.

She was handcuffed and lead down the stairs, tears streaming from her eyes. She shot a furtive look at Coco, keys dangling in his hands, but his shrug told volumes—he had no idea why she was being arrested and was powerless to do anything about it.

"Where are you taking her? What is she being charged with?" Charlie demanded. But his pleas were ignored as she was placed into a squad car that disappeared into the night. The arrest, from start to finish, was completed in less than fifteen minutes.

Coco, dazed and visibly shaken, came inside and sat on the couch. "The police have been asking me questions all week about you and Vali. They also wanted to know about Esteban. They asked about your boat. But the police are always poking their noses into everybody's business. I didn't know what to make of it. My books were in order. I thought they were going to tax me more since two people were staying in my apartment."

It made no sense to Charlie. He thought of Esteban and the cow. If Vali was somehow in trouble for that, he would kill Esteban. "It must be a mistake. She didn't do anything."

"It was no mistake. They knew exactly who they were going after and where she would be sleeping."

"Well, tomorrow I will bail her out and we can ask her."

Coco laughed bitterly. "This isn't America. There's no bail in Cuba. The cops can hold her for a long time without even telling her the charges. It's not the law, but they do it. Sometimes they hold people for a year before they go to court. It's very bad. Perhaps Captain Abrigo can get us some information, but it's hard even for him once somebody disappears into the system."

***

What dignity that is left to the average Cuban vanishes during incarceration. Vali was brought to the local Santa Fe substation after being strip-searched, wrapped in a sheet, and handcuffed to a chair.

Her forehead was bleeding from an officer's "accidental" rough handling.

"Can I please put on my clothes?" she begged.

She was provided a uniform, fingerprinted, photographed, and placed in a three-foot-by-eight-foot holding cell on the women's detention corridor. On one side of the cell, a hinged metal cot was attached to the wall. The concrete floor between the back wall and the bed had been formed into a basin. Within the depression was a toilet, and beside the commode a water spigot with a brass valve. Hanging from the pipe, a small, rusted, galvanized-iron bucket, used for filling the toilet bowl, bathing, and personal hygiene. There were no windows or illumination within the cell, but the lights from the hall shone through the iron bars of the door all day and night. Food was passed through a small iron slot. Nor was there ventilation; midday temperatures would soar to 110 degrees.

Eight cells lined the corridor, four on each side. Communication between prisoners was discouraged, but over time, every prisoner knew the most intimate details of their fellow detainees. Most of the other prisoners had been accused of "crimes against the state"—a catch-all term for economic crimes ranging from pilferage to conversion of funds. *Jineteras* who had exceeded their three-strike warning were generally shuttled off to work farms after three or four days.

When Olga Valesques was transferred after thirty-seven days in holding, Vali's stay at sixteen days became the longest. Prisoners came and went, some to prisons, some to trial, and some were released on probation. Many had been in the system before and assured Vali that her accommodations in Santa Fe were far better than anything she could expect in the general population of any one of a hundred prisons scattered across the island.

Vali learned she was entitled to food and gifts brought to her by family members. She would watch as other inmates received clothes, food, medicine, and photographs during the visiting hours on Sunday.

"My mother. Please let me see my mother," she pleaded. "My mother needs me."

A guard scoffed at her. "We have spoken with your mother. She wants nothing to do with you. You have been abandoned by your friends and family. Nobody wants to be near a child molester."

That's what she was being charged with? No one had told her! After two weeks, this was the first indication of the charges levied against her. She found the news to be both distressing and a reason for optimism. First, she had been wrongly accused. It was a mistake. She had never injured a child, nor would she allow one to be injured in her presence. She was entitled to an attorney who would point out to the judge that someone, somewhere, made a mistake and she had been wrongly arrested. Although it might take a week or two, once she got into court, the charges against her would have to be dismissed. She could go home and take care of her mother. She would be able to go home and resume her career. Surely her job would be waiting for her since no one else could do Selena like she. It was just a matter of time until she would be released. Surely Charlie and Coco were working behind the scenes.

But time was the problem. She could be transferred at any time. Inmates were incarcerated according to their gender and crime: foreigners were treated the best—they were rarely tortured or placed in long-term solitary confinement. Political prisoners, guzzanos, were housed separately from the general population; torture, both physical and psychological, occasionally combined with the murder of family members, was a part of their "reeducation." Common criminals were placed in the general population, with provisions made for the insane and non-ambulatory. There were further stratifications within the society of the general population, following a hierarchy where those that committed nonviolent economic crimes were somewhere near the top, followed by violent perpetrators such as murders and rapists. At the bottom of the social barrel were child molesters, particularly homosexual child abusers.

Vali learned from her fellow inmates that if she was placed in the general population of a woman's prison, she would in all probably not live to see the inside of a courtroom. She had already experienced the stigma associated with her unfair status as a child molester—as poor as conditions were in the holding facility, the guards always managed to make her stay even more inhuman and degrading. Although the Santa Fe facility was in no way a maximum-security prison, she was kept in virtual isolation. When guards acknowledged her existence, it was with scorn and loathing. Now it all made sense. It explained the food. Rarely did she receive a meal without there being evidence that it contained one or more ground-up roaches. No matter how hard she picked through the rancid gruel, she always had to spit out a leg or antennae. Occasionally it had a whiff of urine.

Her status explained the lack of soap and toiletries, items generally supplied to the other prisoners. And her uniform. Everyone else was issued a clean uniform once a week. And visitors. She was the only one who never received a visitor. At night when she was trying to sleep, the matron would jab her head with a mop handle. She was powerless; there was nothing she could do. There was nothing she could say. Her pleas for an attorney fell on deaf ears.

As she slowly weakened and lost her grip on reality, the guards picked up on her deterioration and taunted her. "You think this is bad, Selena? Wait until you get to Fidel's next hotel."

One Sunday morning, she was awakened from a fitful sleep. Black-garbed security agents shackled her arms and legs and led her to the office. In front of the station was an armored, windowless transport truck known as a *jaula*, the word for vehicles driven by dogcatchers before the Revolution. As she was led down the steps, she had a chance to view the crowd of visitors awaiting entry outside the rolling steel gate. There, pressed up against the chain-link fence, was her mother, holding a cardboard box. *Those bastards! They not only torture me. They torture my family. First Rowena is taken from us, and now, now I am wrongly accused.*

She cried out to her mother as she was shoved into the back of the van. Had her mother seen her? How many days had she stood outside in the blazing sun? *Did they tell her I didn't want to see her?*

233

Or that I was too ill? She had heard the stories, all Cubans had heard the stories, about confessions being obtained by torturing the family members of those accused. Regardless of the truth, what would they do to her mother if she didn't say what her accusers wanted to hear?

Down the middle of the interior of the jaula ran a shiny iron pipe bolted to the roof. Vali's was seated on the bench nearest the cab, her chain removed from one hand, wrapped around the bar and refastened. She was alone and assumed others would soon be shacked beside her. Instead, the rear door slammed shut. As she sat, trapped with her hands secured above her head to the unyielding bar, the temperature began to rise. Within minutes, it became difficult to breathe. As the sun rose over the dusty parking lot, the van became an oven. Vali screamed in the darkness. She could hear people outside, going about their business. *Can they hear me? Did you forget about me?* Then it became obvious. They had brought her out, knowing her mother would see her daughter being led into the van and slowly cooked to death. She screamed for the next hour then passed out.

Vali awoke chained to a metal frame bed in the infirmary of the decrepit Monto Negro Prison for Women, a needle carrying saline solution taped to a vein in her right arm.

"Water, please, can I have some water?" But when she drank, it was like drinking sand since tap water did little to replace the puddle of sweat, vomit, urine, sodium, and potassium that had leaked from her body during the five hours she had been left in the van. Three days later, she and four other prisoners were transported to dreaded Guanajay Prison, the largest woman's prison in Cuba, twenty-two miles to the west of Havana, five miles southeast of Mariel. She still didn't know exactly what she was being accused of.

Guanajay was a complex of five whitewashed-concrete human warehouses, each consisting of four stories and a collection of outbuildings that resembled barbed wire chicken coops. An outer wall, with wooden gun towers, encircled an inner perimeter topped by broken glass and concertina razor-wire. Guanajay had achieved infamy and had woven itself into the popular lexicon. Mothers would warn their daughters, "If you are not good, you will wind up in Guanajay." Some even thought it to be a myth, an urban legend similar to the chupacabra, designed to scare children into compliance or the setting for stories told around a campfire. But it was no myth, and its reputation was well-deserved.

The jaula jolted to a stop. The rear door opened. Six security officers formed a cordon, as if the shackled prisoners had a chance of escaping from the inner court of a maximum-security prison. Vali shuddered as her eyes adjusted to the light. Behind her, the iron gate was closing between the two guard towers. Through the interior partition, she could see the administration building and behind it the bleak and peeling walls of Pavillion #3. From each barred window, multiple arms emerged, giving the illusion that the women inside were packed like sardines.

Vali, along with her eight companions, were told to stand against a wall. The case against each was read aloud, and they watched as the attendant listened to the charge and assigned a cell accordingly. Five of the women were charged with theft against the state, which usually meant embezzlement, three were drug-related, and Vali was accused of prostitution and harming a minor.

They were herded into a room with dim lights, stripped, and cavity searched by a female guard. The women were provided with clean, pressed shirts, shorts, and a pair of sandals. The room smelled of fermented vomit, fungus, and decay. All eight were led by a plainclothes security officer into a steaming corridor. Flickering incandescent lights without sockets, perhaps fifteen watts, were hung from naked wires protruding from the moldy ceiling at regular intervals. As the metal door swung open, Vali could hear muted screams and groans echoing through the labyrinth of darkened corridors. The guard read from a clipboard and hauled each prisoner to a predetermined cell.

"So much for the crooks and druggies." He turned to Vali. "We saved the best for last. We have something special for you."

The third and fourth stories of Pavillion C were *galleras*, dormitories approximately twenty feet by thirty feet, designed for twenty-four women but often holding twice that number. Iron beds were stacked to the ceiling in a futile effort to accommodate the overflow. On the second story were *tapiadas*, punishment cells designed to hold one, sometimes two prisoners. Below them, on the basement level, were the dreaded *gavetas,* the drawers, six feet in length, four feet high and four feet wide, infested with rodents, cockroaches, and other vermin. Unlike galleras, the tapiatas and gavetas were sealed chambers where the light from the corridor was controlled by the *llaveras,* literally, the guards with keys. After months in the heat and darkness, prisoners would lose touch with reality and start the process of losing their minds. Guards often used sedatives to suppress their screaming.

Vali's eyes adjusted to the dark. "Please, let me call my mother. She doesn't know where I am."

"Don't worry about your mother. Soon you will have nothing to worry about. For your own good, you are going to have a private cell. We have looked at your files and determined if you were put into a cell with other women, they would tear you apart. This is not in keeping with socialist tradition, and we are forced to place you into protective custody. It's for your own good. You will find that your stay here will be much more comfortable if you don't make trouble."

Vali was led to her gaveta. Her four by six-foot-long cell was located on the far end of a dimly lit corridor, second level, inches above another silent prisoner who may or not have been alive. She gagged when the steel door was swung open. The overpowering smell of feces, mold, tears, and rat urine marinating in the stifling heat immediately turned her stomach. She recoiled. "No! No! I'm not getting in that thing!"

The guard cautioned, "It's a bad idea to give me a hard time. I will help you up."

The prisoner instinctively pulled back and broke away from the llavera's grasp. "No. Please! I smell rats. You can't put me in there. I didn't do anything wrong!"

Wham. The llavera's club caught Vali above the left eye, and she fell to the slimy floor. Subsequent blows broke her nose and fractured both her arms, her ribs, and her kneecaps.

"I told you that you would be much more comfortable if you didn't make trouble. Now, get up, and get yourself into the cell."

Wracked with pain, Vali crawled to the cell door beneath hers. Her arms were on fire, and she was nearly blind. The edge of her cell, only four feet above the floor, seemed as high as the summit of Everest. *Smash.* Another blow between her shoulder blades knocked the wind out of her and made it hard to breathe.

"You are lucky. Most child molesters don't make it this far."

Weakened and recovering from dehydration, she pushed herself up against the rusty surface like a snake, trying to propel herself upward. *Whack.* Another blow sent her hamstring into a cramp. She succeeded in getting her hands to the edge, but when she placed her weight on her knees, she screamed out in pain.

The guard went on. "I can tell them you fell down the stairs. A lot of the guests in this hotel fall down the stairs. Get up there."

Now highly motivated, she tried to escape to the relative sanctuary of the dungeon. Vali finally got her feet beneath her and leaned into the cell. Transferring the weight to her palms, she slowly bent forward and crawled into the darkness, being careful to protect her knees.

"Hurry up. I don't have all day."

As her feet were about to clear the edge, the llavera, looking for all the world like a professional baseball player, brought the full force of the bat to Vali's right heel, sending a shock wave of pain that momentarily eclipsed the combined agony of the other injuries.

"Don't worry about it. You are not going to need your feet for a long time."

As the thick metal door was shut and bolted, Vali was seized with claustrophobic terror. She was seriously injured, writhing in pain, trapped, without light, without food, without hope, hidden somewhere within the stinking bowels of Guanajay prison.

CHAPTER TWENTY-FOUR

"We need to find out where she is and bail her out." Charlie paced in front of the thick mahogany desk behind which sat Guillermo Zaras.

"We don't have bail. This isn't America." By the look of him, Guillermo Zaras could have been practicing law for Morgan, Lewis, and Bockius in Miami. Both his manner and his dress were impeccable. One of two thousand lawyers on the island, it was nearly impossible for Charlie to comprehend that the modern, urbane, articulate gentleman in the leather chair was a cog in the wheels of Byzantine oppression. "According to our legal system, she can be held for several days without being charged. What color was the uniform of the arresting officers?"

"Black." The scene, every detail, was burned into Charlie's brain.

"That's unfortunate. Those were agents of the State Security Force, a division of the Ministry of the Interior, not the local police. Apparently, your girlfriend has caught the attention of someone in Havana. Jaimanitas, you say, that would be the Santa Fe holding facility. Valentina Olivera?" He picked up his telephone and speed-dialed a number. Charlie tried in vain to interpret the questions in Spanish as the attorney furiously scribbled the answers he received on a yellow legal pad. He hung up and turned back to Charlie.

239

"It's a mistake, you know. They arrested the wrong girl. If we can't bail her out, then let me hire you to represent her. Is that possible?" Charlie asked.

"That would not be in her best interest. I would have to disclose your involvement to the court. Her association with an American would not be looked upon favorably. It would be better if I was paid by the family."

"They don't have any money. How are you usually paid?"

"We are paid by the state." The tone of his voice suggested that this should have been a foregone conclusion.

"How can that be? That's a built-in conflict of interest. It was the state that arrested her. You can't possibly argue effectively against"—Charlie struggled to find the right word—"your employer."

Mr. Zaras swiveled in his chair and pondered as he gazed through a stained-glass casement window into the rose garden, "It is worse than that. We cannot in any way disparage the state or impugn their motives. When we are in court, we are in a straitjacket. If we show disrespect, or even raise our voice, we could find ourselves in the cell next to our client. You know, we all watch *Law & Order* and are familiar with the aggressive, antagonistic defense. It is not that way here."

"Then what do you do?" Charlie was getting the feeling he was playing against a stacked deck.

"We make sure the system is performing properly," Zaras explained. "The police are people. They make mistakes. Occasionally, they arrest the wrong person. Often the police are overzealous when they bring the charge. We review the evidence to make sure the charges are in accordance with our laws. For instance, our system recognizes mitigating circumstances, and we are often able to bring information to bear that lowers the accused's sentence. The defendant is allowed to respectfully put forward their argument to the court. They can call witnesses and present evidence. Since the average citizen is not schooled in the law, we are appointed by the court to do it for them."

"If I gave money to her family and the family then retained your services, would you have to report that to the court?" Charlie wracked his brain for a way around the rules, wishing Vali were here to help him navigate this maze of bureaucracy.

"I would have no idea about the family's finances or from where they get their money. That's not my business. The family will have to bring her food, clothing, and any medicines she may need. If I were retained by the family, I would apply to the court for a substitution of counsel."

Charlie tried to digest the information. "Excuse me. What was that about food and medicine?"

"And blankets, sanitary napkins, soap, shampoo, and other toiletries. Vitamins are always helpful. She is going to lose a lot of weight."

"What are you talking about? You said she would be formally charged in less than a week."

"Yes. That is required by law," Zaras said.

"So why would she need vitamins? Why would she be losing weight?"

"The arresting charges are severe" —Mr. Zara paused, referring to his list—"endangering the life of a child, entering a child into prostitution, prostitution, and unjust enrichment. They seem to be confident they have the right girl. I will know more when I review the evidence and prepare for trial. Formal charges might be different. Usually, as they investigate further, charges are added, or modified."

"Added? Can I see her?"

241

"No. Only family. You can see her at trial." Zaras looked apologetic.

"When will that be?"

"Anywhere from three months to a year. I have got to tell you: when you see her, she will not look the same. She is in the system, branded a child molester, and will probably be sequestered from the other inmates. In the prison population, she will be the lowest of the low. Although it is unconstitutional, she could be tortured or killed by the guards or the other women. It happens. It would be good if she could work in the fields, sunshine, and fresh air, but then there are the other women. You may find it interesting that few inmates die in prison. Just before they die they are taken outside, some to the prison hospital, so they die outside. Then it doesn't register as an in-prison death, looks better to the world community, even the firing squads—"

"Are you insane? We've got to get her out of there!" Charlie, who had stilled, resumed pacing.

"Get her out? Most difficult. There are ways if one has enough money. It happens. I can't be involved with any of that."

"What if I marry her and get her off the island?" Charlie asked.

"That would work. There are no prohibitions on marriage. But you must wait for her to finish her sentence."

"How long will that be?" Charlie's gut clenched at the memory of Rowena in the hospital. He felt the same sensation now—helpless, desperate, impotent.

"Well," said the attorney, calculating the numbers in his head, "if what you say is true and she has never been in trouble with the law before, and with good behavior, maybe fifteen to twenty years."

***

"The police have been at my house asking questions about you," said Coco as he withdrew a Bucanero from the refrigerator. "They have also been talking to your neighbors."

"That makes sense." Charlie, who had returned to the apartment to find Coco there, was unconcerned. "After all, they yanked a girl from my bed in the middle of the night. I imagine they are talking to all her friends as they try to build a case against her. She's innocent, you know. She didn't do anything wrong. Maybe the fact that they are asking questions means they don't have a case."

"I don't think that is it. They are also asking about your friend Esteban. Captain Abrego said they wanted to know if you were around on a specific night, some time back in July. They reviewed my records to see if you stayed here that week. They wanted to know if I had a photograph of your face, if I had photocopied your passport picture, and if I had looked inside your refrigerator. It does not make sense. Crazy questions. Captain Abrego likes you, and I know he put in a good word."

Charlie didn't need any more complications. He was starting to panic. He took a trip down to the marina to tell Jenna and Allen to pack up and be ready to leave at a moment's notice. He didn't miss the relief on either of their faces. Charlie visited the man at the Hotel Sevilla who Esteban had introduced him to during the cash flow debacle and began to put his plan in motion.

Three days later, a car pulled up in front of Charlie's little house. Two plainclothes policemen emerged, presented their identification, and apologized for the inconvenience, asking the Yuma to accompany them on a short drive to the country. Suddenly all the pieces of the puzzle began to fall into place. Charlie's stomach tied itself into a knot. His pulse quickened, as did his respiration rate—if he had been hooked to a polygraph machine it would have blown up. He tried to be cool, act cool, think cool, but he was on the verge of throwing up his breakfast. If he were arrested, Vali had no hope. Her mother could do nothing but crumple into deeper despair. Charlie checked on her daily, and that morning, it had taken her a long time to get up and come to the door.

Charlie knew the police were trained to look for the slightest indication of knowledge of guilt—some were even trained in subliminal perception—but it didn't take a professional to see he was shitting in his jeans. He felt transparent, as if they could see straight through him—he was aglow with guilt by the time they had placed him in the back seat.

They retraced the path Esteban had taken on the night of the butchering. When they turned to the farm road and began to follow the shiny, new barbed wire, he was able, for the first time, to patch together the mosaic of images previously gathered in the cone of their flashlight and the glow of the night sky. He could see the entire pasture and its relation to gate—it was huge—how could they possibly have stumbled onto the carcass of a dead cow? There was the patch of woods where the car had been hidden. The collection of wooden workhouses was much closer than they'd appeared at night.

They drove past the tube gate and made the left turn, eventually stopping in front of the house where Charlie had passed uncomfortably close to the elderly woman carrying a flat of eggs. The officer occupying the passenger seat knocked on the door of the farmhouse and led that same lady to the window of the patrol car. He motioned to Charlie to lower his window. The lady's eyes drilled like a laser beam into his, as if he were a ghost or worse. Her shaking finger rose from her side—she was now a *bruja*, a witch from hell and she pointed an accusing finger, the same finger of death from the depths of Inquisition that had condemned so many over the ages.

"Es el! Es el!" *It's him! It's him,* shrieked the bruja. The hag was locked like a bird dog onto a quail and was still pointing when Charlie looked back as they drove away. They then traced, with uncanny precision, the route used by Esteban to escape detection. Apparently, his unorthodox path had produced the opposite effect. Villagers were used to a pattern that changed little from day to day. An unfamiliar '56 Chevy traversing a wagon trail at the break of dawn was something odd, therefore memorable. And remember they did when news of the slaughter spread through the sugarcane telegraph. Residents were all too eager to pin the rap on a mysterious getaway car, freeing themselves of suspicion and removing the police from their own doors.

As they passed pedestrians going about their business on the dusty roads, the police would stop and request they look at the squirming foreigner in the back seat. Villagers were quizzed, "Have you ever seen this man before?" Time after time they were answered with shrugs and blank stares. This was repeated perhaps fifteen times before they emerged onto the main highway in Sibonet. Charlie felt like an animal in a cage. It seems the police knew everything except the identity of the light-haired passenger in Esteban's car. Now that mystery had been solved. As they returned Charlie to his little house in Jaimanitas, they seemed most pleased with themselves.

Charlie struggled to control his growing sense of dread and panic. He didn't know what was going to happen, but his addled brain focused on the fact that he couldn't spring both Vali and himself from Cuban prison at the same time.

CHAPTER TWENTY-FIVE

Charlie had a million questions and went directly to Coco's house. As he told his tale, Coco's face became grim. Raquel squeezed her husband's hand and looked as if she were about to break into tears.

"The police know everything!" Charlie concluded. "What should I do? I can't get into trouble, not when I have to figure out how to get Vali out."

Coco seemed as if he didn't know where to begin. "There's someone you have to talk with," Coco said. They drove to the house of Ramon Villamonte, an attorney in Miramar. Villamonte invited them in, and they all took seats in his office.

"I am not a criminal attorney," said Mr. Villamonte, "I structure contracts, international trade with other countries and foreign relations. But we study criminal law. What's up?"

Coco explained about Charlie and Esteban's midnight adventure. Ramon listened and took notes. "Were there witnesses?" he asked.

"An old lady recognized me. She saw me in the car as we were driving away," Charlie answered.

"Did you leave any fingerprints at the scene?" Villamonte kept scribbling.

Charlie reconstructed the events in his mind, the bushes, the road, crossing the road, climbing the gate. "The gate! That's metal. I grasped the top bar with both my hands to get over the gate."

"Then they have your prints. When they book you, they will take your prints and compare them. They are in no rush. They know you can't leave the island. Also, they will have Esteban's testimony." The man fixed Charlie with a stare that was matter-of-fact. There was no emotion there. Charlie's fear ratcheted up.

"Esteban is my friend. He will never turn me in," Charlie scoffed.

Coco looked at the attorney. They exchanged a look that Charlie took to mean *the Yuma doesn't have a clue*. Coco turned to Charlie. "They will torture Esteban, not just physically but psychologically. They will threaten his family. Who is he going to protect, you or his little girl? With three pieces of hard evidence, they will have no trouble justifying the arrest of an American."

Ramon sat back in his chair. "You know, I heard about that killing. Very messy. Those were the cows from the university. You know, Cubans joke they can get more time in prison for killing a cow than a human. But it's not a joke. By extrapolation, a cow, in the eyes of Fidel, is worth more than a human. Really pisses off the Cuban people. You want coffee or anything? This is going to take a while."

Charlie waited anxiously as the attorney's wife returned with three tiny cups of espresso.

Ramon went to his library and returned with his dogeared copy of *Penal Code, Law No. 62*. When he returned, he took a tentative sip of his espresso and began. "First, when a foreigner, even a citizen of the United States, is on Cuban soil, he or she is subject to Cuban law. There are some exceptions. For instance, a diplomat might have limited immunity, and embassy personnel are given some slack, but a tourist, in theory, is no different than any other Cubano. Sometimes when tourists screw up, they are escorted to the airport and told never to return. But not in the case of the slaughter of livestock. It is not a petty crime. And particularly not in the case of this steer from a herd in which Fidel himself had expressed a personal interest. The penalty is crystal clear—slaughter major livestock and spend from two to five years in prison, transport the meat from a slaughtered cow and tack on more time. That goes for everyone, from generals to campesinos, mothers with starving children to idiots here on vacation. They are very strict when it comes to livestock."

Charlie felt his heart drop into his stomach. He started to speak, but Ramon held up a hand.

"That's not good," he said. "It goes on. Whoever sells, transports, or in any manner whatsoever trades with major livestock meat illegally shall be subject to a punishment of deprivation of freedom for a period of from six months to two years, a fine two hundred and fifty quotas, or both. As I understand it, you brought the animal to your friend's house?"

"Just the legs," Charlie said, his throat so dry that he could barely get out the words.

Ramon nodded soberly. "Here's a little more. Whoever knowingly acquires slaughtered major livestock meat illegally shall be subject to a punishment of deprivation of freedom for a period of from three months to one year, a fine of one hundred to three hundred quotas, or both. Did you bring any home with you?"

"No. I have no use for a side of beef. You should see my refrigerator."

"What about your friend? Now, this is very important. Does he have a criminal record?"

Charlie explained about Esteban's making-money scheme during his tenure with on the cruise ships and the fallout.

"That's not good. Another economic crime." Villamonte clicked his tongue and lifted his espresso cup, testing it to see if it had cooled.

"But that was a couple years ago," Charlie offered.

"Our system never forgets. Might as well have been last week. A previous offense opens the door for the prosecutor. We have a catch-all law, hard to get around on the second offense, under the provision of *dangerousness*—considered the special inclination which an individual has to commit crimes depicted by his behavior in manifest contradiction to the rules of socialist morality. It's subjective. Depends a lot on the judge. What kind of a house does he have?"

"Very nice. Three stories, in Sibonet. We have been working on the tile."

"That's not good either. Better if he was living in a shack. They are going to take his house into consideration. If it looks like he has been living beyond his means the prosecutor will try to hang him on, let's see, right here, Article 149, Illicit Enrichment, 'increases his property ... in an amount not proportional to his lawful income'—two to five years in the clink. Your friend had cause to fear simply because he lives in a larger house that was improved by his revenue earned from the proceeds of prostitution aboard the ship. That's not good for you either."

"But I didn't have anything to do with the cruise-ship scheme! And I didn't do anything wrong!" Charlie protested.

"You mean you didn't *intend* to do anything wrong. You butchered major livestock, transported it, and did your best to conceal the crime. How did you carve up the carcass?"

"We used my fish fillet knife." Charlie didn't want to hear what the attorney was going to say next. What he'd heard already was bad enough.

"Your knife? We have a law that addresses that also. Article 214, possession of a knife, or any other sharp or blunt tool … destined to commit an offense. This will all come out in the trial. It's your actions they will look at, not your intent. We have a lot of foreigners in our jails for doing a lot less. All these charges can add up consecutively, so it *is* technically possible to get more jail time for killing a cow than a person. Authorities also have the power to confiscate all or part of the property of anyone involved in black market cattle dealings."

Charlie blew out a shaky breath. "Then why didn't they arrest me on the spot?"

"If you were a Cuban, they would have. From what you have told me, the only positive identification was from a crazy, old bruja. They know you can't get off the island, so there's no rush."

"What's the big deal about cows?"

The attorney lit a cigarette. "The government is very sensitive about the cattle industry. Before Castro took over, the average Cuban ate about seventy-five pounds of beef every year. They were big meat eaters, among the highest in the world. Now beef is available to the Cuban people through the rationing system at the rate of one-half pound per person two or three times a year."

Villamonte's face softened somewhat. "It was a thriving industry. My grandfather was a rancher. The cattle industry represented about twenty percent of the population of Cuba. Three-fourths of all land in Cuba had cattle. But it wasn't just ranchers—the industries related to the cattle industry—real estate, export, banking, milk, cheese, butter, canned beef, hides, tallow, forage, veterinary care, fertilizers, weed killers, disease prevention, trucking—it was huge, it was right up there with sugar. My grandfather was a Castro supporter. So were his friends. Castro had promised prosperity. Then out of the blue came the 'Laws of Agrarian Reform,' which allowed the government to seize my grandfather's land without paying him a nickel."

"Why would they do that? Destroy an industry?" Charlie was incredulous.

"I don't know. Control? Power? Why do communists do anything? Seizing the land was just the beginning. The cattlemen were the first organized group to rise up and defy Castro. They were there when President Kennedy refused to use air support at the Bay of Pigs. That was a disaster. Leaders of the resistance were rounded up. Most served time in prison. Some were executed. Others were allowed to finish their terms and immigrate."

"And the cattle?" Charlie asked.

"Cubans never forget," Ramon said. "Some people feel they have a right to the cattle. That's why the government is so tough when it comes to guarding the few cows they have left. Nevertheless, a lot of them were eaten during the starvation of 1994. So the government obsessively controls the relatively small amount of meat that is still produced: the vast majority of our beef is devoted to extracting dollars from tourists, very little is allocated to Cuban citizens."

"Oh my God. I just figured that we would have to replace the cow." Charlie could feel the noose tightening around his neck "What can I do?"

"There's not much you can do. The police have your name and passport number. If you try to fly out, they will detain you at the airport. They check all the boats that come and go from the marina. There is no embassy here to protect you. You will probably need someone in Florida to conduct your affairs while you are away."

251

Charlie looked at Coco, who said nothing. Without a word, Coco stood, and Charlie followed, carrying the ever-growing burden of dread and foreboding.

***

The sun was going down as they returned to Jaimanitas. Within a week, Charlie's tropical paradise fantasy had become a real-world nightmare. Events were spiraling out of control. Five to ten years in prison—a Cuban prison! Vali was already in there, suffering in who knows what ways. He tried to channel his fear into a plan for survival, but the island itself was a prison. There were guards everywhere.

"When do you think I will be arrested?" Charlie asked Coco, who had shown up at his apartment just after darkness had fallen.

Coco looked at his watch. "They could be here any minute, in a few hours, next week. You may want to call home and say good-by to your mother."

"Don't they need a warrant?" Charlie grasped for any lifeline that he might have left.

Coco frowned. "Did they have a warrant when they arrested Vali? You are lucky. You know they are looking for you. Usually, they just knock on your door, and you are gone."

"Will you help me? I have to get off this island."

Coco shrugged. "Sure, but they are undoubtedly watching you right now. The CDR lady is just down the street. I will do what I can, but I don't want to end up in prison either."

Charlie tried not to panic. He tried to channel his fear in a productive manner. A plan was crystalizing in his brain. "I am going to need some of my clothes, my knife, my face mask and snorkel hidden somewhere accessible to the channel. I will write a note, telling you I am leaving to spend a few days in Pinar Del Rio, put it on the table in front of the couch. Then I need a place to hide along the canal, near the El Laurel. I will pay whoever hides me. I will pay them well. I will make them rich."

Coco thought for a moment. "You remember Guillermo, the guy that was helping me fix the air conditioner? His family owns one of the houses to the west of El Laurel Restaurant, right in front of the entrance channel, the address is 26416, big blue house. It is being completely remodeled. They work on it occasionally but always return here in the evenings. It's easy to find from the water. There is a range marker in the backyard—it's the house all the boats aim at until they make the left-hand turn into customs and immigration. It is fully walled but open in the back to the lagoon and the channel— right across from customs and another guardhouse. But you don't want to stay there. You can't swim from there to your boat. It's too far."

Charlie felt a spark of hope. "Just get me to the water, and I will do the rest. Before I spend ten minutes in jail, I would swim to Key West. You get me in there, and I will do the rest."

CHAPTER TWENTY-SIX

The next morning, Raquel went at the usual time to mop, clean, and replace the towels and sheets. On her departure, she left the note and inserted the items Charlie requested into her laundry bag. With his clothes hanging in the closet and the food in the refrigerator, it appeared that he was still occupying the apartment.

Coco dressed Charlie in baggy pants, a floppy shirt, worn shoes, and an oversized baseball cap to cover his head. With his possessions in a pillowcase, Charlie walked west on Avenida Quinta, past the guarded entrance to Marina Hemingway, looking for all the world like a worker trudging home from a hard day's labor in the sun. Coco passed him in the Lada after having obtained the gate key from Guillermo's bother. He left the gate at the harbor house ajar. As Charlie approached 26416, he adjusted his speed, so when he slipped inside, there were few, if any, witnesses. He located the key to the side door, which had been hidden beneath a concrete frog. It was a large house, but the windows had been removed, and logs held the forms for pouring the rear porch, ready to receive rebar and concrete.

As soon as he looked through the windows, he jumped back, pressing his body against the wall. Just as Coco said, the white and blue Customs and Immigration Complex was located across the canal and slightly to the right. He estimated the distance at five or six hundred feet, but since they had binoculars and a small observation tower with one-way windows, there was no way to tell if there were eyes upon him.

Charlie recollected the hospital where Rowena had died. He remembered thinking that if this was a hospital, he would hate to imagine the conditions inside a Cuban prison. As he waited for nightfall, sitting amid shards of broken concrete, dusty rubble, and discarded TuKola cans, he reveled in the bounty of his freedom, the beauty of the sounds of the road, the loveliness of the green leaves, and the ability to glimpse the bay with its canals and its connection to the timeless sea. He knew that at any moment an officer could appear and put him in a box. This might be the last time for everything. But even as he was free, he could not be totally at peace until Vali was free also.

The property was separated from the lagoon by a concrete bulkhead, attached to it a deteriorated dock that went halfway to the channel. In the corner, growing where the side wall met the bulkhead, was a bush that flowed over the edge, its branches kissing the tops of the tiny swell that made its way into the lagoon from the sea. He waited until dark. It was under the protection of this overhang that Charlie slipped into the harbor. He left his passport and house key on the second floor, replacing them in his pockets with concrete aggregate stones to reduce his buoyancy. With just the top part of his head and the tip of his snorkel protruding above the surface, he had the water signature of a small duck. But now, with a journey of over a mile to reach his boat, a mile through one of the most heavily guarded ports on the island, what was the proper way to proceed? If he went up the center of the canal, he would be visible from both the houses on the right side and the military installations on the square island in the center of the marina. If he went on the residential side, the south side, he would be forced to swim under the well-lit dock at El Laural and the customers enjoying their dinners on and beside the dock. That would never do. But the guards on the other side walked the concrete edges with German shepherd dogs.

Charlie swam slowly to not leave a wake. He headed directly across the lagoon, which was only about two feet deep, to the ship channel, which was about twelve feet, toward the industrial bulkhead surrounding the rectangular man-made island: the futuristic residential area of the original Marina Barlovento.

Charlie had studied the marina. He knew every inch of it. The Customs and Immigration Complex occupied approximately five hundred feet on the south side, the left side, of the island. The facility was strategically located to separate the docks of the marina from the ship channel entrance. It was impossible for a boat to leave the marina without passing in front of the complex. After dark, the marina went into lockdown; no boats were allowed to enter or leave the harbor. Yachts arriving after dark were required to remain at sea and outside the ship channel until the facility was opened in the morning. Conversely, boats could not check out of the marina until the buildings were manned and operational, usually at 7:00 a.m. At night, eight mercury-vapor lights on high aluminum poles illuminated customs concrete apron. The lights were placed to penetrate the gin-clear water in front of the bulkhead; fish could be swimming on the bottom of the dredged channel, fifty feet away, twelve feet down.

The lights were set back slightly from the concrete edge, casting a shadow that was enhanced by an overhang of fifteen inches. This provided a darkened path of about two feet, running the entire length of the quay, but it was by no means the cover he sought—here the channel was lit up like an Olympic swimming pool. Charlie inched his way toward the lights. He tried to pull himself along, but every crack and crevice in the deteriorating concrete had been colonized by large, black sea urchins, each covered with a thousand spines that embed themselves into the skin at the slightest touch.

Within minutes he was beneath the noses of the guards—and their dogs. He prepared himself to be challenged. He would pretend to be a visiting yachtsman looking for lobster or going for exercise. That could work—everyone knows the Yumas are crazy. They never do what they are told. Even if they ordered him to stop, he would continue toward the dark waters between the marina and customs' blaring lights. Would they shoot him? It was unlikely. Would they mobilize forces to pluck him from the water? Yes. Indeed, that was far more likely. But the guards never looked over the edge, and Charlie made it to the entrance to Canal Number Two in about twenty minutes.

The *Bora Bora Express* was located approximately halfway up the canal, across the road from the swimming pool at the Hotel Aquario. The canal was well lit and patrolled by guards on both sides. Yachts were moored directly to the bulkhead. To prevent their fiberglass hulls from grating on the rough concrete, they employed fenders. Therefore, there was always a space between the boat and the dock that was generally hidden from view. But between each boat was a space that was utterly unprotected. Charlie crabbed along the crawl space beside each yacht, only feet from the captains and crew above. He would then hyperventilate and swim underwater to the safety of the next boat. Without dive weights, it was difficult to stay submerged—more than once his feet splashed the surface as he tried to propel himself under. It took another half hour to reach his boat.

"Allen," Charlie whispered near the stern. He waited. "Allen." His words were echoed in the confined space of water, concrete, and fiberglass. They would never hear him. He swam to the center of the vessel and knocked on the hull beneath the surface of the water. He heard muffled movement, then Allen's low voice.

"What the hell was that?" Jenna's voice this time. Charlie knocked again. *Thump. thump thump.*

"There it is again," Charlie heard Allen say. After a moment, Allen appeared at the starboard rail and peered into the black water.

"Allen." Charlie whispered, "It's me! Lower the dive ladder and tell me when it's OK to get aboard."

Ten minutes later, Charlie was safely in the cabin, toweling himself dry, telling his story, describing his plan. "Anyone come poking around the boat?" he asked.

"Yes," Jenna said. "A guard did come by earlier, asking if we had seen you. He's our friend. We give him drinks all the time."

"He's not your friend," admonished Charlie. "But perhaps we can use him. Tell him I have gone to Pinar Del Rio for a week or two. That you have to take the boat back to Florida to renew the insurance. Tell them I will stay in Jaimanitas in my house waiting for you to return. Do we still have the ziplock bags?"

"We have lots of ziplocks," Allen said. "And there's no way we can hide you on the boat. They are checking everybody, and if you have become a fugitive, they might confiscate the boat when we try to leave."

"That's a chance we will have to take. I've taken out all of the cash that I can and still avoid suspicion. Tomorrow, go to this address"—he grabbed a nearby pen and scribbled the address of the Hotel Sevilla — "and get cash, as much as you can at one go. After you get the money, have a talk with the marina director. Maybe give him a box of cigars. We need him on our side. Kiss his ass. If anyone, the guards, customs, the police, gives you a hard time, stick with the story and hand out hundred-dollar bills. I am going to need the dive bag, the black one. You have anything to eat? A can opener. I am going to need a can opener. Let's plan to leave the day after tomorrow. Have you heard the weather?"

"It's going to be blowing all week." Allen sounded puzzled. "Excuse me. *We* are leaving the day after tomorrow?"

Charlie explained, "As tight as their security is, there is a vulnerability we can exploit. Every morning the *busciandos,* the divers, walk down my street, enter the ocean and fish the reefs. They are great divers. They come back with lobster, snapper, triggerfish, everything. They have been doing it for years. Nobody notices. It's not a threat to the regime. It's obvious they can't swim to Key West. All the fishing boats out there are under governmental control, so they are not a threat either. Once I am in the ocean, I will look just like one of the spearfishermen. If there is any kind of sea running, divers become invisible a minute after they enter the water. You have the chart?"

Allen retrieved and unfurled chart 11013 on the dining settee.

"US boats leaving here typically clear customs at Key West," Charlie said as he placed the parallel ruler over the entrance to Hemingway Marina and struck a line to Key West—117 miles away—then walked it to the compass rose. "Twenty-three degrees. That's where you will find me. On a heading of twenty-three degrees—out maybe a mile or so."

"In a five-foot sea?" Allen pushed back at the idea. "That's what it has been running all week, five feet, flopping tops and whitecaps everywhere. I am supposed to see your coconut-sized head somewhere out in the ocean in five-foot seas. It ain't going to happen."

Charlie thumped the table with an open palm. "We can make it happen. I am going to need the hand-held VHF radio and the Garmin GPS. I will tell you my coordinates and, when I see your bow, direct you right or left."

"That's right in front of the hotel. They will be watching. If we stop to pick you up, they will see and send out the patrol boats. You know, those things move at fifty knots. Then we all go to prison." Jenna sounded less than enthusiastic.

Charlie nodded. "I thought about that. You won't have to stop, just slow down a little bit. We will use the half-inch nylon line with a bridle, just like Dope-On-A Rope that we do in the Bahamas when we hunt for fish. We will lead it through a snatch-block on the port toe rail and run the line back to the port jib winch. We could lift an elephant with that rig. The port side will be hidden from view of the hotel. Anyway, look at it as a dress rehearsal. When we come back to pick up Vali, it will be a little more complicated since she doesn't know how to swim."

"Are you out of your fucking mind?" Allen shouted, lowering his voice after a look from Jenna. He whispered vehemently, "*If* we get out of here at all, it will be a freaking miracle, and there is no way I am ever coming back."

There was an awkward silence, broken by Jenna. "Do you love her?"

Allen said nothing. Charlie looked at Jenna. "I do. I wouldn't be risking everything like this, I wouldn't be asking you to do the same, if I didn't."

The sparks of hope in Charlie kindled into a small, unsteady flame. "I am going to need my dive bag, some food, my fins, five pounds on my dive belt. Can you charge up the VHF tonight and make sure there are new batteries in the GPS? Wrap them up together in ziplocks so they are super watertight. We need to work out some sort of code so it sounds like we are fishing—the guys on the roof undoubtedly scan the entire VHF frequency band. Oh, and can we throw in a couple beers and some water? I will be back tomorrow night to get the electronics. And see if you can get a report from some of the fishermen about the offshore currents."

***

Charlie crawled over the stern, now with his weight belt, and silently slipped into his three-foot-long fins. Instead of bobbing on the surface like a beach ball, he was now neutrally buoyant and became, for all practical purposes, a human seal. He slid effortlessly below the boats. To breathe, he balanced himself perfectly an inch or two below the surface so that only the tip of his black snorkel was above water. Even if he were spotted by a guard, he could dive and emerge a hundred feet away, breathe for a few seconds, and then go another hundred feet. He was free and moving swiftly through one of the most heavily guarded security zones on the island.

He emerged under the bush in his new backyard and made his way invisibly into and through the darkened structure. Charlie shook the dust from a carpet, which he crafted into a bed on the upstairs veranda. He was naked, hunted, and alone in an alien environment far from his home. He was putting his friends—those he had brought with him and those he'd made since arriving in Cuba—in danger, risking their lives. He had never appreciated his freedom with such clarity. It was freedom on a cellular level. He beheld the majesty of stars and sky above him and felt he was connected in some way to forces that were beyond his ability to comprehend. He marveled at the world around him—sound, color, hunks of cement on the floor, his own heartbeat. It could all be gone in a second. At any moment, he might be discovered and stuffed into a box.

He lay awake, waves of nervous nausea ripping his insides. What a trip it had been. He had come to this country to experience the culture, hoping for an adventure, but now, through a series of bizarre events, he was living like a Cuban citizen—scared out of his wits, hiding from the law and doing his best to get out of the country. He realized he was instantly at one with twelve million other potential prisoners, subject to the same omnipresent repressive ideology with the common denominator being fear.

That night as he watched the stars and enjoyed his beer and his freedom, he thought about Vali, ran his plan to free her over and over in his mind, and fantasized about the life they were going to have in America.

CHAPTER TWENTY-SEVEN

S he listened as footsteps approached then stopped in front of her
gaveata, her tiny concrete coffin.

"Valentina Louisa Olivera," the words echoed in mocking
proclamation throughout the moldy halls of the dimly lit dungeon.

Who else did they expect to find in this cesspool? thought
Vali. The lock turned, the iron door swung open, revealing the
llavera and a well-dressed, bespectacled, gray-haired man holding a
fold of papers.

"Good afternoon. I am from the court. Your attorney is here.
He has prepared your case for trial. The court is ready to hear his
arguments. We need to get you ready."

There were festering sores on Vali's knees, hands, and toes—
she had not been able to stand in weeks. The light burned her eyes.
The prisoner was led into a locked chamber adjacent to the visiting
room. She was allowed to shower and put on clothes that had been
brought to her by her mother. A partition had been erected in the
back of the visiting room, which now doubled as a courtroom.
Friends and family were thus sequestered. Defendants, attorneys,
and witnesses were seated in a gallery of wooden chairs. Before the

gallery were two tables, one for the accused and his or her lawyer, the other for the prosecutor and his assistant. A professional judge sat behind an ornate wooden table in the front of the room, flanked by two lay judges on each side.

Her lawyer was waiting in a chair near the partition. It occurred to Vali he looked more like a gay fashion designer—well dressed, about six foot three with five-hundred-dollar shoes.

"My name is Guillermo Zaras. I have reviewed your case with your family, and I am optimistic we can get you out of here quickly." Although Vali had been kept in isolation, she knew that Charlie had been instrumental in finding for her the best possible advocate.

"According to the indictment, they arrested you on suspicion of prostitution. About half of the women here are facing a similar charge. Perhaps a month or two on a work farm if it is the first offense. But your charges also include bringing harm to a minor and entering a minor into prostitution. What can you tell me about that?"

Vali thought about her relationship with children and her neighbors. No, she never even yelled at the kids on the street, perhaps at work? There were no young people there—it was a nightclub. If she was being accused by someone, it was her right to confront her accuser. It would be a lie; the court would become aware. "I would never hurt a child. That part is a mistake."

"Good," said Mr. Zaras, a concerned look on his face. "I talked this morning with the prosecutor. He seems pretty cocky. We need to bring him down a notch or two." Mr. Zaras's optimism was contagious. He exuded confidence, and for the first time in weeks, Vali allowed herself to be cautiously optimistic, too. Attorney Zaras tried to prepare her for court.

"The Cuban legal system had been struggling since the Revolution to replace the existing Spanish Codes of Criminal and Civil Law to one that reflects the ideology of Marxism -Leninism and supports socialist principles. In theory, the Cuban judiciary, that's who I work for, is independent of the legislative and the executive branches of government. However, in practice, we are compelled to toe the party line. Professional judges are appointed by the Ministry of Justice for unlimited terms. He will be in the center. Serving with them are four lay judges, persons without formal legal training, chosen from the general population. Their purpose is to provide the appearance of a court of the people, imbued with the common sense of the man on the street.

"Contrary to popular opinion, the courts are not a prosecutorial rubber-stamp. About one-third of criminal cases are dismissed due to lack of evidence or mitigating circumstances. Therefore, we have a good chance of getting you out of here." Vali's attorney seemed anxious to see the evidence presented by the court. He told Vali that this would be the prosecution's Achilles' heel—the weakness he would exploit to have his client's sentence reduced or eliminated altogether.

Vali's mother was one of those standing in the back of the court, compressed behind the wooden barricade with dozens of other family members. She shuffled in the heat, clutching her purse and straining to catch a glimpse of her daughter. Vali wanted to call out to her, but kept silent, afraid to appear out of order and hurt her chances at trial. A glimpse of her mother's face revealed the toll taken by Vali's incarceration—she appeared gaunt and ten years older. Vali was suddenly angry. Not only had Cuba taken Rowena's life and Vali's freedom, but it was killing her mother just as surely.

Vali's case was fifth on the agenda. The prosecutor used the first case to admonish not only the defendant but also all those who would defy the cause of the Revolution by committing acts against the state and, more specifically, against the comandante who had sacrificed so much to free the Cuban people and expel the agents of imperialism. His rant continued for more than an hour, extolling the perfection of the socialist system and its stated goal as political embodiment of the expression of the highest qualities of mankind. Those who failed in this collective quest and yielded to capitalistic impulses were pathogens, infectious agents that poisoned the system that needed to be dealt with in swift and single-minded resolution.

As such, they were in need of both punishment and reeducation. Thus, reshaped and redirected, they would assume their duties as foot soldiers in the cause of glorious Revolution and thank him when, duly reformed, they realized and rejected the folly of their former existence.

The audience had heard it all before. His diatribe was simply a synopsized rehash of the 24-7 torrent of relentless propaganda streaming from the TV, the radio, the schools, the *Grandma*, and hundreds of billboards, plaques, and signs plastered across the countryside. The accused, thirty-six-year-old Jazmin Juertes, weighing all of ninety pounds, absorbed the full fury of the judge's wrath. Her crime? She had failed to pay taxes on her hair-styling business despite three warnings. Jazmin's attorney argued that the necessary hair-care products and chemicals were unavailable in her bodega and prohibitively expensive in the dollar stores—treading on rhetorical thin ice lest his defense be interpreted as a condemnation of the socialist system. It was a well-structured, logical argument that had the added advantage of being the truth.

Her sentence: three months on an agricultural work farm. *The sun*, thought Vali. *She will be out in the sun. She will feel the wind on her face and watch the birds fly. At night, she might see the stars.* To Vali it seemed a sentence to paradise.

The other cases involved prostitution and embezzlement, which meant theft from the state. Sentences were less than one year. All were petty crimes. Vali was led by her attorney to the defendant desk. One by one, the cases were argued and the sentences handed down. Mr. Zaras was eager to confront Vali's accuser, mano a mano against the prosecutor. It was his specialty. In his experience, the police were idiots, and their tactics Cro-Magnon, at best. They always made mistakes, and these errors, he would identify, articulate, and shove up their collective asses, all the time remaining within the constraints of socialist orotundity. He was one of the best, and he knew it.

"Case number 98-23957, Valentina Louisa Olivera." Attorney Zaras watched as the judge's assistant wheeled a television set that had been facing the wall to a position where it could be viewed by both the judges and the gallery. Beside the TV a small box, connected by wires and plugged into an electrical extension cord. As the prosecutor read the charges, he was handed a remote control. "And we will present only one piece of evidence since the evidence speaks for itself."

He aimed the remote at the apparatus and pressed a button. The eyes of the court were immediately transfixed by images that sprang to life before them. The wooden barricade creaked as onlookers jockeyed for position. On the TV in full digital clarity was the defendant in her character as Selena in a film-clip collage typical of the cutting and splicing techniques used to produce music videos. But it was an X-rated music video.

Between sequences of lip-synching was Vali performing a number of sexual activities. The audience was hushed as they watched Vali giving head to the production crew in the back seat of a car, using a microphone as a dildo, and being attended in a garden by a young girl, a very *naked* young girl. They watched as Vali's crotch was penetrated by the tongue of a pack animal. And then, to the dulcet tones of a Selena love song, they watched as the little girl—Rowena—had sex with the three producers.

"No!" Vali screamed. "No. I didn't know! They took her upstairs! I didn't know!" The judge in the center instructed the attorney to control his client.

"One more outburst and she will be thrown back into her cell."

Vali sprang to her feet, pushing aside the table, her attorney made a grab for her as she ran to the prosecutor. "Oh God! I didn't know! They lied to me!" The audience gasped, then a hush fell over the courtroom as the prosecutor and the defendant, only inches apart, looked into each other's eyes.

"I didn't know," said Vali, softly, crumbling, defeated as she struggled to put together the pieces in her mind before the full power of the Cuban judiciary came crashing down upon her. For a moment, the prosecutor's face softened. He knew the truth that lay in a spontaneous utterance. He knew the truth when he heard it.

If he had rehearsed a diatribe of righteous indignation, looking into the face of tears and anguish, he must have relented, because he spoke with unexpected compassion. "It doesn't make any difference. You brought her into that situation, and it was up to you to protect your little sister."

Vali offered no resistance as she was led back to the table. Her life, like Rowena's, was over. She looked at her attorney. Mr. Zara shook his head and looked down at the table. There was nothing he could say. The prosecutor collected his thoughts as order was restored. Vali tried to not look at the judges. All five were dressed in green military uniforms, dispelling any conceptions about their allegiance. Each was handed a single sheet of paper. On that paper was the offense as defined and dictated by Penal Code No. 62, along with its sentencing guidelines and the prosecutor's recommendation.

Vali was engulfed in a whirlwind of shock and confusion. The treachery of the Colombians was coming into focus as her world dissolved around her. They had lured her with the promise of assisting her new career. Worse, they had ensnared her little sister. They weren't movie producers. They were nothing but perverts who had devised a scheme for acquiring sex on the cheap, then they tried to capitalize on their perversion. They had used her. She had been deceived. Perhaps there was a way to make the court realize she was a victim. She would take the punishment for prostitution. She had always known she was taking a chance when she accepted money for sex—it was a risk she was willing to take. Ultimately, she had been trying to help her herself and her family. Surely the court could be made to understand.

But the horrific images of a drugged and dazed Rowena being gang-raped were burned indelibly into the eyes and minds of all who saw. They would never leave Vali's mind as long as she lived. Vali knew that her pride had played a role—she had harbored dreams of being a movie star, and she had ignored any misgivings that she might have had about the movie. She had been greedy, given in to the money. The prosecutor was correct—it had been up to her to protect her little sister, and she had failed.

The jury conferred for less than five minutes before the professional judge addressed the court. Vali was swimming in a nightmare, the words and the world, the court and the heat and the smells, were contorting around her like a vision from hell. She saw herself through the eyes of her mother as she became disembodied from her thoughts, her mind refusing to accept she was trapped in a chair, in a room, in an out-of-control universe that was exploding around her. Word fragments with the force of lightning bolts were aimed in her direction, impaling her soul through ears that didn't want to hear, an incomprehensible witches' brew of threat and horror. Then time slammed to a stop in a moment of clarity. She heard the words, as if spoken by God himself, cutting through the blizzard of thought and emotion, little words, a snippet, not even a complete sentence: "Seventeen years in prison to be followed by seventeen years of house arrest."

CHAPTER TWENTY-EIGHT

"Thirty thousand dollars," Charlie said.

"How much?"

"Thirty thousand. It's worth thirty thousand dollars to me to get her out of jail. I don't care how you do it. If you can get it done for five hundred dollars, put the rest in your pocket with my blessing." Charlie looked like a homeless person in his baggy pants and worn-out shoes. At that moment, Charlie *was* a homeless person.

The walk to Coco's house had taken twenty minutes. Charlie continued, "I will keep in touch by telephone, and I will give you the phone number of my mother in Jacksonville. It is going to be real simple. When we talk on the phone, we are going to talk about renting your apartment. We will discuss if you think it will be available, when it will be available, and when it will be ready. When you say you're ready, I will arrive with the money. I will try to keep the boat nearby, in the Bahamas or Key West. You get Vali to the house on the canal, and I will take care of the rest. I don't care how you do it. Just get her there alive."

Coco pondered the problem. "I don't even know where she is. And if you are caught, I can only imagine what they would do to

269

you. Twenty years? Twenty-five? She's just a girl. Go meet a nice girl in your country and spend the money on your wedding."

"She's not just any girl. I love her. I haven't even told her yet, but I do. She is going to be my wife. That's all there is to it. Getting her off the island will be a story we will share with our grandchildren. Remember: it was you who told me that everything in Cuba was available for a price. I am willing to pay that price. Her mother will know where she is. I have given Nicole money to hire an attorney and bring clothes and food. Also, Captain Abrego, he's a friend of yours, put him on the payroll. He can work his contacts within the security forces."

Coco stroked his chin and looked at the ceiling. Charlie could see he was already thinking.

***

Charlie entered the water at sundown. With fins and a weight belt, he completed the swim in half an hour. He made it unnoticed aboard the *Bora Bora*.

"We will drop the twenty-three and the eighty," Allen explained, breaking down the code he had devised. "The first numbers of the latitude, which is twenty-three and longitude, eighty, a mile or so off the beach, will not change, so they become extraneous information, and we will drop them. Therefore, we will concentrate on the next six numbers, latitude first, then the next six numbers of longitude. We will communicate on channel sixty-eight. That's the one used by most of the fisherman. Since our conversation will be monitored, every number will be reduced by one—a zero becomes a nine, a five becomes a four and so forth. Say you are at latitude twenty-three, oh-six, oh-three, eighteen, that would become ninety-five, ninety-two, oh-seven—the numbers you tell us, we just round it up by one and compute your location."

Allen continued, "The current kicks in at the hundred-fathom contour line, heading northeast at about one-half knot. At that rate, you should swim straight out from the coast. By the time we rendezvous, you will have drifted pretty close to our rhumb line of twenty-three degrees. And here—Jenna, can you hand that to me? We made you a harness. I have attached a snap-shackle to the end of your tow line. Just hook it to the ring, and we will winch your sorry ass aboard on the port side. You should be hidden behind the cabin. What could possibly go wrong?"

Jenna broke in. "Oh, the police were here this morning looking for you."

"They were at my apartment, too," Charlie said as he looked up through the cabin windows, half expecting to see police on the quay. "Coco said they arrested Esteban two days ago. I need to get off the boat. This is the second place they will look." Charlie refocused, hurrying to get everything said so that he could leave. "I am a little worried about the speed. Let's go with main only. If the genny is out, you will never be able to slow down. Put the fishing rod in the starboard holder. That gives us an excuse for slowing down—it will look as if we caught a fish. I will direct you when I see your sail, steer left, steer right, sounding just like we are fisherman closing in on a school of baitfish."

Charlie ran a hand through his hair. "It's going to be hard to listen to the radio while I am swimming. Starting at seven fifteen, I will stop swimming and put the radio to my ear. I will be listening at fifteen-minute intervals. When you leave customs, how about trying to say farewell to one of your buddies at the marina, put in a call to *Antares*, there is always some boat named *Antares*, as if you were trying to say goodbye to one of your friends in the marina. I will then respond with the coordinates."

It was a plan. Maybe not a good plan, but under the circumstances, it seemed the only plan.

Charlie slipped over the side when the guards weren't looking, retrieving his fins from the dive bag attached to the swim ladder and preparing to spend his last night on the island.

The coast of Cuba west of Havana runs from southwest to northeast at about sixty degrees. Trade winds blowing over the island from the east and southeast should, in theory, be a land breeze. But they somehow curve and parallel the coast, creating open sea conditions where a chart and logic would indicate a lee shore. This was the condition waiting for Charlie—one that he would have avoided had he been sailing—as he entered the water at 6:00 a.m. He made no effort to conceal himself within the harbor, following the left side of the ship channel, above the ledge created when it was dredged in 1953. He headed for sea buoy #2, the last in the series of channel markers. His muscles were charged with adrenaline, and it was hard to maintain the slow and methodical pace as he masqueraded as a local diver searching for fish. Occasionally he would dive, just as they did when they peered into the caves and crevices where the fish hide.

As he left the protection of the harbor, he could see #2 hobby-horsing wildly on its mooring chain in sixty feet of water. *Fucking wind*, he thought to himself, *this would be so much easier on a calm day.* Sea buoy #2 was anchored near a ledge that dropped another fifteen feet. The ledge was usually the limit of the local free divers since, immediately thereafter, the bottom fell away to thousands of feet. By six thirty, Charlie could no longer see the bottom, meaning he was in water over one-hundred-feet deep and dropping fast.

***

The customs and immigration buildings opened at 7:00 a.m. Arriving yachts were searched for drugs and contraband, the dogs they used—German shepherds, cocker spaniels, and beagles—were housed in kennels adjacent to the immigration building. Departing boats are searched for stowaways. This was always done by the staff since dogs can't differentiate between a legal and an illegal person— they smell the same. The *Express* was second in line and instructed to tie astern an expedition trawler.

Two officers reviewed the cruising transire, immigration certificates, US Coast Guard documentation, and the passports that had been spread on the cockpit settee.

One of the officers studied the pile of documents. He said, "Your manifest shows you arrived with three persons. Who is the captain?"

"I am the captain," replied Allen.

"But the papers say the boat is owned by Mr. Sutton."

"That's right. He's my boss, and he is sending the boat to Key West to renew our insurance."

The officer straightened. "The police are looking for Mr. Sutton. Where is he?"

"Right now? Pinar Del Rio." Allen's felt a wave a nausea sweep over his body. They *were* looking for Charlie, just like he'd said. "He should be back in his apartment in a week or so. We will also return about then."

"We will have to hold you here until we find Mr. Sutton." The other officer went below. Jenna went below as well and watched him to make sure he didn't steal anything.

"Do you have any beef?" he asked. Jenna opened the refrigerator and displayed the empty shelves. The cop returned to the cockpit, followed by Jenna, and collected the passports and folder with the ship's papers. Both officers disappeared into the immigration blockhouse. It was now 8:15. Charlie had been in the water for over two hours. Allen tried to calculate his drift. Charlie would now be a half mile closer to Havana.

The sun rose higher in the sky, cooking the cockpit beneath the canvas top. They sat for an hour. Other yachts were cleared to leave, and several were searched by the dogs as they entered. At

11:35, both officers returned with the passports and the file, installing themselves in the cockpit. There was an awkward silence.

Allen had seen the posture before—they had something Allen needed; Allen had something they wanted. He knew the drill. Yet it was a delicate time, a time for diplomacy. Allen couldn't say, "How much money will it take for you cocksuckers to get off my boat?" He tried a gentler approach. "Sir, how many children do you have?"

Although Allen directed the question to both of them, it was rhetorical. The answer made little or no difference. "Please allow me to present to your wife and your babies a little gift from the people of the United States." He reached into his wallet and withdrew four crisp hundred-dollar bills, placing them on the table. Allen sat directly across from the officers. His heart was pounding. The situation was deadly serious.

At this moment, a number of nasty things could happen. He could be arrested for bribery. They could confiscate the boat, put Jenna in jail. Allen couldn't even look at Jenna because he was so damned nervous. Charlie would probably drown since he had already been in the water for nearly six hours. Perspiration ran down Allen's face, and he made no effort to conceal the fact that he was uncomfortable. If that's what the police wanted—to make him sweat, to break him down, demonstrate their power—that's what the police would get. He looked them dead in the eye. On the table was more money than an honest cop would make in fifteen months. But these men were in a position of enormous privilege—they could take the money and still have Allen and Jenna arrested. Or maybe to them, four hundred dollars was peanuts.

It was a poker game with huge stakes. Perhaps the cops had just been screwing with Allen the whole time. The spell was broken when one slid two bills to his companion and broke into a smile. They handed to Allen the documents and the passports—passports containing an exit visa that had already been stamped. The *Bora Bora Express* had been held for five hours as a shakedown.

The engine was started, and they were off the dock within five minutes. As they neared the sea buoy, they headed into the wind and a sloppy sea to raise the main—the forty-foot signal for eyes in a tiny head bobbing somewhere in the Straits of Florida. They called to their friends on the dock, as per the plan, at exactly twelve thirty.

"*Bora Bora Express* to *Antares*. *Antares*, come back please," Allen called. Allen and Jenna waited for coordinates, but there was only silence. If Charlie had anticipated a pickup at twenty-three degrees, a mile offshore, five hours ago, he would have drifted three or four miles toward the east-north-east. Allen plotted a new course that took him much closer to shore and directly in front of the Hotel Viejo y El Mar. There was no other option. They were now about forty degrees off the wind, and the main was luffing, slowing their speed. At this rate, it would take another hour to reach Charlie, and during that hour he would move a further half mile to the east-north-east.

In perfect conditions, the handheld VHF radio was good for about five miles. But VHF is notorious for being a line-of-sight transmission. Its efficacy would be seriously compromised if it were broadcasting, or receiving, from six inches above the water, bounded on all sides by walls of water. Charlie would have to listen, and broadcast, when and only when he was on the crest of a wave.

"They can see us. I know those pricks are watching us." Allen glanced at the sentries on top of the hotel, "Put out the Penn Senator on the starboard rod holder, please." Jenna set the fishing rod out, as they had planned.

At 1:00 they called the *Antares* again, waited, and heard nothing. The skyline of Havana now loomed over the starboard bow. "Great, instead of one hotel to worry about, we now have ten million eyes." 1:15 P.M "This is the *Bora Bora Express* trying to reach our friends on the *Antares*. *Antares*, please come back."

"Ninety-six, eighteen." Numbers crackled over the radio.

"I heard something!" Jenna reached for a pad of paper. She muttered as she wrote, "The nine becomes a zero, six becomes a seven, one becomes a two, and the eight becomes a nine. Oh-seven and twenty-nine—that's all I got!"

Allen tried to make sense of the numbers. They didn't work with 82 longitude, 82.07.29 being well east of Havana. Charlie could not have drifted that far.

Allen thought a minute. "So twenty-three, oh-seven, twenty-nine—that works, we can go north until we intersect with that latitude, then head east. If we keep going east, we are going to end up on the Malecon. Those coordinates should get us to within six hundred feet north or south of our target."

They sailed north to 23.07.29, then due east, sailing along the latitude, just as Columbus had done five hundred years before.

"Go to the bow. Look and listen," Allen commanded Jenna. Now they were motoring directly into the breaking sea. Charlie could have been a hundred feet away and still have been impossible to see.

"I hear something!" Jenna held the radio to her ear. "Left, steer left!"

Allen fell off to port

"Too much! Now to the right!" she cried.

Allen picked out a building in Havana that seemed to be on the line she was trying to describe.

"Straight, keep going straight," she urged.

Allen switched to autopilot and scanned the water's surface.

"I see him!" Jenna instinctively pointed.

"Don't point, for Christ sake! People can see us," Allen hissed. "Just talk me in. We need to keep him on the port side, remember, the left side."

Allen saw Charlie as he was lifted on a wave less than fifty feet off the bow. He aimed directly at him, throwing the tow line as far as he could off the port stern. Allen then swerved, coming as close as he could to their target. Now it was up to Charlie. Charlie swam for the nylon line, but by the time he reached it, it was already a foot or two beneath the surface of the sea. He dove and held on with all his might. The line slipped through his fingers.

"Slow down!" yelled Jenna. "He can't hold on."

Allen dropped the *Express* into neutral, giving Charlie time enough to snap the swivel onto his harness.

"Put it back in gear, or we will foul the prop," yelled Charlie, pushing the snorkel out of his mouth. Allen complied. He looked back to see Charlie being dragged through green water. The tensile strength of the line was over 8,800 pounds, but he wondered if it would break under the strain. Like a huge, struggling frog, Charlie was dragged to the stern, one hand trying to keep his mask from being swept away by the rushing water, the other on the towrope, fins spread wide to keep his head above water.

Allen winched Charlie to the beam where he was unceremoniously slammed against the side of the hull then hoisted uncomfortably to a point where his body was pinned against the toe rail. He was trapped there, the harness compressing his chest and making it hard to breathe. Allen lifted his legs up and over the gunwale while Jenna slacked the line. Charlie flopped on the deck like a dead fish.

"I need a drink," Charlie gasped.

"A Cuba Libre perhaps?" Jenna suggested dryly.

"No, water. I would kill for a glass of water. I lost my weight belt."

Allen threw the *Bora Bora* out of autopilot. "Jenna, get Charlie some water, we are not out of the woods yet." Allen fell off, filling the hard-sheeted main and driving north, toward the ten-mile territorial limit.

"Oh no, here comes a patrol boat," Jenna voice trembled. Sure enough, the black bow of a cruiser blasted through the wave tops, throwing plumes of white water to each side. It was aimed directly for them.

"What can we do?" cried Jenna.

Charlie went to the stern and crouched. "I can get back into the water. You continue to the Bahamas, and I will make it back to shore."

Allen's heart sank as the cruiser bore down. Charlie crouched under the Zodiac, ready to slide back into the sea. But the yacht passed to their bow, headed to the northwest, perhaps New Orleans. On its stern in gold leaf were the words *Black Lace* out of Grand Isle, Louisiana.

***

Allen commanded, "Jenna, release the jib. Slowly!" Jenna moved to do just that, and soon they were flying away from Havana. At this velocity, they were leaving Cuba behind at the rate of one mile every six minutes, but it wasn't fast enough for Charlie. The thought of spending years and years in a Cuban prison for butchering a cow was incomprehensible.

Equally unreconcilable was the thought of leaving the only woman he had ever loved in jail. Without her, he felt like half a person. She completed him. As Havana disappeared over the stern, he knew that their relationship might have blossomed, run its course, and then died a natural death. As Vali had told him, in Spanish, love kills time; time kills love. But being in love is to dream, and his dreams now included her, maybe for a short time, maybe for a lifetime; it would be a crime against nature and humanity not to pursue perfection.

Until this trip, his voyages had been geographic adventures—mountains, cities, redwoods, and tumbleweeds. He thought he had traveled. Yet in some mysterious way, making love to Vali transcended time and space, their bodies fused together as if they were molten glass. They were interchangeable, transparent, connected simultaneously on both a cellular and a cosmic level. Through Vali, he had gained a glimpse into the world's religions, the nirvana of Hinduism, the quest for Buddhist enlightenment, a touch of the rapture. Charlie didn't understand it but having discovered that Vali could take him on a spiritual journey he never knew existed, he was certain that his life would never be complete without her.

If he escaped from Cuba once, he could do it again, and next time he could take her with him.

It had taken almost a week to reach Castro's Island from Fort Lauderdale. Granted, the route was, at best, circuitous. But with the Gulf Stream pushing them at almost four knots, added to their hull speed of eight knots, the two hundred fifty miles to Bimini could be accomplished in a single twenty-four-hour period. They arrived at the Big Game Club at three in the afternoon of the following day. Since the Cuban government had not stamped their passports, there was no record they had ever left the Bahamas. The *Bora Bora Express* entered without a quarantine flag or clearing customs, maintaining, if asked, they had spent the last four months in the southern islands of Great Inagua and Mayaguana. Nobody asked.

Jenna had her bags packed before they hit the dock, vowing never to set foot on a boat again. She said she was headed to somewhere without wind and water, perhaps Iowa or the Gobi Desert. Allen was right behind her, and the trio parted with relieved smiles and a shared hell of a story that they'd be able to laugh about—if Charlie returned from his next rescue mission.

279

CHAPTER TWENTY-NINE

The *Bora Bora Express* sat in a berth on the first inside slip of the Bimini Big Game Club under the loom of the bridge of the *Prometheus*, a behemoth that overhung the outside dock by ten feet. The *Prometheus*, attended by a professional captain and a crew of four, was the fishing toy of Leonardo de la Joya, whom Charlie fast became acquainted with. Lenny, as he liked to be called, was the owner of the largest Toyota dealership in Miami. He had recently entered the markets of Tampa, Orlando, and Atlanta and controlled much of southeast sales and distribution. He enjoyed fishing for marlin in the waters between Bimini and the Northwest Providence Channel. He had rented the outside slip until Christmas, and when he could find the time, he would fly across the Gulf Stream to fish for a day or two.

Lenny was an American success story. Everybody in Miami had heard about Lenny. He had fled Cuba as an orphan during the Peter Pan flotilla. He was labeled a guzzano, a maggot, by his home country and had been raised in Miami by an aunt and uncle. Through power of personality, superior negotiating skills, and a bit of good luck, he had achieved notoriety as a brilliant businessman as well as a cocaine-snorting wheeler-dealer whose parties were epic by even Miami standards. Charlie bided his time in Bimini, listening to Lenny's wild stories, checking in with Coco periodically.

Charlie had planted the seeds of an idea with Coco. He had to fertilize those seeds with cash. He must prepare for the answer that Coco would eventually give. "Yes. The apartment is ready." When and if it came, he was going to need thirty-thousand-dollars cash to grease palms in Cuba, perhaps another five thousand dollars for incidental expenses.

He had to take stock of his finances. Now that he was somewhere where he had easier access to his finances, he could play a little asset shuffle. Expenses at the Big Game Club were adding up quickly. It was necessary to go back to Jacksonville to sell his motorcycle and work or borrow money. Luckily, when Charlie flew Chalk's seaplane to Miami, his passport was in order—his stamps were consistent with entering and leaving the Bahamas. From there he flew home to spend time with his mother.

Charlie persuaded his mother to take a thirty-thousand-dollar home equity loan as a second mortgage on her modest three-bedroom, two-bath located in the suburb of Arlington. Angela Sutton, though cautious at first, was moved by Charlie's descriptions of Vali and his feelings for her, and soon anxious to meet her future daughter-in-law.

His bike, a restored Norton 750, brought $4,200. Every few days he would place a telephone call to Coco. It was assumed the police were listening and the conversation never strayed from the subject of renting a house. Time and time again, "Lo siento. La casa no está desponible ahora." *I am sorry. The house is not available at this time.* Aside from Coco's cryptic replies, Charlie had been unable to get any updates on Vali since his escape. He was feeling more and more desperate.

Charlie considered obtaining false passports. With American passports, he and Vali could pass immigration control at Jose Marti airport and fly Cubana Air to Nassau. But Charlie had no contacts within the forged document community. He would need a new passport since the Cuban government was vigorously trying to imprison the Charles Sutton who had assisted in the slaughter of livestock. But the devil was in the details; he didn't have a photograph of Vali. Cuban immigration *did* have a photo of him, and he was likely to be recognized as he tried to leave. The mere act of trying to obtain a fraudulent passport was, in itself, a felony.

Charlie was forced to adapt his original plan even further. Allen refused to return to Cuba. Allen had openly lied to officials at the marina and was associated with a fugitive who was thought to be hiding on the island. In Allen's opinion, The *Bora Bora Express* should not return to Cuba either since it had been a miracle she was allowed to leave in the first place.

A long, straight road runs along Cuba's barren and desolate north coast. From Baracoa to Mariel, this highway could theoretically be used as an airstrip by a small plane. Again, it seemed to Charlie a feasible concept, but the mechanics were complicated since there were electrical lines that would make landing most difficult. The timing of the pickup would have to be performed with military precision—he and Vali needed to be standing at the spot where an aircraft came to a stop. They would then have to immediately board and take off—how would that ever be possible? How could they communicate with an airplane? Even if they figured out the logistics, Charlie didn't know any pilots, much less one crazy enough to invade a foreign airspace and risk being shot down by one or more MIG fighter aircraft.

He considered using a pontoon-mounted ultralight aircraft that could skim across the surface of the ocean just above the waves. Or perhaps jet skis. Jet skis were quick. He could race in, grab Vali and reach the ten-mile limit before the high-speed patrol boats blasted him out of the water. Or a windsurfer. The radar signature of a windsurfer must be tiny indeed. He could zip in at night on a windsurfer, sail directly to the house, snatch Vali, turn around, and rendezvous with a vessel beyond the ten-mile limit. But according to the group at the marina, there was a new infrared telescope mounted on the Hotel Viejo y El Mar alternately trained on the Rio Jaimanitas and the Hemingway Marina Harbor entrance, specifically searching for the heat signatures of bodies trying to escape under cover of darkness. His mind spun daily, nightly with new, ever-more-elaborate schemes. But what of how he had escaped himself?

Charlie was confident he had found a breach in the north coast security by sliding into the ocean disguised as a Cuban spearfisherman. It had worked once; it could work again. This, combined with the traffic coming and going during daylight hours from the marina, seemed to offer the only plausible opportunity. But while he had been bobbing around in the ocean, he'd had a chance to observe the actions of the numerous native fishing boats. He had been passed by many of them on his way out to sea, close enough to observe the fisherman on board. Most seemed to be diligently engaged in the pursuit of fish, except for one. A white motor launch, perhaps twenty-six feet in length, crisscrossed the inlet time and again. As soon as it reached a point about a quarter mile in either direction from the sea buoy, they turned and retraced their steps. The path of other boats seemed random. Fishermen constantly search for weed lines, follow the frigate birds or seek out current rips. Not this boat. Back and forth, all day, across the mouth of the channel. The more he thought about it, the more he came to the conclusion that the Cubans *were* aware of the potential for escape through the marina channel. He had simply been lucky. On the day he'd escaped, the wind had been blowing and the seas rough. He had been, for all practical purposes, invisible. It might have worked out much differently on a calm day.

Next time, he would bring scuba gear. If and when a fishing boat or a patrol boat—any boat—bore down on him, he would simply disappear beneath the surface, as silent and invisible as the rest of the fish.

By the process of elimination, his path became clear. He needed a different boat, a different crew, a pile of money, two sets of scuba gear, waterproof radios, a waterproof GPS, and a plan to sneak Vali into the United States without getting himself arrested for human trafficking. Jacksonville was about six hundred thirty miles from Havana, after zigging and zagging through the wind and against the Gulf Stream, a sailboat might easily put nine hundred miles on her hull before she reached Cuba. He needed to be closer to the land of Castro.

Geography made the decision easy—he would need to find a boat and crew out of Key West. After some research, Charlie decided that he would not start in the Key West everybody knew, but the workingman's Key West, better known as Stock Island.

It was rumored that anything was possible on Stock Island. Anything, that is, if the price was right. Charlie was counting on it.

If Charlie's research was correct, few tourists and fewer police took notice of the expanse of dilapidated trailers and shabby boating facilities to the left of the Overseas Highway as they crossed Cow Key Cut at mile-marker number four and headed for the island of Key West. One-fifth of Stock Island's fifteen hundred residents lived below the poverty line—the maids, taxi drivers, and topless dancers from Duval Street could find accommodations for as little as $300 per month, which is what Charlie paid for a two-bedroom mobile home on Robyn Lane. Charlie chose this particular trailer since it had a telephone in the owner's name and was within easy walking distance of numerous marinas.

If the dreary harbors and backwaters of Stock Island looked like a smuggler's paradise, it was because they were. It was best not to ask too many questions or wander the sand streets after dark. Charlie was a newcomer and knew his inquiries for a boat and captain would bring unwelcome attention, but the charter fishing boats in Key West wanted two thousand dollars for a ten-hour day and had to be back on the dock by 5:00 p.m. No, Key West was out of the question. Charlie walked the docks of Stock Island and handed out homemade business cards with his telephone number and his address on Robyn Lane.

One night the telephone rang. A gruff male voice said, "Meet me at the Hogfish Grill tomorrow, noon, come alone."

"How will I know who you are?" Charlie thought it a logical question.

"I know who you are. I will find you. Be there."

284

Charlie was at the allocated spot at the right time. He chose a table near the dock and scanned the faces of the patrons. Soon he was joined by a muscular fellow in his late twenties, American, collegiate in his speech and manners, his face hidden by a beard, dark glasses, and a baseball cap.

"What kind of boat are you looking for?"

Right to the point. Charlie shrugged. "Sail or motor, doesn't really matter. But it has to be seaworthy and the captain and crew can't"—Charlie searched for the right words—"be risk adverse. What's your name, by the way?"

"Stan. How much risk?"

"I'm not sure. Might lose the boat. Might do some jail time. But I am willing to pay." The discussion was taking on a cloak-and-dagger air that made Charlie uncomfortable. He was completely out of his element. He felt as though he were playing a part in a B movie. He could hear the words as they left his lips, and he felt like a criminal. "But I have thought it through. I think the risk is minimal."

"Where do you want to go?" Stan asked.

"Cuba."

Stan wasn't, apparently, expecting the answer to be Cuba. He laughed. "There are little or no drugs coming out of Cuba. It is statistically irrelevant. You are new to this business, aren't you?"

"New to what?" Charlie was confused.

"Smuggling."

"Frankly, I am," Charlie admitted. "But I smuggled myself out, kind of a trial run, and I think I can do it again."

Stan thought for a moment. "Well, how many pounds of drugs did you smuggle out?"

"Drugs? What drugs? No. I smuggled myself out. I committed a crime, and they were going to lock me up. Had to get off the island."

Stan took off his sunglasses, leaned forward, and grinned. "Ok, so you are *involved* with drugs in Cuba. Cocaine from Honduras, I bet. You know it all originates from Colombia?"

"Heavens, no. Not drugs. I helped butcher a steer."

Stan was totally confused. "You butchered a what?"

"A steer. Then I helped transport it. It's a big deal down there, five to seven years in jail. I was just helping a friend."

"No drugs?" Stan seemed incredulous.

Charlie spread his hands, turning them palms-up. "No drugs. I don't mess with them. You want to get lunch?"

Stan relaxed, letting down his guard. He picked up a menu. "Then why are you looking for a boat?"

Charlie signaled for a waitress. "For my girl. They locked her up for prostitution. She is not a prostitute. She is wonderful. I want to bring her back to Florida so we can get married. She will be in a house right at the harbor entrance. We will just swim out to sea, jump on the boat and then go to Jacksonville."

"But you said she's locked up."

"I am getting her busted out of a maximum-security prison. That's the hard part. Getting her on a boat will be a piece of cake. What kind of a boat do you have?"

"I don't have a boat," Stan admitted.

It was Charlie's turn to be incredulous. "Then why are we having this conversation?" It occurred to Charlie that he knew nothing about Stan. After a fifteen-minute conversation, Stan knew a lot about Charlie. *Why would a guy without a boat want to get in touch with me?* Charlie thought for a moment then blurted "Oh shit! I am sitting here in broad daylight with a DEA agent! Great. Now I will never find a boat."

"Relax," replied Stan. "I have lived here my whole life. I know everyone, and everyone knows me. If you are not moving weight, we're not going to have a problem. I will pay for lunch if you tell me about Cuba."

Charlie proceeded to describe his adventures and observations over the past couple of months. He talked about Esteban, the police, Vali, Rowena, and their mother. He described the incident with the steer and the strange laws that bear down on the shoulders of ordinary people. He told of his deal with Coco, the code system they had worked out. But there was a new twist. Two days ago, Coco had said, "The house will be available in ten days." Coco was ready to put the plan into action. It had taken two days to prepare and get to Stock Island; now Charlie had eight days to get back to Marina Hemingway.

"How much will you pay for a boat?" asked Stan.

"I am prepared to spend $4,000 to get me there, and $2,000 more to return with Vali back here to Stock Island."

"Would a thirty-five-foot Bertram be acceptable?"

Charlie knew the Bertram line. The thirty-five was the workhorse of the sportfish charter fleet—seaworthy and fuel efficient, it could make the trip to Hemingway Marina in less than six hours. "Actually, that would be the perfect boat. They could stop and fish off the Cuban coast without attracting attention—actually it's much better than a sailboat."

287

Once they were done eating, Stan paid the tab. "Come on. You've got to meet Crazy Joe. He needs the money. His wife is going to have a baby. I am afraid he is about to do something stupid to get money that carries a lot more risk than your job."

Charlie had passed the boat in question, the *Lady Emma*, on his walk to the Hogfish Grill. It lay on a rickety wooden dock covered with engine parts, batteries, and a fully functioning washing machine.

"Joe, you in there?" Stan called. There was a rustling and the gentle murmur of conversation. A heavyset man in trousers and a grimy T-shirt emerged from the sliding doors. He was obviously drunk.

"Hey, Stan—what can I do you for?"

"I have a guy here you need to talk with. He's got a job for you. Can we come aboard?"

"Sure, come in quick. All the air-conditioning is escaping." Joe introduced Debbie, his wife. She was approximately the same age as her husband, perhaps thirty-five or thirty-six, in the sixth month of her pregnancy. Charlie described the plan to smuggle Vali off the island, with details about how he would have to be located and plucked from the ocean. He repeated the amount he was willing to pay.

Joe was unphased by the risk. "That's nothing. You would not believe the places the *Emma* has gotten us into and out of. Sounds like fun. We haven't been to Cuba yet. Everybody else has. When do you want to leave?"

Charlie, though relieved at Joe's acceptance, was uncertain if he should place his trust in the sweaty, liquored-up man in front of him on the advice of Stan, who was a total stranger. Vali couldn't swim. Charlie would already be working at a handicap.

"You realize that if you don't find me in the ocean, not only will I die but my fiancée will also drown? What kind of engines do you have?"

"Detroits."

"How many hours?"

"Less than four thousand on each. They run like a Swiss watch. I am having the port injector rebuilt, and it should be ready to install in two days—that would be Saturday."

Charlie was running out of time. Joe seemed to know what he was talking about. Charlie would have to trust him. "All right, we need to get to Cuba at night, Tuesday night. That way I can get everyone paid off and in position. We can leave anytime after dark, up until midnight, depending on the sea conditions. You are going to drop me off at the sea buoy and wait outside until daylight before proceeding to customs and immigration."

The wind was blowing out of the north the next morning as Charlie returned to Jacksonville. After making carefully planned withdrawals that would fly under the radar, he amassed the proper amount. He wrapped forty thousand dollars, a pack of hundred-dollar bills about three inches thick, into stacks of five thousand dollars each. These were sealed in ziplock bags and bound with rubber bands. The packets were placed in the pockets of his buoyancy compensator, using safety pins as an added precaution in case the Velcro seals were ripped open. He sprayed his seventy-two-cubic-foot scuba tanks black and brought two extra O-rings. Pawn shops provided the paraphernalia that Vali would need—booties, women's fins, weight belt, mask, and snorkel. Attached to his BC was an underwater flashlight and a compass. He memorized the magnetic heading from the sea buoy to the house; it was 140°. He asked Allen to move the *Express* from Bimini to Stock Island since he trusted the winds far more than the old Detroit diesels on the *Emma*. Allen agreed.

"But keep the slip," Charlie requested. "That's important. We need a place to return without being hassled. Leave some of our lines on the dock so they know we will be back."

Monday afternoon. Charlie completed the seven-hour drive to Stock Island in an Avis rental car. Over one hundred pounds of gear was off-loaded to the *Emma*. Charlie peeled seven one-hundred-dollar bills from a stack and handed them to Debbie for fuel and provisions. The GPS coordinates of the Marina Hemingway's outer buoy were uploaded into Crazy Joe's navigation computer. The K-Mart beer-storage minifridge was hauled from its home in the cockpit to the end of the dock. They worked out a code, similar to the one devised by Allen, allowing them to share information over the VHF while sounding like fishermen.

During the first weeks of December, the wind in south Florida is dependent as much on the weather in the Mississippi Valley as the Caribbean. Once the turbulence in the ITCZ, the Intertropical Convergence Zone, has simmered down and ceased producing hurricanes, the path is open for cold fronts to sweep down from the upper latitudes and invade the warm, azure waters of the south. And such was the case on Tuesday, December 8, 1998. The wind had shifted to westerly as a cold front prepared to enter Alabama. Had it been January or February, the wind shift may have forewarned of a screaming norther, but at this time of year, it was just a bluff, a mere catspaw extended by Mother Nature as a playful tap on waters and the inhabitants of the Conch Republic.

The *Emma* left the dock at 8:30 a.m. She followed the day markers across Hawk Channel for six miles into the main ship channel. Once she cleared the bank, Crazy Joe set the autopilot on a ninety-one-nautical-mile course, half throttle to save fuel. Five hours later, the loom of the lights of Havana appeared on the southern horizon. Charlie felt a twinge of nausea. He remembered the first time he had seen the skyline, just six months ago, so excited and ready for adventure. Then, the lights had beckoned with the promise hope and mystery. But now they were the lights of a prison, one that had devoured his friend and had a jail cell open and waiting for him. He would not let the island devour Vali. It occurred that this may have been a one-way trip, his last trip. He thought of Rowena. Adventure was one thing, but this was fucking nuts—returning to a deadly island from which he had just escaped. But in reality, there was no choice. He could not live the rest of his life knowing he had abandoned the only woman he had ever loved to rot in Cuban incarceration.

Crazy Joe had little apprehension. For him and his wife, this was a paid vacation. After hauling tons of marijuana, he told Charlie that dropping off and retrieving a lovesick kid didn't even register on his danger meter. But Crazy Joe had never been to Cuba. He believed the hype he had heard on the docks: free medical, free college, 100 percent literacy, a country without homeless people—a Caribbean Disney Land where all the people lived in utopian bullshit harmony. *Perhaps it's better he didn't know about Cuba*, thought Charlie. He would just blend in with the other Yumas who didn't have a clue.

Four a.m. Three miles from the sea buoy. Crazy Joe throttled back to idle speed. Charlie put on his scuba gear and clamped the weight belt around his middle. Sitting on the swim platform, he had Joe hand him Vali's tank with its attached buoyancy compensator, clipped to it the swim bag containing her mask, snorkel, booties, flippers, radio, and GPS. Due to the approach angle, he was obscured from the view of the infrared telescope on top of the hotel by the hull and *Emma*'s superstructure. By the time he slipped on his flippers, Joe was passing the green flashing light on top of the buoy and heading into the channel. This wasn't the plan. He was supposed to slow down, drop Charlie off at the sea buoy, and wait until daybreak before entering the channel.

Joe's voice rose over the sound of the motors, "I'm going to wait at the customs dock. Done it a thousand times in a thousand banana republics."

In seconds, the *Emma* shot past the sea buoy and surfed the breakers to calmer waters inside the channel. Crazy Joe was deviating from the plan and motoring much too quickly. Charlie was horrified to discover they were adjacent to the eastern breakwater;

anyone there with a flashlight could have spotted him. Caught off guard, he hurriedly nudged the mass of gear over the edge of the swim platform. But the instant it touched the slipstream behind the boat it dragged him from his precarious perch. The blast of the prop-wash dislodged his mask and threw him head over heels like a rag doll. Since both hands were trying desperately to hang on to the bundles, he could not adjust his mask.

The young captain found himself being dragged upside down to the bottom of the channel by a hundred pounds of uncompensated hardware. Pain shot through both ears as the water pressure threatened to burst his eardrums. He desperately needed to squeeze his nose, honk, and equalize the pressure in his ears but dared not release his death grip on the descending cargo.

Although he had been through the procedure a hundred times in his mind, it had not prepared him for the reality of being jettisoned over the back of a boat into total darkness. He had purposely adjusted for negative buoyancy so he didn't bob on the surface like a dead whale. Now, pinned to the bottom of the sea, blind, disoriented and on the verge of destroying his hearing, he regretted that decision. He needed to get to the flashlight to see the compass, so he would know which way to swim, but the knot he had tied in the top of that bag required two hands. A million thoughts needed to be considered at once. He was using air he would need for the escape. White sharks and tiger sharks feed along the shoreline at night, one could be sniffing at his head, only inches away and he would never know. Even if he somehow corrected his mask, to purge it he would have to flip onto his back—but which way as up? A wave of panic shot through his body.

He closed his eyes. Darkness makes more sense if one's eyes are closed. He needed to gain control of his thoughts and his nerves. Getting to the surface would solve three problems simultaneously— he could see where he was going, adjust his mask and switch to his snorkel to save air. To free up a hand, he wrapped his legs around a bundle. Charlie fumbled for the BC's power inflator, located on the end of a flexible tube connected by Velcro to the left side of the vest. All divers learn to do this on day one. He pressed the button and felt the vest quickly inflate. Gradually his body lifted like a blimp from the bottom. A few more bumps of air and he had the buoyancy to drag his cargo with him. The reduced pain on his eardrums told him he was rising. When he hit the surface, he used his snorkel to breathe. Through tiny injections and release of air into the BC, he could maintain equilibrium until only the tip of his snorkel broke the surface. With smooth and even kicks of his oversized fins, he aimed for the safety of the harbor house.

Mindful that his mask might become a mirror and reflect the shine of the security lights to unwanted eyes, he dared not lift his head to look for guards. Charlie went to the dark waters west of the channel. Excitement replaced apprehension. Even if he was discovered, he could switch to scuba and disappear. He was surprised at his progress; he reached the shallows in twenty minutes and the seawall three or four minutes later. He slung his flippers onto the lawn, pushed his gear over the edge, and scrambled beneath the hidden shelter of the overhanging branch. Only then did he dare look back at the island and the guardhouse.

From his vantage point, he could see a tiny pinprick of light emerging from the darkness of the near corner where the security lights did not penetrate. There it was again—the telltale lambent glow of a cigar being smoked by someone concealed in the darkness. That person, or persons, was as invisible as he was. That invisible person was a hunter, waiting patiently, silently for his quarry. Charlie had passed within a hundred feet of a concealed security agent. Had he lifted his head to look, had his mask reflected a single photon of light, he might have been discovered. Fidel had been a hunter. He'd used his knowledge to evade capture time and again. Now Fidel's knowledge was being used to protect the regime—the surrogate eyes in the dark were Fidel's eyes. At one time Fidel had been lucky to evade capture. Now it was Charlie's turn.

Charlie's previous nest was undisturbed. The fugitive could feel his heart crashing in his chest as he tried to go to sleep. Every moment he was on the island could be his last as a free man. He thought of secret agents he had read about, operating behind enemy

293

lines. They would carry little, hidden capsules of cyanide since death was preferable to capture. It seemed a reasonable idea.

Wednesday morning, Charlie put on his Cuban clothes and walked the mile to Coco's house.

His old landlord grinned and clapped him on the back. "I knew you would be back. No one believed me. We have found her. We have a plan. All we need now is money."

"How much are you going to need right now?"

Coco went to his desk and withdrew a paper that looked like the battle plans for World War II. Charlie's plan was taking on military overtones. Calculator in hand, Coco tallied the cost of equipment then the cost of personnel.

"Twelve thousand dollars now."

"What does that get me?"

"Well, a truck, a doctor, lookouts. What do you care? You want the girl or not? You know we are all taking an enormous chance. I have put together a small army, but nobody has moved a muscle until they see the money. Do you have any idea how hard it is to break out of Guanajay? That's just the beginning. The Ministry of Justice will investigate. They are going to talk to everyone. That's the trick—to get her out and not have a dozen other people going to jail. You know, they think you are still on the island, and they are still looking for you."

Charlie counted out twelve stacks of a thousand dollars each. "I am going to need a drink after this. How long will it take?"

"I don't know. It's hard. Nobody was going to commit until I had the money in my hand. Right now we are dealing in the theoretical. The hypothetical. Money makes it real."

"Did Esteban talk? Where is he?" Charlie braced for the response.

"They torture you and threaten your family. You are just a Yuma. Everything Esteban knew about you, the police now know. Don't hold it against him. He has a wife and a little girl. His house will probably be seized, and we don't expect to see him for ten or so years.

"And Vali? Did they torture Vali?"

"According to the doctor, she has been kept in a punishment cell. She sustained some injuries and is recovering slowly. You need to brace yourself. The girl you get back might be very different from the Vali you slept with at the apartment."

"That's all the more reason we have to save her," Charlie said, the back of his throat burning. "I have the rest of my life to put her back together."

CHAPTER THIRTY

There was a shortage of punishment cells. More were being built, but in the meantime, doubling up in the *gaviota* helped alleviate overcrowding. After the verdict was read, Vali was returned to a different cell than she had previously occupied, the cell of Yohana Portillo, a political prisoner. Usually, the *prisonero politicos* were segregated from the general population, but Yohana had a will of iron and refused to be reeducated. By the time Vali was forced into the drawer with Yohanna, the bird had lost the ability to sing—Yohana could no longer communicate effectively. She had been in the vault for eight months and was now utterly insane. Without even a tormentor for company, Yohana's brilliant mind had become disjointed and unraveled, her thoughts no longer connected—they spanned the range of time and perception on a moment by moment basis, without coherence, at once a child, then an angel, or a poet. Vali had heard of a similar situation where the co-occupant was overpowered and had her face eaten by her cellmate who was, in her former life, a nun.

As Vali was shoved into the cell, she could see Yohana huddling in the corner, her knees beneath he armpits, eyes wild and lips moving as if in conversation. The new *gaviota* smelled differently from Vali's former cell. Filthy water came from a half-inch metal pipe that protruded from the wall about a foot above the sewer hole; there was no valve or any way to control its flow. Therefore, when the water was turned on, it blasted to the center of the cell. Occupants had no way of knowing how long it would last since it varied, sometimes five times a day, then no water for twenty-four hours. And when it was turned on, it might last for fifteen seconds or five minutes. There was no way to tell. From this, prisoners had to drink, cleanse themselves and try to guide feces into and down the four-inch hole—in total darkness. If the water stopped in the middle of this process, the hands of the prisoner were covered with filth until the next blast erupted from the wall. It appeared that Yohanna had not attempted to clean the cell or herself in a very long time.

As the door slammed behind her, Vali was no longer able to see her new roommate, but from the smell, she felt she had been locked in the dark with the devil himself.

Aside from visits to the physician, Vali was confined to her cell for twenty-four hours a day. Inmates are required by law to be checked by a physician on a regular basis. While health considerations are cursorily addressed, for political reasons, it is deemed better for the regime if their prisoners die in a hospital. By the time a woman was taken to the hospital, there was a good chance she would ever return.

Vali had been checked by the same physician twice in two months. Both times she was brought to an examination room, under guard, where they would take her vital signs, draw blood, and tend to her wounds. But the third time was different. During the brief time they were alone, the doctor grabbed her jaw and pressed his face to hers. "Next time, stay in your cell and play dead. You hear me?" He squeezed harder for emphasis. "Play dead. Play dead when they come."

As she was escorted back to her chamber, Vali struggled to make sense of what the doctor had told her. Play dead when they come? When *who* comes? His face looming only an inch from hers was strange indeed. What did it mean? But she knew it was a command. A strange and confidential directive. *Play dead*, the words reverberated in her head. Now, locked in with Yohanna, Vali repeated them like a mantra.

Two weeks later. Footsteps outside her cell. The food slot opened, and through it, the beam of a flashlight illumined the cell. Vali had been lying in a thin film of ooze, but instead of acknowledging the intruders, she left her cheek on the concrete and remained motionless. There was rustling. She listened as the slot was closed and the sound of a key entered and turned the lock. She remembered the words, the commandment of the doctor. *Play dead.* Playing dead was easy, all she had eaten for a month was watered-down *harina*, a corn-soup gruel with occasion chunks of fetid meat scrap. She was half dead already.

They pulled her out and, seeing that she was unresponsive, waited for a gurney. She felt herself being placed on a cold metal surface as she was wheeled into the artificial light of a secure holding room near behind the visitor's center. She was lifted by her shoulders and feet to a transfer gurney.

Vali felt a wave claustrophobia sweep over her as thick leather straps, one over her chest, one over her waist, and the third over her feet, lashed her to a new cold surface. On the sides of the strap over her waist were leather hand restraints into which her wrists were lashed. She found herself totally immobilized, bound, restricted—trapped like a rat. It was yet another adventure in horror, but she kept her eyes closed. *Remember: play dead.* The cart's little wheels stumbled over the cracked cement of the loading ramp as she was transported to a waiting jaula. It was nighttime, and the air smelled of burning cane. She wanted to gulp in huge breaths of outside air, but she kept herself breathing slowly, shallowly. It was a sweet smell, different from that of other fires, reminiscent of burning marshmallows since the smoke contained the essence of raw sugar. She never realized how much she'd loved that smell. The legs of the gurney, with Vali attached, folded up and under and slid snugly between the metal seats of the windowless prisoner-transport vehicle. The door was locked and bolted, and she was once again trapped in dark. There she waited for two hours.

Mosquitoes had worked their way through the side vents and were feasting on her face and ankles. She struggled to free her hands from the leather straps. As she stared wild-eyed at the ceiling, she heard the driver's door open. She felt the vehicle shimmy on its springs as an occupant entered. The door slammed shut. The engine started. The vehicle rumbled to the main gate where there was a muffled discussion, then pulled itself forward through a series of laborious gear shifts to a hard-surface road. Vali could hear the whine of the tires and the hum of the drive train.

They stopped three times, presumably at crossroads, each time shifting their way up to cruising speed. Vali imagined the terrain around her—it must be the country since few if any other vehicles whizzed past in the opposite direction.

Suddenly, without warning—smash! Vali and the gurney crashed to the left side of the enclosure. The vehicle accelerated sideways and nearly overturned. The impact knocked the wind out of her and sent a sharp pain through her neck. She knew immediately they had been in an accident. The fuel tank had been ruptured, and she was soon surrounded by the smell of raw gasoline. If it caught fire, there would be an explosion, and she would be burned alive. She heard another vehicle slide to a stop in the loose gravel. She listened as the engine was switched off. A single door slammed. There were muted voices outside. An argument ensued. At any moment, the vehicle could be engulfed in flames—she had seen accidents before.

She screamed, "Get me out of here! Can anybody hear me? Get me out of here!"

Footsteps outside. A commanding voice: "Give me the key." She listened as someone fumbled with the lock. "Help me get her out of that thing before it explodes."

The doors swung open. The driver dragged the gurney backward, its legs springing to the ground when they cleared the bumper.

"What's wrong with her?" A new voice—not the driver's—demanded.

"She's sick. She is on her way to Guevara Military Hospital," the driver explained.

"How sick is she?"

"I don't know. She's almost dead. Just look at her."

"Can she run?" A uniformed police officer had moved into Vali's field of view. He must have been the one in the car that had stopped.

"Run? She can't even stand up." The driver had been injured in the collision, which had been centered on his door. The left side of his head was bleeding where it had been slammed by the window. He favored his shoulder, which Vali thought was broken or dislocated. Yet he complied when the officer commanded that he go to the cab and retrieve his prisoner's transfer papers. The officer placed the papers in his patrol car.

"That table won't fit in my car. Help me get her out of the restraints," the officer ordered.

Vali resumed playing dead, or almost dead. She raised her head and saw that a Ural 4320, a Russian-made dump truck that weighed over twenty thousand pounds, had smashed into the driver's door of the much smaller jaula. The confused and dazed jaula driver assisted as they unbuckled Vali's leather bindings.

The police officer waved a hand toward his car. "Now help me get her into the back of my patrol car."

The driver hesitated. The officer raised his voice. "Look, she is your responsibility. It says so right here in the documents that *you* signed. If she dies, her death will be on your head. We will have her to the hospital in fifteen minutes. Put her in the patrol car. That's an order!"

Vali was lifted from the gurney by the jaula driver and the Ural driver, who had come out of the cab of the dump truck. She was gently deposited into the back seat of the patrol car. The officer slid behind the steering wheel.

"You!" the officer shouted, pointing at the Ural driver. "You were at fault in this. Get in."

The Ural driver climbed into the passenger seat. Seconds later, they disappeared into the darkness, leaving behind a bleeding and bewildered correction official. They drove north through the campo and intersected Avenida Quinta just west of Santa Fe then east toward Jaimanitas. Coco saw them coming and had the gate of the harbor house, Charlie's hideout, open before they arrived. The patrol car backed into the driveway.

Vali heard two words. "Get out." He sounded like a real policeman because he was.

Coco and Charlie assisted as she struggled out of the car and tried to walk. She was half dragged, half carried into the construction site, up the darkened staircase. She was bewildered. This wasn't the hospital. They came into a room illuminated only by the eight mercury-vapor lights located across the channel at customs and immigration. There, Charlie laid her on a blanket, out of sight of the eyes across the channel.

"Vali, I love you," were his first words.

Coco, anxious to get far away from the two most wanted fugitives on the island, left quickly. He had done his job.

***

"I knew it was you." She lifted her arms to embrace him. He leaned forward to give her a kiss and caught a whiff of the cell in which she had been living.

"Good God, we have got to get you cleaned up! I have soap but no running water. Can you make it downstairs?"

"Did you bring any clothes for me?" She plucked at the rags that she was dressed in.

"Just getting you out was a long shot. Coco will bring everything you need tomorrow."

"And a razor. I am going to need a razor. And a toothbrush."

Charlie removed her clothes and led her to the other upstairs bedroom. He estimated she had lost twenty pounds—her ribs were showing; her legs were thinner, as was her face. "We are going to have to fatten you up." Charlie had prepared a proper bed in the hideout, beside it a cooler filled with water, beer, and sandwiches. He reached into the cooler and handed her a tuna salad sandwich. "*Cervesa o cola?*" he asked.

"A beer would be wonderful." When she was through eating, Charlie carried her down the stairs, through the rubble of the construction site, then across the backyard in the shadow of the bushes. When they reached the seawall, he instructed her to wait. He returned to the house and retrieved a bottle of dishwashing soap from the kitchen then hopped into the water. She sat on the bulkhead and swung her legs over the edge. Charlie lifted her and placed her gently in the knee-deep water.

The lagoon was bathtub warm. A beckoning breeze blew in from the sea. Before them, over the darkness of an invisible ocean, blazed a billion stars, guideposts for navigators since the dawn of sea travel. The Big Dipper was overhead. Charlie followed its pointer stars to Polaris, the North Star. North was the direction of freedom. The blinking lights of the channel markers, green on his left, red on the right, were the terrestrial stars that punctuated the edges of the water highway that would be their road to a new life.

"Stand up," he said gently.

Vali complied. Charlie stood behind her and squirted soap on the top of her head and worked it into a lather.

"Could this be a dream?" Vali whispered as she closed her eyes. "Could this be a hallucination? Am I really in my cell right now? This seems real, but it can't be. It has to be a dream." She reached out to touch the side wall of her cell. It wasn't there. Charlie scrubbed her ears and scratched her scalp with his fingers. To Vali, this wasn't real, and Charlie nearly felt the same—that she was back in his arms was *surreal* to him.

"Oh my God. Now I am just like Yohana—completely insane," she muttered, leaning back into Charlie.

Charlie raised her arms and worked the soap into every inch from her fingertips to her armpits. He used the detergent as a massage cream for her neck and shoulders. She lifted her head as he massaged her throat and kept it raised as his hands made their way down to her breasts. He scrubbed her midriff and then her lower stomach.

He soaped her from navel to toes next, hoping that he was washing away a little bit of her ordeal with each stroke. After she was clean, Charlie sat in the sand and had her float in his lap. He swished the soap out of her hair while she swished seawater in her mouth and spit it out, over and over.

"Hold your nose while I dunk you," he said.

"No. No. I am afraid to go underwater." She rolled from Charlie's lap and splashed the soap from her face.

"Have you ever been underwater?" he asked, bracing himself for what he had to tell her next.

"My mother told me that when I was a baby, I almost drowned. That's why I am afraid," she explained.

Charlie pondered the depth of her fear. Was she just uncomfortable with the thought of getting a little water up her nose? Or did she have a full-blown phobia? Maybe the real reason was sharks. Sharks make sense—the fucking fish could eat you. He had to be careful with his choice of words. Somehow or other, in the very near future, she was going to have to conquer her fear and swim a mile underwater. He wasn't a psychiatrist. He didn't know how to make a fear go away. But he had to, within the next forty-eight hours, or they both might wind up in prison, or worse.

"Do you trust me?" he asked.

"Yes. I trust you," said Vali.

"You know I would never do anything to hurt you."

"Yes. I know that."

Charlie had two facemasks hidden beside the seawall. He slipped on his mask. "You've seen me wear this thing before. You remember? Like the divers in the morning on the street."

"I am not going under water. If I do, I will die." Her eyes were saucers in the moonlight.

It's a phobia. Now it was Charlie's turn to panic. The next words he chose might make the difference between life and death. Should he be assertive, logical, or de minimus, make light of the issue—it was nonconfrontational and the least threatening. Yep. De minimus.

"Nonsense," he replied. "I have seen four-year-old kids use these things. It's easy. You just have to relax. You said you trust me. Here, just do what I do. You will see it's not scary at all."

He slipped the mask over his head and had her kneel in front of him. He held her hand. He gradually lowered himself until the water was about halfway up his mask, all the while maintaining reassuring eye contact. "Easy, you try. Put on the mask just as you saw me do." She complied. "Now put the snorkel in your mouth. See? It's easy to breathe. Piece of cake."

Vali was stiff with fear. She knew what was coming next.

"Just sit on the bottom and put the snorkel into the water," he urged. She tried, but as soon as she realized her mouth was under the surface of the sea, she spat out the tube and stripped the mask off her head.

"Vali." Charlie was serious this time. "I have arranged for a boat to pick us up in the ocean. We have to swim under the water to avoid the police. Look, that's them, right there, beneath the lights on that concrete island. Even after we make it to the ocean, they are in boats and watching from the top of Viejo y El Mar. They are everywhere. Vali, we have to hide from them, and the only place to hide is under the water."

She didn't respond. Her eyes glazed over, and she stared off into space just over his left ear. "Have you spoken to my mother?" she asked as if he weren't discussing life-or-death matters with her.

"Yes," Charlie said. "I gave her money. American dollars. Enough to take care of her until we can figure out how to get her to America."

Coco was right. Vali wasn't the same girl he had fallen in love with over the course of a summer. She was shell-shocked, traumatized, glassy-eyed, as if returning from war. She had been kept in a box for three months. It was a wonder she could still form a sentence. And now Charlie wanted her to complete an underwater obstacle course that would challenge a professional. But Charlie knew that the old Vali was in there—the Vali that would do whatever was necessary. It was what separated her from the street girls. Once he got her to Florida, he would bring her back, little by little, every day. Right now, what was necessary was learning how to breathe from a scuba tank and swim underwater. But she'd had enough for tonight.

>25

They returned to the dusty room. Charlie dried her with his only towel, which doubled as a pillow. He put her on the bed and gently lowered himself on her frail body. She welcomed him. He had to be careful since he assumed she did not receive birth control pills during her stay at the Hotel Castro. She wrapped her legs around him and was asleep thirty seconds after.

306

CHAPTER THIRTY-ONE

The sun rose on a dissipating west wind. Charlie watched as the fishing boats left the marina and headed to sea. Local launches and skiffs sailed past the foreign boats being detained and inspected at the customs dock before they were inspected and allowed to go fishing. At seven o'clock a small, white inboard launch made its way through the channel entrance. It turned, as did many of the others, and followed the ledge but never ventured more than a quarter mile from the sea buoy, which was a half-mile swim from the harbor house. The launch tended to stay above the ledge, which paralleled the shore—the same boat, the same course, back and forth. Although there were two rods in the holders on the stern and she looked like a fishing vessel, it was an unlikely pattern for a true fisherman. Vali awoke from a fitful sleep. She was disoriented, but when she saw Charlie beside her, she smiled and wrapped her arms around him.

"I'm hungry," she whispered.

Charlie prepared a Pringles and mayonnaise sandwich with a TuKola to wash it down. He held her by the shoulders and looked her in the eye. "You can't go near the window opening. They have binoculars across the channel at the customs dock. If they see you, they will call the police. Your clothes need to be burned. I will get more from Coco. Today I am going to explain to you everything you need to know about swimming with a tank underwater. Tonight we will practice. There is a boat just outside the channel looking for swimmers, and we must go *under* him. I know it's hard, but it is very important that you focus."

"I want to see my mother."

"You realize that is the first place they will look for you. I'm sorry. That is impossible. We are already much too close to Jaimanitas. We need to get out of here. They are going to tear this island apart looking for you. You are this close to leaving for America. Promise me you will do exactly as I say."

"I promise."

Charlie made the mile walk to Coco's house in the morning, carrying eight thousand dollars in cash. Guillermo returned with women's clothes, shampoo, conditioner, and toiletries hidden beneath his woodworking tools. Once he was safely back at the hideout, Vali cuddled on Charlie's chest as he described the basics of using scuba equipment. She seemed a good student and asked the appropriate questions at the appropriate times. He had some difficult decisions to make. What if she surfaced and was captured? What if she started to drown? There was little he could do to save her—even if he somehow kept her alive, they would both be put into put into a cage until the next Ice Age. If she fell behind, was he prepared to leave her? Charlie estimated her chances of surviving were about fifty-fifty.

That night she practiced staying totally submerged and blasting the water out of her snorkel before taking the next breath. She put on swim fins for the first time. Charlie showed her how to slow kick with an easy rhythm.

"See? Piece of cake. A baby could do it!" he exclaimed. But there was no way to demonstrate how to clear her ears. He could describe it to her, but that was something that always required some practice. Without that ability, they were limited to a depth of less than ten feet.

He placed the tanks, BCs, and the weight belts in the water beneath the seawall. The code was sent to Crazy Joe on VHF channel 73. As Vali slept, Charlie sat in the dark, staring down the channel. If it was up to him, he would leave under cover of night and wait at sea. But Vali could barely walk, much less swim for eight hours. He felt nauseous and was still awake when the sun came up.

At first light, he watched the spearfisherman work the edge of the canal before heading out of the channel entrance. They looked no more than small, black ducks throwing tiny ripple wakes. The ducks disappeared occasionally to search for fish then resurfaced. After years and years of diving, they blended in and became just another part of the natural environment. No one stopped them. No one cared. But there was something peculiar—they were followed by another duck, even smaller, a duck that never dove. Then Charlie remembered. How could he be so stupid to overlook an important detail? Cuban divers towed a floating catch bag thirty to fifty feet behind them. They all towed catch bags. It was the custom. It made sense. If a shark wanted to steal their fish, the attack would be directed at the bag and not the diver. Knives were carried for the express purpose of cutting loose the bag.

Charlie dared leave nothing to chance. A diver without a catch bag might attract attention. The Yuma scoured the house and found a mason's line that he attached to a half-filled TuKola bottle. When pulled behind, the rig should resemble the float used by the local divers. It would have to do.

The *Emma* had been out of the harbor and fishing every morning. It was part of the plan. The first time they cleared customs they had been detained for an hour. According to Crazy Joe, the last time the officials had wanted nothing to do with them and practically waved them through. The plan was working. Radio rendezvous time was set by code for eight thirty. Vali's hands were trembling as she slipped over the edge of the seawall.

"Relax. We're just divers hunting our breakfast," Charlie reassured. Charlie could see the customs officers going about their business only five hundred feet away. Vali tried to assist as Charlie

309

got her into the BC, but she had no idea of the apparatus in which she found herself enveloped. Charlie had her place the regulator in her mouth.

"It's exactly the same as a snorkel, only easier." He listened as she took her first mechanical breath before she switched back to the snorkel.

He buckled her weight belt, slipped on her booties and then her fins. His anxiety made it hard to breathe, hard to concentrate—he had to get a grip on his emotions. Clarity of thought was essential. But no matter how hard he tried to remain calm, his hands were trembling as if the water was freezing.

"*Listo?* Ready?" he asked. She nodded. As they left the bulkhead, the mason's line was payed out behind them. Charlie adjusted Vali's buoyancy and held her hand. They paddled their way to the edge of the channel in less than two minutes. This brought them uncomfortably close to the final guardhouse on the east side of the ship channel. Originally Charlie had planned to traverse this part underwater, but he felt confident in their disguise. Every now and then, he would release Vali's hand and dive, his three-foot-long fins shooting vertically into the air to drive him to the bottom. It was the opposite of being invisible. He remained submerged for about a minute, just like the other spearfisherman. When he returned to the surface, he did so gently, as would a professional. Then they continued flapping their way north, meandering lazily over the edge of the channel as they headed toward the sea buoy.

They approached the jagged breakwater on the east side of the channel. Waves crashing on its serrated concrete edges created a confused and foamy confluence where the harbor waters met those of the open ocean. Charlie had Vali switch from snorkel to regulator. He held her hand, and they kept kicking. Gradually the sea floor fell away, twenty feet, forty feet, then the ledge. He looked up to see the fake fishing boat begin its turn back to the sea buoy. It would be on top of them in a matter of minutes. He turned and held Vali by the shoulders, looking at her, mask to mask, as he slowly pressed her BC's purge valve. She closed her eyes and grabbed him as they sank beneath the surface of the sea. He could tell she was terrified. His mask was inches from hers.

Concentrate on me, thought Charlie. But now they were headed for the bottom. Soon she would feel an intense pain in her ears, and that would freak her out for sure. Charlie bumped a shot of air into the BC. They kept descending. One more squirt of air and they achieved neutral buoyancy at seven or eight feet. Charlie took her hand, and they set off on a compass course of twenty degrees, just east of due north.

They could hear the sound of an engine approaching. Human ears typically can't determine direction when submerged in water—the sound hits both ears at pretty much the same time. But they are acutely sensitive to volume. And the volume of an engine kept increasing to the point it sounded as if they were destined to be run over and ground into hamburger by the prop. Then it began to fade. Charlie scanned in the opposite direction for the fishing lures, or grapples towed behind the launch for the express purpose of snagging divers. There were none. Soon the noise was gone. He looked at his watch. It was seven forty-five.

The continental shelf slipped away quickly to a depth of over a thousand feet. Although the bottom was far away, it had offered a comforting point of reference. Without it they were suspended in blue space, bright turquoise-blue above, purple-blue below. Even the astronauts have something to view when they go for spacewalks. The fugitives had precious little—an enveloping blue nothingness without boundaries. Charlie controlled their depth by monitoring the pressure on his ears. Vali was doing surprisingly well, despite the fact that she must be feeling the same pressure. They slowly pushed their way offshore. Eight ten.

As they sucked air into their lungs, the tanks got lighter. Charlie bumped the purge valve to burp tiny bursts of air out of both BCs. They established an easy rhythm. It was remarkably peaceful and crystal clear—Charlie peered straight down, focusing on a group of translucent moon jellyfish pulsing their way through the abyss perhaps fifty feet beneath them. When he looked up, all he saw was gray. At first, he thought they had stumbled onto the hull of a ship. A gray ship. A gray wall. But the wall before him was moving. On the wall, a distinctive pattern of stripes which he recognized immediately. It was the massive side of a huge tiger shark.

Vali screamed into her regulator and instinctively grabbed for Charlie, dislodging his face mask and allowing it to fill with water. Blinded, Charlie fumbled for the power inflator and scrambled to the surface, dragging Vali behind him. This was precisely the frenzied activity that excited sharks. He cleared his mask and looked down just in time to see a massive head closing in on his stomach. He leaned back and kicked, hitting the fish on the nose. It veered off but circled back. He shot a look at his dive watch—eight twenty-five, five minutes before his scheduled transmission. But this could be considered an extenuating circumstance. Charlie was sure the *Emma* would be listening. He turned on the GPS and held it above his head, waiting for it to acquire a signal. Vali kicked at the shark as it made another pass. On the horizon, the bow of a boat was headed in his general direction. It might be the *Emma*. It might not. He fumbled for his VHF, pressed the button, and yelled into the ziplock, "Left, steer left!"

There was no response.

Once again, he shouted, "Left! Steer left!" Slowly the bow swung to its port, but far too much. "Now right, steer to the right!"

Vali tried to climb onto Charlie's back, pushing him underwater as the shark came in for another pass. With a GPS in one hand and the radio in the other, he had no way of dislodging the terrified woman who was trying to use his head as a life raft. He escaped by going deeper, leaving her flailing on the surface. The shark made its way to a position between the swimmers. As it snapped toward Vali, Charlie straddled its back and gouged at its eyes with his fingernails. The shark thrashed Charlie off and writhed a few meters away. Suddenly, there was more noise, more commotion, and they were tossed about like seaweed by a sudden prop blast of bubbling blue water. Charlie looked up to see a hand extending through the shimmering mercury surface—it was Crazy

Joe's hand. He had seen the commotion from a quarter mile away and rushed to put his boat between the shark and the swimmers. Joe hauled Vali onto the swim platform while Charlie pushed her from below. Then Charlie shot from the water like a penguin and landed on the fiberglass surface.

Gasping, Charlie flopped back onto the deck. "This is the first time in my life I have ever shit myself. Let's get out of here!"

"Relax." Crazy Joe offered his observation, "That shark was just playing with you. He wanted you to give him a fish. If he was really hungry, you would be in its stomach."

Charlie looked over to see that Vali, like her mother, was a fainter. She was passed out cold.

The Detroits screamed as Joe went to full throttle. They were not out of danger; if Joe could see Charlie from a distance, there was a good chance that he had been spotted by the police through their high-powered binoculars. At twenty-six knots it would take about twenty minutes to reach the ten-mile limit. The Cuban gunboats traveled twice that fast. All eyes were glued to the horizon. There were about a dozen boats plying the local waters, but none altered course.

Joe scanned the coast with his binoculars. "I don't think we are being followed. I'm going to slow down and set out a spread."

Charlie just shook his head. Joe was not a worrier. "Once we get into international water, I don't care. We can fish all the way home. But first, let's get out of Cuban waters."

Vali stirred, and Charlie helped her sit up and wrapped her in a towel. She held Charlie's hand as they watched the island disappear over the southern horizon and with it the combined charges of livestock slaughter, prostitution, child endangerment, unjust enrichment, escaping from prison, and customs infractions too numerous to count.

"Where are we going?" she asked.

"*Primero*, Cayo Hueso." Cubans knew Key West by its old Spanish name: Island of Bones.

"Is that near Miami?"

Charlie began drying her hair with the towel. "Well, it's about a hundred and twenty miles, approximately the same distance as Havana to Villa Clara." Charlie tried to imagine the world through Vali's eyes. The only things she had to her name were shorts and a T-shirt, and technically, even those were not hers since both were loans from Raquel. It was hard to imagine. She owned absolutely nothing, not even underwear or a toothbrush. More importantly, she had no papers—no birth certificate, driver's license, or passport. Entering the United States took on a host of new felonies—human trafficking, illegal entry, violations of Treasury as well as a laundry list of acts, provisions, and treaties. But that made little difference to Charlie as he embraced his future wife.

Crazy Joe decided against fishing. They arrived at the main ship channel at 2:00 p.m. where they radioed the *Express*, waiting in the *Emma*'s vacant slip.

Allen had the engine idling as the *Emma* backed to fenders on *Express*'s starboard. Vali and the scuba gear and were transferred in less than five minutes. An envelope containing two thousand dollars exchanged hands. The *Bora Bora Express* was in Hawk Channel ten minutes later. *I love Stock Island*, thought Charlie, as he recollected that the events of the last week were made possible, in part, with the improbable assistance of a DEA agent.

Vali disappeared into the master stateroom bath. Charlie watched as she emerged an hour later, her body as smooth as the day she had been born. He watched as she sat on the edge of the bed, combing her long, dark hair. He could watch her forever. She seemed a neglected flower, blossoming back to life with a little water and fertilizer. The sores on her knees, hips, and hands were already scabbing over. The Vali he knew was materializing before his eyes.

Charlie and Vali hugged, kissed, cuddled, and made love as they sailed through the night, assisted by the Gulf Stream, arriving in Bimini as the golden-hued sunrise burst over the eastern horizon. The *Express* slid into her reserved berth beneath the shadow of the *Prometheus*. Vali, naked, peeked from the companionway at a new and strange land.

"Stay in the cabin!" ordered Charlie. But she had already been spotted by a crew member working on the flybridge of the yacht towering above. The man, gaping, waved. Vali waved back.

Charlie yanked her back into the cabin. She fell back, laughing.

"Allen, can you find some of Jenna's clothes that might fit her?"

He had imagined she would remain hidden in the aft cabin for the week or two it took to arrange her trip to America. After all, the berth in Charlie's aft cabin was infinitely more desirable than being locked in a steaming sewer. Now he realized that would never work. He could not become her jailer. She was anxious to explore her new freedoms, and Charlie would have to hope she stayed beneath the radar of the Bahamian police. Allen, like Charlie, had befriended the crew of the *Prometheus*. They were not a threat, but loose lips...... Charlie began to question the wisdom of bringing her to Bimini. Now that they were here it seemed to add one more layer of complexity.

Charlie quickly compiled a new wardrobe for Vali from the local boutiques. It was outrageously expensive but worth every nickel. Vali was beautiful in the bold prints of red and yellow. She loved the color yellow, and Charlie found a sundress very much like the one she had been wearing the first time he'd seen her. He bought for her a beautiful blue-and-gold bikini although she swore she would never enter the water again. And sandals. Sunglasses. A baseball cap. Lipstick. Over the next week, Vali melded seamlessly into the tourist scene of North Bimini. She would walk to Manny's Market every morning for freshly baked bread. She learned how to use a credit card. One night she discovered the Compleat Angler Hotel and dragged Charlie to its dance floor.

The crew of the *Prometheus* kept the boat in meticulous order, never knowing when Lenny might show up, as he did, two days before Christmas. The crew prepared for an impromptu Christmas Eve party, not one's standard party but one of Lenny's over-the-top, money-is-no-object, full-blown extravaganzas. A private plane was chartered to bring bartenders, a band, a pastry chef, some of Lenny's friends, and a contingent of professional Miami party girls. They all spoke Spanish as a first language. Charlie became reacquainted with the crew as he helped the band set up on the aft deck.

That night Charlie wore his best Hawaiian shirt and pressed shorts. Vali had been turned over to the girls, who took great delight transforming her into a new and improved Selena. Lenny had heard about her act and looked forward to watching her perform.

She had coordinated with the band to play a sequence of her favorite Selena songs, beginning with "Baila Esta Cumbia," a proven crowd-pleaser. Although the *Prometheus* could hold over a hundred guests, the night of the party revelers spilled onto to the dock, where, it seemed, half the island had assembled to drink and salsa. The lively beat of high-decibel Latino music filled the marina. The band gave Vali a sign. She grabbed a microphone and launched into her act.

Charlie could not have been prouder. The SRO crowd danced on every available square foot of bridge, deck, and dock. One song after another. Charlie had never seen her perform, but Vali looked like Selena, moved like Selena. Vali morphed into Selena, and the audience loved it. When she completed her set, everyone wanted an opportunity to meet the mysterious superstar stranger in their midst.

Charlie ended up carrying Vali back to his boat; her tolerance for alcohol had been lost while she had been in confinement. The next day she awoke with a pounding *resaca*, a hangover. Charlie left her relaxing in bed. He shook hands with Lenny when their host from the previous night walked across the dock to inquire about the diva who had so enlivened his festivities.

"Come aboard," he said to Lenny. "Can I make you a drink?"

"It's too early for me," Lenny said in his softly retained Spanish accent. "Where is the little songbird?"

Charlie pointed to the aft companionway door. "Go in. She will be surprised."

Charlie watched as the millionaire descended into his cabin. He heard a muffled discussion, in Spanish, much too fast for him to follow. He thought it good that she had a chance to speak in her native tongue since few of Charlie's friends in Jacksonville would be able to speak with her.

It was Christmas Day. A special day. Charlie had rented the entire Compleat Angler, which was scheduled to have been closed, for a surprise dinner in honor of his bride-to-be. Lenny and the crew of the *Prometheus* had been invited, as well as some of Allen's new friends from the marina. Jenna was even flying back, keeping her promise to not travel the waters anywhere remotely near Cuba again. The whole setup had been very expensive. Charlie had ordered a stone crab bisque, Caesar salad, a full lobster main course, an open bar with unlimited champagne, guava, and queso pastelitos—Vali's favorite dessert—for twenty place settings. To save money, he'd promised to help decorate. Charlie gave Vali a kiss on her hungover lips and informed her he would be gone for a couple hours.

As he was returning, though he was a quarter mile away, he could hear the engines of the great *Prometheus* spring to life. They practically shook the island. When he neared the *Bora Bora*, he was surprised to see the mega-yacht pulling away from the dock. Even as she left, salsa music flowed from her aft deck, across the docks, and onto the pool deck. It seemed the party never stopped on the *Prometheus*.

On its elegant flybridge, Charlie could see the captain working the throttles. Beside him sat Lenny, smoking a cigar. Lenny's arm was around the waist of a girl, a girl in a bold yellow sundress. Her arm was around his neck. As he watched, Vali planted a kiss on Lenny's fat cheek.

Charlie remembered her words, spoken the first day they met. Indeed, she would do whatever was necessary.

THE END

GPS CO-ORDINATES

Las Olas Anchorage, Ft. Lauderdale	26 07 10.25 N 80 00 38.49 W
Boat Slip at Big Game Club Bimini	25 43 33.73 N 79 17 42.92 W
Northwest Passage	25 24 28.52 N 78 07 01.63 W
Coral Heads South of Andros Island	23 21 53.24 N 77 32 55.32 W
Outer Sea Buoy Hemingway Marina	23 05 15.81 N 82 30 26.47 W
Harbor House, across from Customs	23 04 45.26 N 82 30 07.29 W
Slip in front of Hotel Aquario	23 05 20.63 N 82 29 49.50 W
Coco's House Calle 234	23 05 23.71 N 82 29 11.93 W
La Cecelia Bar & Nightclub	23 05 39.39 N 82 27 12.88 W
Hotel Kohly	23 06 34.39 N 82 24 33.73 W
Siboney	23 04 58.68 N 82 27 02.67 W

Vali character's Shack La Loma, Santa Fe	23 03 56.71 N 82 31 05.91 W
The Military Hospital Marionao	23 04 57.40 N 82 25 54.35 W
Necropolis Cristobal Colon (cemetery)	23 07 23.86 N 82 24 08.97 W
El Rumbo, Jaiminatas	82 29 17.37 W 23 05 18.28 N
Hotel Viejo y El mar	23 05 31.45 N 82 29 34.58 W
Swimming Beach, Jaimanitas	23 05 35.06 N 82 29 11.96 W
Restaurant El Palenque	23 05 10.72 N 82 27 45.56 W
La Lisa	23 03 10 .13N 82 26 55. 63W
Guanajay Prison	22 55 17.47 N 82 40 43.38 W
Boat Slip at Stock Island	24 34 01.13 N 81 44 00.95 W
Playa Banes	23 01 53.20 N 82 38 20.01 W

ABOUT THE AUTHOR

Jeff Hartdorn is a resident of New Smyrna Beach, Florida. He has travelled to seventy-three countries, so far. He was an advocate for out-of-state property owners and wrote newsletters for twenty-two years. An avid sailor and spearfisherman, he is currently working on several patents. After an injury and facing one hundred days in bed, he promised his ninety-five-year old mother he would write a book.

Hartdorn has lived with the Cuban people, and many of the day-to day details in Bora Bora Express are based on his personal experience - as are many of Charlie Sutton's more hair-raising escapades.

Made in the USA
Columbia, SC
26 November 2018